BRIDGET DUNSEITH

# DESIDERATA

*or*

# THINGS DESIRED

Merimna Publications

Published in 1999 by Merimna Publications

ISBN 0 9531705 1 9



Designed and produced by
Axxent Ltd
The Short Run Book Company
St Stephen's House
Arthur Road
Windsor
Berkshire SL4 1RY

*To AF*

## DESIDERATA

Bridget Dunseith was born in Belgium and brought up in Portugal. After reading Classics and gaining her PhD, she went into full-time secondary school teaching. She now lectures at University level and writes part-time. ***Desiderata*** is her first published novel, and she has researched and published a full-scale biography of Jessie Chambers, D.H.Lawrence's first love.

**Acknowledgements:** my thanks to Peter Tunnicliff, Colin Martin and John Case.

**Author's Note:** All chapter headings are taken from the Oxford Classical Texts edition of Ovid's Amores ("Love Poems"), Ars Amatoria ("The Art of Love") and Remedia Amoris ("Cures for Love"), edited by E.J.Kenney.

### ERRATA

p.25 line 11, p.236 line 8, p.237 line 30 and p.238 line 16 – for **gymn** read **gym**

p.31 line 5 – for **the hoi polloi** read **hoi polloi**

p.37 line 1 – for "***Quis estis?***" read "***Qui estis?***"

p.71 line 28 – for **when** read **than**

p.92 line 19 – for **seried** read **serried**

p.97 line 23 – insert **from** between **ground** and **beneath** and line 26 – for **do** read **does**

p.120 line 7 – for **chords** read **cords**

p.143 line 19 – for **say** read **saying**

p.146 line 12 – for **is** read **it**

p.185 lines 15 and 18 – for **Cornwall** read **Dorset**

p.230 line 13 – for **feels** read **feel**

p.257 line 14 – for **Bogata** read **Bogota**

p.272 line 4 – for **fourteenth** read **twelfth**

# CHAPTER I

*coeptis, mater Amoris, ades (A.A.I.30)*
*"favour my enterprise, mother of Love"*

When I took up my post at Dons, a public school for boys, I was old enough to be the youngest's mother and young enough to be the mistress of the oldest. The latter thought has surprised me: I am not given to sexual reflection.

On my husband's death two years before, I was twenty-eight. I had loved Antony but was not enamoured of him. We had been married five years when he crashed and died at the controls of a small plane. I had lost a friend more than a lover, and a sense of the futility of things drove me back to college where I gained a teaching diploma to add to my degree in Classics.

I suppose Dr. Graff, Head Master of Dons, had taken pity on my widowed state when he, Francis Marks his Deputy, and the director of studies whose name is irrelevant, interviewed me.

"Why do you want to teach boys, Mrs. Farthing?" he had asked after some preliminary questions. "I see from your curriculum vitae that your teaching experience has been in girls' schools."

I faced all three of them in the Head Master's study; they looked businesslike and impartial in their dark suits and ties. They were watching me and waiting for a reply, so I answered, "I'm curious to find out how boys' learning of Classics is different from girls'. It would give me a new perspective to see how the two sexes approach the same subject."

They had seemed satisfied with my answer and Dr. Graff turned to his Deputy. "Have you any questions you'd like to put to Mrs. Farthing?"

Francis Marks, who reminded me of an ageing retriever, had tired but kindly eyes. He gave an encouraging smile before asking, "What would you say are the disadvantages of teaching in a boys' school?"

"I can't think of any." But my reply had lacked deliberation, and silence hung heavily in the room.

Continued Mr. Marks, "Does filling the post of head of department with three male colleagues in a supportive role bother you?"

"No, but it might bother them."

For some reason, all three men laughed. "Truthfully," said Dr. Graff, "We had intended filling this vacancy with a man, not out of any partisanship which, as you know, is illegal but for the simple reason that a woman is unlikely to want to coach rugger or cricket. But perhaps your talents stretch in that direction?"

I had smiled. "I'm afraid not." And that, I believed, was my downfall.

I'd already begun to doubt the wisdom of applying for a post in a boys' school. It seemed to me, as I sat in the room scented lightly with beeswax polish and hushed by a thick red carpet and panelled walls, that the gap between the sexes was more pronounced at schooling level than it ever would be in later life.

Now it was the director of studies' turn to question me. "Boys approach things differently from girls. How would you cope with a class of twenty-five adolescent males with sex on the brain first, and learning Latin and Greek a long way behind?"

I shrank a little. How indeed would I? This time I did pause before saying, "Many of them will, presumably, go into the professions. They will have to realise that any person they come across in a professional capacity is, one hopes, a professional first and male or female second."

They nodded and shuffled the papers before them; then, having agreed amongst themselves that there was nothing more to ask, Dr. Graff wondered if I had any questions. It was diplomatic to show interest, so I enquired about Classics in the school (extremely popular), its success rate (very high), and the precise nature of a departmental head's duties (various but not taxing). My interview had then come to a natural conclusion.

Dr. Graff put his papers to one side. "Well, Mrs. Farthing, I understand that our present head of Classics has shown you round the school and you have met the other three in the department. Now, is this the sort of post which would appeal to you?"

My reply was sincere. "Very much so."

"Good. Thank you for coming to see us. We'll be in touch within the next few days."

We had all risen and shaken hands, and I left the room feeling my answers had not altogether found favour. But two days later came a written offer of the post. I accepted.

Dons was in Sussex near the town of Deme. Eastbourne lay some fifteen miles away and to London it was about an hour and a half driving. The history of the school went back to a sixteenth century churchman called Frederick Samuel Don who was sympathetic towards those lads whose background condemned them to a life of grinding labour. He had set up and funded a local school and made provision in his will for such funding to continue for so long as he had descendants. Since his marriage to a squire's daughter had borne six sons this posed no difficulty. In time, Dons opened its doors to mentally gifted boys from all backgrounds. When I took up my post as head of the Classics department, Dons was an outstanding public school in the same league as others ranking top through tradition and academic prowess.

It had been built on the cloister-theme, with gardens, playing-fields and deep Sussex country all around. New wings were what architects termed 'sympathetically designed'. There was a fine Chapel and a library containing, behind glass, mediaeval texts. Dons was home for thirty-six weeks of the year to some five hundred boys.

I lived in. My own house left me by my father before I ever married was in Westmorland, and that had been my base since widowhood. But during term, the school offered me a small upstairs wing in the main house, close enough to the lower school but sufficiently separate to escape feeling on top of them. My rooms looked east over the front drive and west into the school Quad.

Having given notice of my intention, I moved in the day before most inmates were due back. I wanted to walk round at my leisure without bumping into staff or boys. Atmosphere was important to me and I needed to pick up and savour that of classrooms, staff quarters and grounds without another's interpretation. The canine equivalent is to go about sniffing and raising a leg.

A hideous cat with a voice like a corncrake chose to escort me. His black-and-white marking had been so unfortunately placed that from a distance he looked as if a dog had taken indiscriminate bites from him. I thought Pelops – after the myth where he was murdered and served up as dinner for the gods – would be an apt name for him. Each time I had finished absorbing a room I found myself asking him by look, "Finished?" Whereupon he would stalk out of the door first, tail ramrod stiff, and hang respectfully back while I entered another. At the end of the inspection when I had returned to the foot of the stairway leading to my quarters, he left me with a backward glance which seemed to say, "Satisfied?" I nodded in reply. He and I were to see quite a lot of each other.

From five o'clock the next day, scores of cars rolled up, disgorged sons and baggage on to the drive and drove off again. Forsaken, new little boys blubbed. Asserting themselves, older ones yelled. Sixth Form prefects and housemasters called, advised and directed. Approaching the bereft with seeds of comfort, matron and her assistants in white bent and straightened like four doves. And my apprehension grew.

At seven that first evening there was a welcome supper for resident staff. We had a dining-room away from the boys and on this forty of us converged. I would have preferred to prepare and eat a meal in my own quarters, feeling the school pulsating into life around me; but I, like every new member of staff, was expected to attend.

It does not do to call the assistants in your department subordinates, but if one may judge by their behaviour that is what my immediate colleagues were. I had met all three at my interview and had not been impressed. On this, as on many subsequent occasions, they showed me I was not welcome. One did his lacklustre best to greet me, the second jerked his chin wordlessly and the third turned his back. My solitude growing, I looked for some women to whom to relate, but the four who were present had integrated with the men by becoming loud and aggressive.

Conspicuous in my loneliness, I concentrated on the baggy suits (science and languages), the knee-buckled corduroy trousers (art and music), the wrinkled tracksuits (games staff) and other sartorial gear (without category). I wondered why, in the way that gestating sheep standing before a wattle fence had produced striped lambs, teachers did not assume the professional trappings of their career. I caught sight of myself in the glass over the coffee-table; my late husband, Antony, had once said he loved me first for my looks and second for my style. I was flattered but regretted that, so far as he was concerned, my brain never came into it.

Now everyone was taking a place at table. My subordinates – let them be known as the Three Graces – had slipped from my side of the room and stood, ranks closed, at the far end. Dr. Graff rapped a spoon smartly on the table till silence fell.

"Good evening, ladies and gentlemen," he began affably. "I hope you've all had a good summer. Without preamble, we have five new members of staff this term, and I'd like to welcome Mrs. Jessica Farthing as head of Classics –" he waved a hand in my direction, "– Mr. Tim Laing to Maths, Miss Maureen Johns to Art and Mr. Rupert Cotton to French. I'm sure you'll all join me in wishing them well." There were murmurs and some craning of heads to scrutinise new staff, then he concluded, "Before we sit, could I remind you that we have a full staff-meeting tomorrow at eight-thirty sharp, and at nine this evening our first fire-drill. Thank you."

Noisily we took our seats at table. I did not know who sat either side of me, they mumbled their names so. But some sort of stilted conversation was made over the soup, warm quiche and tinned fruit salad, and I decided that all my meals, save lunch, would be taken in my own quarters.

After the summer holidays – and some staff had the now liver-coloured vestiges of burning suns – I had expected to hear conversation about travel, foreign mores and experience. Not so. The thing that absorbed these people was school: old boys, new boys and the ongoing; timetables, work programmes and detentions. As I was strange to it all there was little for me to contribute.

I ate in silence. The quiche smelled of metal; the salads were gritty; black dots peppered the mash.

Noticing my disenchantment, the colleague on my left said, "The boys have a menu. We will tomorrow." Those were his only comments.

Later, between the quiche and pudding, my companion on the right began, "Classics, eh? What, the works – Latin, Greek and Class Civ? I was hopeless at it. But they're pretty good here. It began to die when I stopped doing it, ha,ha!"

Next, a plump woman in a too-tight overall waddled in and out preparing the coffee-table, while another, almost her double, cleared our plates.

"Are they twins?" I asked my colleague on the right.

"Who?"

"The waiting-staff."

He peered at them over his spectacles. "Good Lord, no. All the working-class look the same."

I thought of my gardener in Pomeroy, a born-and-bred Cumbrian who lived in Doomgate, supported the gipsy fair and tended my cottage-garden as necessary. He was a member of the working-class. I thought of my cleaner when Antony and I lived in Milford, a devout Baptist and deeply proud of 'her' Surrey hills; she too was working-class. Neither of them looked remotely alike. Teachers could be self-opinionated.

In two's and three's we rose from supper and wandered towards the coffee-table. As I waited my turn, the Head Master came up to satisfy himself that I was comfortable in my rooms; and had I been given my timetable?

"Yes," I replied, "But I have no idea where to go for lessons."

He laid a reassuring hand on my sleeve. "Don't worry. The Deputy will take you under his wing tomorrow." Dr. Graff made to leave my side, but I had another query.

"The fire-drill, Head Master. Where do we go for that?"

"I knew I had forgotten something!" He clapped his hands and conversation straggled into silence. "For newcomers' benefit, fire-drill this evening will commence with a continuous bell. Please make your way to the front drive and, if you are a head of form, take a list of those in your class. You will need to make sure that every boy is accounted for."

I was not a form-teacher so this did not apply to me. Now, house-staff had begun to leave the room. I decided to go, too, hoping that I would make a better start with the boys than I had with my colleagues.

At nine o'clock the fire-bell rang. I tossed on a wind-cheater, once Antony's, for it had started to drizzle. Beyond the corridor leading to my stairway which was out-of-bounds to the school, little boys darted, piping in chorister voices. They tumbled down the two flights of stairs to the front hall where a housemaster ordered them to form ranks in silence outside.

The sweet night air was thrown into darker relief by the building which blazed light, and the older boys shifted in curiosity as I walked past them to join the knot of staff standing beside the Upper

Sixth. We waited. The bell clanged on, then stopped. Feet scuffed the gravel, throats were cleared, coughs sawed through the dark. At last, Dr. Graff and his Deputy sauntered out. Everyone stood in silence. Then, to our astonishment, a figure in nothing but a bath-towel round his waist padded from the house.

There was a suppressed titter among the boys, then full-blown laughter. Unaware of the youth behind him, Dr. Graff glared at the ranks till his attention was caught by the semi-nude figure. He turned and spoke. I heard one sentence, "The lock was faulty," a low rejoinder from the Head Master, then the towelled youth ran the gauntlet of some five hundred laughing boys and took his place among the Upper Sixth.

He stood in the warm September rain, silent and rather proud.

"W-hoi!" shouted the younger boys and a catcall made a piercing arc through the muggy gloom. He planted his bare feet wide, folded his muscular arms across a well-developed chest and gazed stoically at the clock-tower roof.

"You look a nut, Forsyth!" came a voice from the ranks.

"Shut up, Pilkington!" yelled a master.

The Deputy roared, "Silence!"

By now, form-staff had started checking off the boys on their lists. During this movement, I went up to Forsyth and tossed Antony's wind-cheater over his shoulders. "You'll catch your death," I murmured. His eyes met mine and he smiled faintly.

At last the entire school was accounted for. Dr. Graff, his Deputy and form-staff briefly conferred, then the youngest boys were told to begin the return into school. As they went, the fourth formers flung their heads round in Forsyth's direction, giving wolfish leers. His expression impassive, he watched them straggle away.

Only the Lower and Upper Sixth remained now. Then they strolled in groups back to the house. "Bad luck, Alex," cried one boy. "Why do they always have fire-drill when a chap's in the bloody shower!"

He grinned and I heard his voice properly for the first time. "Sod's law – and a lock that won't work!" Then he turned to me, drawing off the wind-cheater. "Thanks," he said as he held it out. Clasping the bath-towel firmly, he made off after the others.

I watched him go, and understood why the younger boys had cried, "W-hoi!"

"That's Dons' Classics Scholar, Alex Forsyth," said a voice.

Turning, I found the Deputy at my elbow.

"We haven't met since your interview. I'm Francis Marks." He shook my hand and we fell in step towards the house.

I was still struck by Forsyth's deportment. "Tremendous sang-froid," I murmured. "It's not every young man who can join hundreds dressed only in a bath-towel."

Francis Marks laughed. "If he wasn't out of the top drawer, I doubt he'd have shown his face!"

"Oh? What does his father do?"

"He's a high-ranking member of the diplomatic corps in Bogota. The mother's out there, too, but there's a sister at school in Gloucester. He's Oxbridge material, you know."

I smiled to myself. 'Oxbridge material' was a cliché among those in secondary education; it was as if a particular boy or girl were a different texture, weave and finish from other pupils.

The Deputy saw my expression and his face lifted. "It's er ... good to have a woman among us."

"I'm not the only one!"

"No, but –" and he lowered his voice, "– they're not of your calibre. I do hope you won't find us boorish, Mrs. Farthing. It's so easy for an all-male school to become uncouth. You will remind us that there is a prettier side to life."

Flattered, I laughed.

With a flourish he was opening the door for me as he added, "Sorry you had this for an introduction." He wiped his feet vigorously like a dog in the grasses. "You'll be all right the rest of the evening?"

I hoped he did not think that as a woman I would need molly-coddling. I smiled reassuringly, and we parted.

# CHAPTER II

*qui silet, est firmus (R.A.697)*
*"the one who is quiet is strong"*

The staff meeting was brisk, to the point and, for me, useful. We were given dates for our diaries, new boys were discussed, summer exam grades praised, parents' evenings allocated and, by ten, we had flapped into our black gowns, taken a hymn book and made for the Great Hall.

The school was already assembled, kept in check by a dozen prefects and the head boy. All stood as we paraded, fat, thin, stocky or shapeless on to the stage to our seats. The music master bent crow-like in his gown over the piano and, at a signal from the Head Master, struck the first chords of the school hymn.

I remembered it from my own school days, though we had sung this one only occasionally. It was particularly apt for a boys' public school – a good resounding tune full of punch. There were five verses to it, but Dons' governors had reduced it to three. We sang now in full throat, and later I was to hear the typical schoolboy parody on the same lines as 'While shepherds washed their socks by night...' Dons' fraternity was no less irreligious:

*'God is working His purpose out as year succeeds to year,*
*God is working His purpose out of that we have no fear;*
*Nearer and nearer draws the time, the time that shall surely be*
*When the earth shall be fill'd with the glory of God as His daughters swim in the sea.'*

I thought of Antony as we all sang. He had had a good voice and I used to hear him in the kitchen as he peeled potatoes, rolling his r's theatrically over a Gilbert and Sullivan tune. Sometimes he'd act the fool and parody, 'Three little maids from school are we-ee, locked up in the lavatoree...' Our union had been more of a companionship than a marriage in the true sense of the word. We could laugh together, which was good, yet our relationship lacked fire. This disappointed me more than it did him; but perhaps it made for a tighter bond.

The school hymn over, we all sat. Dr.Graff went up to the lectern and addressed the boys. I, and the other newcomers, were welcomed again and as he mentioned further items, I took the opportunity to survey the blur of faces gazing back at us.

There was the school Billy Bunter, sweaty, flaccid with piggy eyes; the Beanpole, all elbow and kneecap; the Swot, bespectacled and watchful, hopeless at sport but immensely bookish; the Don Juan wearing his uniform like a Savile Row suit; the Thoroughly Bad Egg, coarse of feature with a mouth shaped like an obscenity; and poor Master Acne from whose face chickens must have taken pecks. And somewhere in between these stereotypes of young malehood were scores of indeterminate boys – plump, lean, tall, short, dark, fair, pale, sanguine, spruce, smelly... Some fifty out of five hundred probably cleaned their shoes and changed their underwear daily, but all were growing up in certain discomfort of mind, body, spirit. I wondered where Alex Forsyth was.

And so, with assembly over, the process of education began. Adults left first and we retraced our steps to the staffroom. There, Francis Marks came up to me as I contemplated my timetable.

"All set? Can I call you Jessica?"

"Of course."

"And I'm Francis. Right, who've you got first?"

I looked at my timetable. "The fourth form, room twelve."

"Follow me!"

I caught up a modern text full of hideous cartoons and beautiful Graeco-Roman sculptures and went with the Deputy.

We walked abreast. "It'll take you a little time to know where everything is," he said, barely diverging from his course as scurrying boys, met with our marching wall of adulthood, flattened themselves against the corridor.

"Morning, sir. Morning er..." they said politely. For a while I would be "Er." Teaching was either an ego-trip or a body-breaker. I wondered as we paced to my first class which would be my experience at Dons.

Lunch was in preparation already; it smelled of lasagne or pizza, I could not be sure which. Mid-morning, it was unappetising and did nothing to complement the arched windows and doors of the cloistered building.

"Ah!" I had caught sight of a furry animal which from a distance looked chewed into. "There he is again!"

Francis glanced at me in surprise. "Who?"

"That black-and-white cat."

"Oh, Nisbet. Yes, the boys found him one day behind the cricket pavilion. The kitchen fed him some milk and he's stayed ever since. Dons wouldn't be the same without Nisbet." He had halted before a glass-paned door and now flung it open. The bellowing of what sounded like a football crowd hit us. As we entered order prevailed. I faced twenty-five fifteen-year-old boys like a box of liquorice allsorts.

"'Morning, fourths," said Francis. "This is Mrs. Farthing, head of Classics." He and I exchanged brief smiles and he left me to it.

The moment between the door shutting and my taking command, a soft wolf-whistle sounded from along the back row. Should I ignore or nip it in the bud? I nipped it.

With deliberation I put down my books on the staff-desk. Then my eye ran the width of the back row, "Who did that?" I asked levelly. Silence and foot shuffling. "I asked, who did that?" I saw an arm dither into the air. "Right, would you all open your books at page ninety-one." There was a frantic scrabble, and still letting them stand, I asked the miscreant, "What is your name?"

"Brownlow."

"'Brownlow, Mrs. Farthing.'"

"Brownlow, Mrs. Farthing."

"Brownlow, please translate poem twenty."

Poem twenty was a brief piece by one of my favourite Latin poets, Catullus. In it he reports how his mistress, Lesbia, has asked how many kisses would be more than enough for him. Boys of fifteen may have sex on the brain, but they hate talking about love. I watched this Brownlow squirm and redden to the roots of his hair.

"'You ask ... how many for me ...um ...your...'" he began, then his voice failed.

"Yes, Brownlow, what does Lesbia ask?"

"'You ask ... how many of your ...'"

For some minutes I let him flounder, Catullus, the inability to voice words of love and the name 'Lesbia' exacting their own punishment. Meanwhile, the rest of the class kept their heads down in case I gave up on Brownlow and picked on someone else.

"Oh, do stop!" I exclaimed at last. "All of you, sit down." The gladiator had bettered the arenaful of animals.

Single lessons lasted forty minutes. In the final five of this one I told them what to expect of me and what I wanted from them. It was, if you like, a list of terms and conditions. "First," I began, "I am hot on manners. Not everyone can do Classics, but all can learn how to behave. So, when I enter the room I expect you to stand in silence. I also have a name. Please use it. If you want to attract my attention, you will put up your hands. Further, I regard requests to go to the lavatory with suspicion; if you can't contain yourselves for forty minutes then you had better see matron. In addition, poorly presented work lets you down and is an insult to me." I scanned the room and was pleased to see them attentive. "Finally," I added, "From the nature of Brownlow's whistle, you are aware I am a woman –" There came some sniggers. "I can't help my sex, no more can you help yours. So, let's put our differences out of our minds. I have been engaged to teach you Classics, and that is what aim to do." They were hanging on my words. "And what can you expect of me? Well, I think I am a patient person; I will not humiliate you if you do not understand an aspect of Latin or Greek. If you genuinely cannot hand in written work or prepare for a test because of a valid reason, then I shall be lenient. But if you are shirking, watch it! Any questions?"

There was a hiatus, then they chorused, "No, Mrs. Farthing."

With a nod to them all, I gathered up my papers and walked out.

☙ ❧

Adrenalin carried me through that first day, and by three o'clock I was wondering if I could make it to end of school. The last slot on my timetable read AF and I could not make head or tail of it. I dithered at my desk in the staff study, waiting for Francis Marks to enlighten me.

He entered just after three, looking benign as usual. "How's it going?" he asked solicitously.

I felt I had a friend in him. "Not bad, thanks. But what is AF and where do I do it?"

He smiled. "AF is not what, but who! It's our gentleman of the bath-towel – Alex Forsyth."

"Of course. How could I forget!"

"Quite so. Now, as for where you teach him poses a slight problem. As you are a giving a one-to-one tutorial, space for it has always been difficult. Your predecessor taught him in his own quarters, but you may object to teaching Forsyth in yours."

I was taken aback. "Why should I? Is he infectious?"

The Deputy laughed. "No, but you're a lady and he's male."

*Here we go, the English disease – sexual coyness; they can't call a spade a spade, or if they do, it's spade, fork and everything else in the garden shed.* Briskly I said, "I don't think I have anything to fear from Alex Forsyth. Where is he?"

Francis went to the door and opened it. "You there, Forsyth?"

A voice replied, "Yes, sir."

Francis shut the door again and turned to me. "He's all yours."

I gathered my papers, feeling ruffled over the Deputy, Alex Forsyth and a society so sex-ridden that innocent daily activities became subject to prurience.

Alex Forsyth stood waiting in the corridor with an armful of books. He was a good six inches taller than I and manly in his dark uniform. I looked up at him. "We have already met," I said, and he grinned in acknowledgement. "When you get to university," I went on, "you'll have seminars in your tutor's rooms. Do you object to having tutorials in mine?"

"Not at all. Mr Rowland used to." So simply spoken and without embarrassment. I need hardly have raised the matter.

I marched him, because I was still nettled, to my quarters. We climbed my stairway and entered. I hesitated over closing the door. My eyes scraped his backview. *No; he's had enough publicity for twenty-four hours.* Firmly I shut the world out.

"Did you have a bad time of it after last night?" I asked, placing my books on the table.

He gave a smile. He had white teeth and the most unusual hazel eyes. "They ribbed me a bit..."

I motioned him to a seat by the window. "It's too early for something stronger than coffee – I gather you are eighteen?"

"I'm nineteen."

"Good."

He remained standing until I had taken a chair. Such manners were arrestingly old-fashioned. "Now," I continued as we settled.

"Tell me a bit about yourself. For instance, your ambitions and where you want to go from here."

I listened and watched, half the tutor half the woman, the logical part of my brain absorbing the information he gave, the aesthetic side assessing his person. He wanted to read Classics; *he is the most good-looking young man I have ever clapped eyes on.* He would shortly be applying to Oxford – Balliol if possible – and the careers master was looking into the forms for him; *his head is well-shaped, the dark hair lying across his forehead giving him an almost slickly handsome look were not his expression surprisingly contemplative.* "I thought some branch of law after that," he was saying; *he has fine hands, the nails clean and trim, the fingers long. There's no doubt that this young man is out of the top drawer, from his well-spoken English to the shine on his shoes.*

"Are your parents supportive?" I asked, taking out my A level folder and efficiently shuffling some papers. Even if he had not been good-looking, Alex Forsyth was blessed with an expression that was remarkably pleasing.

"Yes – though they are rather far away."

I knew where, from what Francis Marks had told me the night before but I asked anyway.

"Colombia. But I've a sister in Cheltenham."

"You go to your parents in the holidays?"

He shook his head. "No. My father doesn't think it's the place for us. He worries that we'll have our luggage planted with drugs. We often go to Wiltshire where my aunt and uncle have a farm. Otherwise, my sister and I end up at my parents' flat in London."

To me, this seemed a loose family arrangement. Gently I asked, "How often do you see your parents?"

"They try to come over for a few weeks in the summer. But we're in touch by letter and 'phone."

Antony and I had had no children, and I could not help thinking that if this young man were my son, I would be around him like a bee at honey.

We had reached a natural pause in our conversation. I regarded him steadily and his eyes did not slip away as would so many young people's. I suddenly smiled and then his gaze did fall. "Well, Alex, you've told me a little of yourself. Is there anything you would like to ask about me?"

There was a remarkable stillness about him, unusual in a person of his age; he didn't fidget or twiddle a foot or clear his throat. It was as if all physical activity were concentrated in his mind. He reminded me of some finely-tuned animal whose body is motionless while its senses remain acute. Now he replied, "Everyone is interested in a new teacher. But there are areas we cannot probe. So -" his eyes met mine and he grinned, "You tell me what you think I should know!"

I laughed, liking this Alex Forsyth more each minute. "Right, here goes. As you see, I'm resident staff. I've taught only in girls' schools before, so Dons presents a bit of a challenge. I'm a widow and my home is in Westmorland not far from Penrith..." I paused, wondering what else might be of interest to a young man. "Ah, yes! I drive a black VW convertible, have no close relatives to show their disapproval, am besotted with Classics and...and... one day would like three sheepdogs called Happy, Go and Lucky."

I was beginning to sound a little ridiculous, but that was my intention. Alex evidently liked it for his face flickered with humour. I coloured, sensing that while my capacity as a tutor remained unproven he, in his turn, was assessing me as a woman. At any rate, we both had established that we could work together. There was between us what is best described as 'a rapport'.

Sobering, for it was time to be professional, I opened the Classics syllabus. "Now," I began, "Which Greek prescribed texts have you started?"

"Demosthenes 54 and 56; Euripides, selected passages from the *Bacchae*, and I've chosen the topic 'Aristophanes and War'. I'm also taking the Greek prose composition paper."

This was good. "What about Latin?"

"Prose composition, Cicero's *In Catalinam* and Catullus."

"And how confident are you in all these?"

"I'm least happy with Catullus. Mr Rowland didn't like him – said he was a sexual deviant."

My jaw dropped. "Extraordinary. Does it matter what Catullus' sexual orientation was? Good heavens, he leaps at me each time I open his poems! Did Mr Rowland support his opinion?"

"He said he didn't like the way things were going with a certain Iuventius, and was suspicious of the emotional reaction Catullus had to one Licinius."

I made an exasperated noise. "I'm surprised Mr Rowland had the stomach for teaching Classics at all. Did he ever discuss Greek homosexuality?"

"Not with us."

I said no more. Classics was in no danger of being dropped from Dons' curriculum. But in those schools where it was foundering I blamed its teachers for failing to build bridges between the ancient and modern world, and for not addressing social issues common to most civilizations.

I looked at my watch. It was ten to four. "Well, Alex, what I propose to do for the rest of our tutorial is this: we'll check that our timetables coincide then I'm going to give you a past paper to prepare for next lesson. How does that sound?"

"It sounds all right to me, Mrs Farthing."

According to our timetables we would meet every day for a double lesson, and in my rooms. His work-load seemed colossal and I asked if he could stay on top of it.

"I think so," he replied positively.

"What other A levels are you taking?"

"English, and French."

Alex Forsyth was not only a splendid-looking young man but also very clever; I liked people with brains.

# CHAPTER III

*loca sola caveto (R.A.579)*
*"beware of solitary places"*

A failing of mine is to take an instant liking or dislike to a person, based purely on chemical reaction. To justify myself, I should say that my first impressions are invariably correct and backed up by later acquaintance. To Rupert Cotton, the new French master, I took an immediate dislike. Unctuous, he was the sort of person who on entering a room fills it with his own oil-slick. Well into his fifties he had thinning greasy hair, glasses, a large full-lipped mouth and the disgusting habit of hawking during his rare silences. According to him, he was God's gift to education.

Engaged by the modern languages department to assist in teaching French, he soon made every member of staff aware that he was a past-master at Spanish, English and Latin, too. He had done everything there was to do, and met everyone worth knowing. Not content to have a *sotto voce* conversation with one or two people, he would stand in the middle of the carpet, shove his hands in his pockets and, jingling money, address the room at large. His speech was very Queen's English, very grammatical and very sententious. After one of his 'addresses', I wanted to emulate the Roman practice at bathtime of taking a strigil to scrape his oil-slick off my skin.

He was bombastic, laughed uproariously at his own witticisms and liked to pay insincere homage to those with academic clout. One day early on in the term, he came up to me and asked if the Latin word *dum* could mean only 'while'; without waiting for an answer he recited a chunk of *Stabat mater*, pronouncing the c's in Italianate Latin. Then he peered at me as if to say, "Aren't I a Clever-Clogs?"

I wasn't impressed. I told him stiffly that *dum* could also mean 'until', but he should consult the Lewis and Short Latin Dictionary.

"No, no, no," he protested. "Your ignorance is my wisdom!" and he burst into solitary mirth.

Strange thing, this body chemistry; I wondered why one shrank and grew spiky like a sea-urchin at the sight and proximity of a particular person, yet mushroomed in the presence of another. Throughout my time at Dons, Rupert Cotton would always have the former effect on me, just as Alex Forsyth was to do the very opposite.

☙ ❧

By Thursday that first week I had met all my classes. There was only one word to describe the little eleven-year-olds: enchanting. They slept regularly on their back hair which, next morning, stuck out like a bird's nest; and they came to early lessons with their faces blunted by rest. They had big, wondering eyes and piping voices, and having just left enlightened preparatory schools, knew the four conjugations and five declensions like parrots.

The second years, at first, were overawed by me. They sat in silence, only speaking when spoken to, flushing to the hair-line if they made one mistake, and sitting straight and attentive in their seats.

Learning to swagger a little, the third years were pure fun. Not yet tortured by beer-blossom pimples and fantasies of girls, they made intelligent observations and were cheeky without impudence.

The fourth years continued to be as on first encounter. However, once feeling the crack of my whip, figuratively speaking (I regret), they watched their p's and q's although insubordination was never far from the surface.

As for the fifth formers, all the woes of the world lay heavily upon their shoulders. They had sexual problems and parent problems, GCSE problems and glandular problems. Everybody was against them – "Nobody shall help me – I will drown!" was their personal credo. Fortunately I shared this group with my departmental colleagues, or the Three Graces, who as males of a sort were better equipped than I to deal with fifth year phobias.

The Lower and Upper Sixth were an entirely different kettle of fish. They studied Classics not through parental pressure but because they liked it. In all, I took only fifteen for literary appreciation and verse translation. They were bright lads and responded well.

Finally, the head of Classics' 'perk' was Alex Forsyth. I had sole responsibility for his Latin and Greek and, therefore, his admission to Oxford. If he failed to gain the necessary grades, it would in effect be my fault.

The rest of my time was spent in administration of the department: making phonecalls, writing letters, composing relevant reports and curbing expenditure. As I settled in, I wondered what I had done with my day as Antony's wife. A partner in a stock-brokers' in the City, he had required me occasionally to attend functions. "I want you there and I want to show you off," he once said. I felt like a prize racehorse and did not much care for it. But wearing good clothes and being deferred to did wonderful things for the confidence. After running the gauntlet of sniffy wives and their money-drunk husbands, a staff-room of dedicated but somehow frowsty teachers bothered me hardly at all. No colleague deferred to me at Dons because, I assumed, I had lost social status by becoming widowed; and, worst of all, I was female. But I continued to wear nice clothes and to consider my appearance. It drew a certain swashbuckling gallantry from the boys and gave me what is generally termed 'the feel-good factor'.

I did, however, miss the society of women. Those among the staff were too busy pretending to be male or, like the art teacher, Miss Johns, enjoyed misplaced panic attacks relieved only by the skilful extrications of male colleagues. I spoke occasionally to matron but that was always about the boys because for her, as with most school staff, life ceased beyond the gates of Dons.

When therefore Martha Verall, a cousin of my late husband and then good friend of mine, invited me to her London home for half-term, I accepted at once. Martha was fun and a happy divorcee. She, too, was childless and neither of us minded one whit. There were so many women giving forth blood, bitterness and babies that we felt privileged to be free of our sisters' trials.

"I envy you being with All Those Boys," she wrote in her letter of invitation. "Can you throw me a virile sixth former? There must be several down your way. Talking of virility, I shall arrange a surprise evening for you when you come at half-term. It'll probably be more of a treat for me than you, but I couldn't possibly go alone!"

In small doses, my so-called cousin was good to be with. But I was glad she lived in London and I, during the holidays, up north; Martha, like champagne, was bubbly but she lacked depth.

I had no duties at weekends and two evenings a term supervised the younger boys at prep. But shopping on Saturdays in the nearby town of Deme proved a hollow experience; every corner turned, every doorway entered was an unsolicited rendezvous with Dons' boys. While the evenings lasted, I tried walking round the school grounds. Again, I bumped into knots of familiar lads and, next day, colleagues wondered why I walked at all.

In desperation I went off one evening in the car. Within moments public footpaths between knotty oaks enticed me, and after parking I struck out through nets of midges that wailed in the late sunshine. "Autumn suits you," Antony had once said. I asked him why. "You seem particularly mellow – dreamy, if you like." "I'm not a dreamy sort!" "Well, reflective, then. In spring you're skittish, in summer vigorous and in winter you remind me of a furry creature that wants to sleep." I had laughed, not entirely displeased by his comment. "Have you noticed, Jess," he went on, "how we're sexually inactive during the winter?" We hardly had sexual intimacy at any season, but I did not say so; a non-committal "Ah!" seemed better. "I think that left to their own devices," he added, "married human beings would just sleep and eat like wild animals, and hang the reproductive bit." I had made no reply to that; perhaps I had slept and eaten because he, when not working or flying his light aircraft, wanted to do little else.

With Dons behind me, and only the rooks like pacing parsons for company, I followed my nose down a footpath. In the hedge late-flowering honeysuckle and blackberry beads twined with hips and haws. Far away, a train clattered along the line, and nearer lowed a cow.

The path took a gentle bend which I was about to follow when I heard the sound of jogging feet. I stepped up to let the runner pass and Alex Forsyth pounded into view.

"Mrs Farthing!" he cried, coming to a stop.

With one female glance, I took in his chiselled torso under its singlet and the strong downy legs in running shorts. The scent of male skin salty with sweat routed that of honeysuckle.

Perhaps he misunderstood my scrutiny for he bent forward, hands on knees, and between drawings of breath, said, "It's one of the perks of sixth form life."

I recovered myself. "What, meeting members of staff on jogs?"

He looked up, and seeing that I spoke facetiously, straightened with a laugh. "We're meant to run in pairs, but..."

I cocked my head. "But?"

"The others are half-hearted athletes."

"You're very brown," I observed quite reprovingly to cover admiration of his physique.

When disconcerted he dropped his eyes. "I help my uncle on his farm."

"So this is what you do when not at your studies. Surely you also pump iron!" Such personal remarks ashamed me, but this was my first encounter with vital young manhood, and it was affecting me strongly.

He pushed the hair from his damp forehead. "The school gymn is well-equipped. I train there often."

It showed, my word; he had the body of a Greek athlete. I remembered the drizzle gleaming on his shoulders that first night of term. Now the sweat brought a sheen to his upper lip. I looked away.

"Well, I'd better get back," he said.

I nodded and moved aside, and he started to jog again.

Then I heard his call. "Mrs. Farthing? Will you be all right?"

I knew what he implied and was touched. "Yes, Alex, thank you."

He raised his hand, and I watched him disappear.

What had attracted me to Antony? At first, not a lot. We met at the Royal Opera House one stifling summer night. A colleague at the school where I was then teaching had invited me to *Carmen*, and I spent an agonising few hours silently pulling to pieces the art of operatic singing. It seemed ridiculous to me that two or more persons in various throes of emotion should pant, gasp, cry out to one another in full voice, strike melodramatic poses and, whatever the crisis, still manage to reach top C. Music, dance, art and some theatre made sense. But opera?

Deafened and irritable, I went for a breath of air in the interval, and it was then that a man had shut a door on my scarf with me at the end of it. He was contrite. Could he buy me another scarf, a drink, a new neck? Antony Farthing was not a good-looking man; he was too thin and had the English gaucherie. But he dressed sprucely and there was a wholesomeness to him. I agreed to see him again, and again. Eventually, he married me for love and I married him because, so I believed, we were compatible.

As a sexual partner, he achieved things by chance than design, and they left me cold. I was worried then that I was frigid; I responded far better to his conversation than to his love-making. The only person for whom I had ever felt any passion had been one of my university lecturers who became a magnificent but hurtful obsession. But that feeling had been platonic. In my Classics training, I had discovered more of human sexuality from Greek and Roman writers and Athenian vase painting than ever as Antony's wife. The ancients' joy in sex never shocked me; I was merely the objective voyeuse. Perhaps I had become too objective, and whatever Antony had done – which was invariably unimaginative – would never have fired me.

I walked on down the footpath feeling a sudden loneliness. The woods in the distance were grape-blue; a flock of crows crawled like soot-smudge across the sky; October sun was lukewarm on my back. But I had to see where the track led. Or was it to walk where Alex had run?

# CHAPTER IV

*adfluit incautis insidiosus Amor (R.A.148)*
*"Love glides with stealth upon the unwary"*

Within five weeks of starting term I called my first departmental meeting. I needed to know exactly what and how my colleagues were teaching; it was a fair assumption that they wanted to know what I was doing, too.

I had an office like a boot-cupboard with a desk, table-lamp, telephone, a couple of chairs, several bookshelves and a grubby lead-paned window. Two of the Three Graces had to fetch their own seats, and when we were all inside it was a tight squeeze.

Looking embarrassed, they avoided my eye. I suppose if I had had a wart, glasses and bits of breakfast on my breast they would have found me easier to face. They certainly disappointed my sight. There was a crumpled air to all three; their shirts were a grey-white, one man wore a mauve bowtie, and their trousers shone at the seat. Classics was never crumpled, grey, shiny, and I wondered why so many classicists looked boring.

"We ought to compare notes," I began. Someone smelled of rank he-goat (to borrow from Catullus). I rose to open a window. It caught at one corner and resisted, and no one came to help. I thumped it hard, it flew open and I almost flew out with it. I resumed my seat, grateful for their alacritous assistance and queries as to my well-being. "Now, shall I begin with what I'm up to, or would you like to start?"

Silence. Their eagerness to speak all at once made me decide that perhaps, after all, I should begin. I was brief and to the point, running through the forms I taught and commenting on individual abilities. "Lastly," I concluded, wondering how well my colleagues would accept my final suggestion, "I would like to bring in the Cambridge Latin Course and run it alongside traditional Latin."

This moved them to speech.

"It'll water down our results!" cried Allan, the oldest of the Three Graces.

Said Bowtie, "We've been traditionalists for centuries!"

He-goat (I suspect) declared it was the wrong sort of progress.

"Right." My voice was brisk. "You've all aired your views. Now let's examine the benefits of our existing method. It's traditional, yes; it's challenging, of course. But there are boys here who for whatever reason find it hard. Let's encourage those of Alex Forsyth's acumen..."

Bowtie interrupted, "Forsyth's an exception. He's an all-rounder. He's one of those who is both academic and athletic."

"I agree, and we want more of his kind rising in the school. But we need to give heart to those who haven't quite his gifts."

My colleagues were silent. One groped for his handkerchief, shook out all the germs with its crumplings and blew like an elephant into it. At last Allan said,

"The academic standard of the school may go down if we contemplate an easier option. We, as a department, have always prided ourselves on taking less able pupils and turning them into fair classicists. We mustn't make Latin too easy or we'll be out of work."

I realised then their line of thought; they were concerned not with making Latin, indeed Classics, a challenging and stimulating subject for all abilities, rather with holding on to their jobs. "Are you saying that none of you is prepared to start alternative Latin in the first year?"

Bowtie said, "We've started them on the traditional text already. We can't change now!"

"I had in mind next year." I saw they were resistant to change. Perhaps they needed to get in a huddle to discuss it. I let the matter rest. But there was one final point on my agenda with which they would have to concur. "You've probably heard that the school is introducing a teachers' appraisal scheme next term? The Deputy will be assessing me and, gentlemen, I shall be appraising you. Thank you." This was yet another shock for them. Rising glumly, they trailed off. I glanced at my watch and blew out my lips. It was nearly time for Alex's lesson. Now for some real fresh air.

There was no doubt about it, but he was gifted in Classics. His Latin and Greek prose was both confident and polished; his rendering of the original languages showed accuracy and a talent for

English usage; he spoke appreciatively of classical authors and his comments were mature and succinct. He did not fear silence, which I found restful; if a point needed deliberation, not only would he consider it before speaking but would allow me the same luxury.

After that provocative meeting with the Three Graces I felt what was termed in common parlance 'on a high'. I had flexed my muscles, so to speak, before those conservative men, and if they had originally thought I was easy to ignore because of my sex, they now realised their mistake. Rising on this crest, I asked Alex if he would like to stay on after his lesson for a cup of tea. He said, "Yes."

At the stroke of four, subtly our roles changed. Formal school was over for the day. I rose and put aside my books; he sat back and loosened his tie. From the kitchen I called, "Would you like some toast?"

He had wandered in behind me, and I was struck by the companionable quality of this small action. "Only if you are having some." Relaxed, though without the slightest familiarity, he leaned against the sink and crossed his arms over his chest. He did not watch me as I brought out cups and saucers and sliced the bread, but I felt him aware of my every move. It was irresistibly flattering.

"Should I tell someone where you are?" I asked, silencing the shriek of the kettle with a flick of the switch.

"Do you mind if I take my blazer off?"

"Not a bit."

He slipped it over the back of a chair, saying, "No, it's school tea now, anyway. Prefects have a good time of it here, you know."

I threw him a smile. "So I've noticed!" I must have balanced the bread-knife precariously. It crashed to the floor at his feet. He moved to pick it up. As he bent and straightened, the blood swayed in his face. I took the knife. Our fingers touched. I broke out in a sweat. Any attempt at hiding my reaction to contact with him would reveal I had felt any reaction at all. Efficiently, I made the tea and watched the grill, and never looked his way. "Do you drive?" I asked at last, vigorously buttering toast.

"Yes. Let me help."

Together we buttered. It seemed so natural – as if we had made tea and talked casually many times before.

"In fact," he was saying, as he cut the toast into 'soldiers' and placed them on a plate, "I learnt here. My father has always said there were five essential things he wanted his children to be able to do."

Fascinated, I looked at him arranging the 'soldiers' in a criss-cross pile. He had well-shaped ears, very clean with a generous lobe. 'Never marry a man with small hands and feet and little ears ', my father had told me. Antony had had large extremities but small ears. "And what are they?" I asked.

"To speak a foreign language, play an instrument, drive, swim and dance."

"You do all of these?"

He turned his head and flashed me his white smile. "I'm working on it!"

We even sat in different seats from those we took when at study. Alex occupied an armchair, I the one opposite. I thought how interesting it was that something good to look at filled the orb of the eye; I had seen such uglinesses as mercifully took up only a small proportion of my sight. But anything nice to feast on – a view, an animal, a loved person – always filled the breadth and width of my vision. They say that when one is interested in somebody, the pupils dilate. I suppose looking at Alex mine had. In his dark trousers, white shirt (he wore cuff-links, a prefect's privilege), and slightly askew tie, he filled my expansive gaze. He had ceased to be the sixth-form schoolboy; he was a potent young man on the verge of the world.

"When did you first learn Latin?" I wondered, passing him the honey.

He took the pot and a spoon. "Thanks. When I was nine. My father was posted in Rome at the time, and I had lessons with a Catholic priest."

Gently I asked, "Is your family Roman Catholic?"

He shook his head. "We believe but don't worship – or rather, I believe but don't worship."

We sat in silence for a few moments, listening to the sound of school life below: discordant blastings as of elephants from the junior orchestra; a raucous conversation between boys in the Quad; the bursar's barking dog; and Matron calling, "Benson? Benson! Have you taken your medicine?"

"Do you like it here, Mrs. Farthing?" Alex asked, putting aside his plate.

"More tea? There's plenty in the pot."

"Yes, please."

I rose and, filling his cup, repeated, "Do I like it here? Well, let's put it this way, I'm finding my feet satisfactorily."

He took his cup. "I've heard things."

"What things?"

He looked mischievous. "A chap who keeps the hoi polloi in order and who may clout the over-bold can't help hearing snatches of conversation about staff. But I wouldn't dream of repeating the uncomplimentary!"

"Then may I ask what the nice things are?"

"The fourths think you're fantastic."

"Strange! I squashed them within five minutes of meeting them."

"Exactly. And the thirds say you're human."

I laughed. "What are teachers if not human?"

He crossed his legs, and I was pleased not to see an expanse of hirsute flesh between sock top and trouser bottom. Not that I objected to his flesh – far from it – but if only men realised that three inches of lillywhite leg was not an endearing sight.

"Dragons, swine or wimps."

"But that's applicable to men. What about women teachers?"

He dropped his eyes. "I'd rather not say."

I felt bold. "Then I'll say it for you. 'Cow' perhaps?"

"Perhaps!" I must have looked put out, for he uncrossed his legs and assured me, "But that has certainly not been said of you."

Over the roof, the school clock chimed half-past-four. Alex glanced at his watch. "I'll have to be going, Mrs. Farthing. I'm on prep-duty at five. Thanks for the tea."

We rose. "You must stay again, some time," I said casually.

He gathered his books and went to the door. "I'll get down to that essay on Callimachus, tonight."

"Good. And if you have any problems over it, let me know."

We smiled at one another and he let himself out. I heard his step go down the stairs and fade along the passage. I went to the window and waited to see if he would cross the Quad below to the senior school. Sure enough he did, and from nowhere a tangle of little boys joined him in his striding. I wondered if they had crushes on senior pupils the way people at my school did.

His chair looked empty. He had left his plate, cup and saucer neatly on the table. In a pensive mood I took the crockery into the kitchen. Then I saw his blazer. Still holding the crockery, I walked round the chair in the thrall of his jacket. I put my burden in the sink and tentatively touched the fabric.

Smoothing the blazer as any member of staff might do when they examine a stray garment was innocent enough. I found a name-tag under the label: 'Alexander Stephen Forsyth' it read. But what I did after that was questionable. I went through the pockets.

Pockets were so intimate. Antony had suffered from hypoglycaemia and was advised by his doctor to munch nuts when he felt the pangs of hunger. I had often seen him stuff a hand into his pocket and nibble like a rodent on an almond. To make me laugh, he then shoved his tongue in his cheek so that one side of his face swelled, hamster-fashion. Among the almonds he had also kept some spare shoelaces and a nasal spray.

It was not nosiness which made me go through Alex's pockets. I only wanted intimacy with him. I slipped my fingers gingerly into the left-hand pocket. They found two pound coins and a used rail ticket from London. In the right was a clean handkerchief. But the inside pockets – ah! that was where real intimacy lay. Ashamed, I eased my hand into the left pocket over his heart. It drew out a chequebook and an envelope adorned with Colombian stamps. There was also a black leather wallet with a ten pound note and a cheque-card. In the right-hand pocket, I found a rather splendid fountain pen, a current train timetable and a diary. This I was tempted to explore, but scruple forbad me.

The dirty deed was done. There remained only the perverted. I slipped off my own jacket and put on his. Hugging it to me, I went to the bedroom glass. The shoulders were too broad, the sleeves too long. But Alexander Stephen Forsyth lived and breathed most of his day in that blazer, and for five minutes I was living and breathing with him. Navy suited us both; I swung this way and that, then closed my eyes, inhaling ecstatically.

When at last, I removed it my scent clung to the collar. Dismayed, I took a clothes-brush and gave the jacket a good valeting. Would he be back for it before the scent faded? I crossed to the window and shook the blazer in the air which wafted gently in.

My behaviour had been strange, and the feeling which prompted it stranger still. I decided to go out for the evening; if I was unavailable he could not claim his jacket and, by morning, perhaps my scent would have evaporated.

I left my quarters and locked the door, anxious not to be seen. Soon I was out in the drive, had climbed into my car and was speeding away over the gravel. I took myself to the cinema. A romantic comedy was showing and into that I escaped. But on my return to school, cruel reality throttled escapism and left me longing for love.

Dispirited, I went up the stairway to my rooms. As I entered, the light shone on a folded piece of paper at my feet. Opening it, I read: *'Dear Mrs. Farthing, I left my blazer in your kitchen. Mr. Marks used a spare key to open up and get it for me. I do hope you don't mind. Callimachus seems all right – Catullus even better. I'll see you tomorrow. Alex Forsyth.'*

I looked for his jacket by the window. It was, of course, gone. But had my scent?

# CHAPTER V

*tacens vocem verbaque vultus habet (A.A.I.574)*
*"a silent look speaks volumes"*

"Got you at last!"

It was mid-morning the next day; I sat in my office with a pile of the fourth year's exercise books. Some of their work was promising. I saw a head round the door and greeted it. "Hello, Francis."

"Busy? Or can I come in?"

The way he shut the door behind him as if to speak in confidence disconcerted me. Was it to do with Alex and his blazer, or to say that a 'proper' room had been found for our lessons?

He sat, hands spread on his knees. "How's it going?"

I pushed aside my books and gave him my attention. "I think all's well." I caught his eyes fixing on an object beyond my shoulder.

"You've cleaned the window! Aren't you in a draught?"

*Oh, come to the point, do!*

He continued, "I like the poster. Not a legacy from Rowland, surely?"

We both stared at the picture of the discus-thrower. I loved its balance, the sense of control before unleashed effort. "No, I've had it for years."

He nodded and now looked at me. "You probably noticed that I came to your rooms to get Forsyth's jacket?"

I dropped my marking-pen so that the colour which went to my face could be mistaken for the attempt to retrieve it. "I did."

"I felt a bit of an intruder."

"Don't worry about it."

"Apparently he had the crown jewels in those pockets."

I knew all about the pockets.

"But why I've really come to see you has to do with appraisal next term." He paused and examined his hands. "Jessica, there have been some rumblings."

"General or specific?"

"Specific."

"Can I guess from which quarter?"

"You could try."

"The Three ... my three colleagues?"

The Deputy sat back and crossed his legs. The gap between sock and trouser showed a bulbous vein, purple against white skin. "Yes."

"Ah."

He looked unhappy. "This is rather difficult..."

I said it for him. "They aren't prepared to have me appraise them?"

It was clear that this type of conversation was part of his task as Deputy which he least enjoyed. He sighed wearily. "I wish that weren't the reason."

"They're being sexist."

"It looks like it.

"I could equally say I refuse to be appraised by you, a man."

"Will you?"

"Of course not! I've nothing to hide. If I have shortcomings – which is likely – I'd be only too pleased to have my attention drawn to them. I would also hope to be given credit for my strengths."

"That's what appraisal's all about! Look, it's a delicate topic and I was wondering if we could discuss it out of school, in a relaxed fashion, over a drink?"

I stared at him; this was unexpected. A faint colour was tingeing his pale face and he looked sheepish. I smiled. "That would be better, Francis. When and where?"

He brightened. "Well, it's half-term next week. Would one evening suit after the break? Monday, the -," he peered at my calendar on the wall, "fifth of November? Unless you intend going to the school bonfire night."

"What happens then?"

"There's a good deal of noise and horseplay, a whacking great bonfire in the grounds, and the maintenance staff set off all kinds of rockets."

"Perhaps I could let that pass."

"It's not my kind of entertainment, either. Let's say eight o'clock in the front hall?"

I nodded and he rose. "I'll remind you nearer the time. Now, promise you won't be upset about your colleagues?"

*Limaces viri!** I drew the pile of marking towards me. "Something told me they'd be resistant."

Francis made a dismissive gesture and left the room.

When he had gone, I stared at the boys' exercises without seeing them. The Three Graces were becoming a problem. What kind of department was ours if its teaching staff were disunited?

Feeling irritable, I went for break in the staffroom. Rupert Cotton, whom I had secretly nicknamed 'Seneca' because of his sententious turn of phrase, was holding forth in Spanish with one of the modern linguists. His deliberate articulation, the way he planted his feet and gently rocked, proclaimed as usual, "Listen to me! I'm fluent in Spanish!"

Miss Johns from Art sat looking up at him admiringly, her custard cream biscuit arrested in mid-bite. Mistaking the language, she chirruped, "Bon, bon!"

I found a chair and hid with my coffee behind *The Times.* It seemed I was hiding rather a lot; not from the boys whom I liked teaching, but from my colleagues. We had little in common; world events were minor by comparison with those at Dons.

The end-of-break bell rang. Up again, and I was off to the first years. I stepped smartly into their formroom, and twenty-five little bodies stood to attention. The shuffling gradually ceased. *"Salvete, pueri,"* I began.

*"Salve, magister,"* they chorused.

No matter that there wasn't a word for school-mistress in Classical Latin; I was quite happy to assume male gender on these occasions. *"Sedete,"* I added, and they sat.

They watched me expectantly, elbows on tables. All enjoyed Latin.

"Revision of question-words, everyone," I said. Then I held up a book. *"Quid est hoc?"*

*"Est liber!"* they chorused.

I pointed to my pen. *"Quid est hoc?"*

*"Est stilus!"*

I moved up to the red-head in the front row. *"Quis es?"*

*"Sum Ricardus."*

---

*'slugs!'

I touched the next two heads lightly. *"Quis estis?"*

*"Sumus discipuli!"*

*"Bene!"* I cried and they all beamed. "Now, will you turn to your neighbour and practise asking each other as many accurate questions as you can. I shall put on the board a list of question-words and the present tense of the verb 'to be'. Out of that you must make some sense." I let them burble happily while I wrote on the whiteboard. "There you are, now off you go."

They were as keen as mustard, and moving among them I was tickled by their voices asking each other as many questions as they had words for. This spoken Latin was an idea I had not discussed with the Three Graces. I had simply adapted the direct method familiar to foreigners learning English and now used it alongside traditional Latin study. The first and second years liked it, it gave them a sense of achievement and helped eradicate the mistaken view that Latin – despite its moods and voices -was a dead language.

I smiled indulgently on them and watched their 'tweety-bird' profiles working at *'quid?', 'quis?', 'es?'* and *'estis?'*. Late October sunshine flooded in through the windows and caught the creeper turning wine-red round the frames. I wondered if among these lads there were another up-and-coming Dons Classics Scholar like Alex Forsyth.

ᘓ ᘐ

I had just reached my rooms for his afternoon session when he knocked. I made myself busy with some books. "Come in!"

He entered, jacketed.

"Hello, Alex. Thank you for your note. I'm glad Mr. Marks found a key." If butter wouldn't melt in some mouths, this piece of humbug wouldn't in mine.

He closed the door quietly; that quiet control was getting to me. "I wasn't quite sure what to do, Mrs. Farthing," he said, coming into the room. "When I was free, you weren't here."

I gestured him to his usual seat. "I should have reminded you before you left." Keeping my eyes down, I sat and began to extract from a folder his latest essay. "Now, you did this well – as always." I passed it to him. He used black ink and wrote in a well-formed rugged hand. "Have a few moments to read my comments, then please say if there are any problems."

Chewing on a knuckle, he looked over his work. And I observed him. I wanted to find something in his person or character to disappoint. For nearly six weeks I had tried to detect a flaw either to put me off or of which to disapprove. Everybody had one: ugly hands, for instance, or stale breath, or pigeon-toes; if by some happy chance they were physically perfect, perhaps they pursued the trivial, had a mean and jealous nature or were vexatious to the spirit. Not Alex. There was absolutely nothing in what I saw or knew of him to dismay me. Even his pockets were irreproachable.

I now scrutinised his bent head. In my experience, young men between sixteen and twenty had rubbery faces, their features smudged with the complacency of youth, their lips full and indecisive, their jaws without definition. Not Alex. Manliness and, with it, a mature expression had come to him early. This was not your run-of-the-mill 'Oxford material'; and he had more grit and savoir-faire than many an older man I'd known.

Suddenly he looked up. Caught by his eyes, my private thoughts seemed all too public. My gaze flickered self-consciously away, then back again. "Any comments?" I managed to ask. *How calm he is, while inside me – riot!*

"Yes. Did Catullus go out of his way to shock, or was it natural to him?"

I considered the poet's obscenities and his irresistible charm. "Perhaps a bit of both. Think of D.H.Lawrence. Some of his poetry is absolutely delightful. Have you read *Tease*? And then think of *The Rainbow* and *Lady C.* which caused a forore. Was he setting out to shock his readers, or was it just one facet of his genius? We could ask the same of Catullus."

"I don't know Lawrence's poems." He sounded regretful. "Do you have a copy of them?"

I rose and went into the bedroom. Antony had given me the Penguin collection as a birthday present. I opened at the fly-leaf and read: *'To my darling Jess – happy returns, with love, Antony.'* "Try this," I said, returning to Alex and holding out the book. My trust surprised me; on principle I did not lend books: they never came back or were returned damaged.

He could not help see the inscription. "This is precious!"

I sat down. "Yes."

"I'll take care of it."

Perversely, I hoped he would not; for then I could fault him.

He left that afternoon with all his belongings; not even a paper-clip was forgotten. At the door we paused. "That's our last lesson till after half-term," I said, picking up a leaf which had come in with my shoes. "Will you do some study?"

His eagerness was touching. "Of course! What would you suggest?"

"That Latin past paper I gave you – could you try the verse unseen for a change. Time yourself, and don't use a dictionary."

"And for Greek?"

"Attempt one of those essay questions I handed you last week. You haven't done the Aristophanes title. No more than six sides, please, and time yourself again."

He nodded and put his hand on the door-knob.

"You aren't going away?" I asked.

"Only to the London flat."

"With your sister?"

"I don't think her half-term coincides with mine. We ... don't get on too well."

"Oh?"

His eyes fell in that disarming way. "She thinks I'm a fuddy-duddy."

"You, a ...! How can she!"

"She won't forgive me for not introducing my friends here. That's what brothers are for, she says. But I don't look to her for girl-friends, so -" He finished on a shrug.

I rose to his defence. "Some people are born middle-aged, but not you. Is she confusing maturity with fuddy-duddyism? You are very mature, Alex."

He straightened his books which were about to slip to the floor. "I don't go in for raveups, you see, and she likes them. Once, I overdid the drink, but never again! So, fuddy-duddy I must be!"

I didn't know what to say – or rather, I did but could not say it. "Your sister has yet to appreciate you," was all I dared.

He gave me a grin. "What about you, Mrs. Farthing. You're not staying in school?"

"No. A distant relative has invited me."

"Good. Well, till next time." He stepped out and with a quick backward look went down the stairway.

# CHAPTER VI

*tua sum nova praeda, Cupido (A.I.ii.19)*
*"I am your new prey, Cupid"*

Staring out of my window at lunch-time the next day, I could hardly believe that it was some six weeks since I had watched cars disgorge boys and baggage at the start of term. Now, cars were rolling up and swallowing the same boys but rather less baggage.

By two o'clock the school was deserted. I disliked the hush, the long dead corridors and silent Quad. Before it depressed me I, too, took my leave. The front hall was empty as I swung open the heavy door. Some gnarled leaves scratched across the flags, and a feline shape with pieces of its anatomy missing streaked after them. "Nisbet?" I called. He stalked back, his demeanour saying: Me? Chase leaves? Never! I crouched and put out a hand. Grudgingly he paced forward, paws turned out like a ballet dancer. Then he went into a paroxysm of affability, pressing himself over and over against my holdall, ears back, throat rattling.

Beyond the hall a door banged. Harassed heels sounded on the flags. Like a goose with her long neck and bobbly nose, the school secretary flapped up.

"Have you seen Dr. Graff?" she asked, waving a piece of paper.

I rose. "Absolutely no one. Where is everybody?"

But she wasn't interested in everybody and went off muttering that some staff were probably still at lunch.

I gave Nisbet a final stroke. He followed me to the step and, with a wave of his tail, saw me off the premises. It started to rain. Turning the car, I made for the London lights.

Martha, my cousin-in-law, had half a house in Hampstead. Well-off in her own right, she had negotiated a handsome divorce settlement and could afford a cleaning woman who came in twice a week. This left her plenty of time in which to amuse herself. She spent hours on the telephone and went to most new shows in the

West End. She was a good antidote for depression until her giddy lifestyle and the attention span of a butterfly made even low spirits seem preferable.

When I arrived, she was unpacking a box of choice groceries. She pecked me on both cheeks and said, "You look well, Jess. How are the boys treating you?"

I sat, suddenly feeling tired. "The boys are all right. It's the men."

"Do you like black olives?"

"Yes."

"What's the matter with the men? Put the kettle on, will you."

I said, "Me," and went to the sink.

"Nonsense! Let me just put all this away, then we'll have a talk."

In between nibbling at a piece of fruit cake, she painted her nails. She questioned me eagerly then listened with half her attention to my answers, fanning out her hands to survey their enhancement. "Do you like this pink?" she interrupted as I described various members of staff.

"Very much."

She peered at my nails. "You have such nice hands, Jess. I like varnish for a few hours, then it bores me. Go on. That Seneca-man sounds dreadful. Any virginal sixth formers ripe for the picking?"

I felt the heat go to my face, but she was too intent on a second coat of varnish to notice. "I doubt many sixth formers are virginal today." *Is Alex virgin?*

"Pity. I like 'em young and I like 'em pure."

I had to laugh. "Tell me about the show you wouldn't dare see alone."

She pursed her mouth, then said, "No. That's Friday's treat. If I tell you now, you'll back out, then we'll argue and someone will go off in a huff."

"Oh, dear. Am I such a fuddy-duddy?" *Alex used that expression!*

She grasped my arm affectionately. "From what you've told me about your ancient Greeks, I doubt it. Did they really paint all those sexual positions on their tableware?"

"Yes."

"Good gracious! Imagine serving your guests today from a plate which shows buggery going on."

"Some might."

She gave me a sly look. "Hmph. Despite it all, you're very moral, Jess – much more than me!"

"I wonder. What's your definition of morality?"

She flopped back in her seat, spreading her dark hair with her hands. "Oh, that's far too deep! Come upstairs. I've got some new clothes to show you."

Much later as I lay in bed in a back room listening to the crackle-pop of impatient fireworks, I considered the ancient Greek definition of morality: for them, it was immoral to scorn the gods, dishonour parents, abuse the position of host or guest, break an oath and to act treacherously. For those attempting to follow, if loosely, Christian tenets then the Sermon on the Mount provided guidelines. But how many believers adhered to them? They swore, were adulterous, worshipped money, made a song-and-dance about good deeds, hated where they should not, did not forgive as they ought, and killed if not fellow men then, indirectly, other forms of life.

I decided that modern society was rotten, had thrown over traditional morality and, as it developed further, was making up a new code to suit itself. And I, I was just as rotten as the rest, sitting in judgment on my colleagues and hankering after Alex Forsyth.

It was out. I had admitted it. Unable to face the truth within the confines of school, once split from the cocoon of Dons I was laid vulnerably bare. I, thirty, wanted a sixth-form schoolboy.

Martha and I spent my half-term pleasantly, walking in the park, window-shopping and eating out. One lunch-time she told me about her latest acquisition.

"It's a flat, Jess, nothing very grand, in Rome."

"Rome!"

"Yes." She leaned towards me excitedly. "You know, or perhaps you don't, that I have a man-friend in the housing business? He deals with properties world-wide, and told me about a little place in a quiet area of Rome. I thought it would be a good investment if I rented it out."

I was pleased for her and said so. "When will you go over?"

"Perhaps Christmas. Come, too! You don't want solitude again, do you?"

I hesitated. My first two Christmases without Antony had been spent at our home in Milford. They had been difficult but I learned how to pass, and despite bereavement enjoy, the festive season alone. It was now nine months since I had sold the house and made Westmorland my home. I had yet to spend a Christmas there.

Martha was watching me, waiting for me to accept her invitation. Then she smiled. "I know that look. There's a 'no' coming on!"

"You're very generous Martha – but perhaps not this Christmas. Antony never liked the north country, you know. He called it wild and woolly. Whenever I suggested a holiday there, he'd go quiet and cold."

"Men!" Damning them with her tone, she raised a hand for the bill. "Well, the offer remains if you change your mind."

There were now only two days left of half-term. I couldn't wait to get back to Dons, and it wasn't to see Nisbet either. When Friday came, I tried to get Martha to tell what she had planned for that evening. She refused.

"Just dress up a little, Jess," she said secretively.

She had already booked a taxi, and at half-past-seven we were driving into the heart of London.

I probed further. "It's not a blind date?"

"Not a good idea, these days."

I fell silent, watching the lights make greasy patches on the wet-liquorice road. "We've had supper," I mused aloud, "So it can't be a meal. Then it must be a show."

She turned to me with a smile. "You're getting warm!"

We had swung into Soho, and were making our way along a street with an air of disrepute. In one doorway sat a couple of homeless men under a grubby bedspread; in another was a pile of crates. Windows wore the bloom of grime and the pavement was tacky.

"It's a pornographic dive!" I exclaimed. The taxi driver must have heard, for I was sure I saw him wink.

We came to a squeaking stop outside a building over which neon lighting flashed the words: *Henny-Penny's.*

"I'm about to corrupt you, Jess," said Martha, opening the taxi door.

As I waited for her to pay the driver, I read the billboard at the entrance. It said: *'For Ladies only – an Evening to Remember! Let some of the Sexiest Men in Town bring you Fever! '*

Martha had arranged a visit to a male strip-club and, before I could re-hire the taxi, she had thrust her arm under mine, was marching me into the foyer and saying, "Come along, Jessica. We're big girls now. If men enjoy girls stripping, we can watch the boys."

There was no turning back. A gaggle of tittering office girls was hard on our heels and a burly man, presumably a bouncer, was holding open an inner door. Swells of loud jungloid music rolled over us as we entered a dim interior. The odour of beer and cheap scent twitched at my nose.

"Good evening, ladies," called a second man, taking Martha's tickets. "Would you like to leave your coats at the desk?"

An attendant with a cast in his eye saw to Martha's, but I hung on to mine in case I needed to make a quick exit.

We now stood on the threshold of a large, low-ceilinged room. It was dotted with tables at which sat women of every shape and size. At the far end was a high platform pulsating with strobe lights which caught and made glitter garlands of coloured tinsel.

Martha had booked a table for two at the back. "I don't mind being mobbed by muscular men," she said, competing with the loud music, "But I draw the line at frenzied women."

Unhappily, I sat down. This show was going to be too obvious, and I preferred subtlety. As we settled, a pretty-boy waiter in black trousers and patent leather party shoes approached. His naked torso was offset by white wrist-cuffs and a dark bowtie. We ordered ridiculously priced drinks then surveyed our fellow 'hens'.

Some were bursting ripely out of sequin-tops; others wore spider-black, against which their peroxided hair gleamed. Many were piranha-types, with mouths for ugly practices. A few middle-aged women sat bemused and twitching nervously. I speculated why they had come; perhaps their husbands offended them, rifting and breaking wind and shovelling in their food before front room television sets; perhaps their dreams had grown arid as they worked cyclopean machinery, and, to revitalise them, came here to stroke with longing eyes symmetrical male flesh.

I did not need this. Athenian vase painting was peopled with naked bodies, cavorting with wineskins and nymphs, and captured in a state of eternal satyriasis. Some time before I had marvelled at X-rated pottery in the British Museum far from school parties waving clip-boards and pencils. More recently, a youth had stood in the September rain in only a bath-towel...

Pretty-boy was bringing our drinks. The music softened, and a dinner-jacketed gentleman with kinked hair, lustrous eyes and a fruity voice stepped on to the platform. The hens wolf-whistled and clapped and drummed their heels on the floor, though I hardly knew why. He was clothed; he was ageing; he was vulgar.

"Ladies, good evening! And what an evening in store for you!" He groaned orgasmically into his microphone. "Biceps..." and the catcalls increased, "...pectorals the size of melons..." squeals followed, "...thighs to sigh for..." and heels drummed harder, "...but before we start the business of getting your pulses pounding, have you heard the one about the actress and the bishop?"

He proceeded to tell half a dozen lewd jokes which the hens loved hugely. Martha and I exchanged superior looks; clearly minds before eyes required titillating. The obscene innuendos came to an end and the music increased as the compère theatrically pulled from his pocket what everyone thought was a condom. The women shrieked as he put one end to his mouth and – blew. It swelled into a pink phallus-shaped balloon. He knotted it, then tossed it to some keening maiden to fondle as he cried, "Ladies, for your pleasure will you now welcome Marc, Laurie, Jon, Hank and Sandy!"

The lights dimmed. The music swelled and on to the pulsating stage stepped five svelte young men in full safari gear. Each carried a whip. I looked at them one by one as they moved effortlessly in a snappy dance routine. Then I almost dropped my glass. For, the young man known in this set-up as Sandy, at Dons went by the name of Alexander Stephen Forsyth.

# CHAPTER VII

## *uror (A.I.i.26)*
## *"I burn"*

I shrank. My drink had been 'spiked'. I was hallucinating. Any youth with his stature and colouring turned into Alex. I looked again. *God help me, it is him!*

I wiped my sweating palms on the tablecloth. The thudding music pounded in my ears, at my temples and bumped out of beat with my heart. Would he spot me among those faces? If he did, how could we possibly continue for two more terms in sober study? Bowtie would have to tutor him, for we would cringe and go dumb.

In my attempt to hide behind the big-haired female in front of me, I missed the show. So, I ducked and craned and bobbed like a panicky hen-pheasant at the centre of a shoot, until Martha noticed my twitchings and shouted, "You all right, Jess?"

I lied, "Yes!"

Those five young men certainly knew how to rouse the libido. They flicked whips, jerked their pelvises and gyrated buttocks in such teasing unison and with such sang-froid that I, if not all the women there, would have made a carpet of myself at their feet. But I wasn't for walking on yet; I still had a sense of perspective, and remembered what Alex had told me some weeks earlier: 'My father has always said there were five things he wanted his children to be able to do – to speak a foreign language, play an instrument, drive, swim and dance...' But this kind of dance?

Greedily I watched him. I had fancied undressing him for some time, though I refused to admit it; he had given me a taste for his body when he stood in the gloom the night of the fire-drill, a yearning for his flesh when our fingers touched on the knife, a need for his intimacy when I slipped into that blazer. And here he was, in a Soho hen-club, strutting his stuff to my cost. No wonder he didn't turn a hair when he passed five hundred boys dressed in a bath-towel. No wonder he trained at the gymn. No wonder he could sit in my rooms so self-possessed. Here was a young man who, used to participating with latter-day bacchantes in Dionysian revels, found no difficulty in sitting near a Penelope in her weaving-room (so to speak).

Did his parents know? Evidently his sister did not, or she would hardly have called him a 'fuddy-duddy'. And why did he do this? Was it the *frisson*, or were there darker callings?

I envied the dancers their clothes. No fiddling with recalcitrant buttons, no tugging on zips with bad bites; but, at a satisfying rip, they pulled off safari jackets and tore away their trousers. The women shrieked as masculine flesh glistened.

Now it was leopard-skin jock-straps and nothing else; and the pelvic thrusts continued in time to the throb of the music. The theme was African, a combination of man-on-safari and Tarzan-in-the-jungle. Suddenly, the strobe lights died and special effects striped the dancers liked tigers. We heard native drums, tropical birds, lions roaring. All five men then knelt on the floor, thighs wide. They looked under their brows straight ahead and began flicking their whips at the audience. Finally they arched backwards, every contour from pectoral muscle to knee zig-zagged with gold and black. There, in mid-arch, with scarcely a stitch of clothing, they ended their first number.

Yells, clapping, whistles, drumming – the hens were ecstatic. We were plunged into panting darkness, and my febrile imagination saw an ancient Greek mountain-side woven with rabid women making their frenzied way behind Dionysus, god of wine and life-force, tearing wild animals limb-from-limb and quaffing their ruby blood... This audience was not much different; given the chance, they'd have had these men-animals and sucked them dry.

"What do you think of it?" shouted Martha, beckoning to a waiter.

"It's excellent!" But I spoke as one stunned.

She was ordering two more drinks. I protested; my senses were reeling already. But she insisted, another ten-pound note exchanged hands, and the music changed tempo.

The second theme was that of officer and a gentleman, all very pukka. The same five dancers stepped soberly about in white uniform, gold braiding and naval hats, saluting, po-faced, to each other. Then the beat increased, and the first item to come off were their white gloves which they tossed casually at the audience. Once the remaining trappings of authority had been torn away, their movements lost decorum, and they gyrated in black leather briefs, exposing one muscular buttock, then the other.

It hadn't taken me long to acquire a taste for male stripping, and though I did not join the cacophony of catcalls and shrieking, I was roused like the rest. Antony, to whom sex but not sexuality was fine, would not have approved of the next number. It involved one dancer who, as a lonely soldier, gazed longingly at the photograph of his girl back home. With each agonised look, he discarded an item of clothing till he stood sinuously moving in a neat g-string of camouflage colours. At last, desire for his girl overcame him, and draping himself across the kind of bed no self-respecting soldier would be seen dead on, he drew up the coverlet, removed his g-string and mimed the actions of onanism.

This proved too much for the highly-charged hens; some leaped from their seats and tried to jump on to the stage, weeping and stretching out to the bed where the busy stripper lay. Martha covered her eyes in embarrassment; I – inured to satyrs in various stages of up-lift – breathed a little faster; and the management kindly but firmly led keening girls back to their tables.

Our choreographer had imagination. Next, we were delighted by a Wild West bar and five hunky cowboys riding invisible mounts (understand girls) in time to the beat. After their usual aplomb at throwing off waistcoats, check-shirts, leather breeches and stetsons, they accomplished remarkable manoeuvres with hips, holsters and guns. Then, and I wasn't sure if they or we were more exhausted, came the interval.

"What an eye-opener!" cried Martha, looking flushed. "Jess, what are you doing?"

I was moving my chair so that I sat obliquely to the stage, just in case 'Sandy' surveyed the scene in the break. My reply was fabricated but credible. "There's someone down there I don't want to see me."

"Who is it? God, your eyes are bright! Tell me who!"

I looked about for inspiration. At various stages of arousal, women were making for the lavatories or thrusting their hands between pretty-boy waiters' legs. "A teacher I once knew."

"So what!" She leaned forward aggressively. "Who do you fancy? I like the dark young man."

"There are two."

"The one who's always on the end."

*That's Alex!* "Ah, not for me! I'll have the...blond, definitely, without doubt, the blond!"

She was looking at me oddly. "You sure you're all right, Jess? It's only a bit of harmless fun!"

Of course it was fun, especially since one of the strippers was a pupil of yours, whom you taught every day, whose innocent eye you would have to meet while in yours burned his nudity.

Women were now returning to their places, looking smug or satisfied or both. They squawked as they sat and smoothed themselves down all set for the next routine. The compère re-emerged as the beat increased and called, "Enjoying it, ladies?" To which came a resounding, "Whoah!"

He was chased off by a row of five city 'gents', and after this number bowlers, pin-stripe suits and furled umbrellas would never be the same again. The strippers proved that Eden's fig-leaf was quite old hat when they demonstrated the uses to which the urban bowler could be put. These athletic young men were superb, superb to look at and superb movers. Their polished bronze bodies reminded me of the ancient palaestra, where equally athletic young Greeks would exercise naked; and many a spectator's pulse must have quickened, then, to see youths disport in the dust, as ours were thudding now – with one essential difference: these young men's movements were not a preparation as originally were the Greeks' for battle, but for defeat of the female in a strip-club.

When we reached the final number, I was in a state of tachycardia which nothing except blindness and deafness would cure; and my condition worsened when five dagger-wielding Arabs in head-dress, robes and nothing underneath moved towards total revelation under the light of a desert moon. The tempo quietened to a slow erotic thump, and the audience began clapping in time to the beat. I gripped the table. This was leading to the 'full monty'. I could not stay for total knowledge of Alex's anatomy.

I rose with my coat. "Martha, I'll wait for you outside."

"Jess!" She looked at me, then the stage, then at me again. "Anyone would think you'd never known a man!"

Turning away in case I was recognised from the platform, I stumbled for the foyer. Outside stood the bouncers. I was propelled, as it were, through the door on a drum roll and a shriek, and they turned in surprise.

Said one, "You've missed the best part!"

Making for fresh air, I called back, "I've seen it all before!"

In the street, the neon sign mocked me with its lurid pulsations – on and off, *Henny-Penny's*, on and off, *Henny-Penny's*... There was a roaring in my ears, a blindness to my sight. Dizzy, I leaned against the wall.

"If you've seen one, you've seen the lot!" Martha observed cryptically as she joined me, pulling on her coat. "You poor innocent!" She began rubbing me between the shoulder-blades. "Come on, we're going home."

We sat in silence as the taxi took us away. It had been raining again, and the current which blew through the window was sweet. I wondered if I should tell Martha that it wasn't my innocence but a startling piece of knowledge which made me leave when I did. But one explanation would lead necessarily to another, so I said nothing at all.

When home, she apologised. "I should never have taken you. Opera would be more your style."

I curled my lip. "Opera! Thank God you didn't! No, I enjoyed *Henny-Penny's*, thank you very much. But titillation is better than the...the bare facts."

She grinned. "Some bare facts they were, too! Let's have a night-cap."

It was nearly midnight when we retired to bed. I could not sleep. I relived the show over and again, the spotlight of my eye on Alex: Alex as Tarzan, officer, cowboy, city 'toff' and Arab, Alex sometimes clothed, but more often semi-nude. And when those images inflamed me beyond comfort, I concentrated on the young man at school.

How could I keep up a diffident front now? Whenever I looked at him in his uniform, I would have the x-ray vision to see beyond the blazer, shirt, prefect's tie and trousers to the sculptured body beneath. I would be at a pleasurable though unfair advantage, and his innocence would compound my guilt.

Phrases of music still thumped in my head; the way he had moved blazed on my eye. If he could do those things for a horde of women, what might he not do to one in the privacy of the bedroom, to – me? I pushed my head under the pillow to escape the fantasy, but it followed me into the stuffy dark.

Rest, that night, was impossible.

Dawn crept like a grieving widow upon my junketing visions. At seven I rose, determination and shame at conflict; I had decided to see the show that evening; once more; alone.

Downstairs as I boiled a kettle, Martha scuffed into the kitchen in gown and slippers. "You're up early, Jess. Any tea for me?"

I took out a second cup, drily asking if she had had pleasant dreams.

"Garbled and in technicolour. And you?"

"I hardly slept."

She sat down with a yawn. "Just behave yourself when you go back to Dons tomorrow!"

"A uniform helps." But my smile was thin.

At breakfast I casually mentioned that I'd like to browse round shops in the afternoon and probably have supper out. I treated her to lunch, yet I felt treacherous. Not even buying her a present in return for her hospitality improved my self-respect. I tried cerebral activities; hours in bookshops and rather less at a gallery, but I was in a physical frame of mind.

Seven-thirty never seemed to come. Earlier decisiveness turned to indecision; did I really want to see the show again? If so, why? Were my reasons healthy? How would I like it if someone with whom I had purely formal dealings knew the contours of my body? Was I on the slope to perversion? *Jessica Farthing, you are becoming a pedant.* I made for *Henny-Penny's.*

At the box-office a sour-faced man looked wordlessly at me through the partition. I had found that in certain circumstances, a deviation from what is termed received pronunciation can smooth one's way. "Should I have booked?" I whined.

"How many for?"

"One."

"You'll have to share."

I nodded, paid and slunk through the same doors that Martha and I had passed the night before. My table was already occupied by two raunchy females. They must have had native leanings because they were tattooed, studded and clamped on nearly every piece of visible flesh they owned. As I sat, they eyed me with suspicion but their attention was soon drawn to the same pretty-boy waiter who had served before. They stared at his flies and grimaced over his rear, but he bore it all with good humour.

I recognised the musical beat, but the mood of the clientèle was different. On Friday night, young women in suits with squiggly hair and drain-like mouths had come straight from work. This evening's audience were out to indulge their basic instincts, to ogle the dancers, drink themselves silly and, later, to have repeated coitus with any male on whom they could descend.

At last the fruity-voiced compère appeared, recited his jokes, blew up the phallic balloon and announced five strippers – but no one called Sandy. I scrutinised them all. None was remotely like Alex. What had happened to him? Perhaps he was scheduled to perform only on Friday night. Disappointment was my first reaction; then anxiety took over. Suppose a spectator, rabid with lust and drink, had accosted him the night before and left him bruised, bitten, incapacitated?

This time, the show was too loud, too obvious; and I suffered. When the second theme ended, I slipped out.

"Had enough, miss?" asked a bouncer, kicking his heels in the foyer.

"I've a splitting headache!" Then, on impulse, I added, "Where's the stripper called Sandy?"

He looked surprised that I knew an entertainer by name. "I don't know, miss." He craned his neck and called across to the ticket-box, "Bert? Where's Sandy tonight?"

"Who?"

I cringed as the question was repeated even louder. "Sandy, one of the strippers. This lady wants to know." The bouncer turned to me again. "Have a word with Bert over there, love. What he doesn't know about the lads isn't worth knowing."

I smiled self-consciously and moved across to the box-office. Sour-puss had mercifully gone. A cheery little man grinned through the window at me. "Sandy's sick, love."

I held the sill. "Do you mean sick as in vomiting or ill with a cold?"

His grin became a little fixed. "Sorry, love?"

When at a loss, resort to the vernacular. "Is he sick like throwing up, or sick like with 'flu?"

Comprehension swept across his eyes. "I dunno, miss. All I do know is that at five-thirty he rings up and says he won't be stripping tonight."

I paused, then lowered my voice. "Will you give me his 'phone-number? I'm a friend."

A wicked grin widened his features. "Our lads have lots of – ahum – friends! Sorry, miss, we aren't allowed to divulge their numbers." His manner was descending to the wink-and-elbow-jerk, and if I wanted to leave *Henny-Penny's* with any dignity, I had to leave then. Drawing myself up, I thanked him and walked out.

In the street, my imagination ran riot: he had been set upon the night before by not one virago but three; they, in orgiastic frenzy, had had their way with him in every conceivable fashion, had lacerated his fine flesh with their foul nails and left him for dead; no wonder he couldn't strip that night! Even now he was lying in a muck-sweat, infected, diseased, Aids-ridden...

I found a telephone box and dialled Directory Enquiries.

"What name, please?" came a voice.

"It's a London number, operator. Forsyth, A for Alexander, S for Stephen."

A recording said silkily, "The number you require is -" and I wrote it down. But in my own bacchic frenzy I had not thought this through; it was unlikely Alex's father shared the same initials, even more so that Alex would be listed. Yet some action was better than no action. I dialled.

The number was ringing, and next a cultured male voice said, "Hello?"

"Alex?"

Pause. Then, "I think you've dialled the wrong number. There is no Alex at this address."

I apologised and returned the receiver to its cradle.

The triumph of reason over emotion – that is what the ancient Greeks had revered; yet there was I, prey (as all women were, in their view) to the chaotic forces of nature, I who had always prided myself on logical thinking. I pressed a hand to my forehead as if to push back emotion. How would I have explained myself had that voice been Alex's? Reason put hands on hips and laughed me to scorn.

Slowly I made my way back to Martha's. Thirty-six hours remained before I could know how Alex was.

# CHAPTER VIII

*tacitae flammae (R.A.105)*
*"secret flames"*

School was sane. I was back in my rooms by Sunday evening and spent a few hours preparing lessons. The atmosphere bubbled with returning boys; doors banged, feet pounded, lips whistled. They seemed glad to be back.

I was. It promised to be a busy second half of term with two parents' evenings, sessional exams and preparation for the Carol Service. Most important of all, Alex had already sent off his application form to Oxford and would probably be summoned for an interview in December. My part in this process had been to select some of his marked work and send it with the form. Now we waited.

I had not forgotten my meeting with Francis Marks; what would be the outcome of that quasi-social occasion I had yet to find out. But before then – Alex.

On Mondays I taught him for an hour immediately before lunch. There was no notice on the staff board to say he was ill, so I waited as usual for him in my rooms. Punctual to the minute footsteps approached the stairway leading to my door. They came up effortlessly – but then they would. There was a pause, perhaps he was shifting his books. Next, a knock.

"Come in!"

Alex, not 'Sandy' or an Arab or a city gent, but Alex the Sixth-Form prefect entered.

It was on the tip of my tongue to ask if he was feeling better, but I was not meant to know he had been ill. Instead I scrutinised him, as only females can, quickly and taking in all the minutiae of his person.

"Good morning, Mrs. Farthing." He approached with a smile. Perhaps he was a shade drawn? What had those sluts done to him?

"Hello, Alex. How are you?"

"Well, thanks. And you?"

"Very! Take a seat. How was half-term?"

I watched the curve of his body bend itself to the chair, and recalled the tight brown skin across his stomach, the sensual thrust of his loins. Something in me became cold, formal, distant.

"I did quite a bit of work. But it ended on a ropy note."

My reaction was sharp. "Oh?"

"I ate something late on Friday night which disagreed with me and was sick as a dog."

"Ah!" And that was laden with understanding. Swiftly I added, "Poor you! So, you recovered in solitary splendour?"

"Totally. Virginia never showed up which was, perhaps, just as well."

I said another "Ah!" and felt foolish. This would be a perilous hour; the ancient Greeks advocated reason, and dismissed the advantages of the circuitous female mind. I would need to look at Alex with the reasoning part of my brain; but I would also see him with a new form of knowledge. And there female deviousness came into its own.

Settling opposite him I examined my edition of Catullus as if I had never laid eyes on it before. "I rarely eat out," I said lamely, "for that precise reason." I raised my eyes. He was looking at me a little astonished by the length of time my observation had taken to come. I coloured. Perhaps I should be frank – only up to a point, of course. "Do I sound a bit odd to you?"

Making a humorous sound, he glanced away. "No!"

"Because I sound odd to me. Holidays! That's what it is! They do not agree with me! I'm a workaholic. I love work." Our eyes met again. I saw them as they had been, looking out into a rabid audience, smouldering, inviting. I rose abruptly. "Excuse me," I said and went into another room.

When I returned I had schooled myself. The woman was suppressed. A cold male Stoicism had taken over. I sat down again opposite him. Tactfully he kept his eyes lowered. And we worked. But I felt humourless. The sparkle he had once given me was quenched. I barely looked at him, though my eyes did once caress his feet. I had seen too much, now knew too much. They say innocence is bliss; well, knowledge can be burdensome.

The lesson passed uneventfully. His work was excellent and I said so. He received my praise in an unusually subdued manner.

Was he still feeling unwell? When it was time to stop for lunch, neither of us made light conversation as we normally did. In silence he gathered his papers and I piled up mine. He was nearly at the door when he stopped and turned.

"Mrs. Farthing, have I offended you?"

I was opening the window to the November sun. Surprised, I faced him. "No. Why?"

"You seemed ... cold."

*Lacrimae rerum.** In taking the rigours of reason too far, I'd given the impression that he had offended me. Coming forward, I apologised. "I'm sorry, Alex. I'm a little preoccupied, that's all. I'll endeavour not to be cold tomorrow!"

He grinned and left. *Cold?* If only he knew.

☙ ❧

In the staff-room after lunch, Francis Marks reminded me of our rendezvous that evening. "Is eight in the hall still convenient?" he asked over Seneca who was pontificating about the best way to sit a horse and stay there. What else could he do so well? Absail down a wall of fire?

I assured Francis that the time was perfect and, retiring now from Miss Johns' panic attack, made for my office. The day passed pleasantly enough. I was obliged to crack my whip over the fourth years who thought they would try a new performance with which I did not agree. Then, after school supper at seven, a new form of excitement tingled in the air. It was Guy Fawkes night which promised a bonfire, fireworks, popcorn and pyromania generally.

Except at term beginning and end and exeats, the front hall was out of bounds to all boys save prefects. A little before eight o'clock, I was standing beside the portrait of Samuel Don, an eighteenth century descendant of the original founder. I expected Francis Marks any moment. Prefects passed by in two's and three's, and a little self-conscious, I turned to examine Samuel Don's face. He had the stern eye and hooked nose of an authoritarian. One did not trifle with a gentleman of his sort. I was wondering if there were any extant members of the Don family when a voice at my elbow exclaimed, "Mrs. Farthing!"

My heart kicked. It was Alex.

---

* literally, 'the tears of things', Virgil, Aeneid Bk.1.462

"Are you coming to Guy Fawkes?" His eagerness was touching.

I smiled. "I'm afraid not. It's compulsory for you?"

"Yes. Prefects have to circulate to keep an eye on idiots."

"And what might these idiots do?"

"Start conflagra -"

"Jessica, I've kept you waiting!" Francis Marks had come upon us.

I glanced from one to the other. Interrupted, Alex probably felt snubbed, so I finished his sentence for him, "Start conflagrations like Nero!" And to Francis I said, "No, I've only just arrived."

"Good." Frowning, the Deputy turned to Alex. "Shouldn't you be outside, Forsyth?"

"I'm on my way, sir."

Between them I sensed a spark of friction. How to dampen it? I moved towards the front door; Francis would surely follow.

He did, asking, "Your car or mine?"

"Yours." I was manoeuvring him to the vanguard.

"This way, then." He marched ahead over the gravel, and Alex brought up the rear. I looked behind. Our eyes met. An indefinable expression was in his.

"I'll see you tomorrow, Alex."

He nodded and turned away.

Francis was not a good night-time driver. He sat tense behind the wheel, peering down the funnel of his head-lamps and accelerated fitfully. He drove a tired grey estate car. Everything about Francis Marks seemed tired, from his eyes and general appearance to his possessions. Even when we had arrived at, and found a table in, the pub the papers which he drew out had lost their crispness.

He bought me a glass of lager and himself some beer, and after a deep draught began, "Forsyth coming along well?"

My tone was light, uninvolved. "Very. I need explain something only once and he has grasped it."

"Your predecessor didn't like him."

"Why not?"

"Said he was cocky."

I stared at Francis. "I find him most unassuming. Now, Smithers in the upper fifth's cocky."

My colleague played with the coaster under his glass. "Perhaps it was a personality clash. Women either bring out the best or the worst in a man. I dare say you see only the best in Forsyth."

I looked into my drink and made no further comment. Next door, fruit machines chugged and a cascade of coins fell into the metal cups. Then there was ribald laughter and a tune began on the juke-box.

Francis looked kindly into my face. "Well, we haven't met to discuss Forsyth. Have you settled in with us now?"

I hesitated. The teaching posed no problem; it was my Classics colleagues. Whenever I tried to talk to them an unseen barrier came down between us.

Noticing my hesitation, Francis smiled. "Your silence speaks volumes!"

"Yes, I have settled in, I like the boys and my work but – I can't help my sex!"

"Thank God for that!" He paused, trying to fit the lower rim of his glass into a ring on the coaster. "I've heard only good of you, Jessica. The boys tell their parents and the parents tell me. Several have said what a difference you have made to their lads' understanding and enjoyment."

This was gratifying, but I remained unmoved. "I'm sure it's team-effort."

"Hm. You'll know what I mean at the third form parents' evening in two weeks' time."

We had still not come to the point of our meeting, and I wanted to deal with it quickly. "Francis, what exactly does one do in teacher-appraisal?"

"Right." He leafed through the papers in front of him and passed me a sheet. "Ideally, you appraise those in your department, I appraise you, the Head Master appraises me and an external head appraises Dr. Graff."

I gave a laugh. *"Quis custodiet ipsos custodes!"*

He blinked. "I know what that means, but remind me."

"'Who will guard the guardians'."

He opened his mouth to speak but the door crashed open and a couple wandered in. They saw us and more sober inmates, and the man cried, "Blimey, wrong bar!" before he and his girl crashed out again.

"Are the governors ever appraised?" I asked, when peace had returned.

"Heavens, no. The governors are beyond reproach!"

I curled my lip. I had a healthy disrespect of school governors. What were they? Ageing men and women who had either held down jobs in industry or none at all; who came to school functions and were treated like potentates; who ate and drank well at the school's expense, then spent a somnolent afternoon expatiating on policy and finance when they hadn't a clue how to clean a white-board. They were patronising, insensitive and usually dense. In my view, a school was best run by its staff, pupils, some parents and external teachers – in short, people who knew.

I doubted, however, that the Deputy would share my opinion. He broke in on my thoughts with details of appraisal. "First, an initial meeting is arranged with the person you're appraising," he said. "You agree a time to sit in on a lesson. Then you observe that lesson and have a further meeting to discuss it. Next, you draw up a statement which addresses issues relating to the appraisee, agree it together and, if necessary, suggest areas for improvement. After that, you sit tight till you hold a later meeting to review the situation."

Our eyes met, then we both laughed. Strangely, Francis also coloured.

"May I say what I think?" I asked, sobering. He waved a hand in a theatrical manner which I understood as assent. "The whole procedure is ridiculous!"

"Quite." He removed his spectacles and rubbed an eye. "But we've got to do it." Almost boyishly, he tossed back the remainder of his beer. "Have another?"

I declined, and when he had returned from the counter I continued, "Why can't we do it the old way? Tell a teacher they are good or bad, and if bad, sack them?"

"Oh, that's cut-and-thrust! You must nanny them through the rough patches, and reward them with a bonbon when they've improved." Francis Marks did not think much of the appraisal system either, but we were stuck with it.

"So," I began, pushing on to the neighbouring table the tacky ash-tray from ours. "I have three colleagues, male, who refuse to be appraised by their head of department, who is female."

"And that's one of the reasons why we are having this drink."

It had not occurred to me that there were others. "Reasons?" I echoed.

He shifted, embarrassed. "I'll mention that later."

"Then what shall I do about my colleagues?"

He sighed, clearly disliking the whole situation. "The Head Master has spoken to them. They remained unmoved. They implied they'd walk out if ..." his voice trailed away.

I understood. "Do you know, Francis, I've never acted the little tin goddess with my colleagues. We've had one departmental meeting which, I felt, was democratically conducted, but I could hardly drag a word out of them, and when I did, they were inflexible. I would like some support!"

He stretched out his hand but did not touch me. "I know, Jessica."

For some time we sat in silence. A conversation, presumably between farmers, reached us from the other room. It concerned set-aside farming. "It's bloody stupid!" cried one irate voice. "All that ground sitting idle just to please a few white collars who don't know the difference between a tup and a ewe!" They had my sympathies; bureaucracy should become more empirical.

At last I said, "Dons doesn't need the sort of publicity brought by three Classicists walking out. And I'm not resigning because of some sexist men. There's only one answer."

Relief flooded across Francis' face. "Yes?"

"We compromise. You sit in on their classes with me."

He scratched his neck, murmuring, "We hadn't thought of that! Jessica, I take my hat off to you!"

"Ah, but will they agree?"

"They'll have to. Or the matter will go to the governors. Yes, that's an excellent compromise. I'll make a few written comments during their appraisal so they can see it's a combined effort... Oh, do have another drink!"

I smiled and shook my head; I still had marking to do – an essay from Alex. And now the main reason for this meeting had brought a result, there was little else to say. We discussed our respective half-terms, and conversation grew progressively stilted. Weariness overcame me. This was, after all, a staid pub despite the irregular chunterings of the fruit machines and sentimental Country and Western music on the juke-box. The last thing I wanted was to be staid with them.

Apologetic over our silence, Francis gazed into the middle distance. His was the face of a middle-aged retriever, kindly, brown and a little droopy. I imagined him naked; he would have the white puckered buttocks of the sedentary man; his calves, I knew, were knotty with veins; his chest, though hollow, probably had slight breasts. I had noticed a spare tyre bulging over his belt. At that point I stopped, my powers of observation striking me as cruel. I switched to Alex and recalled his chiselled body; there was nothing to spare on him – everything was firm, proud, capable.

To stay longer seemed pointless, and boredom was increasing my fatigue. Francis' glass still stood half full and I looked pointedly at my watch. He noticed and asked, "Sure I can't buy you another drink?"

"No, thank you. I ought to get back – work to prepare!" I found Alex in work, in Virgil and Thucydides, Ovid and Aristophanes, as hero, soldier, lover and young man about town. In seeking my books, I sought him.

Only when Francis and I parted in the school hall did I remember that he had not told me the other reason for our meeting.

# CHAPTER IX

*possessa ferus pectora versat Amor (A.I.ii.8)*
*"cruel Love makes sport of hearts in his thrall"*

Whatever had caused the friction I felt between Alex and the Deputy, there was no sign of it the next day. When Alex stepped into my rooms in that controlled way of his, the first thing he did was to return my collection of D.H.Lawrence's poems.

"Did you enjoy them?" I asked, taking the volumn. It was in the same perfect condition as before. *Oh, Alex – do put just one foot wrong!*

He stood by his usual chair and a beam of sunshine glanced across his shoulders. It brought out the male fragrance of after-shave, nothing strong but, like much of Alex, provocatively subtle. "Yes. An incredible use of language!"

I thought I would test him. "Give me an example."

He chewed on a knuckle. "There's the poem where he writes of – and perhaps I misquote – of his *'kisses steaming wasteful into the night's black nostrils...'*"

"A powerful image. I see night as a black mettlesome stallion." *What's your kiss like, Alex?*

He came nearer. "And elsewhere, there's something about sparrows and sin."

I paused, my brain doing three things at once: delighting that his enthusiasm matched mine, trying to recall those particular lines, and wondering if my eyes gave anything away. Then slowly I recited:

*"'... I did not dare look up,*
*Lest her bright eyes like sparrows should fly in*
*My windows of discovery, and shrill 'Sin!'"*

"That's it!"

"It's from *Snap-Dragon.*" At last, I looked at him.

He sent me a little smile to which I responded. A bond seemed to link us; we shared not only our studies, but also something which stretched beyond the tight sphere of school and examinations. His reaction to Lawrence showed he saw much of what I saw; and I enjoyed much that he enjoyed. A sense of happiness overcame me.

I was stroking Lawrence's book of poems; perhaps my expression reflected my feelings, for I suddenly looked up and found Alex's eyes on me.

He said, "I realised its sentimental value and took care of it."

Sentimental value? Ah, yes – Antony's gift. Yet it had not been of Antony I was thinking, but of Alex and how his hands had held that book, his eyes had followed those poems. "Thank you, Alex." I sat, and he took his usual chair. "I see I can trust you with more." An enigmatic statement, and he could interpret it in any way he chose. I gazed out of the window again; *we really should get down to Classics.* I continued, "To me, there is a similarity between Catullus and Lawrence; no part of the body is taboo. They write straight from the...the gut, about anything and everything. I suppose people can't take that." I turned back to him. "Learning, Alex, is about opening the doors and letting the light in."

He looked at me steadily, then his eyes seemed to darken. "I think you're wonderful," he said.

A flush from my heart (so it felt) crept all the way up to my hair-line. I could not hide, nor hide from, it. I burned in front of him. Should I make light of it? But why? I had thought him wonderful for weeks, though my wonderful was rather different from his wonderful. After that Rowland-man, I dare say I was bloody marvellous; idiot, calling Catullus a deviant, and thinking Alex cocky!

I made no comment, nor did I change the subject; that would have suggested his admission was inconsequential and out of place. It was neither. So I allowed him the luxury to see his compliment make an effect. When my colour had subsided I asked, "Are you reading a lesson at the Carol Service?"

He sat back. "No."

"Would you like to read a passage from Virgil?"

Chewing on his pencil was not a habit, yet he bit on it now. I saw his white teeth and was affected by the movement of his lips. "Yes, I would. But how is it relevant to the Carol Service?"

I told him about a pastoral poem of Virgil's, often referred to as the Messianic Eclogue; for the poet foretells the birth of a child, believed by some to be Christ, who would restore the world to its past glory. "That, at any rate, is how some interpreted Eclogue Four. Now, if I speak to the Head Master, and he agrees, would you be happy to get up there and read Latin?"

Alex grinned. "Try and stop me! You'll help my pronunciation?"

"Of course." I hesitated, thinking of all the work he had. "It will mean coaching after hours."

"I can cope."

When he left, my head was full. His words, 'I think you're wonderful' kept recurring. At least he liked me! Then there was the matter of priming him for his Latin reading; perhaps, subconsciously, it was a ploy to see more of him.

Whatever, Dr. Graff gave his consent and the coaching went ahead.

I told no one else. Whom Alex informed was up to him. But it seemed right that Dons' Classics Scholar should read a piece of Latin at his final carol service. He came at different times, immediately after school or, like the first meeting, when supper was over. That had been a preliminary session when we looked at the poem in question, translated it and discussed the background. We would meet for an hour.

"Would you like a drink?" I asked once, desperately hoping he would say yes.

He did. "I've told my parents about this reading," he added, drifting into the kitchen behind me.

"And what did they say?"

"You want my father's precise words?"

I looked at him anxiously. "I hope he doesn't think you've bitten off more than you can chew."

He took the glass I handed him, our fingers just brushing. "He said 'Blast'."

"Oh dear!"

"No, not that kind of blast, but the blast which means 'Hell, I wish I could be there.'"

"Ah!" We had returned to the sitting-room. Deviously I took his seat because my need to touch the things with which he had most recently been in contact was growing importunate. He absorbed this phenomenon briefly, then sat in my chair. I sipped my sherry as a cat might drink cream; to be female and governed by nature had distinct advantages (*pace* the ancient Greeks). "There is no chance that he could come over?" I added.

"No."

"Then he won't be at the Upper Sixth parents' meeting next term, either?"

"I'm afraid not."

"Do your uncle and aunt ever come?"

He shook his head and his eyes fell away from mine. We were silent. The lower school bed-time bell rang, Nisbet (presumably) let out a feline shriek in the Quad and the bursar's dog yapped something which could be interpreted as: "Serve you right! Serve you right!" – or ruder.

"Are you like your father or your mother?" I asked casually.

"My father, so they tell me." He balanced his right ankle on his left knee, and I smiled to myself. Body language never lies; he was holding himself as might any young man at ease with his companion. I felt gratified. And just as one guest king, who having done something visibly strange with cutlery, was kept company by his host in this strangeness, I kicked off a shoe and tucked my stockinged foot under me.

"I admire my father," Alex continued. "Some things I do I know he would disapprove of, but –" He finished with a shrug and a grin.

Aha! *Henny-Penny's!* "And your sister? Who's she like?" He had beautiful hands, long-fingered intelligent hands with perceptions of their own; he kept the nails clean and blunt-cut. I began to imagine those hands exploring another body, a fantasy so intense that I missed what he said about his sister. But I wasn't really interested in her; she had called him a fuddy-duddy and for that I tossed her from my mind.

"And you, Mrs. Farthing," he suddenly asked. "Who are you like?" His glass was empty. I rose, slipped on my shoe and offered him some more. "Just half, thanks."

Returning to my seat, I assumed my previous position. "I have no close living relatives, only some cousins in New Zealand, but apparently I take after my paternal grandmother – a combination of opposites, often in conflict."

He gave me an appraising look. "I haven't been aware of conflict!"

"It's a private battle," I replied softly and avoided his eyes.

When he left me at half-past nine, I wondered how wise it was to have him in my quarters after school hours. Dr. Graff had probably told Francis Marks about the Latin reading; what Francis did with this information was his affair – though it might end up by being everyone else's, too. I could support any murmurings my colleagues voiced, but might Alex not be mercilessly 'ribbed' by his? There was only one alternative for everyone's peace: to conduct these meetings in my office downstairs.

As I prepared things for the next day, I mused on what Alex's study-bedroom was like. Sixth-formers had private rooms in a wing at the other end of the building and were overseen by the senior housemaster. Did he have 'pin-ups' on his wall like most young men? What kind of woman did he admire? At any rate, he had called me 'wonderful', though it was probably on the inspiration of the moment. I would be sensible and accept it as that.

Now a muggy November night enveloped me. I felt hot. I wanted to show love but lack of opportunity left me feeling impotent. *'Water, water, every where. Nor any drop to drink.'* I was surrounded by over five hundred males and could be demonstrative with none.

A moth dived between the curtains into my room and collapsed against the lamp-shade. I tried to rescue it, but it insisted on its light-besotted blunderings. Slowly I undressed in front of the glass. Once, Antony, sitting in bed in striped pyjamas, had looked up from his book as I performed the same ritual and said, "You've got a beautiful body, Jess." It was spoken as you might say, "The forecast is rain for tonight." A lover-husband would have leaped from his bed to relieve me of my remaining clothes; but he merely scraped me with his eyes before returning to his book.

Bit by bit my sexuality had gone underground. The love-scenes I witnessed in films were so frenzied and insensitive that I began to believe that was the nature of all sexual activity. In any case, Antony and I jogged along adequately without it.

How would Alex make love? Was he still virgin, his sensuality channelled into stripping from time to time at *Henny-Penny's*? I took a shower, then lay down naked. Someone had defined sex as a celebration of the body. Did that mean no sex was no celebration? What had Antony and I celebrated? Not a lot. He had juddered upon me more, I suspected, for his convenience than mine and, at times, I felt he regarded my body as a penetrable piece of flesh, a sort of skewer-and-kebab affair, rather than a sentient thing. Without doubt, sex performed badly was best performed not at all. Perhaps Antony had sensed his shortcomings which explained the infrequency of our congress.

I could have asked for what I wanted. Once I did, and he was exasperated. "You shouldn't have to tell me, Jess! It's like giving directions – 'no, not there, here'. I am not a lost pedestrian in need of guidance to the post office!" But he was.

I was no feminist wanting to rip my man's clothes off, yank him to the floor and straddle him. There were some areas where a man should lead and if, in time, the woman went with him, neck-and-neck, then that was the way it should be. From what my experience was worth, I much preferred to be the violin from whom the player produced harmonious chords.

I looked at the semi-circles of my breasts. They did not hang, when I stood, like milked cow's udders. They were – how should I put it – interior-sprung, not large but firm and conical. I had a long waist and small navel like a pucker in an otherwise smooth pool. And what a ridiculous term, the mound of Venus, for the female pudenda. The Portuguese called it 'little dove', while D.H.Lawrence referred to it as 'fig'.

Had Alex read that particular poem? A shiver ran down me. Dragging the coverlet across I hid my face and fantasised about him as officer and gentleman, Arab, sixth-form prefect sharing with me intimacies indescribable.

# CHAPTER X

*arte regendus Amor (A.A.I.4)*
*"Love must be guided by skill"*

The third form parents' evening was a tedious business. It began at seven-thirty when Francis Marks shepherded new staff to their tables and parents to new staff. We were placed round the Great Hall, far enough from a colleague so that we did not succumb to chat, but within earshot of conversations with parents. On my table stood a prim white notice saying: 'Mrs. J.Farthing, Head of Classics'. Fortunately, and perhaps by design, the Three Graces (namely, Allan, Bowtie and Catullus' Goat) sat a long way from me.

Francis fussed around. "Are you warm enough, Jessica?" He laid his hand against the heater at my back. "It is on."

"Just about, thanks." But I was more intent on looking at the Sixth Form prefects walking sprucely among parents. And Alex? Where was he?

"How many parents want to see you?"

I consulted my appointments list. "Forty. Is that normal?"

"For Classics, yes. Look, I'll get one of the prefects to fetch you a cup of coffee. We do like to keep staff at least watered on these occasions!"

I smiled at his little joke. His attentions were, I felt, becoming noticeable. Since our drink the week before, he had gazed at me mournfully with his retriever eyes like one wanting to wag his tail but uncertain whether the response would be a pat or a reprimand.

Someone had told me he was a bachelor, had once set his cap at the then school matron but was rejected. I felt he was now wondering if I might consider becoming Mrs. Marks. Billets doux had started to appear in my pigeon-hole written in his spidery hand and always beginning with: 'I thought you might like to see this...' It seemed that he combed the daily papers for all things classical, whether it was a letter in *The Times* from a Girton scholar or details of archaeological finds. Did he assume that I never read the papers; or was it his way of saying: 'Look, I'm thinking of you!'?

Fortunately, he was now called away and I sat, conspicuous and rather vulnerable, in an area that was becoming ever more crowded. I had some marking to do and was on the point of embarking on the correction of an execrable translation of Hannibal and his elephants when a voice to my left exclaimed,

"You've got no coffee!" Alex was looking down at me in indignation. "Haven't those mutts seen to you yet?"

I smiled. "Who are the mutts?"

"My fellow prefects. Honestly, they're useless. I'm late because my father has been on the 'phone. He's worried about Christmas arrangements. What would you like, Mrs. Farthing – tea or coffee, weak, strong, sugar or none, milk or without?"

"Weak coffee with milk but no sugar, please." Since he lingered, I went on, "Do you always act as waiters at parents' evenings?"

He began to back off as a large couple bore down on me, and said over his shoulder, "It's called service to others!"

I saw and spoke to the Joneses, the Higginbothams, the Wilberforce-Gibbses and the Steiners of this world; I listened to the pretentious, the homely and the patronising; I looked at the well-dressed, the dishevelled and the vulgar. Most parents were pleasant, some just civil. Twice Alex came and went with cups of coffee, and by ten o'clock I had a headache.

I used the same patter for many parents: 'He's coming on well,' or 'He has a flair for Classics.' No sooner had one couple left their chairs when another sat down. This on top of a full teaching day was, I felt, an imposition.

Gradually the hall emptied. I had seen all the names on my list and could retire blissfully to my quarters. I was gathering up Hannibal and his elephants when Francis plodded towards me looking peevish. "Jessica, can you spare me five minutes?"

Five minutes could be more. I replied, "I'm rather tired, Francis. Can't it wait till tomorrow?"

"Not really. Let's go to your office."

Stiffly, because he was becoming a bore, I left the hall with him. He attempted to make conversation as we walked down deserted corridors. The little boys were in bed; the others in their houses. There was a silent fullness to the atmosphere. "Now, Francis," I began, easing my books on to the table. I did not offer him a seat.

He fiddled with a cup of paper-clips which irritated me. *Oh, spit it out, do!* At last he observed, "You should keep a watch on Forsyth."

I swallowed. "Why?"

He took out a paper-clip. "I caught him several times this evening staring at you."

I had to laugh. "A cat can look at a king, Francis!"

"Not in that way."

"What way was it?"

"Almost ... calculating."

"Poor chap! He was probably calculating the right moment to slip in between parents and ask me about a pig of a Plato essay I set him today."

A sniff escaped him. "I'm not so sure. We need to be careful. Most of our Sixth Formers are well-developed young men, and Forsyth is more mature than most."

I laughed again. "Francis, what are you suggesting?"

The bent paper-clip had become a hunch-backed pin. "It is irresponsible of us to expect you to conduct one-to-one tutorials in your private quarters. It was all right for Rowland for obvious reasons. So, I have decided to move Allan's small group from here and place him elsewhere. Then you can give all Forsyth's lessons in your own office."

This was risible. Smartly, I leaned across and shut the door just in case the wall outside had ears. "Forsyth is one of the most self-contained young men I have met," I began. "He is discreet, chivalrous and hard-working. It would offend him to know he was being moved down here for propriety's sake."

Francis raised a hand and closed his eyes at me. "Really, Jessica, we should never have suggested you teach in your rooms. On behalf of the school, I apologise. It will be more convenient for you here – you'll be near your other classes and the staffroom, and it's better all round in case of an emergency."

The more I argued my case, the more adamant he became. Reluctant to descend to the undignified, I said at last, "Very well. When will this happen?"

He replaced the paper-clip no longer fit for its purpose. "Tomorrow."

"Will you tell Forsyth, or shall I?"

"I will."

There was nothing more to be said. I opened the door, bade him a good night and left him.

From that moment, I began to question my role at Dons. I had thought myself happy, only because Alex was responsible. But, in two terms, he would be gone. What was left me then? A good job wasn't everything. For true fulfilment one – at least, I – had to be satisfied, mentally, physically and spiritually. Was I really accepted at Dons? Despite political correctness, I was being stigmatised by some for my gender and, quite possibly, my looks. That I was an able Classicist made no difference; had I been male and handsome, no one would have disputed my right to be there. But in an academic environment female good looks and brains were incompatible. The most successful beauties have been brainless, and the most successful brains have been plain.

Slowly I switched on the lights in my sitting-room. I looked at Alex's chair then at mine, at the Christmas cactus spurting pink flames from its leaves. We spent five hours a week there, reading, talking and discussing Classics. I think he enjoyed his lessons. I loved them. The quality of my teaching and the extent of his learning should not be affected by a change of room. But I felt it would.

ᘓ ᘔ

At eleven the next morning, I duly stood outside my office waiting for Allan to emerge. I heard his excitable talk, the effete way he pronounced his r's as w's. Evidently he advocated tutor- rather than student-centred classes. Now twelve large fourth formers tramped down the passage towards me. My instinct was to back against the wall, so loud, so big they seemed. I stood my ground. I was the bollard, they the traffic, and they would go round me.

Some had younger brothers in the school. "Did you see my parents, Mrs. Farthing?" asked one.

"Yes."

"And mine?

"I did."

Then a voice mumbled something and there came a suggestive guffaw which, I sensed, was directed at me. I thought how unseemly was this hanging around in the passage with a posse of louts (and more to follow) bearing down on me. Francis had done me a great disservice by altering my teaching room.

At last Allan issued from the office with two Lower Sixth members. He shot me a black look and hurried, slightly knock-kneed, down the corridor. The air in the office smelled of fetid breath. I flung open the window and wretchedly sat, waiting for Alex.

Five minutes passed. A hush descended on the building as lessons continued around me. A male voice rose in the middle distance then sank. Elsewhere, laughter lifted to a crescendo and tailed off. I left my desk and looked up and down the passage. Only a slinking low-slung figure paced across the floor. It was Nisbet. He halted as my head appeared in the doorway and looked at me as if to say, "Only thou and I are sane in this place," then he paced on. Another five minutes passed; still no Alex.

Seizing my books, I hurried along the corridors to my rooms and, as I expected, there he was outside my door sitting in the gloom on the top stair.

"Mrs. Farthing!" He rose to his feet.

I steamed up the steps like Nemesis. At the top, while I took out my key, we crowded together. I was panting more out of fury than effort.

We entered. "So, Mr. Marks didn't tell you?" I shut the door and faced him.

"What was he to tell me?"

"That our lessons had, from this morning, been transferred to my office downstairs."

"No. Why the transfer?"

I flung a reply over my shoulder. "Suddenly it lacks propriety."

He stood where he was. "Then, shouldn't we go down?"

"No!" I snapped, following it with a gentler, "We stay here. You've wasted ten minutes and I've wasted ten minutes and we aren't wasting any more. Have a seat."

He came further into the room. "And my Virgil practice for the Carol Service?"

"We stay here!" Our eyes met. Suddenly he grinned and we laughed as conspirators. In the spring I would look for another post. Dons without Alex would bury me alive.

# CHAPTER XI

*ingenii est experientis Amor (A.I.ix.32)*
*"love demands guts and initiative"*

I did not see Francis Marks at lunchtime nor, for that matter, Allan. But at the end of school, the former sidled into the staff-room for tea. He looked sheepish and attempted to hide behind the urn as I approached.

My tone was, quite naturally, reproachful. "You didn't tell Alex Forsyth of the new arrangement!"

He coloured. "It slipped my mind, Jessica, what with one thing and another." We stood before the table where brown bread and butter shone oily in the lights. "Let me pour you some tea," he added, placatory. He rattled cups, saucers and teaspoons as he continued, "Er ... we'll have to go back to the former arrangement, I'm afraid. Allan's unhappy about being shifted from your office. He's always taught there, you see."

I took the tea he handed me. "I suppose he thinks it was my idea?"

"I told him not. Bread and butter?"

"Thank you. So, let's get this straight: I resume teaching Forsyth in my rooms as before?"

He shunted the jam bowl towards me and thrust a spoon into its red viscosity. "I think that would be the best plan after all."

I smiled to myself, and for once was grateful to one of my department.

"Would you like to come to Sunday lunch?" My astonished look led Francis to continue, "You haven't seen my house, have you? One of the perks of the job. The only thing they left out of the package was a company car."

He was being facetious but to please him I smiled. "The trouble is, I can't return the gesture."

"Oh, good heavens! Buy me a drink some time. You will come?"

"I'd like to." We had moved away from the table as Seneca, expleting verbal wind as usual, pressed down on us from, so it seemed, all sides. "Which house is it?" We found a corner table and Francis sat, perching his plate on a bony knee.

"To the left of the senior wing as you come up the drive. It's the only one with the yew in front. Have you any dislikes? I'm quite a dab-hand at the Sunday roast."

I bit on my bread, butter and glutinous jam. "Pork. And sprouts. Otherwise I am easy to please."

"So, pork and sprouts will be off the menu. Will twelve-thirty suit?"

I said it would before Seneca, deciding he would join us, moved in our direction. I shrank. I was allergic to the man.

"God!" he began, curling a foot round a chair leg and drawing it beneath his posterior. "Why won't these boys see the relationship between Latin and modern languages? I'm sure you do your best, Mrs. Farthing."

Mrs. Farthing did, and frankly had no difficulty in that direction. Without comment, I watched him take a noisy draught from his teacup and waited for his next pearls of wisdom. They came.

"Classics is so useful! It civilizes wild breasts. It hones the rugged mind." Now came some tooth-sucking. "I had thought it was making a return. But, it's dying."

I bristled. "Pah!"

"My dear Mrs. Farthing, colleagues in other schools tell me so."

"Well, with respect to your colleagues, Mr. Cotton, they are misinformed. There is a new Latin scheme for primary schools, adult returners are taking to the subject heart-and-soul, students can reach GCSE standard via distance learning, and Oxford is marrying various branches of Classics to the most surprising disciplines."

When contested, he squeezed his face up in a deathly rictus. "Perhaps, but in schools it's floundering. State education doesn't offer it."

I contradicted him.

"Not to A level."

"Some do, especially enlightened colleges of FE."

"Well, I've learnt more Latin since school than I ever did in it. My one regret is not knowing Ancient Greek."

*Ignare!** I thought it judicious to leave that little tea-party before Latin invective became Saxon-expressed. I got up, saying, "I do hope, Mr. Cotton, you don't tell your various classes that Classics is dying – when it isn't."

He looked at me indignantly. "Certainly not. I'm all for it!"

"Good. Because it is mischievous talk like that which will do no one any good. Excuse me, gentlemen." The man should have been gagged, but he'd only pontificate in that oil-slick voice of his through some other orifice.

"I want you to be the first to know."

It was Friday evening. Alex and I had just been rehearsing his extract of Virgil for the Carol Service. I was pouring some lager, for it was half-past six and time for a drink. "And what's that?" I handed him his glass, waiting (and praying) for the brush of his fingers. We often made contact this way; it meant nothing to him, of course, but for me it was magic.

"My application to Oxford has been processed and I've got tests and an interview in December."

I was delighted. "And this is to read pure Classics?"

"I wouldn't contemplate anything else!"

"Have other colleges or universities made contact?"

He released his tie and top button, and I had sight of the well between his collar-bones. *'Pectorals the size of melons...thighs to sigh for...' Henny-Penny's* featured often in my rooms those days. "Not yet," he replied." But I've set my heart on Balliol. Mrs. Farthing, I want to thank you for making it all possible for me."

I was touched. "It has little to do with me, Alex. It's entirely through your own hard work and ability."

He looked serious and, if I could believe it possible in a man, almost emotional. "Not altogether. I felt I was getting nowhere with Mr. Rowland. You've peeled off the layers and led me straight to the core of Classics. You've been the only one to show me the writer beneath the words."

I smiled at him. "Now I'll have my say! You've a receptiveness and an attitude well beyond your years. There have been times when I have forgotten you were the pupil and I the teacher. We've

*'fool!'

had some rattling good discussions which have widened my perceptions of classical authors. Dear me, I sound like a school report! However –" I raised my glass, "– I propose a toast. Here's to your success at interview and to us for the rest of our lessons together." Was that unguarded? I glanced at him, but he looked only reflective. "You've told your parents the good news?"

"I will, later."

"And have you decided on your Christmas holidays? You mentioned the other day that your father was worried about arrangements."

He loosened his tie further. I liked men with released ties; it suggested to me rising heat but restrained passion. "I think so. I suppose I'll be in London. My parents can't get home, and my sister says she's staying with friends."

He'd be alone? He was a mature nineteen, but a solitary Christmas seemed rather cruel. "You won't have anyone?" And I stared at him in concern.

He shrugged. "I don't mind. My aunt and uncle in Wiltshire would have me if I really wanted company. They take in everyone. There's no peace! What I'd like best of all is a tranquil Christmas, the great outdoors and all that, with wild places, no crowds and food when I like it."

An idea in embryo began incubating in my mind. A gentle hint would hurt no one. "I've always thought a London Christmas must be exciting," I said carefully. "All those bright shops, the bustle and festive atmosphere. Quite different from Pomeroy..."

"Pomeroy? Isn't that where they hold the gipsy fair? I didn't realise you lived there!"

"It was only a bolt-hole while I was married. Antony hated the place."

Our eyes met and held. It was as if the idea developing in my head were meeting a similar notion in his. It was up to me to express it. "You won't know what I'm thinking now, Alex."

"Try me!"

"Since you want a country Christmas and I would love a city Christmas, why don't you spend it in my Pomeroy cottage -"

"And you stay in my parents' flat?"

"Precisely."

He leaned forward. "I'd like that very much!"

"What about your parents? Would they mind my staying?"

"They'd be delighted! They know how supportive you are."

From the depths of the building the supper-bell suddenly rang. Alex finished his drink and straightened his tie. "I must go," he said. Then, on impulse, he stretched out his hand. "Thank you, Mrs. Farthing, for absolutely everything!"

I gave him mine and, liking the firmness of him, looked long into his face. Then our clasp broke, we both rose and he left me.

☙ ❧

I did not really want to have lunch with Francis Marks, yet I had no reasonable excuse. Living on the premises, I was easy prey. For a while, I toyed with the idea of cancelling it; however, it occurred to me he was growing a little jealous of Alex and his tutorials with me, and if I accepted his invitation it would keep him sweet and put him off the scent.

Sunday dawned glass-bright. It had rained and turned much colder, and drops hung trembling from the trees adding to the winter glitter. Sunday was the least structured day of the school week. The only compulsory occupation was morning service in the Chapel. After that, the boys played sport or music, those prefects who drove went out in their cars and supervision was in the hands of housemasters. I had heard rumbling among staff about the boys being bored, and it was an issue raised at a meeting. But Dr. Graff was adamant. "Young people must learn how to structure their free time," he had said. "Many of them will face periods of unemployment, so one day in the week when they are compelled to fall back on their inner resources is a positive exercise."

Seneca, his voice as unctuous as ever, put in the saw, "'The devil finds work for idle hands to do.'"

"Hear, hear!" exclaimed the head of science who, because of his wild hair and shaggy beard, I privately called Archimedes. "I found a goldfish impaled on a compass-point last Sunday."

Miss Johns gave a little shriek. "That's from the art room aquarium! How awful."

The Head Master asked stiffly why he had not been told. Silence. He turned to Francis Marks. "Did you know?"

"Yes. But I felt it deserved ignoring. Make a point of these things and they're inclined to recur."

"So that, Head Master, is how the boys structure their free time," said Seneca with the suggestion of a sneer.

Dr. Graff was inflexible and insisted that if any further cruelties occur he had to be told; free time should be used constructively, he said, with which we all agreed. And nothing more was done about sabbath ennui.

The Sunday I went for lunch with Francis was fine enough to encourage the boys outside after Chapel. They flocked about the grounds filling in time before one o'clock. This was unfortunate because my approach on, and entry into, the Deputy's house caused an inordinate amount of interest. There were Whoi's! and catcalls which made me wish I had never consented to the invitation.

Francis heard my footsteps and swung open the door. "Hello, Jessica," he said. "Take a seat in the sitting-room – first door on the right. I'll just deal with this foul bunch."

From the window, I watched him stride up to the ten boys outside. "Pilkington!" he shouted. "Take your hands out of your pockets. One is permissible, but not both. And you, Scott, tuck in your shirt. You look like a lager-lout." Then he ordered them all into a row with their backs to his house and cried, "Stand easy! Now, here you will stay till I say otherwise. And no talking!" He came back to the house and slammed the door on them.

From my place in the sitting-room I heard him mutter, "That'll teach them!" He appeared in the doorway. "Sorry about that, Jessica. Smutty little devils! What will you drink? Scotch, gin, sherry or lager?"

I asked for a lager and he went to a cupboard near the window. "You've heard the good news about Forsyth?"

"That he's been called for interview at Oxford?"

"Yes. He'll go far that young man, if he doesn't grow too big for his boots." He came across the room with my drink and I adopted the policy that silence on certain topics was golden. But for some reason, having been the first to bring up the subject, he would not let it go till he felt like it. "Any others who might be as good as him?"

"Jamieson in the upper fifth is promising." I sipped from my glass, just as determined to remain casual about Alex as Francis was to pursue him and his so-called arrogance.

"Yes. And an altogether different cup of tea to look at!" (Jamieson was bespectacled, a touch spotty and so thin he could be mistaken for a ruler.)

My reply was non-committal. "Quite."

Francis had flung himself into a chair from which he continued with Alex. "I hear Forsyth's reading some Latin at the Carol Service. A good idea of yours, Jessica, or did he suggest it?"

"I did." The sound of hissing steam came from the kitchen. He rushed out to see to it. I relaxed and casually looked round a typical bachelor's sitting-room. There was a lot of brown in the books and furnishing, and not a plant to be seen. The one bright thing was the coal fire whose flames pattered like butterfly wings. A grandfather clock ticked its weary heart in the corner, and there was the slight smell of fusty papers. I glanced through the window. The ten 'sentries' still stood with their backs to Francis' house.

He returned saying, "Lunch won't be long. Do you mind eating in the kitchen?"

"Not at all. Francis, the boys outside ..."

"Can stew another five minutes!" He peered truculently at them. "I won't have them embarrassing my guests on my Sunday. So, only two more weeks to the end of term. Tell me, what's your impression of us at Dons?"

I knew what he meant, but it made me feel a visitor rather than an active member of the school. I did not challenge him; I needed him for a reference. "I like teaching male minds," I said.

He crossed his feet at the ankles; his shoes were weekend wear and scuffed. "Hm. Classics is still predominantly a male subject."

"I think it always will be considering there are no Greek and Roman women writers of note."

"Pity. When I was at school we did Caesar and Virgil only; and the pattern verb for the first conjugation was not *amo* but *laudo* and the first declension pattern noun was *regina* not *mensa*. 'To praise' was better than 'to love', and I doubt one could decline the word 'queen' today without a snigger!"

I laughed. "And I've had to change the second declension pattern noun from *annus* to *dominus*."

"Oh?"

"One wretched child in the third year insisted on pronouncing it 'anus'. For a week I had nothing but 'anus, oh anus, anus, of the anus, to/for the anus, by/with/from the anus'."

Francis found this hilarious and thumped the arm of his chair till the dust flew. "And how did you nip that one in the bud?"

"I told him that if I heard 'anus' one more time, I'd pin the word writ large on his back and he'd wear it for one whole day."

"Appropriate in a boys' school!"

I understood the implication. "Have there been any incidents?"

"Yes. Behind the sports-hall. He was a lower sixth-former who bribed half-a-dozen first years to meet him there. We expelled him. Anyway -" he slapped his knee and jumped up to look out of the window. "Good! They haven't moved!"

I thought the 'sentries' had been punished enough. "Won't you disband them, now?"

"No. School lunch is at one. I'll dismiss them at five past. That way, they will be late for food and get order marks. Now I'm going to drain the peas."

At one, we heard the school lunch-bell. The sentries outside shifted and looked over their shoulders at Francis' house. No one dared move. Francis called me to the kitchen. He had laid the table with care. A bowl of peas, carrots, roast potatoes and a joint of lamb steamed appetisingly. He began to carve.

At five past one, he bade me not to wait and left the room. I heard him open the front door and call, "Right, lads, dismiss!" And twenty heels shot across the gravel.

It was a good lunch, well-complemented by a bottle of Bulgarian wine. We talked very little of school, which I appreciated. Eventually, conversation turned to the Christmas holidays and he asked me my plans. I was sufficiently vague, and he told me he was intending to spend his with his sister in Dorset. "If you've enjoyed your lunch," he added, "then I have her to thank. When it seemed I would never marry, she took me in hand and showed me how to roast, boil, steam, blend – the lot!" He looked pleased with himself and pleased with me for sitting with my feet under his table. "What is it about a woman that makes things perfect!" he concluded.

"Male imagination."

He laughed. "Good heavens, Jessica, you can be stringent!" But I did not feel it. A sleepiness was coming upon me. It had been a busy term and most nights I lay wakeful during the small hours, thinking. If I sat beside Francis' fire in the afternoon, I might fall asleep.

Much to his disapproval, I washed up and when we had had coffee he suggested a walk. The sun still shone and the chill wind would be bracing. He put on a trilby and we set off down the drive, I hoped, unseen.

The country was superb; great rolling Sussex hills over which tree skeletons climbed and, lower down, intimate lanes. We walked for an hour, and when we returned the sky was deepening for night. "Come in for a cup of tea," Francis begged. It was the fire more than the tea which enticed me; and there was little left to talk about now. We drank our tea and had a slice of cake and made desultory comments while mesmerised by the flames. I thought of my cottage at Pomeroy; I would tell Alex to light a fire whenever he liked – there was plenty of wood and coal; and he must choose which of the bedrooms he'd prefer; mine had a double-bed, the guest room a divan.

"Jessica?" Francis had risen to join me on the couch. He placed his elbows on his knees and pressed his finger-tips together. "Have you ever thought of remarrying?"

I started out of my soft reverie. "That's a bolt out of the blue!"

"I'm sorry. But if the chance presented itself, would you consider it?" He turned to look at me out of brown droopy eyes; more than ever I saw him as a kindly retriever.

I turned back to the fire. "It would depend on the circumstances."

"What if I asked you?"

Considering his recent attentiveness, I was not altogether surprised. "In that case, Francis, I would say it was for convenience."

One hand left its finger-tip steeple and lightly touched my arm. "Don't presume to know my mind!"

"Sorry! It's a failing of mine. But, to be honest, marriage hasn't entered my mind."

He looked hangdog. "I see. Well, I'm proposing anyway! Look, I don't want to stay at Dons forever, nor be Deputy till I retire. I'd like a headship somewhere and a wife to support me in my work."

Whatever my dreams were, they certainly did not feature my becoming a head-master's right hand. Gently I said, "I think you would make an excellent head, Francis."

"Perhaps. But I'd still need a woman beside me. Jessica, you'd complement me terribly well!" A warm paw was now laid on mine. I didn't like it. I had fed myself with visions of a young male whose torso was as strong as it was firm, of sexual intimacies suggested in a

Soho strip-club and carried out in the bedroom. Francis Marks' canine attributes, though lovable in a dog, were unattractive to me in a mate.

I said, "I like you, Francis, but anything deeper is not possible."

The paw was removed. He rose and seemed to shake himself. "I've been too blunt." He began moving round the carpet. "And I've taken unfair advantage of you. I intended asking you only for lunch, not marriage; that was meant for another time. But you looked so receptive, so right sitting here before my fire, that I was carried away. I'm sorry."

It was an apt moment to leave. I, too, rose and smiled at him. "Thank you for a most enjoyable day."

He fetched my coat and assisted me into it. "Thank God you aren't one of those ghastly women who say 'I can manage – I haven't got a broken arm'!"

"But that's what men are for," I retorted with a sly look, "To open and shut doors and generally smooth a woman's passage through life!"

"You try telling the Modern Ms that!"

At the open door we paused. There was the smell of coal smoke and the bite of frost. "Keep warm!" he called as I crossed the gravel to the main building. I raised a hand and went in.

# CHAPTER XII

*vix a te videor posse tenere manus (A.I.iv.10)*
*"I can barely keep my hands off you"*

Alex went to his Oxford interview early in December and was away for two days. On my advice, he took with him some further copies of his record of achievement and the two essays I had marked. If his interviewers were going to refer to them when they met, it was only fair that he should have access to these papers at the same time.

Before he left, I gave him a further tip. "Don't stress your academic leanings, Alex. They've got proof of that in these essays. Talk about your athletic interest, your hobbies, for example, swimming or – dancing." I was not beyond the occasional slyness.

He had kept his sang-froid. "I could certainly mention the athletics."

I wondered what Oxford would say if they knew he flexed his muscles in a rather different fashion in Soho.

On his return to Dons he looked cautiously hopeful. "The papers I sat posed no difficulties," he said, "and I think they liked my interest in my uncle's farm. We had a long chat about combine harvesters and contract farm-workers, which led to the journeymen hay-trussers of Thomas Hardy's day."

"Excellent! Smack them between the eyes!"

He grinned. "I didn't want to knock them quite out. Anyway, they implied that any offer they might make would be conditional on my gaining two A grades in Latin and Greek, and B in my other subjects."

"In that case –" and I pulled my books towards me, "– we'd better get on!"

End of term was now almost here. He had a final rehearsal of his Virgil reading in the school Chapel. We entered when the rest of the school was at prep. I had told the duty master what we were doing, just in case he saw the lights on and thought of hauntings or, worse, vandalism.

It was a fine building, long and narrow with pews that creaked like old bones in bad weather. Plain windows soared to the roof, save one whose red and gold was repeated in a bright aisle carpet and an array of chrysanthemums. On the altar stood candles, fat and buttery in stalwart holders.

I switched on the altar lights. Slowly out of the dim nave Alex and I walked towards the glow. "Did you say you were religious?"

He stopped, his eyes circling the nimbus before us. "Not in a churchy way. Are you?"

"I hate religion – any religion – being knocked. Apart from that, I hope but am not convinced."

He was straightening a prayer-book. "Mr. O'Hare, the school chaplain, gives good sermons. Did you know he read Classics at Cambridge? Last Christmas he talked to us about Horace sacrificing a kid to the *fons Bandusiae*."

I had not properly met Mr.O'Hare. I asked what point he was making through a pagan reference.

"That religious practice, however strange to others, must be respected. He said that society in Britain was such a hotch-potch of different beliefs that the only way to accept the status quo was through tolerance." Alex turned to me, his face lighting. "I can remember how he began that address. My word, we all sat up!"

So, Dons did have a few interesting staff-members. "How did he begin?"

Alex looked at the pulpit, then at me, then at the pulpit again. "Like this." In a few quick strides he was up the pulpit steps. For a moment he stood there, hands resting on the surround, then leaning slightly forward in the manner of vicars, he began:

*"'Oh Bandusian spring, brighter than glass,*
*Worthy of sweet wine and flowers;*
*Tomorrow to you I shall sacrifice a kid*
*Whose brow, swelling with its first horns,*
*Destines it for love and sparring.*
*But not so: for the young of a sportive flock*
*Will dye with red blood your cool gushings.'"*

I stared in astonishment at him; what else was stored in that mind of his? And I was still staring when he left the pulpit and returned to the aisle, saying, "You look amazed. That's just how we all were!"

My speechlessness continued; I was astounded not so much by the Chaplain's choice of quotation as the striking image of Alex in the pulpit. Would law be the right career for him? For a moment I saw him as a priest. I recovered myself. "Well, if the Chaplain borrows freely from Classics, I think I'll come to Sunday service!"

"He is good, Mrs. Farthing. He makes a point of talking to all the forms in school to find out what they're studying. Then, somehow, he'll weave a sermon round a topic we can relate to. Last year's Upper Sixth were studying Horace for A level."

"Right, now let's see what your reading of Virgil's Messianic Eclogue will do for parents and school alike!"

Prompted, he picked up his book and went this time to the lectern. I slipped back into the shadows until only he occupied the light.

He did not pose now, but stood grave and erect. Then he began. Just once I corrected him; the rest was perfect and I said so, but did he want one more go since that would be the last? He agreed, and as he read it for the final time before the Carol Service, I wondered what the future would hold for this exceptional young man. Dare I ask him to keep in touch when he went on to Balliol, as doubtless he would, and I – heaven knew where?

The final week of term was upon us. This was the boring part. Lessons gradually wound down, and years one to four wanted to play word games. The fifths were sullen and were interested in nothing; so I gave them a classical word-search which they pretended was beneath their dignity but since I had introduced references to the homosexual Harmodias and Aristogeiton and the rape of Lucretia, they rather enjoyed the exercise after all.

Alex's final lesson was spent exchanging instructions about our respective pieds-à-terre and not much else. "Here is a spare set of keys to the cottage," I said, handing him what had once been Antony's. "Keep the home fires burning, Alex, so use plenty of wood and enjoy yourself!"

He took the keys. (We did not brush fingers this time.) "I think I will! Thanks."

I needed to ask where I should sleep in his parents' flat but dithered a while; mention of bedrooms in the context of Alex was rather too close to the bone. Tidying a folder which did not need it, I casually asked, "Which room should I have in your place?"

"There's my parents' which is unmistakable, Virginia's all teddy-bears and celebrities, and mine – well, you'll know it when you see it. Take your pick!"

I had already. "And you're sure your sister won't be spending Christmas there?"

He made an exasperated sound. "As sure as I ever can be with Virginia. She told me she was staying with friends in Cheltenham when I rang her yesterday. They're partying up to the eyeballs, apparently, and she loves her parties. Look, this is the communal front-door key ..." He was holding up one, "And this is the key to the flat."

I took them and asked if anyone knew of our holiday arrangements.

"Not likely! They'd make a meal of it just as they made a meal of your Sunday with Mr. Marks."

"Ah! I thought as much. There's something incestuous about being resident in school. You can't smile at someone or have a meal with another without its signifying more!"

His eyes slipped from mine. "It's none of my business, but some chaps are saying you and Mr. Marks are secretly engaged."

"Tosh!" But he deserved a fuller reply. "We will treat that idea with the contempt it deserves! Now," and I became efficient, "The best rail route to take to Pomeroy is from Kings Cross to Leeds, then the scenic Settle-Carlisle line across the Pennines. It's rather a trek, I'm afraid. Does that put you off?"

"You should know me by now, Mrs. Farthing!"

It was an innocent enough comment, but I had the impression it conveyed rather more. Teased, I studied my hands then dismissed it; young men were given to quipping. I changed the subject. "We've got an extraordinary staff-meeting followed by tea with the governors on the last afternoon."

"Bad luck! We can go after the Carol Service."

"I know. But staff have been bribed, as it were, with the promise of a Christmas tea which –" and I was naughty to say this in front of him "– will be made all the more delightful by the governors' presence."

He grinned. "You don't like governors?"

I think I looked bullish. "Shall we say I question the talents of those who become them. But enough of that! I shall stay on in school till the next morning, and when you start your journey north, I'll be just about beginning mine to London."

It was a good arrangement; but I could not help feeling guilty. Teachers and pupils did not usually exchange homes as we were doing; it smacked of an intimacy which should not have existed. On the other hand, Alex was no longer a boy. He was old enough to vote, to marry, to buy alcohol and tobacco, to see adult films and to make a will. Where and how he spent his holidays was certainly not Dons' business.

Two days after, term ended. An electric atmosphere sizzled through the school. There was horseplay among the boys and still more among the junior masters who, by dressing up as Scrooge and the spirits of Christmas Past, Present and Future, tried through various methods to frighten both staff and pupils.

I called a departmental meeting to recap on the term's work and to exchange notes on any plans for field trips. My colleagues expressed no ideas. "I feel we ought to arrange something," I said, wondering if they had been so apathetic under my predecessor. "For instance, I had thought of a British Museum visit for the fourths, and Fishbourne or Bignor Villa for the lower school." I looked at all three faces, but the men sat eyes down, silent. I tried again. "A short play might be fun, too. We could commemorate Julius Caesar's assassination in March, and take a few boys from the fifths and Lower Sixth to act it. I don't mind writing the script or even directing, but I can't do both."

This was met with dead-pan expressions too, until Allan remarked that the fifths had too much on their plates with public exams looming. I said very well, let's choose boys from the fourths.

Bowtie responded with a shrug and, "We could try."

I grew impatient. "I like your enthusiasm! Have any of you some better ideas, perhaps?"

"Field trips are popular," put in Catullus' Goat, and that was the only concession he made to my thoughts on the matter.

It was the shortest departmental meeting I had ever attended. "Thank you, gentlemen," I said tersely, and picking up my papers I walked out.

On the last evening, we ate a Christmas dinner – boys in their dining-room, and we staff in the room adjoining. There were paper hats for everyone. The Deputy's tilted over his brow making him look tipsy. Mine was unobtrusive and a flattering shade of blue. The kitchens did us proud with everything traditional, from stuffing to brandy-butter. I wondered if Alex would cook himself a Christmas lunch. This school meal had been mine, and on the big day I would eat simply.

There were no lessons the next morning. Till break, each form cleaned out and tidied their lockers; after break they smartened themselves up before filing into Chapel for the Carol Service.

The occasion for horseplay was now over. On everyone sat an air of sobriety. Cars of all shapes and sizes rolled on to the rear games field and disembarked fathers, mothers and siblings. In the Chapel, the school was directed to the left, visitors on the right. The first four rows were reserved for staff.

In the staffroom we finished preening. All wore formal gowns with hoods. I liked wearing mine; it was an academic status symbol. I ceased to have a gender. I was A Mind.

# CHAPTER XIII

*augent secreta furores (R.A.581)*
*"secrecy increases passion"*

"Can I sit next to you?" murmured Francis Marks as we gathered in the front hall before filing in two's into Chapel.

I smiled my consent, thinking how schoolboyish grown men could be.

"You look wonderful in your gown," he added after some scrutiny.

Was he just being complimentary? I glanced at my colleagues who wore their gowns like sacks; they drooped at the rear hem, or slipped off a shoulder no matter how much they were twitched and yanked. The art mistress had high heels in which she walked hen-toed, and kept tossing from her neck masses of dyed black hair. She reminded me of one of the Erinyes. Seneca fancied himself, lifting his arms like a Roman orator while declaiming in his unctuous way.

Now it was time to file into the Chapel. "Are we ready?" called Dr. Graff. Like children we arranged ourselves in a crocodile, no one observing any particular order or rank save that I walked with the Deputy immediately behind the Head Master. No doubt the boys would make something of that. To the strains of *Once in royal David's city* we entered the Chapel and paced down the aisle, seried ranks of boys on the left, a motley crowd of visitors to the right, and ahead, the stalls incandescent with a befrilled and surpliced choir.

We took our places in the first four pews and examined our service-sheets. When the shuffling and creaking had stopped and the whole congregation stood vigilant, from among those shining apple-faces in the stalls a fluting voice sang the first two verses of *O little town of Bethlehem.* I taught that child, a messy little beast who flicked his pen to draw the ink; there had been blue splodges everywhere, on floor, boys' backs, books and my shoes; now he had to write in pencil which he hated. Still, his was a superb voice, full-throated and clear like a blackbird's. I wondered as I listened when political correctness would have its way with all words containing 'black', so that we had darkbird, darkberry, dark sheep of the family, dark magic, darkhead, darksmith...

The service-sheet now required us to join in the singing, and fluting Darkbird was swamped. The very bowels of the Chapel seemed to rumble, and a fraction – always a costive fraction – behind the organ, the congregation strained at its voice.

When was Alex due to read? I cast my eye down the sheet. Ah! Almost at the very end of the service there it was: *Virgil, Eclogue IV, lines 4-23. Reader: Alexander Forsyth (Upper Sixth).* My translation was printed beneath the Latin for the benefit of the untutored.

Some ten minutes passed during which the choir sang a Christmas piece and the head boy read the lesson. Then we all sang again, after which a bespectacled child who could hardly see over the lectern lisped his way through the Annunciation of Mary. The Chaplain came next. Mr. O'Hare had always been of the staff but not in it, and I was looking forward to the address of a fellow Classicist who drew, in a back-sitting-up way, on Horace's *fons Bandusiae.* He was now entering the pulpit and settled his hands in precisely the way Alex had shown.

The coughing and creaking ceased as he began: "Our celebration of Christmas has its origins in a pagan festival called the Saturnalia. The Romans celebrated the Saturnalia for seven days in honour of the god Saturn, who represented a civilized and golden age. It took place roughly in the third week of December. It was a time to close everything down in favour of merrymaking: schools shut, businesses stopped, the courts went into recess. Slaves were allowed to say what they liked about their masters, gifts were exchanged and gambling with dice was permitted." He paused and looked intently round at us all before continuing, "I've been thinking very hard about this over the weeks, and in my travels through the parish and beyond, have been made aware how we are really twentieth century Romans celebrating not Christmas but a latter-day Saturnalia. For what do we do? We shut our schools and businesses, and the media – let's call them modern slaves – say just about what they like of their 'masters', that is, people in the public eye. And what mad gift-getting, too! Shops are bursting with things you can buy and just as quickly give away, and the gambling with people's lives and happiness is embodied in the self-indulgent drinker who becomes a demon. What excuse do these people use? 'It's Christmas!' they say. But I say, 'No, it is not. It is the Saturnalia.'" He raked us with his eyes again; and the congregation sat tight. His voice lightening, he went on, "The early Christians were a sensible lot. They knew that Christ's birth would, by comparison with the Saturnalia, be a rather wan affair in the calendar. How much wiser to attach it to an already established festival whose accent was on closing down and cheering up. So they placed Christ's birthday near the festival of Saturn. Saturn the Roman god and Jesus the Christian Saviour were conveniently celebrated at the same time. It barely mattered whether you were giving presents because it was a pagan custom or because it symbolised the Three Kings presenting the gifts of frankincense and myrrh to a Child-God in a stable. Now, some two thousand years later, there has been a shift in emphasis. The Saturnalia has dropped from the calendar and the twenty-fifth of December is big news and big business. Though few people have heard of the grand Roman festival and most know of Jesus Christ, the noisy spirit of the Saturnalia has drowned Christ's quiet birthday. In our mad rush to go partying, gift-buying, eating and drinking, in our obsession with closing down and cheering up, we forget that in all this noise, quietly a Child was born.

"In every one of us is the pagan and the Christian, the loudness and the hush. As we all leave for our separate homes today, may we remember, for Christ's sake, the festival He put in our calendar. Let us all enjoy the season not as followers of Saturn, but as believers in Christ."

I turned slightly to Francis on my right and caught his eye. We both raised our brows in approbation while Mr. O'Hare cleared his throat and asked us to sing the next carol on our sheet. And, as that came to an end, my heart began to pound: it was time for Alex.

We sat, and the pews creaked under the weight. From the corner of my eye I watched for Alex coming, as he should, down the central aisle. But he seemed to have taken his cue late. The creaking and coughing and shuffling ceased. I – the entire Chapel – waited. Only the heating soughed through the vents.

I turned towards the aisle. Others were turning, too, their faces speechlessly questioning.

"Where is he!" hissed Francis in my ear.

A little boy behind hacked at the air with a series of saw-toothed coughs. Someone's stomach rumbled, then a sneeze was suppressed. The clay-like quality of the flesh has its moments.

I began to turn red. My heart doubled its beat. To Francis I said in an undertone, "I haven't seen him today. Can he be ill?"

"Then it's sudden. He was handing out service-sheets earlier."

By now, everyone was craning their necks, and the silence rustled with whispers. *Alex! You've let me down!* Unable to bear the suspense a moment more, I rose, stepped past those seated on my left and walked up to the lectern. Facing the congregation I said, "Alex Forsyth is unable to read today." Like calmed waters, the crowd subsided. The crisis for them was over, and I began: *Ultima Cumaei venit iam carminis aetas...*

I read with my lips and my eyes, but in my head I heard his voice. As I came to the finish and concluded, "Here endeth the lesson", an emptiness filled my heart. That should have been Alex's reading; we had worked hard to perfect it; but he had failed himself and let down me.

Numb, I returned to my place. Francis nodded with grim satisfaction. And for the remainder of the service I was an automaton following the actions and noises of everyone else. One word dominated throughout: Why?

We sang the final carol, and the service was over. Staff left first; the boys would follow and finally the visitors. The Michaelmas Term had officially ended. Once outside, Francis took control. "You go into school and see if he's there. I'll watch the boys as they come out. Young Forsyth's got some explaining to do!"

Mortified, I hurried away.

"You filled the breach well!" oozed Seneca at my elbow; but I had no time for his oiling.

Inside the school I paused. Could Alex have left an explanatory note in my pigeonhole which I had failed to see? Or one under my door? Or was there no explanation because he had been taken ill? With my gown billowing behind me, I ran to the rack of pigeon-holes outside the staff-room. Mine was empty. Two-at-a-time, I took the back stairs to my rooms. I unlocked, but there was no note on the floor. What now? Should I wait, or go to my office in case he turned up there? Even now, news could be flying from mouth to mouth, and I the last to hear it.

But my office was empty. Dispirited, I entered, leaving the door ajar. I wanted to howl. Miserably, I looked out of the window at gowned colleagues flapping like cormorants in the breeze as they saw cars off down the drive. Among the boys at least, Alex's misdemeanour was fast becoming submerged by more immediate concerns.

Nearer, doors banged, voices called, footsteps pounded past the door, then "Shit!" cried a boy as something crashed to the ground. Now, other steps approached, irritably. At my office they stopped, and I turned.

"Ah, there you are," said Francis, coming in. "I can't find him anywhere! Matron hasn't seen him, either. What the hell is he playing at? You've looked upstairs?"

"Yes."

As we discussed the situation, Francis growing more agitated the more dispassionate I remained, a shape filled the doorway. Alex stood on the threshold, hand raised to knock.

"Forsyth!" shouted the Deputy.

I leaned across my desk as Alex walked in. "Are you all right?"

He was white, his eyes dark with wretchedness and in silence he looked first at me then at Francis.

But Francis would not wait for his reply. "For God's sake, what got into you!"

Alex's voice was husky. "I chickened out, sir."

"Not ill?" I asked.

"You 'chickened out'?" cried Francis. "You don't chicken out of your commitments! You face them like a man!"

"Yes, sir." Alex held himself well, hands behind his back. I could not help thinking that if he had 'chickened out' of the service, he was taking this situation with remarkable courage.

Francis continued his tirade. "You've upset the continuity of the service by your 'chickening out'. You've put Mrs. Farthing to great embarrassment, and brought a last minute panic on the school. What got into you!" He was growing melodramatic now, throwing his arms about and spitting and, by comparison with self-contained Alex, looked slightly ridiculous. It occurred to me that his irritation would have been less had it been another boy; but it was Alex of whom, I was sure, he had been growing increasingly jealous, and I felt that he enjoyed berating him in my presence.

I couldn't bear it although Alex stood his ground, punctuating the Deputy's comments with polite affirmatives. "Oh, please!" I cried at last. "We're getting nowhere! Perhaps there is nowhere to get! Deputy, let me handle this. Alex and his reading are my responsibility, and it's not fair that you should work yourself up over it."

Francis jerked his gown round the back of his neck. "Very well. I've got parents to see and the Head Master will need to know Forsyth's about." He brushed past Alex, then pausing in the doorway added waspishly to me, "Do what you have to do!"

I gave a heavy sigh and sat down. "Shut the door Alex, will you."

He closed it quietly and I motioned him to a seat.

For some moments I remained silent, my eyes on the desk between us. A breeze rustled the creeper outside my window; cries and greetings came across from the drive as still more boys left for the holidays. Someone honked their car-horn; a woman laughed like a jackass. Raising my eyes as last, I said, "Alex, what went wrong?"

"I chickened out!"

"So you've already said." I looked hard into his face, feeling there was more to it than that. "But why? You were so confident the last time we rehearsed it."

He broke eye-contact. "I was all right until Waring started singing *O little town of Bethlehem*. That pulled the ground beneath my feet."

I was watching his features. They twitched, and for one terrible moment I thought he was going to break down. Gently, I said, "Do Waring or that particular carol have a significance for you?"

He looked at the floor and gave a brief nod.

"In that case, shouldn't the Head Master and Mr. Marks know?"

"Mr. Marks should know, but Dr. Graff wasn't Head Master at the time."

This silenced me. Up till then, I had thought it strange that Alex could perform erotic floor-shows with incredible sang-froid, yet balk over reading sober Latin at a carol service. Now I knew this was not the problem. "Do you want to tell me about it?"

"No." It was a polite but firm negative. "That is –" and he leaned towards me "– not now. It's irrelevant, Mrs. Farthing, to your tutoring me."

"But Alex! It isn't irrelevant to what happened this morning! I had to read your piece for you! What am I going to tell colleagues when they query it, as I'm sure they will?"

He looked pained. "Do you think bad of me?"

"No."

"Have I disappointed you?"

"No – well, if I'm honest, yes."

He sat back. "Then I'll tell you!"

I put out a hand. "No, don't. Tell me when the time is right for you. I accept that you had your reasons and, knowing you, they must have been valid. It's just such a shame that after all our work you never got to do your bit."

He paused, before saying with deliberation, "People's memories are short. In a way, that helps me, but at a time like this, I wish Mr. Marks had remembered!" He hesitated. "It's a bit of a nerve to ask a favour, Mrs. Farthing, considering... But I'm going to, anyway. If you want to know about that significance you mentioned earlier, will you please not ask the Deputy?"

I was taken aback. "I won't ask anyone, if that's what you'd prefer."

"I would prefer it. One day, when it's right, I'll tell you myself."

Suddenly the lunch-bell rang. We both rose. "When are you leaving?" I said.

"At two-fifteen by minibus to the station."

"I suppose you'll be ribbed again after this morning?"

He shrugged. "I can take it. Look – none of this affects our plans, does it?"

"For you to stay in my place, and I in yours? No."

"Good!"

I watched him stretch for the door-knob; his hand was shaking slightly. "I think you've been overdoing it, Alex," I said. "Go up north and have a rest. And –" now this caused me some effort, "– if you meet some nice local lass, ask her to dinner!"

He gave a laugh with not much humour in it. "Unlikely! But if I do, I'll tell you."

We exchanged a brief, almost conspiratorial, look and then he left me. For some time I stood reflecting. Alex seemed too young to have secrets, and yet here was another to tease me. He had let us both down at the Carol Service, and a small part of me insisted that my image of him was now tainted. The reality was he intrigued me even more.

# CHAPTER XIV

*Militat omnis amans (A.I.ix.1)*
*"Every lover is a soldier"*

"Funny choice of address." Bowtie sat in a chair and stretched out his legs. We had all finished lunch and were drinking coffee in the staff-room. My nose was in the paper, behind which I saw a lot and heard more. I had caught Alex's name at table, but missed any qualifying remarks. Perhaps people would elaborate now.

Said Seneca from the coffee-pot, "I thought it rather good, myself."

Bowtie took a noisy gulp from his cup. "Well, first we are told to be less Roman in our Christmas knees-up, then we have a reading from Virgil. Surely the second cancels the first?"

Seneca oozed over to Bowtie and stood swaying and deliberating as he sucked on his teeth. "Whose idea was the Latin?"

I said from behind the paper, "Mine."

"And a good one, too!" Francis Marks had come into the room and I winced, wishing he would not assume that I was incapable of championing my own cause.

Bowtie sounded aggrieved. "I didn't say it wasn't, Deputy."

Seneca eased into the chair beside Bowtie and pulled methodically on his fingers till the knuckles cracked. "To return to your observation," he continued, "I think the address was apt. Virgil's talking about the start of a new golden age at the birth of a boy. I don't believe the Chaplain has anything against celebrating Christmas, provided we use moderation."

Now Mr. Sproat, head of technology, entered the debate in his twangy voice. "I don't pretend to be Christian, and I'm going to drink myself into a stupor à la Roman."

"You should know that one alcoholic drink warps so many brain cells," observed Miss Johns, teetering about in her high heels like an inebriated duck.

"What gives you the idea I have any?"

The promise of a lively conversation was here reduced to inanities. I found it always the same with teachers; someone threw out a provocative comment, a reply was tossed back and you were on the point of progressing to a full-blown discussion when a numbskull punctured it.

I turned my attention to the paper. There was the obligatory Christmas murder, drink-driving, two indecent assaults and a terrorist bomb-blast; an oil-slick was spreading in the Red Sea (had Seneca stretched that far?), inflation was rising, unemployment was down and a horse had been sexually mutilated. I looked for a ray of sunshine in the weather, but freezing fog was forecast.

Francis hovered round me, not sure whether to speak or leave me alone. To ease his indecision, I glanced round my paper and asked where the extraordinary staff-meeting would take place. He told me in the library at a quarter-past-two.

I liked the school library. Apart from a wide range of academic and fiction books, it had every serious newspaper and magazine a reader could wish; and behind lock and key, some yellowing Mediaeval manuscripts about 'pieces and parcels of land'. The room was lit by long windows, and button seats and tables stood in quiet alcoves. Overlooking all, busts of Plato and other great thinkers contemplated readers with some severity.

When I entered at five-past-two, the tables had been pushed together in the centre with rows of chairs around. The top seats were reserved for Head Master, Deputy, bursar and school secretary. Remaining staff could sit where they chose. By two-fifteen the room was full. Talk buzzed irritably. No one knew the reason for this meeting and most wanted to be off on holiday.

Dr. Graff and his immediate colleagues entered and took their places. Without preamble, he thanked us for attending. "Tea, I am told, will make it all worthwhile." There was a pause for polite laughter. "Now," he continued, "As you know, we held a governors' meeting last Tuesday. I won't bore you with the ins and outs but they have seriously discussed whether we should follow some other public schools and open our Sixth Form to girls."

This was quite unexpected, and reaction showed it.

"Girls?"

"Girls!"

"Heaven forbid!"

"Standards will fall."

"There'll be sex behind the bicycle sheds."

"If girls come, I go."

Anyone would think girls were a species to be hated, feared, mistrusted or all three. As a female outnumbered by males I found their reaction humiliating.

Dr. Graff raised a hand and the hubbub ceased. "I read your immediate response clearly, and half expected it. However, we do all need to think this through in a logical way. I don't have to cite those boys schools which have taken in girls, and how they have benefited from that step. Let's consider it rationally for Dons, then we'll have a show of hands."

"Head Master," began the head of languages, "Are all the governors in favour?"

"Yes."

"And when – if we decide it is right for us – would we let girls in?"

"Probably the autumn after next."

"It would involve quite a shake-up," commented one of the pastoral staff. "I mean, we'd have to move around the boarding-houses and install a house-mistress."

"Yes, but it would be physically possible. We have the room; it would involve just a shunting effect." Dr. Graff paused and glanced round at the few women staff. "Would any of our present women teachers be prepared to take on house-mistress' duties? You would, of course, receive additional remuneration."

I dropped my eyes and remained silent. In two years time I would not be at Dons.

One of the French assistants had raised her hand. "I wouldn't mind, Head Master."

"Thank you, Miss Shaw. Any other comments?"

"Well," began Mr Sproat of technology, "Since you ask, I for one don't much like the idea of having a bunch of menstruating girls in the school."

There was a murmur of protest. I doubted I had heard him correctly. But I glared at him, for he sat opposite, and I felt the heat rising in my throat.

He went on, "They'll start having crushes on us staff and become emotionally involved with the boys, then there'll be tears, manipulation and at some stage we're bound to have eating disorders."

"Steady on!" squealed Miss Johns. "Are you a misogynist?"

Or homosexual, I thought. I had begun turning my pencil round and round in my fingers, a sign that I was pulling out mental ammunition for return fire.

"Not at all," denied Mr. Sproat. "I'm merely facing facts. Girls will distract, and be distracted by, the boys."

Here Francis expressed an opinion. "Shouldn't we look at the advantages? Isn't it possible that with girls in the Sixth it may encourage more boys to stay on rather than leave after GCSE?"

There were murmurs of assent and much nodding. "Yes," agreed Archimedes, vigorously breathing on his spectacles, "I think it would give the boys a broader vision of later life. There's too much male-bonding already from childhood. And when they leave secondary school, they gravitate to still further single-sex groups. Having girls here might prepare them for a society where women are a formidable part of the work force."

This was all very positive, but my ire was crackling. I stared across at Mr. Sproat who bit rabidly on a lip and looked sweaty. Then, in the lull that followed, I let him have it. "Mr. Sproat," I began, my voice trembling with indignation, "As one of the minority in this school, I find your comments about menstruating girls tasteless and unnecessary. I could just as well ask what girl would wish to join a lot of masturbating boys. Perhaps I should remind you that if girls did not have the menarche, you would not exist."

Miss Johns bounced in her seat like a delighted toddler. "Oh, well said, Mrs.Farthing!"

I was unaware of any other support I received because I was watching a dull red spill into Sproat's face. And I had not finished yet. Addressing the whole meeting, I continued, "However, let's rise above male and female biology. I've been at Dons for only one term, and I am convinced that the school has as much to offer girls as girls would offer it."

Someone clapped and there were voices calling, "Hear, hear!" I had nothing more to add. Neither had Sproat, but just once I caught his eye. It was venomous.

The matter was discussed for almost an hour, and when Dr. Graff asked for a show of hands, most were in favour of opening the Sixth Form to girls. There the meeting ended. I never tasted that special Christmas tea, nor had the dubious pleasure of circulating among the governors; for, at three-thirty when the others drifted along to the dining-room, I decided that I had had enough of everyone and went to my rooms to pack.

☙ ❧

It was good that I had not intended driving to London that evening; a fog pressed hard on the heels of night and squeezed it by the throat. And packing for the holidays was not high on my agenda, after all; I felt tired and dispirited. Used to self-analysis, I knew the cause of the latter; for, although I would be spending three weeks in his London flat, sleeping in his room surrounded by his possessions, twenty-one days without sight of Alex crushed me.

I bathed and put on casual clothes, and was considering something to eat when there came a light tap at my door. Would they (whoever 'they' were) never leave me alone? I wrenched open the door and found Francis blinking at me from the stairway.

"You weren't at tea," he began in an apologetic voice, "I wondered if you were all right. It was awfully good!"

My invitation lacked welcome. "Won't you come in, Francis?"

With a canine bound he was up the remaining stairs and into my sitting-room. He looked round. "Homely! It needed the woman's touch."

"A drink?" I asked, offering him a seat.

"No, thanks. I've had enough tea, sandwiches and Christmas cake to keep me going till breakfast." He sat and I perched. "Jessica, why didn't you come?"

My reply was stringent. "Since working here, I've noticed myself getting on the defensive. It's ridiculous! I don't need to justify my work or opinions."

He put out a hand in a conciliatory way. "No, you don't. But as you are one of the few women in an all-male school, perhaps you feel it's necessary. So... you didn't come to tea because you felt you may have had to defend your courageous comments at the meeting?"

I shrugged. "Something like that. But I've surprised myself. I would never have dreamed of speaking that way while I was married. In other words, Francis, I'm learning to fight hard for myself. It's *Jessica contra mundum.*"

His look was tender. "Does the world seem that hostile?"

"Sometimes."

He leant forward, elbows on knees. "Come with me to Dorset! My sister would love to meet you! You wouldn't have to fight anyone or anything there, and you'd find the world is – gosh, I hope my Latin grammar's up to the mark – *tecum* 'with you', is that right? – rather than *contra.*"

I laughed. "Good memory! You're very kind, Francis, but I've made other arrangements."

"Break them!"

"Ah, no!"

He pulled disconsolately at the corner of an eye. "Jessica, I've hinted already how I felt about you when you came that Sunday to lunch. You need a man to give you what you clearly lack. Hell, I'm not such a bad chap, am I?"

I looked into his kindly face and made all the right noises. But next to Alex, he was – uninspiring.

We talked a little longer, then mercifully he left me. I had an early meal and retired soon after. And during the night, I dreamed that in the middle of a governors' meeting I had leaped on to the table and begun to strip to the basics. Then, quivering what in common parlance are called my 'assets', I offered to take them on individually or en masse.

By morning, the night's fog had turned to a cold yellow drizzle: an English winter's day at its worst. I longed for steamy heat, talc-pale beaches, the bell-notes of tropical birds and colour to burn upon the eye. But this was Sussex, and December.

Before anyone could stop me, I was up and off to London. As I drove, I thought of Alex making tracks for Cumbria; his was by far the longer journey. The morning rush hour had ended by the time I reached Piccadilly, but Christmas shoppers were starting to emerge. With some relief I turned towards Green Park and into a side road.

He had given me directions and used Brown's Hotel as a focal point. This I found easily enough. "Once you're at Brown's," he had said, "you're less than five minutes away." I drove more slowly now, much to the annoyance of a taxi-driver behind, and coming across a metered parking bay, slipped in. I would find the flat on foot.

Park Mansions was one of those terracotta-red buildings with gables and lead-paned windows. The Forsyth flat was at the very top. "You can see over Green Park, at least from my room," Alex had told me.

Feeling like an intruder, I turned the front-door key in the lock and entered. A plush carpet met my feet and there was subdued warmth. Marble-topped tables shone in the hall with a poinsettia on a stand. The lift whirred down obedient to my summons. It had an old-fashioned grille which you hauled and crashed shut, and a slight rocking motion as it ascended.

On the top floor there was another deep carpet and, this time, a potted palm. I had only three doors to choose from; the first one I approached was the Forsyth flat. Cautiously I unlocked and stepped in.

An elegant sitting-room opened out from a vestibule with mirrors to reflect the light. The furnishings were melon-gold; a splendid array of dried flowers fanned against cream walls and there were rugs and capacious sofas. Mrs. Forsyth had taste.

Slowly I made for the first door on my left. It was the dining-room. I passed through to the kitchen and pounced on a note propped against the bread-bin which read:

*'Dear Mrs. Farthing, it's nine-thirty and I'm just off. There's stuff in the fridge.*

*Please help yourself to the cupboard. Fresh linen's in my room. I'll ring this evening at about 6.15. Alex.'*

I glanced at my watch; he had been gone just over ninety minutes. There was nothing to welcome him in my house: no food, no heating, no note.

Now I looked for his bedroom. True to his word, his sister's room was all teddy-bears and posters of bean-pole men in T-shirts, grimacing with eyes closed into phallic microphones. His parents' restrained room came next, and I examined a group photograph on the dressing-table. I saw a handsome middle-aged couple flanked by Alex, aged about sixteen, a vacant-expressioned girl, presumably his sister, and a younger lad the identity of whom I did not know.

The door of the final room was ajar. Gently I pushed it wide. It was smaller than the other rooms, but brighter. To my left was a large bookcase to which I was instantly drawn. Alex's childhood books were there and I took one out. On the flyleaf in an immature hand was written: *This book belongs to Alex. So there.* Smiling, I replaced it and skimmed the other shelves. They were crammed with Greek and Roman authors and books about the classical world. Because there was no room, the huge Latin and Greek dictionaries – Lewis and Short and Liddell and Scott – sat on the floor.

I turned to his dressing-table. Over it hung a lethal-looking sabre with a gold tassel. On the table itself were a glass dish with numerous cufflinks, a bottle of subtle-smelling (for I took a sniff) aftershave lotion, a manicure scissors, a photograph of a rugged man grinning from a tractor (the Wiltshire uncle?) and a china monkey picking fleas from its belly.

I passed round the bed on which were laid clean linen and two towels, and moved across to the cupboard. I opened the door and a full-length glass reflected, as much as it reproached, me. He was a tidy chap. All the shelves, well-stocked with shirts and jumpers, were in immaculate order. I did not investigate the drawers beneath. On the other side of the cupboard hung jackets, a couple of suits and trousers for all occasions. Below these was an array of shoes and a whip. Aha! I had last seen that in his hand at *Henny-Penny's.*

Of everything in that room I could have made a sexual object simply because I was sexually involved with Alex. His books, of which his mind was a product, affected me on several levels, so too did his clothes seen and unseen. My occupancy of his bedroom with all its evocative things could end by making me as raving as the women who hankered for him at the strip-club.

A few hours in Regent Street followed by a brisk walk through Green Park brought me to my senses. Then I began counting the hours till he contacted me. At a quarter past six the telephone rang. I sauntered up to it, though my spirit reached it first and waited, fluttering, for me to catch up. There I paused; it did not do to be too eager. At last I lifted the receiver and almost drawled, "Hello?"

"Mrs. Farthing? It's Alex. Have you settled in all right?"

"Ah! Alex, hello! Yes, I have. And thanks for the stuff you've left. Was your journey smooth?"

"Without a hitch. This is some cottage!"

"Have you located everything – switches, plugs, linen, matches, the lot?"

"Yes, and I've lit a fire. I hope you don't mind."

"Of course I don't. And food?"

"I bought some at the late shop in Pomeroy. The views are great, so's the air! Do you like the flat?"

"Very much. I was thinking –" and I gave a little laugh because I felt embarrassed though about what I wasn't sure, "– there's something reminiscent of the town mouse and country mouse in our exchange. Have you made plans for tomorrow?"

"I want to sleep late and walk miles. By the way, I've brought up some work."

"You're remarkable!"

His laugh came down the line so low and abashed that for a time I was in torment. A pause followed which I hurried to fill briskly, "Now, if you find those walks too solitary and the sheep uncommunicative, you will say?"

"And what happens then? I muck up your holiday."

"Not at all. I may find crowded London lonely."

He received that with silence. I coloured. Had I suggested more than I should? The silence continued. "You still there, Alex?"

"Yes. I was just taking in what you said."

"What I mean is this: we've got to be perfectly honest. If after a week you've had enough, you must say so. And I'll do the same."

"Agreed! Well, I'd better be going. Someone's outside this box hopping from foot to foot. I wonder why. Happy Christmas!"

"And you, too!"

With the replacing of our receivers my lifeline was severed. Disconsolately I wandered into his room and started making up the bed. Then I lay on it to dream, fitting my body as he might lay his. Eyes wide, I stared up at the ceiling thinking acute thoughts of him several hundred miles away. Surprisingly, I slept, and when I next woke it was half-past-seven and time to eat.

# CHAPTER XV

*mora semper amantes incitat (A.A.III.473-4)*
*"delay always goads lovers"*

Christmas Eve was only two days off. Naturally I had heard no more from Alex and shrank from making contact in case he felt I was mothering him. I was now into my London stride, shopping in the morning and visiting a gallery in the afternoon. I even had the temerity to drop in at *Henny-Penny's* to ask after a stripper called Sandy.

A man different from the one I had previously seen spoke to me, and his wink was bigger, cruder. "Sandy's ever so popular with the ladies, miss!" (Wink-wink.)

I wanted to find out what he had told them. "He does still work here, then?"

"On and off. Apparently he's gone away. Told management he couldn't make it for a while. They don't seem to mind. He's that good at his gyr... gyr-what's it called, that management says he can ring them and come whenever. Sorry to disappoint you, miss!" (Wink.)

I went on my way with photographic 'stills' to distract me, and the same questions in my head: why did he strip? How did he get the training? When did he train? Did anyone in his immediate circle know about it?

In Tottenham Court Road I was jostled by young adults of his age. They slouched along, whinnying or croaking, mouths hanging loose or jaws ruminating on gum. When they laughed, it was an opening of the mouth to let out a mirthless cacophony, the kind of amusement that never touched the eyes.

What was it about Alex that, despite his descent into titillation, he still maintained an air of probity? It put me in mind of some classical poets who insisted that although their muse was lewd, their lives remained blameless. Alex could be inspired by a wanton Terpsichore, and lead a sober life. Perhaps his upbringing had had something to do with it; abroad for the first stage of his life and tutored by Catholics, he had a polish only top-drawer expatriates gained. It was a heightened form of 'savvy', an asset in diplomatic circles but sneered at in Britain as 'stand-offish'. I hoped Oxford would not squash it.

When I returned to the Forsyth flat, the afternoon post had left me a Christmas card from him with the additional line: *I'll phone on Christmas morning*. That was the best present I could have hoped for.

The next day dawned frosty. I had bought a paper before breakfast and was reading it in the kitchen over a second pot of tea, when there was a thump in the hall outside the flat-door. Cleaners at the common parts? Then I stiffened. Someone was pushing a key in the lock. Next the door, thrust violently from outside, crashed open against the wall. "Oh, God," wailed a female voice. "Alex must be here!"

A girl's figure filled the kitchen doorway and a pony-tailed young man in a baseball hat peered over her shoulder. In astonishment the girl cried, "Who are you?"

Hiding my surprise better, I replied pleasantly, "A friend of Alex."

She looked round. "Is he here?"

"No."

"Where is he?"

"In Pomeroy."

"Where's that?"

"Westmorland."

She turned slightly to her companion who hung his head over her shoulder as a horse hangs its head over the stable door. Understanding of the situation came slowly to his eyes, then he pushed past the girl and pounced on the teapot with the one utterance, "Tea!"

"Make that two, will you, Jasper? Mugs are in the cupboard. No! Not that one – next along." The girl, who was about seventeen, turned back and eyed me with suspicion. "So. Where do you fit in?"

I had taken an instant dislike to this madam, and without replying, said, "You must be Alex's sister."

"I've got a name."

"You haven't introduced yourself."

"Virginia."

Meanwhile, equine Jasper had found the mugs and was slopping (my) milk into them.

"Virgin! Virgin!" he chanted, throwing her a leer.

"Shut up, Jasper." She returned to me. "Do you know Alex well?"

"Quite."

"Are you sleeping with him?"

"No."

"There's your virgin, Jasper – my prudish brother!"

But virginity was now far from Jasper's mind. He was peering into the 'fridge and had snatched at some cheese and a cucumber. Then he began cutting doorsteps of my loaf.

Virginia stretched across the table for her tea. "Where did you and Alex meet?" She had long straight mid-brown hair that she constantly hooked behind an ear, and which just as often fell away again.

"I teach him."

She gave a little shriek. "You're a teacher?"

"Yes."

"Oh, God, Jasper!"

I did not see what either God or Jasper had to do with it, but I let that pass. The latter's mouth was, by this time, full of cheese-and-cucumber-sandwich and, spitting crumbs, he asked Virginia, "Want one?"

She shook her head. "I'm not hungry. When you've finished pigging-out, will you go and buy that booze?" He had approached and was exaggeratedly chewing all over her. "God, your manners are atrocious! Stop spitting crumbs!"

He nodded, sniffed and chewed vigorously as he ranged round the kitchen, lifting up things, poking at others. He wore baggy trousers whose crotch hung too low, so that he looked liked an overgrown toddler with a full nappy. When he spoke, which so far had been with Neanderthal brevity, I imagined it would be in stumpy words with that curious flat 'a' so popular among the young.

"So," Virginia addressed me, "you teach Alex, he's up in Pomeroy wherever that is and you're down here. How long are you staying?"

"Till term began, I thought."

She heaved a sigh and tucked the limp hair round both ears. Then, leaning on the table she gazed across at me. "I've changed my plans. I was going to spend Christmas with a girl-friend. But she was rude to Jasper. She can be as rude as she likes to me, but I won't have her insulting him. Me and Jasper decided to come here. We've planned a small party for tonight, so –"

I knew what she was suggesting, but said nothing. I took a sip from my now stone-cold tea and watched Jasper slouch out into the hallway.

"Which is your room, Virginia?" he called.

Still waiting for the answer which I was purposely slow in giving, she flounced out after him.

Virginia was typical of seventeen-year-olds. Very conscious of her hair, she was leggy, slim and slightly hollow-chested. She wore black woollen tights and heavy shoes and a short skirt with a denim jacket. A friendship-bracelet, a thing made of thread which was grubby and sucked, wound about her wrist. There was no similarity between her and Alex; she had not his striking looks nor self-contained air. Yes, her features were regular but her expression lacked lustre. The only makeup she wore was charcoal eyeliner. Like most of her peers, she seemed neither female nor male but androgynous. If that was what equality between the sexes was doing, you could keep it.

Through these thoughts, I could hear low tones.

"Who is she?" Jasper hissed.

"Don't know, don't care – but she's too pretty for my liking!"

"Get rid of her!"

"What a bloody nuisance Alex is giving out invitations to his teachers, of all people!"

"Look, we don't want her here. She stinks of authority!"

"Okay. I'll try again." In her normal voice, she added, "Here's some money. Buy lots of cans and loads of crisps. I'll make sandwiches later."

Jasper banged the door as he left and Virginia returned to the kitchen. She sat and drained into her mug the last drop from the teapot. "We'll be noisy tonight," she said. "My parties always are. You'd be more comfortable elsewhere, I think."

I did not need her to tell me. But I feared for the flat. It was none of my business, however, and I gave her the answer she wanted.

"I'll go to a hotel," I said, putting together my crockery; I would wash the things I had used, but not hers or Jasper's.

Then came the final hint. "Jasper and me'll be here till we go back to school."

"Very well, I'll make other arrangements."

"Haven't you got a home?" Her voice was sharp, and while I moved between table and cupboard I saw her eyeing my wedding-ring.

"Of course."

"What do you teach?"

"Classics."

She gave another of her uncontrolled squeals, then quoted, "'Latin is a dead language, as dead as dead can be; it killed off all the Romans and then it did for me.'"

I turned and faced her, longing to take a slipper to her pert androgynous bottom. "Latin is only as dead as those who try to learn it."

Her silence showed she did not understand. She shrugged. "I hated Latin, and couldn't do Greek for toffee. But Alex, dear Alex, is brilliant at both. In fact, he's brilliant at everything – so they tell me."

I began drying up my things. "Why are you jealous of Alex?"

She gave a giggle. "I'm not jealous of Alex!"

"I rather think you are. You haven't a nice word to say about him." I glanced over my shoulder.

She was absorbed in digging her thumb-nail into the grain of the wooden table. For a moment she looked like a ten-year-old. "He has to be different," she observed at last. "He's a swot and a goody-goody and never puts a foot wrong. His exam marks have always been top and he walks off with all the prizes. Just once he drank too much. Did I gloat! My father was decent about it, though, and told him how to hold his drink. But when I came home paralytic, Daddy was furious."

"And your mother?"

"Oh, she hasn't said much since . . ." She caught herself up with a little shake of the head which released the curtain of hair again.

Since what? I wondered but did not ask. "Perhaps your father was angry because you were under-age?"

"So was Alex! And his girlfriends, though since he never tells me about them I can only guess, are probably –" she paused and, lifting her nose, said mincingly, "ladies who haven't heard of flavoured condoms."

Alex enjoying recreational sex with girlfriends? I ground my teeth. And yet, he must have had a few, but at Dons there was enforced celibacy, and it suited me to know that while under the school's roof he lived the life of a monk.

"I don't believe you know your brother very well," I observed at last, wiping down the draining-board. "He is extraordinarily circumspect for a young man of his age."

She had come up beside me, waiting to wash her mugs. "What does circumspect mean?"

"It comes from 'dead' Latin, and means looking at things from all angles and acting with caution."

"That's Alex! He's nothing but a fuddy-duddy."

I smiled as across my mind flashed the vision of a young man in a state of erotic undress, thrusting his loins at libidinous harpies. "Oh, surely not!"

Virginia waggled the mugs under the hot tap and shook them free of water. "He's worse than a maiden aunt."

I ignored that comment and reverted to my vacating the flat. "I'll book into a hotel for tonight. But do you mind if I leave some of my things here till tomorrow? Then I shall move out altogether."

She now smiled, quite pleasantly. "That's fine. I'd invite you to my party, but..."

"Don't think of it. I'll just take the sheets off my bed, then leave you."

While I tidied Alex's room, I considered the options. There were only two: the first to return to school and batten down the hatches there; the second, to go up to my own home in Pomeroy. Aphrodite (desire) and Athena (reason), who at times when I was vulnerable would try to inveigle me into their separate camps, began to argue their case. The most reasonable course was to go home. *But that would put Alex out,* said logical Athena. *Ah, but wait!* sibilated Aphrodite; *need Alex move out at all? Can't you stay there – together? What a preposterous notion!* snapped Athena; *you teach the youth, you must therefore observe the boundaries of teacher and taught.* Aphrodite smiled her slow seductive smile: *but,* she murmured, *before teacher and taught, you are male and female; anyway, who says you are incapable of observing the boundaries and staying under the same roof – credit me with some principles!* Athena met that with a haughty laugh and no more was said. It was left to me to decide. But I knew, and the two forces inside me knew, whose persuasion I would follow.

There was a hotel in Bloomsbury, not far from Russell Square, which could accommodate me that night. They gave me a single room on the first floor over the street. After the Forsyth flat it was spartan, but adequate enough for twelve hours. I spent the rest of that day restlessly deliberating when I should contact Alex with news of his sister's appearance. Athena and Aphrodite made much sport of me, each attempting to win me over, till I couldn't take it any longer and drowned their voices with the cinema. But after the film they started again and went at it all night long. Only when I gave in to Aphrodite did I have some modicum of peace.

I waited till ten o'clock the next morning, then I telephoned Alex. He sounded buoyant, was sleeping like a top (lucky him!) and walking miles, but he had a problem with a Greek translation, he said. I laughed and took my cue. "Alex, I've also met with a problem."

"Oh? What?"

"Your sister and one Jasper turned up at the flat yesterday morning. They held a party last night and want to stay on till they return to school."

He drew in an exasperated breath. "Virginia is the most indecisive person I know! She assured me she was staying with a friend. I'm awfully sorry, Mrs. Farthing. Were you disturbed?"

"No. I stayed in a hotel."

"You didn't! Not only is she indecisive, she's a cuckoo!"

I smiled. "I'm going to the flat now to get the rest of my things... Alex, I've got no alternative but to come up to Pomeroy."

There was the briefest of silences. Then he said, "Of course you must. I'll clear out."

"Ah, no!"

"Honestly. I'll 'phone my aunt and uncle. They'll be glad to see me."

When put to the test, Aphrodite had less grit in me than Athena; I wanted to persuade Alex to stay on, but the words failed.

"Will you get here this evening?" he asked.

I looked at my watch. I hoped to make a move by eleven o'clock. Using the motorway with very short stops, I calculated I would arrive between five and six. "Talk about musical houses!" I added.

He laughed, apologised again for his sister and our conversation was cut short by the pips. I hadn't been able to ask what the problem was with his Greek.

☙ ❧

With mounting horror I stepped into the Forsyth flat. There were cans everywhere, dirty crockery, saucers used as ash-trays and bits of crisps and sandwich on the carpet. Someone – I could not tell whether male or female – was asleep on a sofa; two persons lay on Alex's bed, still in their boots; the bathroom stank of vomit; the kitchen was disgusting, and Virginia and Jasper lay naked on her floor. The only room they had not had the gall to pollute was Mr. and Mrs. Forsyth's.

I went up to Virginia and threw over her a night-dress. Then I shook her and said loudly, "You'd better start cleaning this lot!"

She stirred, blinked and sat up. Hooking the hair behind an ear, she looked about her, dazed. "What time is it?"

I was acerbic. "Ten-thirty. I'd get rid of your friends if I were you and put this place in some order."

She disengaged her legs from Jasper who lay sweetly snoring, and hauled herself to her feet. When she saw the sitting-room she burst into tears. She looked as Iphigenia might have looked, awaiting sacrifice at her father's altar: long tousled hair, wet frightened eyes, her limbs showing through a shift. Only, Iphigenia had a purity Virginia lacked.

After some prodding, she managed to get the others to leave which they did with alacrity once they saw me (who 'stank of authority') and the chaos they had created. On Jasper she merely shut the bedroom door. Then snivelling and staggering she did exactly as I told her. She gathered up the crockery which I steeped in boiling soapy water. Then she collected the remnants of food, taking the vacuum cleaner to the debris. We opened windows and shook out cushions, and lastly I handed her a bucket of disinfectant and bade her clean up the bathroom.

All this took over an hour, after which I stood on the threshold grimly pleased to see the flat as it was when I had first arrived. I turned to Virginia who sat ashamed and tearful on the couch, gazing into a mug of black coffee. "My advice to you," I said tersely, "is this. Reserve parties like these for the time when you have your own place."

Her face crumpled. "It got out of hand!"

"That's obvious."

"You won't tell Alex?"

"I'll have to explain why I am not staying here any more."

"But you won't tell him what has happened?"

"No."

She gave a cowed "Thanks", and I said nothing further. But as I went down in the lift, I wondered how parents who had produced Alex managed also to produce someone like Virginia.

Once free of London I drove fast. And I knew why; I wanted to get home to bask in the aura Alex had surely left behind. The weather was quiet; it was one of those December days when a weak sun shines from an anaemic sky. But pockets of congested traffic held me up, the air grew progressively colder and my journey seemed interminable.

With two half-hour stops and one of fifteen minutes, I succeeded in warding off exhaustion. Then, as darkness fell, fatigue slipped over me and by the time I was driving up the road to Pomeroy, six o'clock felt like two in the morning. Strangely, my thoughts turned to my own upbringing, probably because the street-wise Virginia was on my mind.

I had been what you might term a 'forces child'. As a high-ranking officer, my father had taken my mother and me, an only child, to various postings round Europe. For a year or two during my early adolescence, I attended an international school in Germany; but worried that the instability of his career might have an effect on my education, my father decided (with reservations on my mother's part) to send me to school in England. At Malling Priors where I boarded, I learnt the value of privacy and self-reliance. Of the first there was little, but the headmistress encouraged a good deal of the second. Boarding was not fun. Bells tyrannised us: a rising-bell, assembly-bell, change-of-lessons-bell and lunch-bell; an afternoon-school-bell, end-of-school-bell, tea-bell and prep-bell; a supper-bell, chapel-bell, recreation-bell and bed-bell. Each bell twitched us into a different activity, and if stress had been given as high a profile then as it was later on, all the boarders would have needed therapy.

Our digestions were occasionally upset by the school cook, and prefects forced us to eat all the food on our plate. To ask for the salt or pepper was discouraged since we had to learn how to see to our neighbours' needs. Some girls never learnt, and 'footsie' beneath the dining-table took on new connotations.

There was a death among my classmates but we were not offered counselling; and an expulsion of a senior girl for reasons only rumour could supply. She had, apparently, subverted one of the weaker members in her class by squatting, quite naked, on a mirror in order to become familiar with the otherwise unseen (unless you were an acrobat) parts of the female anatomy. Miss Timson, our headmistress, who to judge by the number of times each week we were called to chapel had conventual leanings, was deeply shocked by such curiosity. The 'perverted' fifth-former was dismissed.

Mostly, however, we were exemplary girls save for the odd moments when there was a spell of stealing others' toothpaste for smearing on tumescent breasts. Hearsay had it that dentifrice made them grow to grapefruit proportions. Another time, someone had sententiously informed us that peanut butter caused cancer, and we – who craved its salt-sweet fattiness – could not get rid quickly enough of our personal jars.

When my final sixth-form year came to an end, I shook with relief the dust of Malling Priors from my feet. Although I rarely complained, my parents knew that my boarding years had not been the happiest. As a form of consolation prize for having endured a prickly youth, they bought a small stone house in Westmorland, initially as an investment but which they presented to me on my twenty-first birthday.

From the moment ten years ago I left the train at Pomeroy station, I had fallen in love with the place. The way it spanned the broad river Eden and rose up to the castle on the hill, its annual gipsy fair when high-stepping ponies were taken to the water to be soaped and rinsed before sale, the tremulous call of sheep mingling with assertive bantam crow, and the sweetness of the air blowing off the freckled Pennines went straight to my heart.

The first thing that struck me as I now left the car was that air. It carried tangy woodsmoke and the pungent odours of the cow-yard. My house stood fully detached with strips of garden either side and a good square of land fore and aft. It was white like most in the area, with deep windows and black-painted 'spines' at all four corners. Built to last, it had a sturdiness which no amount of bitter winds huffing and puffing off the hills could shake.

My neighbours to left and right looked snug with their warm windows. So too would I the moment I entered. With some impatience I turned my key in the lock and went in. The first thing to greet me when I switched on the light was a pot cyclamen; propped against it was a note: '*Dear Mrs. Farthing, just a small gift to apologise for my sister's change of mind, and to thank you for letting me stay here. Till Christmas Day, Alex.*' My 'fridge was well-stocked, everything was clean, and kindling lay ready on the hearth. For a while I stood at a loose end; Alex was everywhere and yet nowhere. I felt cheated of him. Upstairs he had used the spare bedroom, for his sheets lay carefully folded on a chair. I glanced round my room; the double-bed mocked me. And as I went about the trifling things that needed to be done, I mused on how I had changed since I was there last.

Where was Alex now? What new plans had he made? Had he been gone long? I put on some music, but it stressed the minor key and made me wistful. I lit the fire; it sulked. Then someone knocked at the front-door.

I went, thinking it could be a neighbour. But a young man stood on the step.

It was Alex.

# CHAPTER XVI

*quo fugis? in populo tutior esse potes (R.A.580)*
*"Where are you going? You'd be safer in a crowd."*

He said, "I've been hanging around at the pub to give you time to settle."

I motioned him inside, doing my best to compose myself so that my "How nice to see you!" sounded luke-warm.

He left his bag in the hallway and went through to the sitting-room. He looked – and yet was not quite – the familiar Alex. In school uniform he was a youth; but in the bomber jacket, chords and walking boots he now wore he was very much the young man. He turned to me without taking a seat. "Mrs. Farthing, I'm awfully sorry to barge in on you when I'm supposed to have cleared off, but my uncle's invited someone for Christmas I really don't want to see. I wondered, is it too much cheek to ask if I could stay here one more night and then, tomorrow, go to the London flat?"

As he was speaking I watched him, trying not to convey my extreme satisfaction at the sight of him. He looked well; Pomeroy agreed with him. I said, "Your sister and her boyfriend will be there."

"That creep, Jasper!"

"Is he a creep?" Alex smelled slightly of the pub, but I caught the fresher masculine fragrance of his skin.

"All he can say is yeah and nope in between chewing."

I smiled. This description fitted well the almost-moron I had met. "I have a far better suggestion, Alex. Stay on here."

He did not often flush; but he flushed now.

I continued in an even voice, "You can do as you like, when you like. You can walk all day and sleep all night, or sleep all day and walk all night. You can cook your own food when you want it, and pretend I am not even here, although someone recently said I stank of authority!"

He took all this in, then cried, "It's an imposition!"

"No, it isn't. You say you cannot go to your uncle's, so it would mean playing raspberry –"

"Gooseberry."

"Sorry, I'm a bit tired – gooseberry to your sister and her boyfriend the rest of the holidays."

He glanced away. "You have enough of me all term. You don't want a Dons reminder here, I'm sure."

"I like Dons!"

His hesitation was obvious. "Well –"

I waited. His eyes caught mine as if to make quite sure I was being honest. Then he smiled. "If you want me to push off, you will say?"

"You bet! Now –" I became brisk, "– for tonight, will you share my dinner, although since you bought it it's really yours?"

"Let me help. What can I do?"

I went out into the kitchen, found a bottle of rosé wine I had kept over from my last visit, and returned with it and a corkscrew. "You could open this."

He crouched at the hearth, twisting the corkscrew home. Then I watched him place the bottle between his firm thighs and carefully pull. His sexuality was too much for me and I quickly went from the room.

He had left a quiche in the 'fridge, so we ate that and salad, followed by biscuits and cheese. We talked easily, like friends, exchanging news of our separate activities. When he asked whether I thought Virginia and Jasper would behave in his parents' flat, I merely said I believed so.

"My sister's irresponsible," he continued, refusing a third glass of wine. "I know she's only seventeen, but boarding-school is supposed to teach you something! Perhaps I should go back ..."

To lose him now was a cruelty. "'Two's company, three's a crowd'," I quoted. "You'd all have a hellish Christmas."

He chewed on a knuckle. "Does she know you've come up here?"

"No. I told her very little."

In silence, he stared at his wine-glass. I watched him, thinking how well arran jumpers suited dark men. "Do she and Jasper sleep together, you think?"

My eyes slipped away. "I can't really answer that. But, to change the subject, you never told me what the problem with your Greek was!"

"You're on holiday! Wouldn't it keep till next term?"

"Not if it's stopping you from getting on."

He went out into the hallway where his bag still sat, and returned with a text of Aeschylus. He stood beside my chair, opened the relevant page, then leaned on his hands as I read the passage he indicated. I took my time, for my eyes would leave the Greek to stroke his fingers. No part of him touched me, yet I felt enveloped in his presence.

By now the wine was going to my head; and when he took his place again at table, a lull came over the remainder of our meal. I rested a temple on my hand and closed my eyes. He quietly began washing up, and his firm tread going from table to sink and the swish of the brush through suds and water, soothed me. I must have dozed for five minutes.

When I awoke, I apologised and stood. "Hardly the way a hostess should act!"

He looked at me over his shoulder. "If I'm to do my own thing, then you mustn't feel you need act the hostess."

"Perhaps! Thanks for washing up. Now – if you don't mind I'm going to prepare my room for the night. Do whatever you like: go out, stay in, play music, watch television, tackle Aeschylus – anything! I'll be finished in the bathroom within half-an-hour."

I bathed, shielding my nudity which was preposterous; but my thoughts made me vulnerable. Because I was in love with him and he was downstairs, I felt I should not have a body through which to be tempted. Antony had never had that effect. Once early in our marriage I appeared in a black basque. He had taken one look and cried, "For God's sake, Jess, put some clothes on!" I supposed wives were not meant to act seductively: it was reducing a 'decent' relationship to the casual encounter in a bordello.

I dithered in the bathroom longer than intended. What exactly was my role in that house? Was I Alex's hostess, Classics tutor or simply fellow occupant? The last thing I wanted to do was to fuss over his well-being, for I had no maternal instinct and shrank from motherliness when my feelings were far more complex. At last I came out on to the landing and hung over the bannister, calling, "Good night, Alex!"

He appeared from the sitting-room and looked up. "Thanks for everything, Mrs. Farthing."

I waved a hand in answer, and vanished into my room. By then, of course, I was wide awake, and Aphrodite and Athena homed in vigorously. The former stressed how provocatively close Alex was, and threw in for good measure a few mnemonics which hailed from *Henny-Penny's; soon,* she continued, *he'll be climbing the stairs and passing your door, he'll go to his room and prepare for bed! So?* retorted Athena coldly, *it's what most people do at this time of night; you read sex into everything! Because it is in everything!* sibilated Aphrodite. To squash this bickering, I tried to read, but I read with one ear cocked. Not much later, Alex did indeed come up the stairs and pass my door. Then he took a shower, (Alex – naked!) for I heard the water rush in the loft. When he quietly shut his bedroom door, my thoughts and desires blurred into imaginings during which I thankfully fell asleep.

The creeping of grey beneath my curtains and the cool whistle of a robin told me it was dawn. The clock from Pomeroy church struck eight. Morning was magic to me. I often thought of the obscenity of being shot at dawn. Dawn! Just when life was beginning, the system warming up, plans being made, opportunities opening out. To be annihilated then, on the edge of the day's promise!

I had been in the kitchen for some time when Alex appeared. He was in dressing-gown and pyjama-bottoms, and I felt oddly gratified. I asked myself, should I keep him at a distance or ... what?

"Hello, Alex. How did you sleep?"

"Very well. And you?"

"I also. Tea, coffee or neither?"

"Whatever you're having."

I made a pot of tea. Then I surveyed him. "Are you a morning person, Alex? Or do you function better at night?"

He grinned. "It all depends on who I'm with."

I did not expect this and flushed. "Because we need to talk about Christmas arrangements, but I won't choose a time when you're in a state of somnambulism."

He pulled out a chair and sat down. *"Somnus ... ambulare.* Well, I may look as if I'm sleepwalking, but I ain't!"

I passed behind him to the cupboard. He had brushed his hair and it was damp at the ears where he had sluiced his face.

"I'm a morning person, actually," he continued, nodding as I pushed the teapot his way. "Though, I quite often prepare work for a particular tutor till midnight."

"Me?" I stared at him. "Do I overwork you?"

"Sometimes."

"Then you must say!"

He laughed. "I'm only winding you up, Mrs.Farthing. Pathetic schoolboy humour!"

I said, "Oh," and went rather quiet. This was going to be hard, much harder than at school where we had specific boundaries to observe. But here, I was unsure about the limits, and doubt left me vulnerable. He could treat the present situation with good spirits; but I, burdened with a secret love, saw only the gravity.

I prepared my breakfast in silence, without looking at him again. My boiling egg rattled in the pan, and while it cooked I went out into the garden. The air was sweet, sweet with damp and woodsmoke and vegetation. I had less than half an acre but it grew most things: bulbs in spring, honeysuckle and roses in summer and an appletree for the autumn. Now, in December, it had dropped the last of its fruit and apples lay as browning shells in the grass. From the valley not far away a bantam flung its thin crow; nearer, a truck from the local gypsum works thundered down the road. This for me was home.

On my return to the kitchen, Alex had disappeared. But at my place was my boiled egg with a smiling face drawn on it. I went to the foot of the stairs. "Alex? Thanks for taking my egg out."

He came from his room pulling on a jumper. "I thought you were a bit down. It's meant to cheer you up!"

It didn't – much.

As it was now Christmas Eve, we decided quickly on the next day's lunch. It would be 'the works', as they say: turkey, all the trimmings and plum pudding. With so much to carry, I said I would drive to the shops. Alex asked if he could come too. When we were ready, he walked round my car with some admiration. On impulse, I said, "You drive, don't you?"

"Yes."

"Then, here are the keys." I held them out and he looked at me in disbelief. "Go on! I'm properly insured. You drive us to the shops! But on one condition."

He took the keys, his fingers just brushing mine. "What?"

"We don't go round corners on two wheels."

He gave his striking grin. "I wouldn't dream of it!"

He didn't either. He was deft, competent, careful. I took immense pleasure in watching his hand on the gear-stick, and feeling in his control. Once parked, we split up for half-an-hour. There was no bookshop in Pomeroy but the local stationers sold a variety of things, and I bought a book-token for Alex. In the grocer's, my hand reached out for a bottle of sober red wine. But it preferred to close round some champagne, and it was the cue the voices in my head were waiting for. Aphrodite spoke first: *that's a lover's drink.* Athena squashed her: *no, it's a celebratory drink.* Said Aphrodite: *lovers drink champagne after good sex!* Retorted Athena: *racing-drivers shake and spew it over their fans.* Aphrodite: *but you're not a racing-driver!* Athena: *no, and a lover neither.* Obsessive natures were given to hearing voices; Joan of Arc did. I listened to mine – and chose the bottle of champagne.

After lunch which Alex insisted on cooking, he strode off alone. The sun came out and I spent some time in the garden. By tea, he still had not returned. I went up to his room for reassurance.

He was neat without being pernickety. His shaving tackle adorned one part of the dressing-table, a pile of books the other. Mostly they were from school. I moved to the bedside table, curious to see his choice of night reading. It was Flaubert's *Sentimental Education* which I did not know, and I turned to the resumé on the back. When I reached the words '...this story of a young man's romantic attachment to an older woman', I almost dropped the book. I turned hot. Was there some connection I should grasp? Was Alex's choice of reading purely coincidental, or could it be that, like Flaubert's hero, he also felt drawn to a woman some years his senior? Could he be interested in me?

For the first time I began to see things from his point of view; here was a sixth-former under my tutelage who, despite his status, was treated like a mature adult. I talked to him as an equal and listened to him as a friend. Intent on concealing my feelings, I had not observed his other than sensing that he genuinely liked me and, on one occasion, being gratified to hear him call me 'wonderful'. Then, at times when I needed support, he had so often been there: as I waited for Francis Marks in the hall on Bonfire Night, Alex had come and spoken to me; while couples milled around at a parents' evening, it was Alex who noticed I needed refreshment. Now, that same young man was under my roof, drawing faces on my boiled eggs and at the wheel of my car!

Downstairs, the front door opened. I thrust back Flaubert and went into hiding in my room. Alex came up the stairs. He passed my closed door. My face blazed. This was a provocative situation. *Cool it!* sneered Athena: *I thought you were in my camp, but you fantasise, which is regrettable. Don't let your obsession with him cloud your perceptions; that young man's got younger fish to fry!* Aphrodite remained strangely quiet.

I came from my room. My voice was light. "A cup of tea, Alex?"

He emerged on to the landing with, "Yes, please," and followed me downstairs. "I've got something, Mrs. Farthing," he added.

Relief (why was I relieved?) flooded over me; his 'Mrs. Farthing' tripped too often and too easily off his tongue to mean anything other than it should; the man who loved would probably call me nothing at all.

I turned at the foot of the stairs, smiling. "And what's that?"

He passed me and went to open the front door. He had stood on the step the previous evening; now there was a Christmas tree.

"And these!" He was bringing in both the tree and a box of coloured baubles. "My Christmas present to you!"

I was delighted, and felt a little foolish; I should not have gone to his room and read so much into Flaubert.

Alex handed me the box and looked into the sitting-room. "Where would you like it? In the window, perhaps?"

Like most Westmorland houses, mine had deep window recesses with broad ledges. I thought that overlooking the garden would be best, but we would need a flower-pot filled with earth. He would not let me do the spade-work, and as I made tea I watched him attack the ground with energy. One of the beauties of youth should be its vigour; of that he had much. But most of his peers slouched through their adolescence like so many scarecrows, depending on a cocktail of repetitive music and drugs to give them vitality.

After tea I hung the baubles, and was standing back to admire the effect when he said, slightly abashed, "And I found this." From his pocket he drew a sprig of mistletoe.

"Ah!" My exclamation was a shade hearty. "All you need now is the girl!"

We faced each other. With eyes on the sprig, he said contemplatively, "I thought, perhaps, I might kiss you."

Astonished, I had a flash-back to my university days and an infatuation for a Classics lecturer; I was twenty-one and my finals were over; I had gone to his study and asked, "May I kiss you goodbye?" He drew himself up. His reply was cold, "I'm afraid that's not possible." Then he had opened his door as a dismissal. Humiliated and bruised, I left. I never saw him again.

Fear or embarrassment, even both, could have made me react in the same way to Alex's request now. But I was kind. Sweating in the explosive situation, I said, "Of course." And waited.

He lifted the mistletoe above our heads. He looked down at me. His eyes paused at my lips then moved to my cheek. I prayed he would not kiss me on the mouth.

Then he snapped the tension between us with the comment, "How pathetic!" Tossing the sprig on to a seat, he turned away.

I heard him go upstairs and wondered, with a mixture of relief and disappointment, what had made him change his mind.

Later when he came down again, our conversation was stilted. He looked preoccupied while I did my best to appear normal, but then I had maturity on my side. By dinner time, he was his old self and talked of his father telephoning at about eleven the next morning; was that all right?

I said, "Perfectly," and should not he, in his turn, check on Virginia?

"I rang her this afternoon. She wanted to know where I was. Was I alone. If so what was the matter with me. She told me about meeting one of my teachers at the flat. She ticked me off for issuing indiscriminate invitations. I said Jasper was one big indiscrimination. End of 'phonecall."

I was laughing, for he told this little anecdote in such a dead-pan staccato way. "And what will you say to your father?" I asked.

"The truth. Would you rather I didn't?"

"Perhaps you shouldn't tell him I'm here as well."

"Why not?"

I lifted my shoulders. "Well, sixth-formers don't usually spend their holidays with members of staff."

"A few chaps at school do! There's a Japanese in the Lower Sixth who hasn't a guardian here, and he regularly stays with Mr. Greenwood."

Delicately I pointed out that the Japanese boy's host was male.

"And Matron takes Sahid Ahmed home with her!"

"In that case, Alex, I'm plain old-fashioned!"

He looked at me curiously, but not unkindly. "Did you go to boarding-school, Mrs. Farthing?"

"It was more of a Carmelite convent."

"In what way?"

I put my elbows on the table and thought a moment. "To start with, we had to respect the seniors and hold doors open for them. If we didn't they'd put us in the corner."

"Lord! Go on."

"Only those in dormitories without heating were allowed hotwater bottles, so the rest of us froze in winter. The headmistress employed no cleaning-staff because we all took part in a rota of cleaning, dusting and dining-room duties. As for the menu, there was no choice; if you disliked a particular dish, you had to lump it. Then, one girl became anorexic, and we weren't allowed two small helpings at the same meal. Once or twice we had pork. I was neurotic about getting a tape-worm and when no one was looking, managed to twitch my portion of pork on to the floor."

Alex grinned. "Was it discovered?"

"By the cat."

"Another Nisbet!"

"Yes, but this cat belonged to the kitchen-help who was mentally deficient."

"Did that make the cat mentally deficient, too?"

I sniggered. "No, but it looked unsavoury, like its owner."

"Mrs. Farthing, you are not politically correct!"

"I hate being politically correct!"

He laughed. "What else?"

I glanced at the dark window. "We had chapel night and morning and sang depressing hymns like *Now the day is over, night is drawing nigh* ... Then, to gain mass attention, several girls went in for fake fainting fits. The headmistress would be asking the Lord to forgive us our trespasses when there was a crash, and someone passed out at the moment of being shriven. In the end we all got used to these *frissons* of excitement and continued with our requests of God while ignoring the skittles. Every Sunday we walked two miles to the local church, and two miles back in a sort of Noah's Ark formation. We wore hats and gloves and called 'Car! Car!' each time one approached. In church, during the boring sermon, I learnt my Latin verbs while smoothing the creases from bits of coloured silver paper. We saved these from tuck." I paused to glance at him. "Do you want me to go on?"

"Yes!"

"If we cheeked the prefects, they gave us bits of the Prayer Book to learn. I had to memorise the Collect, and always came unstuck half way through."

"So you cheeked the prefects?"

"All the time! I had long hair in plaits to my waist," I continued. "It took ages to brush and do, and I felt that once a day was enough for any self-respecting schoolgirl. Not so the games teacher. At tea, when we all lined up in the front hall before filing in for white bread and seaweed jam –"

"Seaweed jam?"

I smiled. "Schoolgirlese for greengage jam; it was very green and very glutinous. Anyway, as we filed in, this games teacher would give us the once-over. I sort of slunk past, aware that wisps had escaped from my plaits after lacrosse or dancing or whatever, and she'd bark, 'Jessica Stanton, go and do your hair!' So, off I'd trot to my dormitory to brush and plait. That didn't worry me, but what did was entering the diningroom with one hundred and seventy girls seated at tea, having to walk between the chairs up to the head table, and then wait for the games teacher to acknowledge and dismiss me. I hated drawing attention to myself!"

Alex blew out his cheeks. "And yet you chose to teach!"

"One of life's little ironies. But, enough of me." I dismissed my memories with a shrug. "How do you want to spend Christmas Day?"

"How do you spend it?"

I paused thinking back to my Christmases with Antony. They had been passed quietly, and always in the environment of his choice. But now, it seemed irrelevant how he and I had spent any holiday. In fact, I was thinking of Antony less and less, and while it was true to say that there were some things I would not have done had he not been in my life, there were many I never could do because he was. As his wife, I had gained and lost. Increasingly, and with a twinge of disloyalty, I was beginning to appreciate how much I was gaining as his widow.

I suddenly looked at Alex and saw mortification on his face. "I am sorry, Mrs. Farthing. That was a tactless question."

"Not at all. Antony and I spent sober Christmases – and last year I had a solitary chop."

He looked as if he were unsure whether I was being funny or not. I was and I wasn't. But I smiled and cautiously he asked, "You mean, you were solitary, or you had just one chop?"

"Both."

What was going on in his head? His expression was inscrutable. "Last Christmas I was in Wiltshire," he said eventually. "My uncle and aunt adopt people as they adopt animals. Each time I visit, they have more hens and geese and dogs than they need. They never have quiet Christmases because they invite local people who are either at some crisis of their lives or appear to be friendless. If you lived near, they'd invite you."

"But I'm not at a crisis ..." (*liar!* hissed Aphrodite), "... and I have a few friends."

Gently, Alex said, "To them, anyone expecting to be alone at Christmas is without friends."

"I like my own company," I observed.

He looked away, murmuring something that contained the word 'rich'.

"What did you say?"

"I said it was because you were so rich." And he appeared embarrassed.

I smiled again. "How's this for a Roman maxim? *We are not rich according to possessions but according to the wealth within.*"

"That sounds like Seneca!"

"Quite. So, back to tomorrow. Suppose we have lunch at about one, and do whatever takes our respective fancy round that?"

"Agreed!" And there our conversation was interrupted by the telephone.

# CHAPTER XVII

*vir prior accedat (A.A.I.709)*
*"let the man make the first move"*

It was Martha from Italy. "You must come one day, Jess!" she cried with some excitement. "I feel greedy enjoying this alone. There's a superb young man in the flat below, all eye-lashes and curly hair, and plenty of others outside!"

I almost said that I had a young man in my very house, who had rather more than eyelashes and curly hair, but that would have been provocative.

"Are you lonely?" she continued on a more subdued note.

I assured her strenuously that I wasn't.

"Fancy shutting yourself away among those bleak Cumbrian hills."

"They're not bleak, they open me out, and it's Westmorland actually."

"Ah, well, each to his own. Did you get my card? And when do you go back to school?"

"January the seventh."

"I fly home on the tenth. Give me a ring after that, and we'll have another weekend in London."

"Good. But no more strip-clubs!"

"I thought you enjoyed it."

"I did. But once seen never forgotten!"

"Perhaps a French film, then. There's an erotic one coming to Leicester Square, soon."

"Surely a surfeit of Italians will do?"

"Killjoy!" Martha's acute interest in the opposite sex was quite open and therefore merely frivolous. When her back was to the wall, so to speak, she was straight-laced. Now I dissembled; I admired in secret and once my feelings were engaged they were deep and strong. I hoped Alex knew I liked him; but I doubt he felt I loved.

We spent quietly what remained of Christmas Eve. I fretted that it was too quiet for him. As we sat after an evening meal on either side of the fire, he reading, I preparing a scheme of work, I suddenly asked: "If you had the chance to do whatever you liked this very moment, what would it be?"

He lifted his eyes to mine then dropped them showing, as always, that he was disconcerted.

"Should I rephrase that?"

He gave a smile. "No. But do I have to answer?"

"Sorry, perhaps I was probing."

"You weren't. It's just that you wouldn't believe me if I said."

I scrutinised him, wondering if he wanted to tell me that it would be dancing at *Henny-Penny's*. "You see," I continued, "Most young people would find sitting by the fire with an older woman on Christmas Eve unadventurous to say the least."

He looked away again, a smile – this time quite raffish – lifting his mouth. "It needn't be unadventurous."

My jaw almost dropped. Sometimes Alex spoke and reacted like a man at least ten years older; then he was my peer and I did not know where I stood. Silence was my best cover, so I returned to work.

A few minutes passed before he spoke once more. "My sister always said I was a fuddy-duddy. Perhaps she's right."

I snapped, "You are not!"

"But, Mrs. Farthing, how do you know?"

Should I tell him what and whom I had seen in a London club? *Careful!* warned Athena; while Aphrodite urged, *Let him have it!* I put aside my papers and began, "One evening last half-term, a cousin of mine arranged a night out. She took me to a club in Soho, called *Henny-Penny's*." I looked at him and paused as a flush had started to heat his face. "This was a male striptease club, and five handsome young men performed the most provocative routines I have ever had the pleasure to watch." The flush now glowed in his neck. I continued, "Among them was a dancer called Sandy, whom I know rather better as Alex Forsyth."

He said, "Oh, Jesus," and covered his face with both hands.

I rose to feed the flames. Looking over my shoulder, I saw him dig the heels of his palms into his eyes. His mouth, uncovered, filled me with desire.

At last he showed his face. "Were you disgusted?"

"Far from it! I was as stimulated as all the shrieking sirens there, only I didn't shriek." I had sat down again. "But, I hasten to add, I did not stay for the full monty."

He was running his fingers through his hair and still avoided my eyes. "How did you keep it hidden from me all these past weeks!"

"The same way you've kept it hidden... My word, Alex, you've got rhythm! Are you sure Oxford is right for you?"

He laughed, looking rather more comfortable.

"Well?" My attention was full on him. "Are you going to tell me how it all started, or is this another one of the mysteries you'll keep for a better time?"

He looked in my face and said significantly, "I think now is the best time for this one." With deliberation he closed his book. "My father has always wanted his children to be able to dance – among other things. I think I told you? Well, there was no opportunity at Dons, and for a while I felt it would defeat me. Then, during a spot of personal trauma when sympathy was getting on my nerves, I had to find release through a new identity." He broke off, and while he found the words to continue, I wondered what this 'personal trauma' might be. But I did not ask; for Alex, things had to be right, and what was right for one divulgence was not necessarily right for another. "It was in the holidays about this time three years ago, when I saw an advert in London wanting young chaps to train as dancers. I went along, they took me on and gave me training – jazz turns, isolations and all that stuff. Does this mean anything to you?"

I pulled a rueful face. "I'm more au fait with *pas de chat*."

"Ha! Ballet. That's beyond me! Anyway, those sexy movements they taught me brought the relief I wanted, and when I went back to school, and all kinds of things had to be grinned at and borne, I found a new skill helped." He cleared his throat. "By then I was seventeen and being put on course for Oxford. That was fine by me, but after Dons I wanted a car to get me around. So, for the hell of it, I applied for a job at *Henny-Penny's*, and blow me, they gave me one. They're pretty decent. They know I'm still at school and can't always come when they whistle. They also pay well. So," and he shrugged, "It's not quite the line of dancing my father had in mind, but I can tone it down to the circumstances. Best of all, I can start buying a car quite soon!"

I had been watching him, my chin in my hands, fascinated by what he was telling me. But there were one or two things I wanted to ask. I put them carefully to him. "Am I probing, Alex, if I ask about what you called your personal trauma?"

He shot me a look. "No, you're not, but it wouldn't fit the present situation."

"Point taken. Then can I assume there is a link between it and your missed reading at the Carol Service?"

"You can. By the way, was it difficult fielding comments after I chickened out? No staff save Mr. Marks, as you know, said anything to me."

I reflected a moment. "Strangely enough, no one spoke to me about it either. You were right – people do have short memories and, I'd say, brief attention spans." I left it at that. In his own time he would tell me, or not. Now, there were other questions I knew I could ask. My tone lightened. "How do you feel on that platform with all those women swooning over you?"

He grinned. "It's an ego-trip. You feel incredibly powerful. The other chaps and I don't discuss it much, but I reckon we all get the same kick out of it, or we wouldn't do it. Really, it's the music you respond to, that fantastic beat which starts here –" he made a fist of one hand and pressed it against his sternum, "– and then radiates outwards and all over."

I knew all about that sensation, but it wasn't just rhythm which caused it in me. He did.

"Mrs. Farthing?" He leaned towards me. "Do I disappoint or disgust or shock you?"

I caught his eye. "Would it matter if you did?"

"Yes."

I sent him a smile. "Let's say you have greater dimensions than most young men of your age." I, too, had my secrets and, like his, they needed the right moment for revelation.

He seemed relieved. "No one except you knows about *Henny-Penny's.*"

"I shan't breathe a word! So, now you know how I know you aren't a fuddy-duddy."

No more was said. Ostensibly we returned to our previous occupations. I could not speak for him, but my scheme of work went awry. Third-year schedules were constantly interrupted by visions of a young man in various states of undress and, not so very long ago, of his mouth visible beneath the heel of his hands. In the end I gave up.

Inevitably there was a restraint between us as we parted for the night. I sensed he felt uncomfortable knowing that I had seen him in a vastly different guise from that at Dons; and I was worried that this knowledge could spoil the working relationship we enjoyed.

I read in my room for an hour, but my concentration lapsed often. I found myself asking if he had kissed many girls, what sort of girls appealed to him, was he still virgin, did he have erotic dreams, and had he ever dreamed of me? Not conducive to rest.

Outside, the temperature dropped. I felt cold, but it was an inner cold. I was hungry, but it was emotional hunger. I began to shiver, and longed for the fire. The church clock struck midnight. It was Christmas Day. Unable to support my inactivity any longer, I crept downstairs to the sitting-room.

With a couple of logs and careful use of the bellows, the fire soon picked up. I drew a long padded bench to the hearth, and sat directly in the light of the flames, wondering if Alex found me fuddy-duddy. So many women were strident in their demands, but all I could ask of him were essays on classical literature and well-executed pieces of Greek and Latin prose. In my capacity as his tutor I had the right to ask for no more. Then the bitchy Aphrodite got stuck in: *you're the one who's a fuddy-duddy*, she said, *and you're a throw-back to Victoriana! Stop being stuffy and hook him!* Athena, cautious and rather cold, protested: *have some sense! Suppose Alex takes fright at this new Mrs. Farthing and you ruin his chances of good exam grades?* Aphrodite gave an unfetching snort: *then he's not a proper man! What real man will shrink when a good-looking woman with an enviable body makes a pass at him? He's had enough uglies reaching for his private parts, but how flattering if you, his tutor, did!*

There was a movement at the corner of my eye. I jumped guiltily, for Alex was leaning against the door-jamb. How long had he been there?

"Insomnia," he remarked. "You, too?"

I moved up on the bench, saying irrelevantly, "It's warmer by the fire."

He wore pyjamas and dressing-gown, but his feet were bare. "Thanks," he said, sitting down beside me. "By the way, Happy Christmas!"

"And to you!"

Silence. The gap between us was not too close for familiarity, and not too distant to be unsociable. For my part, it cried out to become narrower.

The silence continued as we stared into the flames; they were like crocuses, sun-yellow with an orange base. Tiny red sparks clung in shoals to the chimney-back, then darted away into the sea of night.

"Your husband didn't like it here, did he?" he suddenly asked.

"He preferred the tidiness of Surrey. He tried to like it, but then after two days would go home."

He turned to look at me. "Did you stay on, or go with him?"

"Mostly I went. Once, though, I stayed, and he protested by eating cat-food."

"No!"

"Oh, yes. Antony liked tidy well-behaved places and tidy well-behaved women. In his opinion, this part of the world was neither."

He appeared to consider my words. "So, how would you define a well-behaved woman?"

"The same way you define a well-behaved man – I suppose." I warmed to the idea. "I mean, you don't pick or suck your teeth in public, or burp, or twang your braces or suspenders, or slurp your soup or break wind." Seeing him bent forwards, laughing, I added as an anti-climax, "But I'm sure you know all that."

He straightened. His breath was fresh with recent toothpaste. "You do make me laugh! Did he laugh, too?"

"Sometimes, though like most men, he preferred it if he was the funny one."

Stuffing his hands into his dressing-gown pockets he stretched out and crossed his feet. They epitomised Greek beauty in that the second toe was longer than the big toe. "I don't mind who makes me laugh," he said.

I tossed him a look. "You're a New Man, Alex... Of course, we had our dark times."

A question entered his eyes.

It was something I had never spoken about, not even to Martha. "During the early years of our marriage, I had two miscarriages," I explained. "After that, we decided not to have children. I have no maternal instinct, you see."

He turned back to the fire. "I reckon my mother hasn't, either."

"Oh?"

"When I was younger I used to puzzle why she went off to far-flung places with my father, leaving us at boarding-school and, in the holidays, with an aunt and uncle."

"Perhaps she felt it would be too unsettling for you to be carted round like baggage. Does it still bother you?"

He shook his head. "So many chaps at school moan about their mothers, say they fuss too much, which makes me glad I've learnt independence early. All the same, I think Virginia could do with our mother round more."

Privately, I thought so too; that girl would turn rotten if she did not have some parental guidance soon. I eased forward and poked the fire. More shoals of sparks vanished up the chimney's maw. "Did you ring her again, today – yesterday? How did she sound?"

"Tearful and inquisitive. Jasper had a hangover and wouldn't talk to her and she paid me the compliment by saying that at times like those even I was better to be with than him. Then again she wanted to know where I was, what I was doing, was I doing whatever I was doing with anyone else, was it male or female and why did I never tell her anything." He sighed. "A most unsatisfactory brother."

My eyes clung a little too long to his profile, and he turned so that I was plummeted into hazel waters which could challenge, query, smoulder, flash, smile, sympathise, scorn, grieve and – for a moment I thought – love.

I rose gasping, so to speak. "What did you tell her?"

"Not a lot, but that I was staying with a friend." He saw my smile. "What's funny?"

"Nothing! Just that it is much more flattering to be called 'friend' than 'tutor'." I felt his eyes on me and thought it wise not to meet them.

"Does it worry you, me staying here with you?"

My mouth opened then shut, probably fish-like, as I struggled to find the right answer. It did worry me because although I was mistress of the temptation, my feelings would not be schooled. But if I answered 'yes', he would probably pack his things and leave. So I lied. "No," and our eyes held.

Slowly, as if to himself, he said, "Why are you so –"

No adjective came. I was caught in his eyes. I prompted him. "So..?"

"Devastating!"

My heart began to race. The distance between us was narrowing. He leaned closer and closer, till his mouth pressed long and gently against mine. I could not respond, cluttered and confused by fear-boldness, need-sufficiency, sex-without-sex, heat-frigidity, joy-despair, Aphrodite-Athena, mind-over-matter.

Now he drew away, leaving me cheated of a kiss, for he had kissed me not I him. I raised my hand behind his head and returned his mouth to mine.

# CHAPTER XVIII

*porrigimus victas manus (A.I.ii.20)*
*"I surrender"*

His kiss grew hotter. He caught my hands, we rose and leaned against each other. "I never realised!" he said.

I swayed a little and was steadied in his fierce embrace. "I worked hard so you wouldn't."

"Why!"

"Complications at school."

"Damn complications and school!" Then he was kissing me again, while against me his body grew taut, virile.

When I was able, I said, "Is this the mistletoe kiss?"

With his teeth he was drawing back the collar of my dressing-gown till he had found the bare hollow of my shoulder. "It's something I've wanted to do for weeks, but dared not. And I've been trying to find out these last few days what you felt, but your light was always amber and I kept stalling!"

"Nice metaphor," I whispered against his mouth and said no more; I couldn't get close enough to him – even words got in the way.

"When did you start to care?" he asked, his arms strong around my back.

I thought. It had been a steady mental assessment, first inspired the moment I saw him. "When you appeared in a bath-towel."

He grinned. "Mine was before then!"

"Before! How?"

"When you came for interview. There were six of us in the library. Mr. Rowland showed you round, and when you'd gone, we made bets on whether you'd be chosen or not. I thought, 'Whoi, fancy being taught by her!'"

I gave him a playful punch. "Which way did you bet, and how much?"

"I bet you would be chosen and put down two quid."

"So, you made a bit out of me?"

"Towards the down-payment on my car!"

I was hot for him. The warmth of the fire added to my temperature, and for his piece of cheek I deserved recompense. I began to take my dues, untying the belt of his dressing-gown; then I lifted his pyjama top and slipped my hands against his chiselled flesh. *Watch it!* cried Athena. Chorused Aphrodite and I: *you shut up!*

The kissing began again, and when he asked how far he could go, I said, "As far as you like." With that, he lifted me like a doll and carried me up to my room. Gently he laid me on the bed. I opened the bedside-drawer and pressed a small packet into his hand. Antony had never felt the man in my house.

Discreetly, Alex went away for a moment. I flung off my dressing-gown and waited, wondering how much I would need to guide him. Soon he returned. The stair-light was on, the bedroom door ajar. I saw little more than his silhouette as he lay down beside me.

When he left my lips, he began on my body. He found my breasts and drew with his mouth on my nipples, then slowly progressed down the rest of my frame, his hands and lips producing sensations I had never experienced before. Despite a pleasurable confusion of the flesh, my mind was sharp; so this was what was meant by the biblical words: *with my body I thee worship.*

Now the rising current of his attentions carried me on and on, till the banks broke and I rose with the flood; while he, my great bank-breaker, gave a low groan of release, and together we enjoyed the depths of high-water.

I found his lips with mine, and over and again tasted his salt-sweat. When he had gently withdrawn he lay beside me, till our pulses quietened. We slept.

At dawn I woke first, watching the light bring definition to his face. During our consummation he had been in control. But now, I wanted to take my secret pleasure of this man-boy whose impeccable 'Mrs. Farthings' had, over the months, duped me so well. Careful not to disturb him, I rose on an elbow and leaned over. I hung against his torso as I touched his mouth with mine. Suddenly a hand cupped one of my breasts and held it as you might weigh a peach. His lips returned my kiss, and we simply had to re-inforce the contact we had made several hours before.

By nine, we were ravenous. We took a shower, but that brought a new setting with untried sensations and breakfast was not till ten. At last, hunger drove us downstairs, and as I laid the table the telephone rang.

Alex cried, "That'll be my father!" and answered it.

Reluctant to hear his conversation, I went away to dress. In the looking glass I gazed back. It was the same Jessica Farthing as the day before, yet different; this one felt broader, deeper, higher.

"Mrs. Farthing?"

What was this? Had we regressed? I went on to the landing to look over the rail. "How can you call me that after all we've enjoyed!"

He laughed. "Just testing!" Taking the stairs two at a time, he reached me and caught me in his arms. "Jessica!" he whispered against my ear.

"That's better."

"My father says thank you."

I strained away from him. "What for? You haven't been explicit, have you?"

"I can tell Pa anything. He's broad-minded."

"Yes, but not that broad-minded, surely!"

"I told him how we had intended exchanging premises for Christmas, but Virginia proved the fly in the ointment at the time, that I'm staying here with you and how well you and I get on!" He was gently walking me backwards.

"Alex! Be serious! Please!"

"What's the matter, Mrs. Farthing?" The two-step continued.

I became mock threatening, "No breakfast, *ergo fames!*"*

Which merely elicited, "We must make love in Latin!"

"Forsyth, no breakfast!" I had never called him by his surname before and it had the effect of sobering his spirits but heating his passion. The kettle bubbled on, ignored, and when we went down eventually the kitchen was like a sauna.

---

*'therefore starvation!'

I sounded firm enough, but my look was indulgent. "After breakfast, Alex, I would like to know, first, what you really told your father and, second, how and when you learned your art of love."

His reply was cheerful. "Done!"

From the stove, I asked, "How do you like your fried egg – bare or in a *chador*?"

"Let's try *chadored*!"

With a deft flick of the spatula, I turned the egg on its face.

Only when we had eaten all we could manage and sat opposite each other, relaxed and a little somnolent, did Alex begin to answer my earlier questions.

"I told my father about everything, except our sleeping together," he said, twisting on the marmalade top.

"Really?"

"Really. But he's more concerned with Virginia, and was going to ring her immediately after me."

Tentatively I asked, "And did you speak to your mother?"

"Yes, but she never says much. My father's well-being is what matters." It was said without rancour or jealousy. Perhaps Alex felt, as I, that women were either mothers to their children or wives to their husbands. It seemed Mrs. Forsyth was the latter. Alex could support this; but Virginia? "Are you sure you want me to tell you the other thing?" he added.

"Quite." Even if he learnt his skills with the viragos after his strip-shows, I would rather know than remain in ignorance.

He began, "My aunt and uncle farm land in Wiltshire, as I told you. It's not an easy life, and as a side-line my aunt keeps a few horses and gives riding-lessons. Ever since my father's postings have taken him out of Europe, Virginia and I have always spent our holidays on the farm."

My interruption was indignant. "Surely your parents had leave?"

"Oh, yes, and then we would holiday together mostly in London. Anyway, I began to help about the farm and gradually took on more and more. I'm not horse-mad, but my aunt persuaded me to groom the mares and help when riders came along. As a perk, she gave me a small self-contained flat over the stables. It was about five hundred yards from the house and Virginia thought that as she was the only girl in the family she should have had it. So there was a bit of a rumpus about that."

I put my hand out and touched his. "If this is going to be difficult perhaps you don't have to say how you learnt the – how shall I put it – expertise you showed me last night."

He looked surprised. "Was it expert?"

"Terribly!"

"But, as a married woman, didn't you ..."

"It wasn't a communication of love or need. It left me hungry and disenchanted."

He remained silent a moment. "Well, I want to tell you. You have a right to know. To continue, I was about sixteen and wandering about the farm almost naked save for a pair of shorts, when a rather faded woman came along to learn riding. My aunt introduced her as the local doctor's wife who for some reason had had a nervous breakdown and was advised to do something therapeutic. I felt sorry for her. She seemed limp and wretched. She shrank when the horses pranced and jumped as they blew through their nostrils."

I could not help say, "Is that what being a doctor's wife does for you?"

Alex smiled. "I never saw the doctor in question. Apparently, he was one of her problems: he worked all hours in an oncology unit and when at home drank like a fish. Anyway, at first she came once a week in the morning, when all the bossy little girl riders were at school. Then she progressed to twice a week and next it was four times. She'd have her lesson in the paddock with my aunt, then hang around with the horses in the stables. Bit by bit, she grew more confident. She even gained some bloom. We thought it was animal-therapy ..."

"But, of course, it was Alex-therapy."

He gave an abashed laugh. "It seemed like it. When I returned to school, she asked me if I would be back the next holidays. I said yes, and when the time came, she took to having her lesson in the evenings, so that she was around while I stabled the horses for the night. Next, she had given me a present and stupidly I asked her up to my flat for a drink. Things went from there. She burst into tears, said how unhappy she was except when I was about, that she hated being a doctor's wife and she hated him, and I thought cripes! I'm landed in it now."

"Just for offering her a drink?"

"Hang on, it wasn't just a drink I gave her!" He blew out his lips. "Sexual curiosity makes a chap of seventeen vulnerable. Friends at school were boasting about losing their virginity, and everyone in my year seemed street-wise save me. I was fascinated by the whole topic, and yet the girls I knew left me cold. It was then I learnt how to dance sexily and I felt better about myself. If my friends had sex, I simulated it."

He stopped so I encouraged him. "Go on. This is better than a good book!"

Placing his elbows on the table, he continued, "This woman – let's call her Mrs. Medic – threw herself at me. She came back later that night when no one could spot her. She was in a state, her face red with crying and she had the shakes. She told me she fancied me and wanted to make love. At first I thought crumbs! what a first-time partner! Anyway, I offered her some coffee and she quietened down, and then the chance to find out what I had wanted to know for ages presented itself."

I looked away. "Was it Christmas-time, by any chance?"

"Yes."

I thought, here was another Christmas; and could a second older woman be throwing herself at him?

"You look down!" he cried. "Have I upset you?"

I shook my head. "Not at all. It's just that Christmas seems to be a rather active time of the year for you."

He sprang from his chair and was round the table to me in a trice. "I shouldn't have told you! She means nothing to me, but she did help me learn what I know now, and I gave her a little comfort!" He pulled up a chair and sat beside me, my hand in both his.

Caustic jealousy fizzled in me. Bleated Athena: *You see what happens when you ... Oh, go and play with your spear!* cried Aphrodite and I. "When did you last sleep with Mrs. Medic?"

"August."

I thought of her passing her hands as I had done over the firm lines of his body, marvelling at his cleanness and vigour. My husband had been a stale stockbroker; hers a workaholic doctor; no wonder we found the fine Alex dynamic. Cautiously, I began, "Who's the person now staying at your uncle's you said you'd rather not see?"

His hold tightened. "The very Mrs. Medic! And why? Because I've met you!"

"Ah!" I said, and no more.

Stroking my fingers, he continued, "When I rang my aunt to ask if I could come for Christmas – that was the day you were due here – she told me Mrs. Medic and her husband had agreed to separate for a breathing space. Apparently, she had no one to go to, so my aunt asked her to the farm. No way was I going there under those circumstances. Besides, you put all women in the shade."

This was said in such a matter-of-fact way that I laughed. "Does Mrs. Medic know about *Henny-Penny's*?"

"No one but you knows."

"Will you go on with the floor-shows?"

"If you don't object."

"No."

"It's purely the means to an end."

"Am I the means to an end?"

In answer, he passed a hand lightly under my sleeve so that I shivered, and drawing me to him gave me a lingering kiss. At first, I could not respond, anaesthetized by thoughts of the future.

"She will be very disappointed you aren't around," I observed eventually.

He shrugged. "She'll get over it. I bet I was only an interlude. As for me, the need for discretion was getting a bit of a bind, but at least I can conduct a clandestine affair, now!"

I looked into his face. He seemed so contented, so innocent of the workings of the female mind that I pulled myself together. All that we had shared the previous night was as serious as it was deep. We still had two weeks to enjoy being together. What happened after would take care of itself.

Without doubt, that was the best Christmas Day of my adult life. Alex and I dined traditionally at two, and afterwards drank champagne by the fire. He was touched by my present, and another of his to me – a box of superb Belgian chocolates – was quite unexpected. Then, at dusk, we had a walk through Pomeroy, peering cheekily in at people's lit windows and rating, out of ten, their Christmas decorations.

By eleven o'clock, our thoughts and bodies were merging. And as he varied his loving skills, I could not help pitying another woman who had got there first, but fashioned him for me.

# CHAPTER XIX

*dum licet ludite (A.A.III.61-2)*
*"have fun while you can"*

After Christmas we went out and about. Alex had never been to the Lake District, and since Ullswater was a mere twenty minute drive away we started there. He was the best kind of tourist, buying maps and leaflets and reading out which attractions to see, shutting gates as asked, taking home litter, not disturbing the sheep, and driving (for often I passed him the keys) carefully through terrain whose horizon might suddenly produce a sheep's head, and just as quickly whip it away.

We chose to see four lakes and one reservoir between Boxing Day and returning to school. The rest would wait for another holiday. Mostly the weather was kind; when it drizzled in Pomeroy, at Grasmere is was dry. We rated (like people's Christmas decorations) the towns and their lakes out of ten; and Grasmere came out with top marks.

"What do you like about it?" Alex asked as we sat in a hot tearoom where ramblers had left their cleggy boots by the door. "You speak for the village, and then I'll speak for the surrounds."

"Right!" I paused, staring at a pair of feet under the table nearby, whose shapeless socks made them look like platypus bills. "I like the slate-roofed houses standing tall and surprised-looking."

"Go on."

"The sudden green plateaux among the oaks –"

"That's my bit."

"Sorry. I like the river Gras, or is it the Mere?"

"Neither."

"What river is it on?"

"Pass."

"Whatever... the river which meanders through the village like an umbilical chord to the lake."

He grinned. "I prefer the suprised-looking houses to the birth-chord."

I apologised again. We had walked miles. We had been busy the night before. The tearoom heat after the cold fells was making me comatose, and I gave up. "Your turn!"

He straightened his mouth which I had an urgent desire to kiss, and I asked quickly, "Do you ever smoke?"

"No. Why?"

I leaned across the table to him and said in a low voice. "I have this fantasy of you with an unlit cigarette at the corner of your lips and my kissing you at the same time."

"'Struth! Sounds interesting!"

I leaned still nearer. "You're bare-chested and wearing a naval hat at a rakish angle."

He put a hand under the table and found one of mine. "I can oblige, Mrs. Farthing."

"Do you think I've got a sexual kink?"

"If you do, I love it." He disengaged his hand. "Excuse me." He rose and passed me slowly so that I had the chance to draw my palm along his firm thigh. He left the tearoom, pulling up his collar to the sniper's wind, and looked at me through the steamy window as he went down the road. In five minutes he was back. With eyes full of invitation, he placed a packet of cigarettes in front of me. What he liked about Grasmere's surroundings was left for another occasion.

As the days passed we familiarised ourselves with each other. Between the usual banal things of living, we talked: of school, family, work and love, but never what would happen when he left Dons for Oxford. I believed he loved me; it was in the way he looked at me, in the incredible intimacy of his embraces. But I could hardly expect the Alex of public school to feel the same way when he became the Oxford undergraduate. Adult life for him was just beginning; I was ten years into it.

Now, the start of a new term was only four days off. He and I were finishing tea, and outside sleet fell.

"The Marxist fancies you, doesn't he?"

"Is that what you call the Deputy?"

"Yes. He does, doesn't he?"

"I suppose so. Or he thinks he does. What's my nickname at school?"

"Penny-Farthing, but sometimes Dime."

It could be worse. "And Dr. Graff?"

"Gaffer."

"Miss Johns?"

"Panic-stations."

That was apt. "Mr. O'Hare?"

"Goddy."

"He'd be flattered! What about Mr. Sproat?"

"Not fit for a woman's ears."

"Why not?"

"Because it pertains to what D.H.Lawrence calls *masculine machinery*."

"Alex! I was once a married woman!"

"Very well. Scrote – short for scrotum."

"Ah! And Mr. Cotton?"

"Flopsie."

I laughed. "Of the Beatrix Potter rabbit trio?"

"Yes." Alex was looking at me askance. "Then I was right. I saw it a mile off."

"Saw what?"

"The Deputy fancied you."

Gently I pointed out that one person fancying another did not necessarily mean it was reciprocated.

He turned away. "I'm not surprised he does. That day in the front hall – do you remember? It was Bonfire Night, and I think you and he were going off to the pub."

I did indeed recall the occasion, and saw again Alex's expression as Francis and I had left together. "You were jealous?" I asked.

"As hell. He patronised me. I felt like a third former caught pinching an iced cake."

"I was the iced cake?"

"You were everything!"

I looked at him, murmuring, "Alex, Alex, where will this all lead us?"

"Into the future!"

His boyish enthusiasm cheered me, but I hesitated to encourage it. He was riding on the crest of Christmas and a satisfying relationship. He might regret later what was said and done now. And could I not end like Mrs. Medic, becoming someone he didn't 'want to see'?

"About next term," I began.

He groaned. "There'll be rules to follow?"

"Inevitably. If any of this gets out, your life at school will not be worth living and I shall get the sack. Alex, we must be above suspicion."

He stared at me in horror. "No physical contact?"

"None."

He got up and crouched beside me. "Not even in the privacy of your rooms?"

"No. First, we owe it to your father who is paying a lot of money for your education. Second, you are aiming for top class grades in your exams and a place at Oxford. You won't get A's in Classics if you and I spend our time... cosily."

"I'll burst!"

"No, you won't. You'll channel it into numerous essays and rigorous pieces of Latin and Greek prose. I'll burst instead."

"You will?"

"Yes." I ran my finger across his mouth. "You've given me something no one has ever given me. I've found a new dimension to myself I never knew possible, though I had a shrewd idea it existed. It will be torture sitting with you and yet unable to ... communicate as we have this holidays. But there will be more subtle ways."

"What?"

"I shan't say. Just watch out for them."

He sat back and began to remove my shoes.

"What an emancipated male you are," I added, as he massaged my feet. "But you're frowning. Why?"

"You can still call me Alex, while I must call you Mrs. Farthing!"

"I'm afraid so."

"Oh – sod it!"

"Quite."

"When are you going to send me back to Dons?"

"I shan't send you, but we should arrive separately."

He brightened. "We'll drive together as far as London?"

"It's an idea. You could drop yourself off at your flat and I'll go on to school. That way no one will know we've been together."

He was giving my left foot a final squeeze before putting it back into its shoe. "This next term's going to be terribly difficult."

Our eyes met. "You'll manage perfectly well, Alex. Seeing you manage will help me." I touched his cheek. "Now, would you like to come up here for Easter or –" and this was with a mixture of truth and jest, "– do you think Mrs. Medic will want to see you in Wiltshire?"

He rose and towered over me. "What Mrs. Medic wants she can't have, at least not from this department!"

I caught him by the belt, murmuring, "I wonder which department that might be." But I knew perfectly well, and he knew I knew, and there followed an episode of salacious foolery which concluded in my making him a proposition. "I suppose you wouldn't give me a lesson in your kind of dancing?"

He jumped away. "Good Lord, Mrs. Farthing, you shock me!" But he started unbuckling his belt and gyrating his hips there and then, till I covered my eyes with a peeping-tom hand.

"Not now! There must be music and the right setting!"

He stopped. "Then leave it to me."

For the last few days of the Christmas holidays we had foul weather. It rained, then sleeted and was bitterly cold. We had toured four lakes which left Haweswater reservoir still to see. To do it justice we needed a dry day, so while it rained we drove up to Stainmore above the Eden valley. Sheep, grey clumps of wool, roamed over the grass, unperturbed; but if we came too close, they skittered away, their haunches studded with droppings clacking like castanets. I had last been up there in Spring when the blue bubbled with larksong and lambs cavorted in giggling knots. Now, we bumped foreheads with the clouds, for winter had lowered the sky.

I was preparing lessons in earnest for next term. One evening, while I studied in the kitchen, Alex – who had declared he would work no more that holiday – was in the sitting-room selecting the right kind of music for our movement lesson. I could hear a strong beat, then his voice proclaim, "Possible," or "No good," and sometimes, "Perfect!" and I smiled over my papers. But often I would break off between pieces of Greek and Latin, and dreamily review how this holiday had turned out. Virginia, petulant contrary Virginia would never know how indebted I was to her.

In the middle of one such reverie, Alex appeared in the doorway in that silent way of his. My eyes immediately flew to him.

"I feel randy," he said.

"Then that makes two of us."

He came up behind my chair and put his arms round me. "I can't get enough of you. What am I going to do in our lessons?"

I turned towards his mouth. "Just work, Forsyth!"

"But Forsyth will be thinking of something else."

My pulse was quickening. "A glass of cold water should do the trick."

"Cold makes hot hotter."

"We must be careful!"

"Why?" His mouth was at the nape of my neck. "Your rooms aren't bugged, are they?"

"No. But someone may be on the look-out."

He straightened. "Who?"

I was vague in my reply, and certainly did not mention that I had sensed Francis Marks' jealousy. I changed the subject slightly. "Well, that's one of the subtle ways we can show our feelings."

"Drinking a glass of cold water?"

"Why not? It's the most innocent thing of all!"

"Then I shall be drinking non-stop!" He moved off regretfully. "Right, Mrs. Farthing, all is prepared for your movement class. Please come this way."

He had transformed the sitting-room. The fire was banked high and flickered great dragon's tongues of flame. The lamps had been moved to more subtle corners and the centre of the room was cleared of furniture.

I entered with some trepidation. "Am I dressed right?"

He looked at my shirt and trousers with a nod of approval, but suggested I fling off my shoes.

"You won't laugh at my ineptitude, will you, Alex," I begged, "Nor rouse me too much?"

"Of course I won't laugh, but the other ... well!" Tossing a look over his shoulder, he put on the music. It was the type of rhythm that ran in the primaeval river of your veins, which made your feet tap the ground and, in turn, the earth thumped back her heart beat.

"Just copy me!" he cried over the noise, and standing slightly in front with his back to me he began a series of hip thrusts and rotations.

Like many little girls, I had attended ballet classes. On Saturday mornings, whether in England or abroad, I would don my ballet shoes and a flower-fairy tutu and join other little girls at the local dancing school. There, spaghetti-kneed and starfish-fingered, we jerked, hanging with one desperate hand on to the *barre*, or twirled 'like snowflakes' before mirrors. My prancings were considered by the cognoscenti to be really rather good, and until the age of fourteen I thought I would make a career of dance. But adolescence and peer ridicule soon changed all that. Bookishness took over. When Antony and I married, I hoped we might attend tango classes, for the love of movement was still strong in me. "Tango?" he had exclaimed when the subject was first broached. "Haven't you noticed, Jess? I've got two left feet."

Now I was imitating Alex's gyrations, feeling perfectly inadequate. He kept looking back, shouting encouragement and sometimes praise. But I felt no better. Soon, my defeated expression gave him an idea. He turned down the music, then came behind me and wound his arms round my waist.

"There," he began in my ear, "Move as I move." His pelvis thrust at my back: left, right, forward, left, right, forward. It was all so sensual that I concentrated on him not the beat. "You're so tense!" he whispered against my cheek, "You must flex your knees which unlocks the hips." With his knees he unlocked the back of mine. We stood now like one spoon within another, and though the tension went from my limbs, I still clutched at his wrists. "So tense!" he murmured, and gently disengaged my fingers from his arms. He placed my palms flat against his buttocks which continued to ply their thrusting dance. From the front I was now defenceless; but perhaps that was what he intended. For his hands began to creep up the inside of my shirt to my breasts which he held and caressed. I stiffened at the shock of his cool fingers. But then they moved to that part of a woman which, with deft touchings, makes her fluid.

My tension fled, and we moved to the music as one.

☙ ❧

On our penultimate day of the holidays we drove to Haweswater. It was an area popular with 'twitchers' and the fell-walking fraternity. Its approach was benign enough: through open country along ribbon lanes, before plunging into a wood of low-slung oaks frilled with grey lichen. Soon, these gave way to coniferous trees, and we were driving up and up, catching glimpses of the reservoir on the right. Then down we sped into a bowl whose pewter waters were relieved by the flash of seagull wings.

I always felt slightly claustrophobic when the road came to an end at the car-park, and the steeps swelled bare and rough around me. Alex and I left the car and began walking up the fell at a leisurely pace. Men festooned with obscenely-shaped cameras swung past, their booted feet sounding hollow on the turf. The quiet was supreme, broken occasionally by a voice, thin ewe-bleat and the gush of rills that creamed, so to speak, out of the fell-side. Colours – peat brown and glaucous granite – were unrelievedly sombre till the quilt of foxy fern was touched by ladders of sunlight. Then, water, fell and sky burst with radiance and we were characters in a Blake painting shielding our eyes from celestial glare.

Mostly, the sky glowered with prune bruisings of rain. Alex kept exclaiming at the sight behind and in front. Often we stopped to look back at the reservoir. I said, "How small it's becoming!"

"Are you tired?" he asked, for our ascent was growing slower and we breathed fast.

"A little."

"Then back we go!"

We turned, and arm-in-arm marched down the fell in step. The reservoir grew bigger again, match-box cars (more had parked now) assumed normal proportions, and we were on the last slope when I missed my footing.

I semi-crashed to the ground, for Alex's arm broke the gravity of my fall. A sheep stopped chewing and stared, Alex bent over in concern, people gazing at Haweswater turned to gaze at me. "Jessica! Are you all right?" His anxious voice was tossed among the mew of gulls.

I stood gingerly. "A bit of a wrench," I said, feeling foolish.

He drew me in his arms. "Lean against me and catch your breath."

For some minutes, we stood close and possibly quite dramatic against the frowning fell. An opportunist photographer snapped us. Annoyed, I turned my face away. Alex rocked me as one rocks a sore child. "Can you walk?" he said eventually.

"I'll try." But the pain was acute, so without more ado he swung me into his arms and tramped us down to the car-park. There was applause and one or two whoops. "Do a *Henny-Penny's* for good measure!" I whispered fiercely.

He made a half-humorous noise in his throat and stood me, like an unsteady bottle, by the car as he unlocked. Then he drove us home.

Of course, I was helpless for the rest of the day. He bathed my ankle in cold water and bandaged it, and refused to let me do a thing.

"But dinner!" I cried from my cripple's chair.

"It'll be diplomat's stew."

For a moment I was silent. "Is it peculiar to ambassadorial circles?"

"No. It's diplomatic to every vegetable available; none is left out."

He was so capable. Yes, he nicked his finger with a sharp knife and his eyes wept over sliced onions. I wanted to commiserate, but I said nothing; I would sooner bite my tongue out than be a fussing mother-figure. Once or twice he caught my eyes upon him, and we looked at each other wordlessly. Then exigent boilings and sizzlings drew away his attention, and I was left physically apart but emotionally joined, thinking that to this boy-man, I could be mother, sister, wife, whore and mistress.

# CHAPTER XX

*furtiva Venus (AA.I.275)*
*"secret love"*

The alarm woke us at six. It was cold and very dark, so we agreed mutually to stay where we were till seven. At seven, I said, "*Est tempus ut surgamus.*"

Against me, he asked sleepily, "*Quid?*"

"It's time to get up!"

"*Perii!*"

"I know it's Oh dear! But the party's over, as they say." I rolled out of bed and tested my ankle.

He sat up. "How is it? Can you drive?"

"It's a bit stiff, but that'll probably wear off."

"I'll do most of the driving, if you like."

I twisted back and kissed him, then drew away. It was time to face the fact that the holidays were over, so too all demonstration of our love. At school we had to be like Caesar's wife: above suspicion.

I showered regretfully alone. Then, while Alex bathed and dressed, I cleaned the hearth and, for another time, set the fire which had embraced us in its warmth. As we breakfasted quietly, exchanging the occasional soft look, I said, "I want to thank you."

He seemed surprised. "What for, Mrs. Farthing?"

I smiled. Was he preparing himself for school 'mode', or being humorous? "For absolutely everything. And if anything happens between now and Easter to make you decide you don't want to come here again, or be with me on the same footing as now, I shan't forget what you've done and said and been."

His reply was quick. "Nothing will make me change my mind – unless you change yours." He stretched out a hand, and I grasped it. "And I want to thank you. I feel ... a man. Sort of sexually wise. It's fantastic!"

Our drive south was uneventful, and my ankle bore up remarkably well. We took it in turns at the wheel and stopped every so often for a rest. I hated motorway driving; it felt as if I were a greyhound coursing along a limitless track, magnetised by the hare (read car) in front.

I dropped Alex off in London. "Won't you come to the flat for a breather?" he asked, as we sat despondent over parting.

"Virginia and Jasper?"

He looked grim. "I'll deal with them."

"Do we want to parry questions?"

"Not much."

"Then I'd better leave you here."

We touched hands, and he left the car. "Can I ring you this evening? Eight-ish?"

"Please!"

"When's my first lesson?"

I pondered a moment. Timetables seemed desperately irrelevant. "I've got a staff-meeting tomorrow at eleven, and you all return in the evening, so it'll be Thursday at three."

"Two whole days to go! Oh, cripes!" He shut the door and came round to my side.

I rolled down the window and said something I had yet to say. "I love you."

He bent to me. "And I love you."

Someone in a car hooted their horn at our private moment.

"Shut up, you bastard!" muttered Alex against my mouth. Then he straightened and moved to the safety of the pavement, and I drove slowly away.

At Dons, only Nisbet witnessed my return. He gave me an old-fashioned look which seemed to say, "Ah. You again," before merging with the shadows in the corridor to my stairs.

I entered my rooms and switched on the lamps. Domestic staff had cleaned and polished and left me fresh linen, but they had ignored the pot-plants. I watered them sparingly, and wondered if my request for basic supplies had also been forgotten. But there were eggs, milk, bread and butter in the 'fridge as I had asked; although supper was available for resident staff that night, I would eschew it.

Later, when I should have slept, rest proved elusive. For a while I was in that semi-state between wakefulness and sleep, when reality becomes contorted; I saw a grey worm-like road snaking always ahead of me, and there was one car which I desperately tried to overtake, though it wasn't clear why. A nervous jolt relieved me of that vision. Then, a proper vigil chased away sleep altogether, and I began questioning Alex's relationship with me.

Deep down I felt that, whatever his protestations, he would come to see me as another older woman, dissatisfied, lonely or both. I even tortured myself with nomenclature similar to 'Mrs. Medic'; would I be 'Moneypenny' (courtesy of Ian Fleming) or worse, Mrs. School-Marm. Or would he refer to me as Ms. Don, even Mrs. Mentor? I imagined him in some lattice-windowed Oxford room, feet up on the table cluttered with beer cans, Thucydides and Cicero, tossing peanuts at his men-friends while talking about An Affair he had had when in the Upper Sixth at school. None of this was in character, but the small hours have their own ghoul which sibilates with forked tongue.

Francis Marks was oddly stiff towards me when we met briefly before the staff-meeting the next day. I wondered why; we had parted on good terms before Christmas. No one else said very much to me. My Classics colleagues looked as if they had something crawling in their trousers when I asked if they had had a good holiday. None of them enquired after mine. Perhaps it was just as well.

There was little difference between sixty members of staff who gathered for the first time after the holidays and sixty fourth-formers returning to school. It lay only in physical appearance. Most of the teachers that morning gabbled and laughed, exchanging barely any news about their Christmas but flexing their muscles, so to speak, on the immediate concerns of school.

I joined them guffawing in the staffroom. The men, in roll-neck sweaters and denims (scruff-order was permitted till term formally began), had seized the most comfortable seats, and they sprawled, their flies buckling, as they made towers of their feet, the heel of one shoe placed vertically on the toe of the other.

Those of us who were less empty barrels found chairs where we could: Mr. O'Hare ('Goddy') for instance, who smiled at me from the opposite side of the room, Archimedes – my name for head of science – and a few others. Someone had switched on the fluorescent lighting rather than the side lamps, and those who came unshaved looked green.

Now Dr. Graff, spruce as usual, entered with the Deputy on a lead, so to speak. Foot-towers were hastily dismantled, and language which had been in danger of becoming over-ripe, turned squeaky-clean. Head Master and Deputy took their customary places, and silence fell.

"Good morning, everyone," began Dr. Graff giving us an expansive look. "I hope you've had a good Christmas. I'm proud to say that I've become a grandfather."

We congratulated him, and Miss Johns, in her chirruping way, asked, "Boy or girl, Head Master?"

"Boy."

"I hope he's down for Dons!" oozed Seneca.

Dr. Graff was quick off the mark. "We put him on the list four months ago!" Everyone laughed. "Before we start the meeting, I'd like to introduce Miss Josie Meyer who has joined the historians as a probationary teacher. If she likes us, she might stay." He surveyed us, adding, "You here, Miss Meyer?"

A hand wandered up and necks craned to assess the new staff addition. She was a blushing young thing with wispy hair, a vapid expression and eyebrows so widely arching that they gave her a startled expression. I wondered how she would cope with a class of robust young males.

Interest in Miss Meyer waned and she was left to blush unseen, for the Head Master was now addressing a new topic. "Solvent abuse," he began. "The Deputy and I deliberated about raising it last term, but with Christmas almost upon us, I felt any action we might take would lose its impact in the scrum to go home." He turned to Francis. "Do you want to continue?"

Francis nodded. "There have been several reports of boys in the lower and middle school sniffing pots of ink eradicator and felt-tip pens. As from this term, these are banned –" and he held up a plastic bottle, "– while these, which look like pens and do the job just as well, are permitted."

"What about board markers?" asked a voice.

"I was coming to that!" He took the cap off one, put it to his nose and made a face, saying as if to himself, "God knows how anyone can enjoy inhaling that!" We all laughed again. "Now these pens are our responsibility," he continued. "We must not leave them in the classroom where they can be got at. I know it's a chore, but we'll have to take them to and from each lesson. Failing that, they will need to be locked in the staff desk."

Dr. Graff here took over. "So, will all form staff at registration tomorrow morning please examine the contents of their boys' pencil-cases and lockers, and confiscate anything that smells of solvent. Spot-checks will have to be made throughout term, too."

Someone asked what the symptoms of solvent-abuse were.

Matron spoke up. "Constant sniffing, blinking watery eyes, cold sores and woolly thinking. But it can be confused with a genuine cold."

"Head Master, this is the season for colds!" exclaimed another voice. "How will we know the difference?"

Dr. Graff and the Deputy looked at matron. "I would say cold-symptoms last about a week, while solvent abuse symptoms go on longer."

Said Archimedes, "Who are the boys in question. Shouldn't we know?"

Dr. Graff and Francis Marks exchanged glances. "Again, we discussed that," replied the former. "Frankly, I don't think it will do any good at this stage for you to know. I have approached the boys' parents and warned them that if it continues, their sons will be excluded. I hope that's the end of it. You will all need to be watchful. Let me know if some boy's good work is suddenly failing, and he appears to be under the weather." He paused. "Any questions or comments?" As there was none, he scrutinised his list, then continued, "Next on the agenda is crushes."

My face flamed. And the flames grew hotter. I reached into my bag for a handkerchief behind which to hide, but my blush seemed to burn through the cambric. I didn't have a 'crush' on Alex, but the subject was close enough to the bone.

The Head Master was saying, "It's perfectly normal for adolescent pupils in single-sex schools to idolise someone higher up, and I'd call it playing with fire if we tried to stamp it out. However, what is unacceptable is contact of a physical kind. Most of you know about the sixth-former we expelled a few years back for molesting first and second year boys. We don't want a repeat performance. But late last term, matron found a third year boy up to no good with a member of the fifths."

Mr. Sproat was shifting uncomfortably, and in a pause exclaimed, "What do you propose, Head Master? We can't stop this thing at grass roots. You know what the boys will say: it goes on in the big wide world. Moreover, at ages fifteen or sixteen there are bound to be crises of gender."

Supportive noises were made and I had to agree with, however much I disliked, him.

Dr. Graff was doodling on his agenda sheet. From where I sat, the marks looked like octopuses. To my amusement, Francis was staring at his doodlings as if mesmerised. "I take your point," said the Head Master. "We've talked long and hard about this issue with the Chaplain and he has agreed to address the school tomorrow. Mr. O'Hare, do you wish to elaborate now?"

It was like a tennis-match in slow motion: from Dr. Graff heads turned to the Chaplain. "Not really, Head Master. But I shall do my best not to be judgmental – after all, certain members of the Church condone homosexuality."

The meeting continued for another forty minutes, after which we were refreshed with glasses of wine and nuts. Surprisingly, Seneca had remained quiet throughout most of the hour, but once some red wine had cut through his oleaginous silence he sententiously declaimed on what he would do about glue-sniffing and homosexual practices. And he was still holding forth when I sloped off to spend an hour in Deme.

Francis and I crossed paths in the front hall. We said 'good morning' and I was about to be affable when his aloof demeanour withered me. He barely smiled and hurried past as if reluctant to enter into the briefest of conversations. Mentally I shrugged. If he had thought over, and now regretted, his earlier interest in me, then fair enough; I would not lose sleep over it. But it would have been polite to go through the motions of wishing me a Happy New Year.

The day dragged. I took a long walk before tea in order to avoid the boys' return; it would not do to become embroiled with cars, parents, trunks and possibly Alex. In the lane beyond the school grounds early catkins were hanging like green inverted commas. From an ash, a song thrush repeated its breathless notes and a clump of snowdrops made a promise that spring lay ahead.

By seven o'clock, I knew Alex was back at Dons. Somewhere, among all the lights that twinkled, the voices which called, the doors that banged, he breathed, moved, felt and, I hoped, loved me.

The first day of term began at nine with boys and their form-staff breaking the ice after the holidays. This did not involve me, as heads of department were considered too busy with other things. But at nine-thirty we all filed into the Great Hall, staff taking their places on the stage facing the school, with a gradation of younger lads seated on the floor, the middle school on forms, and the seniors at the rear on chairs. My eyes had a wayward desire to wander towards the row of prefects, but I hauled them back and fixed them on the juniors' bobbing heads.

As usual, we started with the school hymn after which Dr. Graff made general announcements, including a welcome to Miss Meyer and a warning about solvent-abuse. Then he invited the Chaplain to speak. Mr. O'Hare had dignity, not the stuffy bad-smell-in-the-nose sort, but the kind which emanates from an inner centredness. He waited for his audience to cease coughing, sneezing, shuffling and tugging at its collars, then began: "In the days of the ancient Greeks, some five hundred years before the birth of Christ, Greek society was for men and about men. Women had their place, of course, but it was a restricted place in the home. On this understanding, men and women jogged along well and, I suspect, few broke the boundaries society had set. Marriage was a convenience, for economic as well as social reasons. Rather than a man fall in love with a girl and marry her, their respective parents arranged the union. This meant that a man's heart was free." He stopped a moment and made eye contact with the groups of boys before him. "While a man respected his wife and felt responsible for her, his love feelings might be directed towards members of his own sex, for it was to other men he best related, emotionally and mentally. Often, an older man loved a much younger one; the older man guided and set an example to the younger, while the younger looked up to, and modelled himself on, his senior. There was no sex education of the kind we have today, so I suggest that this relationship with a socially experienced older man served to teach the boy how to act man the citizen, man the soldier and man the husband."

The Chaplain was speaking without notes and here stopped a moment to look out of the windows on his right. The silence in the Great Hall was profound. I glanced at the faces in front of us; the juniors were wriggling, doubtless lost in their little world of sedentary discomfort and a natural desire to be doing; higher up the school, attention was rapt, while those at the top sat still, self-important, aloof, as if such affairs were beneath them.

Facing his audience once more, Mr. O'Hare resumed, "The most ideal of these man-boy relationships were platonic, that is, sexual activity did not come into it. It was purely a mental and spiritual bond with a good dose of mutual admiration thrown in. Now, in a single-sex school like yours, it is quite natural for boys to admire others, particularly those in seniority who are rewarded with prizes for sport, science, languages or whatever. This attraction is all part of growing up. And those of you more advanced in Greek will know that the word 'enthusiasm' is made up of *en* meaning 'in' and *theos* meaning 'god'. Enthusiasm is being transported by the god within you. It's fine to be enthusiastic over someone: it lifts you out of yourself and makes you work for that person's good. It's fine to want to be like the successful; it's fine to want to rub shoulders with someone who has qualities you admire and wish to possess. But at this stage in your lives, it is unwise to get any closer. It can bring problems at a time when your various rites of passage make you insecure. It also excludes you from wider relationships which may be less intense but, in the long run, more satisfying. So, my message to you all this term is this: by all means admire, but beware how you express it. The world is made up of all kinds of love, and you will know which is the best for you only when you leave here and mingle with the world in general." He nodded, as if adding a final full stop to his address. "Will you now all stand for the prayer."

We rose.

He waited for the noise to subside, then concluded, "Lord God, we pray for the ability to make the right decisions in our activities and study, in our difficulties and in ourselves. Help us to see both sides of every question whether it is purely for our own benefit or for others'. Lord, give us balance. Amen."

The entire hall murmured back, "Amen" and slowly we filed out.

My first class was with the fourth years. I felt empowered, by love, by the holidays, by the spring which would surely come, and as I strode into the classroom it probably showed. *"Salvete, pueri,"* I said to the twenty boys standing before me.

*"Salve,* Mrs Farthing."

*"Sedete,"* and they all sat. I surveyed them benignly but with firmness. Some pairs of eyes slipped away from mine, which I always found disconcerting. Others regarded me unflinchingly. There were several nice-looking lads among them, with clear complexions, pink ears and tidy backs-of-neck.

"Mrs. Farthing," began one who had put up his hand to speak. "Er...*quid est* 'thank you' in *lingua Latina?"*

*"Si unum adloqueris, est 'gratias tibi ago'; si multos adloqueris, est 'gratias vobis ago.'"* This stumped them; they swung their heads like puzzled young bullocks.

The same hand as before went up again. "Mrs. Farthing, *non intellego!"*

*"Vae tibi!"* I cried in mock irritation. *"Audi diligenter."* I repeated slowly what I had previously said and a second hand was raised.

*"Scio, magister, scio!"* cried the boy who was called Mardell.

*"Age, quid est, Mardelle?"*

"'If you address one person it is *gratias tibi ago*; if you address many it is *gratias vobis ago*', Mrs. Farthing."

I praised him, then another hand went up. "Mrs. Farthing, I haven't the foggiest what this is in Latin, so can I ask in English?"

I felt magnanimous. *"Ita."*

"Was Socrates gay?"

"Not as far as I know." This raised a laugh.

"But how do we know?"

"From what Plato has told us. Socrates attracted a lot of male attention, and although he was fond of Alcibiades –" Someone snorted, and I stopped. "What's the matter, Grainger?"

Grainger went red and spluttery. "It's just that I heard once that Alcibiades went round knocking statues' ..." He was overcome with sniggers and the rest of the class sniggered with him.

"We don't know if it was Alcibiades who knocked off statues' phalluses. Is that what you find funny, Grainger?"

They were all rocking and swaying in their seats, casting me sidelong looks to see if I was shocked or embarrassed. I was neither.

"Enough, fourth years!" I cried at last. "I can see you are raring to go. So, we'll start with a piece of translation. Turn to page nine, please."

The rape of the Sabine women had, in my experience, always been popular. While girls had instantly become feminist over the way Romulus and his men tricked the Sabines into marriage, the lads at Dons treated the whole thing with gleeful chauvinism. It was a good lesson; they enjoyed it and I enjoyed it, and I felt a mad if transient happiness. Soon I would see Alex for his lesson, and although it would be no more than mental contact, it was for me a form of disembodied sex.

A new duty had been allocated to me that term. Were a member of staff on a field trip or ill, colleagues were required to supervise his classes should they have a free period at the time. No one liked these duties because they ate into precious moments which could otherwise be devoted to marking, preparation, administration or catching up on the newspapers with a cup of tea. Now every Thursday, I was 'on call' for the forty minutes before Alex's lesson, which meant I had to hang around the staffroom, rather than go immediately to my rooms to prepare for him.

His first lesson after the holidays was worrying me. In the staffroom I could not settle. I picked up one paper and tossed it away, then another and discarded that. I made a cup of tea and let it go cold, and snapped Miss Johns' head off because she slammed the door.

Now Alex's lesson was only ten minutes away. My anxiety grew. Pomeroy seemed a long time ago already; would he not have been sucked into school life by now and was, perhaps, regretting the folly of the holidays? And how was I to react to him? To pretend it never happened would be an insult to us both. It had happened; it happened with extreme heat. To treat it now as trivial would reduce the whole episode to an experiment. The school clock chimed the half-hour. I picked up my books. I would have to take my cue from him.

I had only just settled in my rooms when I heard a knock at the door. "Come in," I called.

Alex entered. He shut the door and leaned against it, his eyes on my face. I could see he was going to take his cue from me.

Easily, I went on, "Hello, Alex. How nice to see you again!" Our eyes clung. I suddenly flushed. I, a woman of thirty, was tongue-tied by a youth of nineteen. Wordlessly he came forward. He held out his hand. I took it. By the clasp and look that accompanied it, we communicated all that needed communicating. Then we sat.

"How's the work coming on?" I asked.

"No problems, thanks, and I've got some very good news!" He was passing me an envelope.

I opened out and read the contents. "Oh, Alex, I am glad!" It was written confirmation from Balliol to say that he had gained a place for the autumn provided he achieve two A grades in Classics. "That's one hurdle vaulted. We'd better get on with the other. There is much to do yet." I paused, curious to know how his night at the London flat had been. "By the way, how's your sister?"

"Depressed. She and Jasper have had a row, he walked out, and she's now got a girl-friend to stay till they go back to school."

"Well! I don't suppose you minded a flat full of bright young things!"

He gave me an old-fashioned look. "I minded quite a lot! Immature girls set my teeth on edge."

What could I say but, "Ah!"

Meanwhile, he was hunting for a piece of paper. Then, using his file as a surface, he bent over and scribbled furiously. In silence, he passed a note to me. It read:

*'After you, they're a pain in the arse. I've missed you terribly. I love you. Can't we meet properly?'*

Below his words, I wrote back, *'And I love you. We must wait till Easter. We can't afford to be off-guard. Forgive me if I act stiffly. Our situation is perilous but so provocative! Please give me this when you've read it.'*

As he returned the piece of paper he sent me a rueful grin.

Those were days of excruciating abstinence. He came, as usual, for his lessons, and we took pleasure in communicating through Classics. But our bodies remembered the times we had been physically generous. Now all we could do was to look across at each other and thirst. I got into the habit of placing a jug of cold water and two glasses on the table near us, originally as a humorous reminder of my advice to drink when passion grew out of hand. I had also promised him other subtle ways through which we might express our feelings. For our mutual release we learnt to use the Greek and Latin languages. But still we exercised caution; for, if his work fell accidentally into my colleagues' hands, they would understand both languages where others did not. He might scribble in the margin a piece from Horace, and write beside it, "I can't quite get this." The snippet was amorous and I knew that he 'got' it perfectly well. Once he quoted Sappho, again pleading assistance over the following fragment:

οἰ μὲν ἰππήων στρότον, οἰ δὲ πέσδων,
οἰ δὲ νάων φαῖσ' ἐπὶ γᾶν μέλαιναν
ἔμμεναι κάλλιστον, ἔγω δὲ κῆν' ὄτ –
τω τις ἔραται ...

... which I translated for him thus:

*'Some say the loveliest thing on the dark earth is an army of horsemen, others an army of foot soldiers, others a fleet of ships; but I say it is the one you love.'*

It was a form of communication which, because of its subtle nature, charged us physically. He at nineteen, was probably at his most sexually powerful; I in my thirties, and having lived as Antony's wife on a diet of sexual indigence, was keen to satisfy my tastes.

Only once we succumbed, and that was simply to kiss. We had been discussing the union of Dido and Aeneas in a cave during a violent thunder-storm. Dido threw caution to the winds while Aeneas believed, incorrectly, that this was the end to his wanderings from Troy. But Rumour, described by Virgil as a loud-mouthed far-flying bird, began shouting out Dido's 'sin'.

Alex and I fell silent. I felt I was sinning, sinning against my position of trust, against his parents, worst of all against him. Young men would be infatuated, but that was no reason to encourage them as I had, perhaps, encouraged him. My throat went dry. I rose and went into the kitchen. He followed and kicked the intervening door shut. I felt him at my back. His arms went round me. He was warm and sexually vital. How he had contained himself during our lessons I did not know. But my breakdown in resolve, broke his. I turned in his arms, and for the remainder of that lesson we kissed and touched and whispered.

Dido and Aeneas were never, could not ever in our present circumstances be raised again.

# CHAPTER XXI

*vigil custos (A.A.III.612)*
*"watchful spy"*

"The very person I wanted to see!" Archimedes had come up to me as I stood in the staff-room a few days later. I was examining the notice-board and saw with irritation that Miss Meyer, the probationer, needed cover, and I was the one to take on that duty.

I turned to him with a smile. I liked Archimedes; he was stable, always courteous and in favour of Classics. "What can I do for you?"

He held a familiar-looking book under his arm. "Nothing really, Jessica. I thought I should tell you I've put Harrison Senior on detention."

Harrison Senior was a fourth year boy and obtuse at Classics, not because he lacked intelligence but because he disapproved, so I felt, of me. He had a habit of gazing at me, his mouth slightly parted and a wondering look about the eyes. The message he appeared to convey was one of admiration. Far from it, for when I told him off once for slovenly work, he glanced away and muttered darkly. This term, he had become uncooperative and would spend my lessons either glowering at me or scribbling obsessively in his rough-book. "What's he done?"

"I caught him defiling his Latin text. He's added beards and masculine parts to female figures. Do you want to see?"

"Not particularly, but I'd better!" Archimedes held out the Latin text I used with the fourths. I opened at the front, and saw scrawled on the fly-leaf: *Latin stinks. So does she.* "Nice message," I added.

"Don't worry. I get it all the time."

I continued to leaf through, and found that the pictures of goddesses in certain states of dishabille had, indeed, been adorned with ink additions, but such additions as would belong to men of monumental proportions. "How have you punished him?"

"He's spending an hour this evening washing phials et cetera in my lab. Do you approve?"

"Wholeheartedly!"

"Good. Oh, damn, look at that rain." We stared out of the window at a sudden shower falling like lances. Humming, Archimedes wandered out of the room, and I took myself off to supervise Miss Meyer's second years.

A note on the staff-desk showed her calibre. She had written almost illegibly what she required her class to do, then added: *'They will need their neat books which are in the staff-study on my bottom shelf, and plain paper for drawing on.'* Now, I had no intention of running off to fetch neat books and hunt for plain paper; she should have made sure all these were provided before she went on her outing. I glanced round at the expectant second years and said, "You will have to work in rough, boys," which they proceeded to do without demur.

While they worked, I wrote beneath Miss Meyer's instructions: *'No plain paper provided and neat books unobtainable.'* And at the end of the class I slipped the note into her pigeon-hole as my explanation. I never gave the matter another thought until the next day I was accosted by the head of history's wife, Blanche Megram.

For some reason, Mrs. Megram (let her be called Migraine) was Dr. Graff's little white hen. All other staff were addressed by their title, but Migraine was always 'Blanche' this, and 'Blanche' that. Had the Head Master not been happily married, I would have had my suspicions. Anyway, as wife of head of history, Migraine thrust a finger into several tidy pies: she was a housemaster's spouse and had mumsie duties; she arranged flowers in the Chapel; she counselled anyone who needed it; she looked after young visiting teachers and foreigners on exchange. In short, she was indispensable.

I was minding my own business in the staff-study when I felt a rush of displaced air at my back, and Migraine was hissing from the door, "Next time, you could tell Josie to her face rather than write her a note!" Catching my astonished eye with hers, she continued, "We're trying to build up the confidence of a young teacher, but your letter did nothing to help!"

My temper rose. "I didn't write her a letter! My comments were added to the bottom of her instruction sheet to explain why things weren't carried out as she wanted."

"She was on a field trip!"

"Then all the more reason to have got her act together beforehand!"

Now came the parthian shot. Hovering in the doorway so that she could turn tail before the battle got too bloody, she added, "You're not beyond reproach! We've had to do things for you that you haven't got right!" With that she whisked out of the way.

I resorted to the best language for invective, *"Oblatratrix!"** Then, with curling lip, flared nostril and fury in my eye I swept down the corridor, scattering six large boys in my path.

"She's in a bait!" stage-whispered one.

Said another, "Cripes! Someone's going to get it."

The fifths 'got it', but not directly. For we were reading an extract from Horace's satires, and I put all my furious energy into explaining his work. When class was over, the boys looked stimulated but I felt drained.

They say things happen in threes. Over the next few days there was proof of this.

Pupils communicated with staff about their work and, in the case of the Sixth Form, handed in essays via a number of pigeon-holes outside the staffroom door. Before my time, there had been talk of placing the rack inside the room since pieces of chewed gum were being zealously stuck to unpopular staff members' pigeon-holes. But like every fashion, gifts of gum lost their impact, and the wrack remained in its original place.

The day after Harrison Senior wrote that I and my subject stank, and made transsexuals of goddesses, and when Migraine adopted the warring tactics of the Parthians, I received a third blow which, of all, was the worst. Lessons had just finished and I was approaching the staffroom for a cup of tea. My pigeon-hole looked full, and in passing I pulled out its contents. There were seven essays from the Lower Sixth, one of Alex's and a single sheet folded in two. I entered the staffroom with a look at Alex's work first and wondering what subtle quote I might this time find which he could not 'get'. While I glanced through the rest, the folded piece of paper fell at Miss Johns' feet.

---

*'yapping bitch!'

"Oops!" she exclaimed, bending to pick it up. Her knees cracked like firewood. "Happy reading!" and she handed it back to me.

I thanked her and opened it. In my hand was an anonymous note painstakingly put together with capital letters cut from newsprint. The words read:

YOU AND ALEX WERE SEEN AT HAWESWATER
IT WAS DISGUSTING

I turned red then my face tightened. Another colleague spoke to me. I answered logically. Forgetting tea, I made for the privacy of my office.

Nausea came over me. I swallowed repeatedly. The sheet of paper jigged in my hand. Even in Cumbria one could not escape Dons. And what had Alex and I done which could be termed 'disgusting'? I never liked a public show of love, and outside the house we had not acted in a passionate way. So what could have been construed as repugnant? Then I remembered how I had lost my footing; Alex had steadied me and drawn me in his arms to catch my breath; it was at that moment that an opportunist photographer had snapped us. Then, since my ankle refused to take my weight, Alex swung me up and carried me to the car while a few onlookers clapped and whooped. The anonymous note was probably meant for my eyes only; but if the writer and photographer were one and the same – and this is what chilled me – when would that picture be publicly displayed in the corridors of Dons?

My imagination began to run amok: Alex would be dragged over the coals; they would sack me; wherever I went there would be sniggers from the boys and censure among the staff; it would affect Alex's grades; he'd not achieve A's; Balliol would reject him; Oxford would close its doors to him; he, so brilliant, would have to join duller entrants applying through the clearing scheme; and it was because I had returned his kiss. I put my head in my hands and wished I were dead.

The wish passed, and I began to consider who the sender might be. I thought of all those who disliked me. First, there was Francis Marks who since the start of term had been extraordinarily cold. Why? He was hot enough before Christmas. Then, there was Mr. Sproat with whom I had wiped the floor, so to speak, at a staff-meeting. Next, my colleagues, the Three Graces, continually made it plain that they resented me and my ideas. Most recently, there was

Migraine, championing vacuous probationers. To a lesser degree, Seneca could even rank an enemy; so too Miss Johns, for had she not picked up the note itself and handed it back with a "Happy reading"? But I dismissed her; given as she was to panic attacks, she would hardly court more. Yes, I had my enemies.

Now I wondered if Alex had received an anonymous note, too. Or did the sender have an axe to grind only with me? I would watch him carefully during our lessons and rely on my sixth sense.

I sat a little longer in my office and the nausea subsided. Tea would still be available in the staffroom. If the sender was there, waiting and watching for my reaction, I would show him, or her, that I did not easily break.

The room was full. A few cracked biscuits lay on a plate, but the sandwiches looked fresh. I poured a cup of tea and helped myself to some food. Archimedes moved up on the couch to make way for me.

"The phials in the lab are nice and clean!" he began with reference to Harrison Senior's detention.

"Good. How did he take it?" I made a show of enjoying my sandwich, just in case someone in the room was scrutinising me.

"In sulky silence. What did you do about the Latin text?"

"'Harrison, here's your book and some ink eradicator. Clean up the pictures and show me when you've done it'," I quoted.

Archimedes was grinning. "And has he?"

"Not yet." Suddenly I heard my name from the door, and turned.

Bowtie was calling me, "Jessica, Harrison Senior wants a word."

"Speak of the devil!" exclaimed Archimedes as I went, cup in hand, to the door.

In the passage stood the boy, taller than I and shifty-looking. He had weak eyes, and the light from the room behind me made him blink. "Do you want to see the book, or shall I put it in your pigeon-hole?" he mumbled.

"Show it to me now," I said. "Here, hold my tea and I'll look through the pages."

A stumpy thumb with bitten quicks curled round my saucer. As I examined his text I was made uncomfortably aware of his proximity. He smelled acrid and his greasy hair hung limp. I finished my inspection, then handed back the book. "Don't ever let me find these disfigurements again, Harrison!" Relieving him of my cup I went back to my tea.

"Well?" asked Archimedes, thrusting his bi-focals above his eyebrows.

I sat down again beside him. "Someone should lead him to soap and water."

"Yes, the smelly little blighter!"

That evening, when alone in my rooms, I considered the situation. First, how to deal with an anonymous note? Would there be more, or just the one? And what was the purpose of it to start with? Blackmail was too dramatic for the circumstances. In that case, was the sender trying to unnerve me, or in some warped way enjoying control over me, or hoping to drive me from the school? Then, I reflected on my position at Dons. In sixth months' time Alex would leave. He made everything there worthwhile. Once he had gone, my departmental colleagues' hostility would affect me more than it had done. I would feel very much alone. So, I could do two things; find accommodation outside school where my life would be more my own, or resign my post altogether. The latter option seemed drastic. I was happy enough in my job; the boys and I got on, and Dons' academic excellence made it a stimulating place in which to work. But would it be the same once Alex had gone? Did not my involvement with him make everything bearable? I began seriously to consider the option of another post.

Such thoughts then led to my contemplating what would happen to our relationship. There was no question about my love for him. I had never loved anyone the way I loved him, and it was doubtful I ever would. But I could not expect him to feel the same. He was not yet twenty; university life with its enormous possibilities was opening out ahead of him. Even if he had a penchant for older women, there would be others with whom to become involved before he decided on one. However much it hurt, for his sake I would have to leave him free. That meant making no claims, extracting no promises, demanding no rights. While he wanted, I would give. Then there would be an end to it.

All this made me wretched. And I came to the conclusion that there was only one life worth living, and that was the life of the mind.

Alex gave no indication that he also had received an anonymous note. We studied and discussed our work as I had insisted we should, and apart from the voluble glances and drinks of cold water and subtle pleas for help with extracts he pretended he could not 'get', he remained a young man without a pressing secret.

A week passed. It occurred to me that perhaps the sender of the anonymous note had intended merely to tell me that he, or she, knew Alex and I were enjoying a stronger relationship than teacher and taught, and there the matter would stop. But it did not.

The second anonymous note was, as before, among the papers in my pigeon-hole. This time, it was suggestive:

WHAT DO YOU BOTH DO IN YOUR ROOM
WHEN IT SHOULD BE HIS LESSON?

Staff and boys alike knew that Alex came to my quarters for his one-to-one tutorials but no one had made an issue of it – except Francis Marks and Allan. The Deputy had thought these lessons should be conducted downstairs in my office, and Allan, who would have had to shift elsewhere, made his feelings on the matter plain. It so happened that no alteration was made, but perhaps the acrimony had stuck. I found myself regularly looking with suspicion at both Francis and Allan, and when I was not damning them with my eyes, I condemned them in my heart.

To all appearances, I carried myself as before and gave nothing away. I did not snap at colleagues, or complain I was under pressure or become over-critical of my pupils' efforts. Detentions were de riguer should the circumstances demand them; I voiced praise if it was deserved. In the staffroom, I was polite but really more interested in the newspaper. To all intents and purposes I was showing the sender of those anonymous notes that he, or she, was dealing not with a Miss Johns who panicked at the slightest provocation, but with someone of very different mettle.

Now, nearly at half-term, the appraisal procedure with which we had been threatened before Christmas was upon us. In ten months' time Dons would be inspected at every level, and Dr. Graff wanted all staff to have gone through at least the first stage of appraisal by then. Francis Marks would be appraising me.

The entire school knew we were gong through self-appraisal. At first, the boys thought they were the ones to be assessed, and when I told my fourth years that the Deputy would be sitting in on one of their Latin lessons, Grainger voiced the fear of many. "Mrs. Farthing, I might make a fool of myself. Can't the Marx ... I mean, can't Mr. Marks sit in on some other class?"

I put on a long-suffering expression. "Grainger, how often do I have to tell you that it is I who am –" I paused; that sounded ungrammatical, so I tried again, "– I who are..."

"You wot is," encouraged Mardell helpfully.

"Thank you, Mr. Mardell." I began to exaggerate my dilemma, on purpose you understand, for the boys loved it when teachers were at a loss or made a mistake. I put a hand to my chin and gazed out of the window, muttering audibly, "I who are, I who is, I who am..."

They started laughing squeaking, grating laughs that went up the scale and down the scale in the manner of voice-breaking boys.

"Aha!" I cried at last, feeling as Archimedes (the real) must have felt when he leaped from his bath with the answer to his difficulty, "When in doubt, turn to Latin. A laurel wreath to him who solves the riddle."

Primers were opened with theatrical gestures; these fourths were great showmen given the chance.

"*Is qui ...*" shrilled one lad, jigging in his chair at the thought of laurel leaves.

I dampened his ardour. "That, Puttham, means 'he who'," and he hunched in his seat like an owl with indigestion.

"*Sum qui...*" cried another lad, waving a ruler above his head, "In other words, Mrs. Farthing and chaps, 'I am the one who'."

A boy in front of him was withering in his criticism. "No, dick-head, Mrs. Farthing said 'It is I who am'."

"Hang on, Jones, I do believe Verey is right." I looked over to Verey who was still waving his ruler about like an antenna. "What's the context, Verey?"

Verey's confidence increased. He bent over his primer. "Well, the book gives an example, *sunt qui discessum animi a corpore putent esse mortem,* and it's followed by C.Tusc.I.9. What's C.Tusc.I.9, Mrs. Farthing?"

"Cicero, the writer of the Tusculan Disputations. Go on."

"And the translation has, 'there are some who think that death is the departure of the soul from the body'. So, if *sunt qui blah, blah, putent* is 'there are some who think', why can't *sum qui* mean as you said – 'I am the one who'?"

I was opening a window and leaning out. Along this particular piece of wall grew a wisteria. It had lost many of its leaves, but I found half a dozen and returned to the front of the class. "Now, Verey," I began, "We don't have any laurel, so you'll have to imagine it." I was twining the leaves into a wreath. "Come up here, please, and accept your crown of victory."

The class began to chant, "Go! Go! Go!", and flushing to the ears, Verey stomped all feet and elbow towards me, ducked his head and received the wreath.

As he returned to his place, I asked them, "Are you still worried about Mr. Marks' presence?"

"No, Mrs. Farthing!"

They might not be, but I was. Francis' manner towards me had not improved; it was no worse, but it still made me wonder what had happened to bring about this change since Christmas. And a few days after that laurel-awarding lesson, he sat in on the class, as arranged, to observe and take notes.

We met the following afternoon to share the experience and he seemed to unbend. "I liked the way you addressed them all," he began. "Your eye-contact was very good, you varied the pace and learning strategies, and left few in doubt about the aims and outcomes. But, one or two boys contributed little. Could you not, perhaps, have elicited rather more from them?"

So far so good. "Which boys had you in mind?"

"That lanky fellow, Hankinson?"

"You mean Harrison Senior?"

"That's the one!"

I thought a moment. "A dark horse," I said. "I've never seen him smile, and trying to get information out of him is like squeezing a dry orange."

A flicker of amusement warmed Francis' face, but my heart remained stony: *How do you spend your evenings – cutting out letters for anonymous notes?* The meeting continued well enough and by the end he had drawn up a document about our observations on that lesson and targets over the coming months, all of which would be typed then signed by us both.

Next, it was the Three Graces' turn to be appraised. Francis spoke to them individually, and classes were arranged when both he and I should assess them. I was annoyed at the need for this arrangement, and told him so. "It's a flagrant waste of two professionals' time," I exclaimed as we stood by the notice-board in the staffroom.

He agreed, but then looked wise. "They wanted it this way, and they'll get it this way – plus extra work! They will have more photocopying to do to provide us both with necessary papers, and it might just show them the error of their ways."

And this was precisely what happened. Men being transparent creatures, they looked ill-at-ease in front of the boys; for, while all other members of staff had only one appraiser, in their classes there were two; doubtless there would be questions why. None of this endeared me to them; their initial recalcitrance had backfired and ended in a *reductio ad absurdum.*

A pattern to my anonymous letters began to appear. I was sent one weekly, but never at the same time. It might be at break or in the lunch-hour or even after school, so that had I wished to keep watch I would never know exactly when. Their message was also growing smuttier. The latest read:

HOW OFTEN? EVERY LESSON?

This was something I would dearly have liked to share with Alex. It involved us both and under normal circumstances he should have known about such letters. But we were not living under normal circumstances, and I dreaded disturbing his peace of mind. His work-load of four A levels was colossal. He was also heavily involved in school athletics. At times he looked tired. I wondered if he lay sleepless wanting me, as I lay at night wanting him.

I could have become neurotic about the whole thing. The thought that someone somewhere was busy working out foul things to say, painstakingly collecting newsprint from which to cut letters, sticking them on paper and then waiting to slip the note into my pigeon-hole made me feel, at times, quite ill. But I persevered. What Alex and I were to each other was nothing to be ashamed of; it was our environment which was wrong.

Half-term was now only two weeks away. Senior boys sat their mock exams while the lower school took sessional tests. There was a lull in teaching before the frenzy of marking which would lead up to the break. I had envisaged ten days without sight or sound of Alex; but one afternoon into the first exam week I was in my rooms at the time he normally came for his lesson when a knock sounded on my door. I went to answer and I found him on the second-from-top step, so that our eyes were almost level.

"Room service, madam," he said softly.

I smothered a laugh. "Hello, Alex. Got a problem with some work?"

He entered wielding a book. "Plato," he said, and I shut the door on the world.

"Can you stay for some tea? How did you find the Latin prose paper?" But he was handing me a note and he remained silent while I read the following:

*'Can we spend half-term at the London flat? Virginia's school has theirs later. We'll be alone! Would you mind if I strutted my stuff at H-P's a couple of evenings? If you do, I won't. I'll strut for you instead. Mille basia undique.'**

I looked up at him and nodded, before writing back:

*'I'd love to. No, I don't mind. Cash in on ALL opportunities! I'll be along at about 7pm.*
*ardens in cupiditatibus.'***

We talked of work and sorted out his Plato difficulty, touching on nothing personal. It was good just to be together, looking in each other's eyes while our minds registered past intimacies. At four, I was about to make some tea when a heavy footstep came up the stairway. There followed a peremptory knock.

"Come in," I called, and Francis Marks opened and put his head round the door.

"Jessica!" he said, then seeing Alex who stood courteously, he added in a rather different tone, "And Forsyth."

I refused to blush or explain Alex's presence. "Hello, Deputy. Won't you come in?"

A disgruntled expression crossed his features as he dithered by the door, uncertain whether to shut or leave it ajar. Clearly he was put out to see Alex with me, and he homed in on that at once. "Aren't you revising, Forsyth? I'm sure Mrs. Farthing has enough to do without attending to you in exam week."

We looked at Alex who stood firm. "Mrs. Farthing is kindly helping me with some Greek, sir."

---

*'A thousand kisses all over'

**'Enflamed with desire'

I could see that Francis had not yet done with Alex; and the piece of paper on which we had communicated about half-term lay visible on the table. "Would you like some tea, Deputy?" I asked.

"No, thanks."

"Alex?"

"A glass of water would do me, please."

I passed behind Francis, throwing Alex a speaking glance. He understood, gathered up all my papers, including our note, and put them on a chair across the room.

"We've got some prospective parents downstairs, Mrs. Farthing," Francis was saying as he perched on the table. "They're German."

I returned from the kitchen and placed a glass of water beside Alex. "Don't stand on ceremony, now," I said with a little smile at him. "Have a seat!"

"Forsyth should hop along," put in Francis. "It's gone four o'clock."

No one tells me whom to have in my private quarters, and I saw no reason why Alex should 'hop along'. "What about these German parents?" I asked as I sat, ignoring his comment.

He folded his arms across his chest. "They've got a seventeen-year-old son who wants to carry on with Latin here. Apparently, by sending him to a British school he can jump the queue back home for a job – but don't ask me how. They're having tea with Dr. Graff now. Would you come down and speak to them in a minute or two?"

Tea with Alex would have to be postponed. I swore silently. Alex tossed back his water, and we both rose.

"If you have any other problems, do come and ask," I said to him as he picked up his Plato.

"There's always the staffroom door, Forsyth," put in Francis trenchantly.

I tightened my lips. "We might as well all go down."

Francis ushered him out first, and he went with a quick 'thank you' to me before vanishing along the corridor.

"Cocky devil!" muttered the Deputy.

I said nothing. My suspicions that Francis was indeed the sender of the anonymous notes had deprived me temporarily of speech.

# CHAPTER XXII

*metuendos esse sodales (A.A.III.659)*
*"friends should be feared"*

Francis and I reached the front hall in silence. He seemed uncomfortable and marched a little ahead of me, with occasional backward glances for reassurance that I was following. I remained laconic. At the foot of the staircase, we halted and looked across at the open front door.

"Hullo, it looks as if we've been superseded," he said, with a frown.

In the drive, hands in both pockets so that their backsides showed broad and flaccid, were the Three Graces joking in a hail-fellow-well-met manner with a Germanic-looking couple and their son.

"Hang on, Jessica. I'd better consult the Head Master." And Francis disappeared into the depths of the building.

There was no point in my joining the party which was clearly about to end. So, I waited and observed. Now hands were being stuck out and shaken; the Germans climbed into their hearse-like car; doors slammed, and my colleagues ducked and grinned in at the windows. Slowly the visitors drew away.

No one listening to anyone else, the Three Graces gabbled into the hall. At sight of me, their spirits dampened and in silence they passed, a posse of male power, without offering any explanation.

They did not know that I was already aware of the Germans' visit, and my icy question took them short. "What's the upshot, gentlemen?"

Bowtie blustered into speech, "The boy's coming this...er... next term."

"But the Deputy wanted me to speak to him."

Bleated Catullus' Goat, "You couldn't be found."

"They had a 'plane to catch," said Allan.

"He's a bright lad," observed Bowtie as if that had anything to do with it.

I breathed in deeply. "Good. But there's the principle to consider. I was asked by Dr. Graff, who sent Francis, to see these people. I have not seen them. You have."

Allan shrugged and began moving off. "Sorry, Jessica. But we tried your office, the staffroom and every conceivable place."

"You weren't immediately available, and you know how impatient Germans can be," added Bowtie, walking on Allan's heels.

Catullus' Goat said nothing.

To press the matter would have been undignified, so I let them go. But I was angry; three little pip-squeaks had decided to take on my role just because I was not 'immediately available'. Boiling, I went to the door to cool off. And where the hell was Francis? I would wait no longer for him.

The boys were at tea, so there was no tide of youth to push against. I made for the staffroom and, in passing, twitched some papers from my pigeon-hole. I hardly dared examine them, but yes, there it was, another anonymous note:

WHOS ON TOP YOU OR HIM?

In one corner of the staffroom the Three Graces were ensconced, roaring their heads off; Miss Johns was demonstrating a highland fling before Seneca who screwed up his face in a caricature of amusement; while Sproat picked his nose over the newspaper. It all seemed so awful that something in me snapped.

I went out again, still clutching papers and anonymous note, and marched towards the administration wing. The route took me through the cloister and past the seniors' notice board. From a distance I saw what looked like a large black-and-white photograph. I drew in a deep breath. Was it of Alex and me at Haweswater? My step slowed. Two members of the fifth came towards me. At the board they paused, bent closer and, heads together, stabbed with derisory fingers at the picture. Sniggering, they came on. I braced myself and strode out. They passed, saying in their normal way, "Hello, Mrs. Farthing." Surprised, I returned the greeting and stopped at the board. What hung there was a black-and-white photograph of a scene from the school play. I tossed the dread from my heart and marched on.

Dr. Graff's secretary was on the telephone, bending her goose-neck to the receiver. Bits of hair stuck out over her collar like farmyard feathers: *Do people look like animals or do animals resemble people?*

She replaced the receiver with a snap. "Mrs. Farthing?"

"An appointment with Dr. Graff, please."

She consulted her diary. "Four o'clock tomorrow?"

It could not have been better.

Dr. Graff liked to drink from fine china. "Have you had tea?" he asked, as I entered his office the next day.

"Thank you, yes."

"You won't mind if I drink mine as we talk?"

"Not at all."

"This –" and he raised his cup, "– was my grandmother's. We used to keep the set in a cabinet. But my wife said we should enjoy it. She's right, of course."

I smiled. "A shoe is for wearing, so a cup is for drinking from."

"Precisely!" Putting cup and saucer to one side, he added, "Have a seat," and took one opposite me. "Now, what can I do for you?"

"I've come to resign my post."

He said, "Oh, dear," and began to stroke his left sideburn with an index finger.

I waited for more, but as he remained silent I continued, "I've been here only a short time but long enough to realise that a boys' school is not the right environment for me to give of my best." It sounded lame, but then I felt lame.

He shot me a look. "It's not a discipline problem?"

"No."

"So, what is it, Mrs. Farthing?"

I told him what he doubtless knew; that my immediate colleagues were uncooperative in every way and how, recently, they had taken over my task of speaking to the Germans. "I don't like talking about people behind their back, Head Master," I added, "But you need to know why I'm taking action. Let's face facts, Classics has to compete all the time with new subjects entering the curriculum. Its teachers need to be united, or it will fall from grace. My colleagues and I are disunited."

He stared into the distance, still meditatively stroking his sideburn. Then he pushed back his chair and crossed his legs. "I find it very sad that despite our endeavours to be politically correct, there are those who for whatever reason won't toe the line. I am aware, Mrs. Farthing, of your uncooperative colleagues and all I can say is that it does them no credit at all." He looked me straight in the eyes. "It is because of them you want to leave?"

I flushed. "Not entirely. I do feel that to give of my best as a Classicist I need to be free of – how shall I put it – constraints placed on me because I am a woman in a male school."

"Constraints?"

"It helps to act as one of the lads, Head Master."

His expression relaxed and he brushed me with his eyes. "We certainly can't call you one of the lads!"

I smiled. "That's the trouble. If I could hurl a cricket ball and absail down the school clock-tower it might help."

He gave a laugh. "I won't be bullied by my staff, Mrs. Farthing. If you do leave us and a woman applies with the men for your post, I shall give her as fair a chance as the male applicants. May existing Classicists take note!"

"Ah, but will you stipulate that coaching of rugger and cricket is a must? That is the sly way boys' schools get round the equal opportunities ruling."

He shot me another look. "I certainly won't, though other head masters do. Now, there must be an answer to your problem. We don't want to lose you."

I had not expected this. My mind was made up; I was going for a range of reasons though I could tell him only two.

He smiled. "You look surprised! We chose you, Mrs. Farthing, out of six final applicants, not least because you were female. Dons needs more women on its staff. We intend eventually to have an equal mixture. Could you and your colleagues have a meeting, with Francis as mediator, to thresh your problem out?"

I glanced away; difficult colleagues wasn't my doing, but I let that pass. "It might work for a while. Yet resentment runs deep. Besides, all these meetings eat into valuable teaching and preparation time."

We were silent a while, he as determined to keep me as I was to leave. More battles! To that with my feelings for Alex, anonymous notes, departmental colleagues and Francis Marks was now added another, and with the Head Master.

"You know girls will be entering the Sixth Form in eighteen months' time?" he asked suddenly.

"Yes."

"We will need women members of staff to act as role models, mentors and anything else. Now, you would be an excellent person for girls to emulate. You're academic and, forgive me if I become personal, extremely decorative. Could I not persuade you to tread water, so to speak, until the girls come?"

A whole year and a half; eighteen months in a school where Alex had lived and come to me for tutorials; and perhaps just as long coping with uncooperative colleagues and anonymous notes. I would not be treading water; I would be *in* a backwater. I pretended to consider Dr. Graff's suggestion, then said at last, "Thank you, Head Master, but I don't think I can wait that long. And there's no guarantee my present departmental difficulties would remain ironed out, even if a solution were temporarily found."

He gave a sigh. "Won't you go away and sleep on it?"

"I already have."

"Won't you have another night on it?"

I laughed but made no comment.

He had begun playing with his letter-opener, and I saw Dr.Graff as a boy of twelve poking, as he was poking now, at an object on the table while a parent told him she had made up her mind to his cost. "Does Francis know?" he asked.

"Not yet."

"Shall I tell him? He's due here at five."

"Please do. But could it remain just between the three of us for a while? I don't want any of the boys knowing; it might unsettle them, particularly the fifths and Upper Sixths."

He assured me that no one apart from the Deputy and he would know. "But once you have found another post and write confirming your resignation, we'll have to advertise. I'll have no control over confidentiality then."

"Of course." I rose. "Thank you, Dr. Graff."

He reached the door first and with his hand still on the knob said, "What a great pity, Mrs. Farthing." Then he shook his head and opened for me.

I was learning well the art of how to be secretive. As a child, my father had drummed into me: *'Let not thy left hand know what thy right hand doeth.'* By contrast, my mother believed in *'tell it to the bees.'* In my own time, I learned what to conceal from my left hand and what to inform the hive, and it worked pretty well.

Since we were now into February, it was the moment to look for new teaching posts. Anyone interested in changing jobs would scan, on Fridays, *The Times Educational Supplement*. However, I needed to be secretive about my resignation. So, at six in the evening, when most staff were in their quarters or had gone home, when the staff-room was warm but not stuffy, I slipped in and made myself comfortable behind the paper. About five minutes later, the door opened and I waited for a comment from as yet I did not know whom.

"What a lot of hot air Rupert Cotton talks!" came Francis Marks' voice.

I glanced round my paper. The Deputy was looking at me sheepishly. We had not spoken since he left me in the hall watching the Germans, and had made no effort to explain why he never returned as he gave me to believe he would. "You should have heard his observations on Platonic love this morning," I said. "Absolute rubbish! Of course, the non-cognoscenti were listening bouche bée."

"Bouche-what?"

I apologised. "Open-mouthed, gawping. I fear it was Cottonic not Platonic."

Francis gave a giggle which sounded out of character; he was so canine in his ways, and dogs do not giggle. I returned to my paper.

"Jessica?" He had sidled closer. I lowered my arms to find him directly in front of me. "The Head Master tells me you're thinking of leaving us."

"That's right."

His eyes slipped from mine; he appeared apologetic now. Apologetic for what? "Can I ask why?"

Rustling the sheets of newsprint, I replied evenly, "I'm not entirely comfortable in a boys' school."

He began pacing round the carpet, one hand in his pocket. I watched his feet fitting the pattern of the rug. It was the sort of thing a child does, and I found it momentarily endearing. I did not want to suspect him of sending anonymous notes; he had always been kind to me. But his attitude to Alex and various trenchant comments certainly made him a possibility. I hardened my heart.

"Is there anything we can do to make you stay?" he was now saying. *Left foot in the red block, right foot in the black diamond... Aha! Now what are you going to do? There are two blocks together. Will you do a hop-scotch jump?* But no; as the pattern was spoilt he lost interest and flung himself into a chair some seats from me. He continued, "You've made such a difference to the Classics department. It would be a shame to leave just when it's becoming noticeable."

"Thank you, Francis, but I've made up my mind."

There must have been something in my manner which silenced him. He got up, sheepish again, and from my position of advantage I suddenly asked, "How was your Christmas in Cornwall, by the way? You never said."

He shot me a flustered look. "Very nice. But what a long time ago!" With that he left the room. *I bet you didn't go to Cornwall at all ! I bet you went up north – to Haweswater ! And did you take a photograph? Will that be your trump card? Triste mentum!* *

It seemed that he was the sender, for no more anonymous notes appeared in my pigeon-hole. I began to deduce what he had done; he must have taken my address from staff records and decided to spend part of his Christmas in Cumbria. By some extraordinary coincidence he had visited Haweswater when Alex and I were there, and from that point started to scheme. But now that I intended leaving Dons, he had scotched his plans.

Then I wondered what had been his motive. Jealousy? Spite? A dog-in-the-manger attitude? My resignation had clearly surprised him and the sending of anonymous notes lost all purpose. Such deductions, however, were flawed.

School exams had finished. Half-term was in five days' time. We were feverishly marking, assessing and teaching; and the fifth anonymous note sat in my pigeon-hole:

DO YOU SATISFY HIM?

The higgledy-piggledy words danced a dirty jig on the white page. To read them made me virtiginous. And at last I knew that here was a situation with which I could no longer cope alone; that,

---

*'droopy-jowls!'

continuing perhaps right up to my last days at Dons, it was probably intended to foul, if not damage, all my dealings with Alex. In other words, if the sender couldn't have me, he would make quite sure that what I had of Alex was spoilt.

To whom to turn? At first there appeared to be no one. Then one morning, down the corridor towards me came Mr. O'Hare, the school Chaplain. As well as his teaching duties he tended the pastoral good of the entire school.

"Mr. O'Hare?" I called as he approached.

"Good morning, Mrs. Farthing!"

A bunch of first formers cut us in two, jabbering about teams and prep and smelling in the dry warm-furry way pre-pubescent boys do. "'Morning, Mr. O'Hare. *Salve,* Mrs. Farthing," they chorused.

*"Salvete, pueri."*

"'Morning, boys. Thompson – your shoe-laces!"

Obediently, Thompson stopped to bend down, and a clutch of lads fell over his posterior. In the hubbub that followed, I asked Mr. O'Hare if I could speak to him on a personal matter.

Without making contact, he put an arm in an embracing way behind my back. It was a comforting gesture and I almost burst into tears. The tensions of not being able to love Alex, of maintaining a detached front, of holding my own against three supercilious colleagues, of keeping to myself the tyranny of anonymous notes which could so easily erupt into total exposure, were near to breaking me.

He looked kindly into my face. "Please do. You know where I live? Left in the lane beyond the school gates, first turning on the right." To my nod he added, "Why not this evening? Come at six, if that suits, and we'll have a drink."

My relief was enormous, and half the burden slipped from my shoulders. We bowed slightly to each other and were parted by an exodus of boys, this time coming from the right. It was class change-over. To escape I turned into the staffroom.

There, Seneca oozed up to me. "The very lady!" he began unctuously. "We're in the middle of an argument," and he waved a hand towards the choir-master, a young man with a pigling-bland face. "How do you pronounce –" then he spelled out, "i-n e-x-c-e-l-s-i-s?"

I hitched my books higher under my arm; ten minutes to go before Alex's tutorial. I had a beast of an essay question for him: *"Discuss the value of any oratory you have read for Athenian social history."* Seneca and his time-wasting arguments seemed insignificant.

But I made an effort. "In ecclesiastical Latin you may find the 'c' pronounced 'ch', hence *in exchelsis.* If it were in a Classical Latin context, I would pronounce the 'c' always hard."

You cannot please everyone all of the time, and sometimes you don't please anyone, ever. My answer seemed unsatisfactory to both parties, and I left them as I found them, arguing good-naturedly.

# CHAPTER XXIII

*saevi dolores (A.A.II.235)*
*"anguish"*

"Mrs. Farthing, do come in!"

I stood under the porch at the Chaplain's front door in a wet darkness that numbed. It was just after six, and Mr. O'Hare had answered my knock.

He moved aside to let me in. There was the scent of beeswax polish and fresh baking, and as I entered the hall a little woman hurried out of a back room.

"Marie, this is Mrs. Farthing from school and our head of Classics. Mrs. Farthing, my wife, Marie."

We shook hands and I was immediately struck by her warmth. After exchanging brief pleasantries, she said, "Ryan, your drinks tray is in the study." She turned to me. "If you would prefer tea or coffee, do tell him!" Then, with a nod, she disappeared into the back again.

"Awful night," began the Chaplain, closing the study door behind us. "I do like my fire in the winter." He drew up a seat for me near the hearth. "Now, what will you drink? I have beer, sherry, whisky, orange juice – or Marie's tea or coffee!"

I asked for some beer, and as he poured, I looked briefly around me. His wife's touch was in the vases of dried grasses and flowers and choice of cushion covers. But all else was an expression of his interests: bookshelves, thin books, fat books, paperbacks and leather-bound, folders, catalogues and a fascinating display of bits of wood; wood that groaned in its contortions, was whistle-thin, knotted and curled, coarse-grained, skin-smooth, carbuncled, warty, green or grey with lacings of lichen.

He noticed my interest, and said simply, "Fun, isn't it?"

"Oh, yes!"

"Marie tells me if I weren't cloth-bound and school-foisted, I'd be along the sea-shore collecting flotsam and jetsam. What would you be doing if you weren't teaching Literae Humaniores?"

"Belly-dancing in a Turkish bar."

He put back his head and laughed. "That's fun, too! I'm glad you don't take yourself seriously, either."

"I enjoy your school addresses, Mr. O'Hare," I began. "The one at Christmas struck a chord, and I thought your recent talk on homosexuality was – sane."

He looked pleased. "One so rarely gets feedback on these things, you know. I gauge my addresses by the silence with which they are afterwards met. If people don't like them, I'll hear about it. Of course, the boys say nothing. It's so easy to talk down to them. I just hope I don't appear moralistic and fuddy-duddy."

I smiled, remembering Alex's use of that expression. "I've sometimes wondered why youngsters don't try talking up to those more mature than they."

He made a dismissive gesture. "Oh, the young are so inflexible! You need say only one wrong word and they damn you forever."

"I wonder what God makes of it all."

"I imagine He's fascinated."

"But what does He do all day?"

Mr. O'Hare laughed again. "You make Him sound like the bored unemployed."

"Well, if you were omnipotent, where's the challenge?"

Gravely he replied, "We are."

I looked at him, thinking this through for a moment. "But," I said at last, "There's no evidence that we do challenge Him. I mean, we're blown up, racked by disaster, infected with disease, oppressed and mutilated with no interference from Him. How can you say we challenge Him?"

He leaned forward and thrust another log on the fire. "The answer is in the Gospel and in those who work on His behalf."

I put my glass down. "Mr. O'Hare, I desperately want to believe. There is much that is spiritual in me. But I cannot believe if I have no evidence. We have proof of thunder in a clap, and of lightning in a flash; so, I believe in thunder and lightning. We have evidence of spring and summer in growth and maturation, so I believe in spring and summer. But where is living evidence of God?"

He smiled. "In you and me, thunder and lightning, spring and summer."

He was merely throwing back at me my own examples, and I looked at him askance.

"See it this way," he continued, leaning his elbows on his knees. "You do a good, generous deed; that is evidence of God."

"Or is it self-interest?"

"I rather think not."

"How simple you make it all sound."

"It is simple. It had to be to get through to Christ's fishermen."

"Ah, but you're talking about Christ. I had in mind God."

"Christ is God – the physical embodiment of God."

"Now that's not so simple!"

His mouth lifted. "D'you know what I think, Mrs. Farthing? I think you're one of the thousands of people who need to thrust their hands into Christ's side before they believe."

I agreed with him, and we fell silent.

"But this is not what you've come to see me about, is it?"

"No." I paused, wondering if I could get away with telling him half the truth. I had a quick look into his face. The eyes blue and kindly, the expression interested but not curious, conveyed a person to whom one could explain much without being censured. So I began, "You know Alex Forsyth?"

"To pass the time of day with, but that's about it."

"I inherited him, so to speak, from my predecessor. We've been thrown very much together, and although it was not the intention originally, he spent the Christmas holidays with me at my home in Cumbria. Someone from Dons must have seen us near Penrith because over the last few weeks I have been receiving these." I pulled a large envelope from my bag and handed it to him. "They don't make pleasant reading."

He scanned the notes with a grimace. "Not nice. Not nice at all. Forgive me for prying, but am I to assume that you and Alex were acting in such a way as to give the sender – how shall I put it – ammunition?"

It was tactfully said, yet I coloured. "We have become emotionally involved. But I don't like a public show of affection. The only time someone could have put two-and-two together was when I slipped on a walk." I explained briefly what had happened at Haweswater.

He nodded. "Women have an enviable sixth sense. Do you have any suspicions of who it could be?"

"I've an idea."

"Staff or boy?"

This drew me up. I had not thought it might be a pupil. "Staff," I replied, with only a little hesitation.

He rose to replenish my empty glass, and as he carefully poured from the bottle so that the foam mounted slowly, he said, "First we must consider the outcome – what this person is trying to do." He handed me back my glass. "He, or she, is presumably trying to make you feel guilty or frightened. They are also enjoying a sense of power over you which is all the keener because you do not know who they are. These notes may peter out. Or the sender may wish to push to the extreme – either to make you leave or humiliate you publicly."

"Going public is just what I'm worried about! I could probably take it, but it might upset Alex so much that he fudges his A levels and doesn't get to Oxford after all."

The Chaplain pulled at the tongue of his shoe which appeared to be uncomfortable. "I don't know Alex as well as his brother, but –"

"Brother?" My voice came out sharp.

He looked at me in surprise. "Didn't they tell you?"

"Tell me what!"

He turned his eyes to the fire. "I suppose you didn't need to know. It was over three years ago."

I could barely contain my impatience. "What was three years ago, Mr. O'Hare?"

"Alex was sixteen when his brother, who was eleven, fell from the train and died."

A heat crept over me. I stared at the Chaplain. And in a flash I recalled the Forsyth flat, where a lad I did not recognise looked out of a family photograph; and how Virginia had referred to her mother cryptically: 'Oh, she hasn't said much since...' before breaking off and changing the subject; and had a brother's death been what Alex meant by his 'personal trauma'? "What happened?" I asked, now cold with shock.

"It was the last day of the Christmas term. We used to have the Carol Service in the afternoon then, but it was changed to the morning by general agreement. Anyway, as usual, a group of boys whose parents were unable to pick them up caught the London train. I remember it was a bleak day. Everyone was in high spirits, and as I saw them off, I praised Forsyth Junior on his excellent singing."

"He was a choir-member?"

"Oh, yes. Had a voice like a flute. He started the service with *Once in royal David's city* just as Waring did last term..."

"Do you mean they had the insensitivity to choose the same carol –" I broke off. That explained Alex's 'chickening out' of reading his Virgil piece. The carol had obviously summoned grim recollections. I said with some bitterness, "He was right. People do have short memories. How could they have chosen that carol when Alex was still in the school!"

The Chaplain gave a sigh. "I have no say in the choir-master's choice of music, and didn't know he had coached Waring in that particular carol till it was too late. And in the choir-master's defence, he came to Dons after Forsyth Junior's accident. But others should have remembered." He smiled faintly. "Perhaps that's why no one fussed when Alex didn't do his reading. They remembered too late."

Francis Marks had fussed! He stood in my office and berated Alex. He had the gall to tell him to face his commitments like a man, knowing perfectly well why he vanished. Jumbled feelings were rushing through me: pity, nausea, rage, indignation, love – and an immense urge to run back to school, to search Alex out, and in front of everyone take him in my arms. Embrace and be damned!

"What exactly happened on that train?" I asked.

"No one really knows. But it seems that Forsyth Junior mistook the reflection of the carriage in the windows for a corridor. He opened the door and fell on to the track. It was a ghastly business. He died on the way to hospital."

I had put a hand over my eyes. "And Alex?"

"He had to cope till his parents flew in from abroad. A terrible thing for a lad of sixteen to endure alone. But he did it."

"What was his brother's name?"

"Gavin."

I gave a low groan; my anonymous notes and departmental problems suddenly seemed paltry.

"So you see, Mrs. Farthing," said the Chaplain, looking at me directly, "Alex matured in double-quick time because of that experience, and if the writer of your nasty little letters does make your involvement common knowledge, I really don't believe Alex will let it ruin his chances."

I glanced away, my mind seared with images of train doors hanging open, figures running up and down the track, a small body patterned with lights from the carriage lying near the line, and Alex – only sixteen – identifying his own brother.

Mr. O'Hare was watching me with eyes full of concern. "We were all there for him when he came back to school in January. He was offered counselling, but refused. He's a remarkably private chap, Mrs. Farthing – but you probably know that."

I had not appreciated how private. No wonder he had turned to dancing and stripping in a hen-club; perhaps the removal of his clothes symbolised the stripping away of memories, while sexy movement was a safety-valve; and perhaps Mrs. Medic in Wiltshire provided him with periods of blissful forgetting. *Oh, Alex! Why did you never tell me?*

I voiced my last thought as, "Why did no one ever tell me?"

"Would it have helped you professionally –" and Mr.O'Hare leaned slightly on this word, "– to know?"

"Not really."

"Some things are best never explained. But I have told you this now because you are emotionally involved, and to illustrate my point that if your involvement gets out Forsyth, who's been through one crisis, will have the grit to get through another. Now, have I or have I not helped!"

I relaxed a little and smiled at him. "Mr. O'Hare, you've not let me down!"

"Good. But, the problem of the notes remains, I'm afraid. On the other hand, knowing what you now know should help you ride out whatever this thoroughly nasty person has in mind. Is Forsyth getting letters as well?"

"I don't think so. I haven't even mentioned it to him in case it rocks the boat."

"Hm. Tricky situation. Well, if it does eventually get out, he'll survive, I'm convinced. How you will manage is a different matter."

I was on the point of saying that I intended leaving Dons in the summer, but changed my mind. Here was another example of the left hand not knowing what the right hand was up to... I now rose. "I'll manage."

He too got to his feet. "Just remember, I'm always here. If you need someone to talk to, if these notes get you down, you come over and – I'll show you my wood collection!"

We both laughed as he escorted me to the front door. "How can I thank you?" I asked, shaking his hand.

"Evidence of God, Mrs. Farthing?"

We laughed again, and I stepped out into the dark.

# CHAPTER XXIV

*'illa' sit in vestris, qui fuit 'ille', notis (A.A.III.498)*
*"in your letters, let 'he' become 'she'."*

That night I ached for Alex, not the ache of love that often kept me sleepless, but the woman's ache over something hurt or bruised which she is impotent to make whole. A young brother who fell from the train – it was appalling. No wonder he had turned to *Henny-Penny's*. He may have liked to think it was to save for a car, but I believed it was his way of blotting out a traumatic experience.

Through the dark hours I fretted to see him. A sore throat which had niggled me for a few days rasped at my tonsils like sandpaper. I felt hot then cold; the room was airless then freezing. I tossed and turned and had visions that were half-dream, half-imagination.

When dawn came, bedraggled like an injured dove limping from shelter, I felt ill. My head throbbed and stiffness gripped my limbs. A virus with these symptoms was going round the school, and I had caught it. There would be no classes for me that day and, the day after, no going to London for half-term with Alex. Had I not felt so feverish, I would have wept with bitterness.

At half-past-eight I telephoned the school office, explained I was ill and could cover be arranged for my classes. No one there evinced much surprise and no one wished me a quick recovery. Thoroughly sorry for myself, I returned to bed.

Through a haze school life went on around me. Bells rang in the distance, boys' voices in the Quad rose to my windows, and from the playing fields I heard the irritable whistle of the referee. Then, mid-morning, a soft tap sounded at my outer door. I called painfully, "Come in!" and matron entered.

"So, we've succumbed," she said, closing the door behind her. She came into my bedroom and stood at the foot of the bed, surveying me. She carried a plastic bag and wore her glasses on a velvet ribbon round her neck. "How do you feel?"

"I could dance all night!"

She sniffed, implying perhaps that sick teachers should be in no state for facetiousness. She moved to my side, her white overall rustling crisply. Without a by-your-leave, she raised my wrist and felt the pulse. "Rapid. Light. Eyes ache when you look up?"

"I'm always looking up!"

She dropped my wrist as you would drop a dead rat. "Mrs. Farthing, you have a masculine sense of humour. Stop it or I shan't let you see what I have in this bag."

I stopped it and she laid her cool palm on my hot forehead.

"Yes," she said, "I think you've got a temperature." From her plastic bag she drew a bottle of mineral water, some foil-wrapped pills and a thermometer. I was about to comment with febrile pleasure on the contents of her bag, when she added, "Pop this under your tongue."

Meekly I lay there, proboscified and silent, perforce. At last, she relieved me of the thermometer and examined it. "Oh, dear, yes! Right, drink plenty, sleep even more and take two of these tablets now. I'll drop by again this afternoon."

"Is that all you have for me in your bag?"

"No. An essay – and a note."

"Whose?"

"You're not well enough to mark the work, but I suppose you should see the note."

"I want both!"

"What you want is a cure! Now, then, let's see."

If I had not known better, I would have believed she was taunting me; for she slowly took out four or five pieces of file paper (the back of the last sheet was blank) and with a little smile was looking at what was pinned to the front. "I have a soft spot for this young man," she was saying, "His manners are so delightfully old-fashioned!"

"Who?"

"Mr. Forsyth."

I flushed under my temperature. My lord, had he been indiscreet?

"Shall I read what he says to you?" She did not wait for my reply, but launched into Alex's letter: "'Dear Mrs.Farthing, I'm sorry you're unwell. I don't suppose you'll be better for half-term, so I'm letting you have that essay now. Matron is very kindly being my messenger; she likes it when I wrap her round my little finger. With best wishes, Alex.' See? Isn't that courteous?"

"Very nice." It was my turn to sniff, but then I was sniffing anyway, and I looked at matron with fresh eyes. *Age? Forty-ish. Looks? Must have been a pretty girl. Figure? Trim, filling out to plump. Legs? Can't see. Background? Middle-class. Soft spot for 'Mr. Forsyth', indeed! And he, capable of wrapping her round his little finger!* Meanwhile, she was leafing through his essay. "So, that's Greek, is it? It looks double-dutch to me. Where shall I put it?"

Something personal from Alex was the tonic I needed. "Here," I suggested, patting the coverlet.

"You're in no fit state to go marking!" And she hung on to Alex's essay and note.

"I shan't mark it! I'll just look at it. Light reading, matron!"

She made a click with her tongue and laid the precious work on my bed. "Now, is there anything you'd like? Some fruit, perhaps?"

"An apple would be nice."

She nodded. From the bedroom door she added, "By the way, the Deputy sends his best wishes. I'll come up again this afternoon." With that she left me.

When she had gone, I looked through Alex's essay on the power of women in Greek tragedy. At first, there seemed to be no subtle message for me, until he was discussing how, in Euripides, Medea talks to Aegeus as if they were equals. Then, he referred to dialogue which was not Euripidean: *When Aegeus addresses Medea, he hides his true feelings in cool words: 'Are you holding up under the circumstances? Can I do anything for you before I leave the palace for Athens? You know where to reach me if need be.'* I smiled and asterisked his comments, then at the bottom of his page, wrote: *You should note Medea's replies – 'Yes, I shall get along all right. Nurse cares for me well. Travel safely, and may the gods protect you!'*

To return him his essay through matron that afternoon would have seemed oddly enthusiastic, bearing in mind my condition. So I said nothing about his work till the following morning when she came a third time to check my progress.

"Your temperature's going down and you look brighter. But –" and she waggled a finger at me, "– no getting up yet! I've brought you some tangerines and a magazine. Had you plans for half-term?"

"I was going to stay with a friend called Sandy."

"Bad luck. What's that?"

I held Alex's essay. "They leave for half-term after lunch, don't they? Could I ask you to give this back to Alex? He should have it in case he's studying over the break."

She thrust out her lower lip. "What devotion to duty! Yes, I'll give it to him. But you do realise you've got to stay there a bit longer?"

"Yes, matron, I realise."

"Good. So many don't – or won't."

It was a particularly nasty virus, leaving one feeling worn out and dispirited. At lunch-time I heard the school empty as pupils and staff left for the long weekend, like so many migratory birds. The sparrows round my roof, however, came into their own, arguing garrulously in the gutters. But not even their squabbles could quell the first blackbird singing flute-like cadences.

Matron agreed I could get up the following morning. I think she was quite glad to have me in school, because when she returned at eleven she brought her knitting and made us both a cup of tea. We sat in my sitting-room and she talked proudly of her family, and was on the point of bringing out a photograph album when someone knocked at the door. It was the school secretary.

"Hello, Mrs. Farthing. Feeling better? These have just come via Interflora."

I looked at her burden. "Flowers? For me?"

Matron had taken the bouquet and as she brought it over, glanced at the envelope attached. "My word, who's going to be chipper now!"

In my arms was a large bunch of spring flowers – daffodils, narcissi, tulips and gypsophila, all tied up in cellophane and ribbon. I opened the small envelope and read: *Jessica, get well soon. With love, Sandy.* I blushed as matron, with touching naivety, peered over my shoulder.

"Ah, that's the Sandy you were to have spent half-term with. How generous of her!"

I laughed, secretly commending Alex on his diplomatic skills.

My strength returned slowly. By that afternoon I felt well enough – though pale and interesting still – to wander the school. I went into the staffroom which looked dead, then to the staff-study which seemed expectant. My desk was littered with a variety of paper: circulars from staff, stray Latin texts, an empty sweet packet. I wondered if I was strong enough to investigate my pigeon-hole. To my relief I found three upper fifth essays and several 'get well' cards from the junior boys. No anonymous notes.

Now what? The restlessness of convalescence was getting to me. I looked out of the window. Fresh air beckoned, a walk seemed possible and the need to communicate with Alex was strong. There was a public telephone box about a quarter of a mile down the lane. Well wrapped up, I aimed for it.

Under the trees in the school drive crocuses were shooting their bright flames; snowdrops, pearly and delicate, drifted across the grass. The light was sharp-bright, and when the sun burst from behind the clouds I winced like a dormouse used to the dark.

It was four o'clock. Alex should be at home in the London flat. Sweating with weakness and anxiety, I entered the telephone box and dialled his number.

"Hello?" It was his voice.

My throat thickened and for a moment I could not speak. "Alex, thank you for the beautiful flowers."

"Jessica!" Then he laughed. "How are you? Where are you 'phoning from?"

"Down the road beyond school."

"What a quick recovery! I've missed you dreadfully."

"And I you." I paused, a little abashed; I was chary about giving away too much. "Those comments in your essay were remarkably subtle."

"So were yours! You were right, there are ways of communicating on a different level."

I smiled and said softly, "Trust me."

"I do! I trust you as much as I trust my father."

This was most complimentary, but I changed the subject. I felt oddly close to tears. "What have you been doing the last few days?"

"You can guess in the evening."

*"Henny-Penny's?"*

"Yes. But what females! They get worse! Their claws are everywhere!"

I pointed out, a little skittishly, that so too had been mine.

"You don't have claws. Anyway, I don't mind where you put yours. Look, it there any chance we can meet before half-term's over?"

"I don't think so. You'll be back in two days. Besides, I may be a carrier of this virus. If you caught it at school, I would be unable to answer for my actions."

"And what actions might they be?"

I waved a hand, trying to sound flippant. "Oh, running into your room every spare moment to check your pulse, and that would give the game away."

He was silent a moment. "I wouldn't care a jot if the game was given away."

"The ribbing you got when you came to fire drill in a bath-towel would be nothing compared to this, Alex!"

"I could take it. I mean, it's not as if you're a married woman or we'd been caught in action. Why shouldn't I fall for you? I'm my own boss even if I'm still at school. I love you and I think you love me, but –" he broke off, "I'm being selfish. You would suffer if it got out."

It was not the moment to tell him I had already taken steps to leave Dons, and no more was said on the matter.

On my way back past Francis Marks' house, the front door opened. "Jessica?" He stood on the step. "I'm glad to see you better. Won't you come in for a cup of tea?"

My reaction was to decline; I still suspected him of writing the anonymous notes. But I was tired of my quarters whose staleness was relieved only by the beauty and fragrance of Alex's flowers. I veered towards him. "So you haven't gone away?"

He stood aside to let me enter. "No. How are you?"

"Better, thank you. It's a nasty germ."

He shut the door behind us. "The Head Master's got it now."

"Oh, dear." I passed into the sitting-room. "Well, look who's made himself comfortable!"

Curled up in a chair by the open fire lay Nisbet. I bent to stroke him. He opened a lemon eye and gazed at me steadfastly. It was a look that said: I-know-all-about-you-and-a-certain-prefect. I smiled, murmuring, "You funny old thing, you get everywhere!"

"Earl Grey or Assam?" Francis asked from the doorway.

"I've lost my sense of taste, so Earl Grey would be wasted."

"And do muffins and fruit cake appeal?"

I turned to him. "In small quantities, yes."

He went out. Gone was the discomfort he had shown the first half of term; he was his usual kindly self. I wondered again if he was capable of devising and sending anonymous notes. I returned to Nisbet, gently scooped him up and sat down with him on my lap. He was the sort of cat you tell things to. So I told him I was really a dog-person but as far as cats go, he was quite something. Thereupon a rattle quivered asthmatically in his throat, he spread his paws and began kneading my thigh. I continued with my nonsense, "A cat in Latin is *feles*, Nisbet, but I can't remember the Greek for it. I rather think the Greeks were too busy sorting out themselves and the universe to bother much with animals. Aren't you lucky you live today with us?"

Francis returned with a tray. "That's exactly what I do when he's here."

"What do you say to him?"

"Mainly stupidities, like how's pussy-wussy, which he receives with a cold stare." He placed the tray on a small table. "Are you warm enough?"

"Perfectly. How I miss an open fire!"

He gestured with the milk jug and as I nodded, he said, "You have one at home? Did you say in Cumbria?"

"Near enough. At Christmas –" and my voice cooled, "– I lit one every day." I watched his expression narrowly as he passed me my tea. It told me nothing. "How is your sister?"

"She's well. She's booked an educational cruise to Greece in May, you know the kind: lectures, guided tours, visits to ruins."

"Oh, yes. You've not been?"

He handed me plate, napkin and knife. "No. When I retire I might." He sent me a sudden pleasant smile and sat opposite.

It was only after tea that he raised the topic of my leaving Dons. "You're quite determined to go, are you?"

Nisbet had come back to my knee, and I now picked a crumb from his fur. "Quite."

"Have you seen any vacancies in the TES?"

"Not yet."

He paused, playing an invisible piano on his arm rest. "Is your leaving here to do with anything general or specific?"

"General."

He blew out his lips. "My word, Jessica, you don't give much away, do you!"

"Not a lot."

The phantom piano-playing resumed. "When the first girls start turning up, they'll need a role model like you."

"So I've been told. However, seventeen- and eighteen-year-old girls don't consider women like me worth emulating. They're into nose-rings, earrings, nipple-rings and navel-rings, oh, and tongue-studs. I have none."

"I'd be very surprised if you had!" He drew a hand over his chin. "It's a phase they go through because their peers are doing it."

This was something I knew already, and I made no comment.

He rose and threw a chunk of coal on the fire. "Have you found what you're looking for?"

I stared at him blankly.

"Let me rephrase that."

But I broke in, "You don't need to. Surely we are all searching for something at different stages of our lives. What you sought when you were thirty is, I assume, rather different from what you seek now?"

"No."

"Then you are static?"

"Not static. Single-minded. At thirty I wanted a wife, and ten years on I want one more than ever!" He was looking at me in such a way that I felt embarrassed.

I had eaten his tea (albeit without gusto), drunk from his cups and was now seated in front of his fire. I ought to have had an answer to give him, but I had none. Instead, I remarked, "You think you want one, but it's all academic!"

He gave a mirthless laugh. "I remember we sat here a few months ago and I ticked you off for presuming to know my mind. And you said it was a failing of yours to think you knew people's minds. I'm inclined to believe you don't know even your own!"

What piffle he was talking. Silence seemed the best defence.

Suddenly the fire spat. He thrust out a foot and stamped on the spark. Nisbet ceased his rattle-snake purr. I made to leave.

"Now, you women are home-makers," he resumed. "Don't you want someone to share with?"

"You forget. I did once."

He was not put off by my reference to an earlier marriage. "Then surely your widowed state must remind you of what you have lost?"

I didn't know what to say that would not be disloyal to Antony. The more I remembered our married life and the closer I drew to Alex, the more unsatisfactory that marriage seemed. I sidestepped the issue. "I don't see myself as a widow, but rather as single again. I was a happy single woman, and I'm happy now."

Francis looked crestfallen. During his silence, I wondered what he thought I might see in him. I saw his underlying decency (anonymous notes or no), his sense of having a worthwhile place in society and a certain affluence. But for me that was no longer enough; I had married Antony for precisely those qualities. It occurred to me that I was becoming increasingly ancient Greek; more and more I was turning from the plain to the beautiful; to feature at all in my life an object, whether sentient or not, had to be aesthetically pleasing. Francis Marks was no Greek god to look at; nor, to compensate, did he have a Socratic fineness. Therefore Francis Marks did not please me.

"I suppose you wouldn't consider marrying me?" he said.

This proposal (of a sort) on a cold afternoon when I still felt fragile after a virus came as a surprise. Before I could answer, he leaned forward adding,

"I didn't get you in here to ask you to marry me. I saw you passing, and on the spur of the moment thought that if I did ask it might just change your mind about leaving Dons."

I was as gentle as possible. "Francis, I am flattered –"

"Teamed with me," he interrupted, "things could improve at the school for you. You'd live here, instead of in those rooms, and together we could face and work out any problems you had!"

Nisbet raised himself on my lap, stretched till he was like a horseshoe with its luck running out, then sprang stiffly to the floor.

I shook off his fluff, saying, "You're very generous, but the problems are in me, not the school."

"Then let me help!"

I was to tell him, was I, that I had fallen in love with my best Classicist, that to remain in the school, living in rooms where he had come for tutorials, hearing him spoken of in the past tense, was an anguish I could not bear? I said, "I respect you, Francis. You have been helpful when I've needed advice and supportive in my work. But a man must be able to offer me more that I can give myself."

He flung himself back into his chair. "Right, let's see what you do have." He was on the defensive. "You have a house in the north. You have a car. You have a fairly well-paid job as far as teaching goes. These are the basics. Don't tell me a man couldn't offer you more!"

All this was unexpected, and I did not feel in a combative mood.

My silence fuelled his attack. "What about the status marriage brings, and a legitimate sex-life?" He saw the heat go to my face and sat, his hands in prayer pose, looking triumphant.

If my suspicions that he could send anonymous notes had wavered, they were strengthened again now. "I've had married status, Francis," I said coldly, "and what you term 'a legitimate sex life'." I paused, affronted that he should be attacking me on his own ground and when I was too low, physically, to counter it. "And in my view," I added, getting up, "they are both overrated." I made for the door. "Thank you for the tea."

I saw myself out and, taking advantage of the open door, Nisbet shot out with me. Together we walked briskly into the main building, cat and woman disenchanted.

# CHAPTER XXV

*scire velim saltare puellam (A.A.III.349*
*"preferably, a girl should know how to dance"*

Quite by chance I bought Tuesday's *Guardian*. It advertised teaching posts but most were in higher education. I was interested to read it because sometimes junior fellowships at Oxford and Cambridge were on offer, and I had always had a secret desire either to work for a higher degree or take on some abstruse research. Without Alex I would need cerebral anchorage or I would spend my life in an emotional void.

And there it was, thick and chunky like a square of chocolate; not a fellowship but an advertisement for a teaching vacancy in a girls public school two miles from Oxford. And, good heavens, another Classics post – this time in Suffolk. I owed it to myself to try for both, but it was the Oxford job which drew me.

Whitemeads School had charitable status and existed to offer 'a good education' to some four hundred and fifty girls aged eleven to eighteen. They wanted an experienced Classics graduate to teach to Oxbridge entrance. The post was full-time, non-residential and was vacant from September.

There was no guarantee I would succeed; but if Alex was going to Balliol and I teaching not far away, could we not meet occasionally, by design or some happy coincidence? I had now to face the question of when and how much I should tell him about my plans to leave Dons. For as long as possible no one, except Dr Graff and Francis Marks, should know. After my formal resignation, however, it could become public, and Alex deserved to be told face-to-face, rather than learn the news from others.

But could I tell him when I was leaving without details of where? And suppose I was successful with the Whitemeads School application, would it not look as if I were following him? There lay the difficulty. I felt he did love me, but that it had the exuberance of the first love affair, made exotic by the attentions of a mature woman who was also his tutor. Enclosed in an all-male school and deprived of a mother's love, naturally he would be quickened by a personable female teacher, particularly since we had been thrust academically together so often. When he began to live in the freer atmosphere of university, where girls and much else were available at the jerk of the chin, might not his tangling with me become an embarrassment? I wanted him to be free to explore love and life as he chose. The last thing he should feel was a sense of obligation to me just because of a happy and fulfilling episode at school.

One step at a time, I told myself. First, I would apply to both vacant posts, and decide what to tell Alex later.

Teachers and taught returned that evening for the second half of term. In class next day, the juniors were enchanting, asking after my health in their halting Latin, "*Valesne,* Mrs. Farthing?"

"*Ita vero, gratias. Sed nunc laboremus!*"

They groaned at my admonition to work, but soon cheered up when I told them we were visiting Bignor Roman Villa soon, and earlier still, they would see the chariot race from the film *Ben Hur.*

"*Estne multus sanguis,* Mrs. Farthing?" asked one lad.

I replied, yes, it was quite bloody at which they raised a cheer. Funny children; I suspected that blood was so divorced from their lives that seeing it spilled had distinct appeal.

Francis' attitude to me since our tea together now became aggrieved. His former coolness was easier to bear than this. As Dr. Graff was still unwell, he presided over the first staff-meeting we had after half-term, and when I raised a query about mock exams he listened with a pained expression. It was quite ridiculous, and I felt nettled; a man who couldn't take rejection was no man at all.

After the meeting, I hurried off to class pulling out the papers from my pigeon-hole as I went. It was an hour with the classical fifth, twelve talented boys several of whom had expressed a wish to aim for Classics at Oxbridge. As I separated printed papers from pieces of hand-written work, another anonymous note looked up at me:

WHO WILL YOU HAVE WHEN HE LEAVES?

Staff desks were a cross between a headless giraffe, a sloping table on stilts and a lectern. The beauty of them was that once the class were seated, no one could see what was under your elbows; for all the boys knew, you could be doing *The Times* crossword, looking at a risqué magazine or writing a poem. My anonymous note was noticed by no one. I coloured a little but continued talking and shifting my papers; but as I did so, something niggled me about the message. It wasn't the ungrammatical use of 'who'; only linguistic purists knew how to use pronouns correctly. It was something else.

I set my class a timed Latin unseen then looked at my book with sightless eyes. 'What about a legitimate sex-life?' Francis had asked during our tea. I remembered flushing, but could not recall his tone of voice. Was that a hint at my illicit relationship with Alex? Was he, despite the good points to his nature, really the writer of those notes? Incarceration in a single-sex school did funny things to staff; what, in the outside world, was insignificant, within the microcosm of a boarding school assumed colossal proportions. No one 'outside' would bat an eyelid at my intimacy with Alex.

Suddenly the niggle about the wording of that anonymous note resolved itself. Francis knew I fully intended leaving Dons in the summer; I would not be in a position to 'have' anyone at the school once Alex had gone. Therefore, Francis could not be the sender.

I confess I was relieved, and not a little ashamed that I should ever have suspected him; but he did 'fancy' me, he had shown a jealousy of, and at times had been harsh on, Alex; of all my suspects, he had the most cause to write foul notes. So, that now left Sproat, one of the Three Graces (or had they combined?), Seneca, Miss Johns and Migraine. The last three were only vague possibilities. It had to be Sproat or the Graces, and I was prepared to bet it was Sproat.

For a time after my virus I remained dispirited. One day merged into another, and though I struggled to be in control of the situation when Alex came for his tutorials, the effort made me all the more depressed. There was nothing but work, and I had missed out on half-term completely. With spring coming, I began to feel restless and stale; my life at Dons had no contrast, and I longed to do something different. An idea came to me, preposterous perhaps, but it would not be quashed.

We had been back after half-term for ten days when I telephoned Martha one evening and put my idea to her. We talked of this and that, when I suddenly said, "Martha, I want to learn modern dancing."

There was a pause, then, "You can't."

"Why not?"

"You're a Classicist. Classicists don't learn things like modern dancing."

But I had detected a smile in her voice. "This one does. This one does all kinds of strange things and at the moment she feels so cooped up that if she isn't let off the lead she'll go barking mad!"

"I see. Well, I must have a part in this grand design. What is it?"

My enthusiasm grew. "You know there's a dance centre near Covent Garden? And you have heard how dancing is quite the rage? I read somewhere that there are dance classes for adults on Saturday afternoons. If I stayed with you each Saturday night as a paying-guest, will you give me house-room?"

"I will not."

I was silenced. Surely she did not disapprove?

"Really, Jessica, you do suggest the most extraordinary things. Of course I'll take you in, but no paying! Are you in love?"

I laughed. "What has that to do with it?"

"Lots!"

As an explanation I said, "I am changing my job."

"But you've only just taken that one!"

"Yes. I'll tell you about it when we meet."

"I think you should! And when is your first dance class?"

"I can just turn up. Next Saturday?"

I heard her sniff before she said with the slightest disapprobation, "So, I'll see you then!"

It had occurred to me that if Alex could perform his sensual routines, then perhaps I should attempt some as well – not in a dive full of leering men, but for my own edification, a sort of spiritual sexuality to help me through periods of no sexuality at all. My mind was constantly being challenged, my body hardly ever. Some years before, there had been much talk about exercise releasing endorphins which promoted a sense of well-being. I had mentioned it to Antony who thought the idea rubbish. "My firm's annual dance is in six weeks' time. I suppose you want to go to that?" I hardly termed scudding round the dance-floor with a left-footed husband an endorphin-stimulating experience, but we went. And it was awful. He so jigged me about that all my natural rhythm was affronted, until a proficient couple glided up to us. She took him in hand and her male partner took me, both of us too surprised to resist. Immediately, my partner and I had skimmed off, using the music to best advantage, while poor Antony was given a halting lesson in the quick-step. When I was returned, glowing and exhilarated, to him he looked resentfully over my shoulder. "You made an exhibition of yourself! And who the hell were they, anyway?"

"I did not! We merely danced. And that's making an exhibition of yourself!" I had nodded in the direction of a girl in red. She was leaning against a table, flinging back her head and shrieking like a siren. As she leaned, her tight low-cut dress pressed against her untrussed breasts, accentuating the nipples. Her skirt, slashed high up the leg, showed her thighs which were brown but puckered like orange-skin.

Antony had shrugged. "One expects that of secretarial staff. But you're A Wife." I fell silent, and spent the remainder of the night musing on the disadvantages of being anyone's wife.

Now, Alex made me brave. It was one of the things I loved most about him. He unlocked me, physically and emotionally. To the things I felt ought not to have been there, he gave glorious release. He never showed superiority or disapproved of anything I did or said, not even when at Christmas my language had become a little Catullun, or in layman's terms, graphic.

I wanted to pay him the compliment of dancing, one day, with him, if not in abandon, at least with a certain amount of panache.

❧ ❧

In school, our role-play as cool tutor and studious taught was growing more authentic by the meeting. Had anyone entered my rooms without first knocking, they would have found Alex as he should be, listening, taking notes or in discussion with me who sat, a good two metres away, surrounded by books, papers and all the trappings of academe. I had often thought that when male and female were together, the female of the species set the tone; a hem drawn high, a collar teased low, a flirty dimple and inviting glance were non-verbal beckonings that any man, if he wasn't blind, could see. I was as capable as the next woman of showing rather more leg and breast than I should, with one essential difference: I was fussy about whom I showed them to. Alex, the virile stunning Alex, was my choice every time, but at Dons, in his tutorials was not the moment. I remained the professional first, and his mistress (to my cost) last.

We could not school our eyes; they spoke a very different part from the one we were acting. And our hands did not always obey our minds, either. If I passed him a book or some marked work, his fingers might close over mine and he would not let go till I took the point. There I'd sit, flushing like a virgin while he watched, with a little smile of power, the colour flame in my face. Right, my lover! I'd say to myself, for that, we'll work you just a little harder and see who triumphs this time! His gaze ignored, his touch avoided, I would throw him questions and points for discussion, syntactical gobbets and teasing translations until he sat back, himself flushed with the effort. Triumphant, I'd look him full in the face: *Now who's on top!*

We were man and woman, tutor and taught, lover and mistress, Mrs. Farthing and Alex Forsyth all combined. This brought a pleasurable *frisson* to our meetings, but it left us hungry and athirst. Our bodies cried out for physical union, but obligations kept us apart.

We were now well into the second half of the Lent term. I had gone over with Alex his mock exams already, and predicted A grades in both Greek and Latin. But fate was fickle, and the gods punished *hubris*. So, with humility we pressed on.

Now it was a Friday afternoon. The rain drummed on my roof and in the Quad boys and sparrows dashed. Alex entered my rooms for his tutorial with a look in his eye which was not usual between tutor and taught. I met it with briskness. It was the only way. "Well, Alex, are you more comfortable with Catullus now?" I had in my hand his latest essay.

We sat in our normal places. *How clean his shoes always are! People say hands give a lot away, but feet must, too.*

He was saying, "Much more. But in my reading round him, I've come across references to someone called Iuventius. Who was he?"

"His boyfriend."

"But I thought he was all for Lesbia!"

I smiled. "Catullus was an unorthodox man. There are poems, not in your selection, addressed to and about a lad who smote our poet painfully."

He made a dismissive sound. "Aren't exam boards being a little coy? We all know about sexual aberration – it's thrust down our throats early enough in school. Why not include a homosexual poem or two?"

"Probably to spare the teacher's blushes."

He laughed, then after a pause said, "Talking of male adulation, there's a fourth former who's giving me the creeps."

I inclined my head attentively.

He continued, "He's always hanging around the passage that leads to the Sixth Form house. And when I go to the gymn, he often peers round the door to watch. I got fed up with it the other day and challenged him."

"What did he say?"

"That he wished he could be like me, or that sort of tripe."

"Then what?"

"I told him to piss off."

I hid a smile. "And did he piss off?"

"Till the next time. There's something obsessive about him, and he looks at me like a spaniel. It's not healthy!"

I asked who this fourth former was, but he refused to say. "It's not fair on you – particularly as you teach him."

I respected his reticence and said, "I had a crush on a girl at school, so I understand how he feels. Ignore your adorer, Alex; that's the best course!"

He nodded and we did not mention Catullus' Iuventius again.

At four, I asked if he could stay to some tea. His face lit, but I gave a gentle shake of my head. He understood that we would still have to observe our role-play, and with a despairing expression began scribbling me a note. *'This is terribly difficult! Can't we meet soon just to touch?'* I wrote back: *'What do you suggest?'* His answer was: *'It's exeat weekend in a fortnight. My parents' flat?'* I said quietly, "Yes," and got up to make tea. London would be a better place to explain my intentions, and I left it till then.

ଓ ଓ

The next day I drove up to London for my first modern dance class. I was nervous, far more nervous than facing a room full of unfamiliar pupils. On arrival in town, I bought suitable dance paraphernalia; then, with trepidation, made for Covent Garden. A lot was going on in the studios there. For a moment I stood outside on the pavement, listening to different tempos drifting down from windows. And I wavered. Then a beat like that which Alex moved to thumped on the air, and I went in through the main door.

Children, youngsters and adults mounted and leapt down the stairs. They moved as if on springs, while my body was knotted and tense. I paused before a notice-board where lists of classes were pinned. That day there were belly-dancing, jazz, tap, contemporary, ballet, tai chi, modern American and disco lessons. Beside each class was the instructor's name and studio number, and a large plan of the building showed how to find the room. I joined the learners going up, and searched for room 11.

A class had just finished, and bodies glowing with colour and sweat piled out into the corridor. A poetic-looking man in leg-warmers and Nureyev shirt followed, giving me a soulful smile as he passed. I went in. The studio was wider than it was long and had huge mirrors on two walls. A buxom wench in a short pleated skirt and bikini-top was operating a 'ghetto-blaster'. As I entered, she looked up out of large brown eyes.

She hailed me in Americanese. "Hi! Modern?"

When in Rome do as the Romans do. "Hi. Yes."

"I'm Francesca, but they call me Fran." She raked me up and down. "You look balletic. Are you?"

"Probably, but I don't want to be at this lesson."

Fran grinned. "In ballet it's –" and she mimicked an imaginary teacher, "– tums in, bottom under, chin up and toes out. But in modern, the more you stick your bum out and jerk your chin the better!"

I had the schoolboy's desire to say, "Cripes!" Instead, I asked, "Am I dressed right?"

Arms akimbo, she surveyed me again. "Aren't you slim! Well, lots of girls wear flirty skirts like mine or tracksuit bottoms if they've got thunder-thighs. What's your name, by the way?"

"Jessica."

"So, Jessica, your footwear's fine, but you'll get the feel of modern dance more if you wear looser gear."

"Like yours?"

"Why not?"

The door had swung open and four young women entered, giggling. Two wore leggings and the others had trousers. I retreated, feeling very much the new girl as another eight people came in. There were only two men, and promptly at three the class began.

We warmed up with knee bends and foot rises. Everything was parallel rather than, in the way of ballet, turned out. Then we flung our arms around and rolled our heads and lunged like fencers. In the back row, I followed slavishly those in front, amazed at their looseness and personal engagement with each movement they executed. In ballet, you attempted to be outside your body, and aimed for a spiritual levitation. But for modern, the soul panted and sweated with the frame. Caught between two opposing disciplines, I neither levitated nor perspired, and it was a source of frustration.

Our warm-up ended with isolations where the rib-cage moved independently of the pelvis. But nothing in my body would be isolated. Fran took pity on me and showed how it should be done. Then she gave me a playful cuff and cried over the beat, "You'll catch on. You've got what it takes!"

After this, she changed the music and the studio burst with a wild beat which would have sent a skeleton juddering. Everyone except for me knew the routine which followed, and I did my best to keep up. But I was like a string puppet in arthritic hands. The beat was inside me, in the thud of my heart and the rhythm of my pulse, but my body would not keep up.

The routine ended. Panting and bending over, we took a minute's rest. "Okay, Jessica?" called Fran.

I gasped back, "I could be fitter."

"Couldn't we all!" said someone and we laughed.

Next, it was run-run-leap-time diagonally across the room. Here I did reasonably well till with a look at me Fran called, "No gazelles, please!"

Confidence broken, I hugged the wall. It was easy for the others to fling their bodies about; they had not been brought up to comport themselves in a seemly manner. I cursed that breeding which emasculates.

At the end of the hour, Fran 'brought us down' (to use her expression), which involved some quiet breathing and stretching exercises. But I was still fired as I changed my shoes and put on my outer clothing.

She swaggered up to me and asked, "Will you come again?"

I straightened, pushing back my hair in a Virginia-gesture. "I'd like to, but..."

She began to wipe her torso with a towel. "But?"

"I love dancing – all kinds. But modern does the opposite things ballet teaches. Will I ever learn these new steps?"

She nodded to show she understood. "Since rhythm is in you, I think you will. I was watching you quite a bit, and yes, I can see you've done ballet because your movements are neatly-packaged, if you know what I mean. Smudge them a bit, let go of the control." She smiled, worried perhaps that I would take offence. "Tell you what, do you have a full-length mirror at home?"

There was one on the inside of my cupboard door at Dons. "Yes."

"Then, between now and next Saturday, stand in front of it and practise the isolations and hip and head movements we've done today. Just ten minutes at a time, and I guarantee that when you come again – if you do – you'll cope better."

I flung on my jacket and smiled back at her. "Thanks. I'll give it a shot!"

We exchanged a cheery good bye, and joining others on 'jacob's ladder' I clattered down the stairs.

I had left for London before the post reached staff pigeon-holes. On my return to Dons on Sunday, it was to find a letter from Whitemeads School near Oxford inviting me for an interview. They gave me a clear week's notice, but I began to make arrangements for my absence immediately. Alex would be going on a school athletics meeting to Brighton the very day I was off, so there was no need to tell him his tutorial was cancelled. Then, the day before my interview I gave Francis Marks and the school office a list of how my classes should be covered.

The morning I set off for Oxford was a fine March day. A hoar frost sugared the ground and made magic wands of the bushes; and, as the sun strengthened, the glittering rind melted and drops shot their prisms. Snatches of bird-song came in through my open car window and the grass gave off a sweet scent. The tunnel of winter was now behind us and nothing, neither frost nor snow, could stamp down the surge of spring.

When I had last visited Oxford – it must have been four years earlier – I had felt trapped. Innumerable doors and gates, mostly closed in the evening, a July heat infested with greenfly and traffic fumes, and jabbering foreign students creating their own particular infestation, had changed for me a city of dreaming spires to a city with claustrophobic fortressing. Now, on a glass-bright Spring day at noon, the city breathed *glasnost*.

My interview was at two o'clock, and to kill time I lunched and reacquainted myself with Balliol, Alex's chosen college. I could see him striding under those learnèd windows. But how and where would I fit in?

Just before two I was driving past a prim lodge up the drive to Whitemeads School. It looked promising and the secretary gave me an auspicious welcome. Leaving me in a side room with the school prospectus, she went in search of the head of Classics. The brochure was the usual thing: colour photographs of happy-looking, fulfilled girls at science, on the games field, in their bedrooms, during field-trips, in class – all smiling and receptive. There was a picture of the headmistress above the school's mission-statement, and a list of costive-sounding governors. Whitemeads' motto was *Omnia sapienter* – Everything wisely. I wondered who ever managed that.

"Mrs. Farthing?"

I twisted in my chair to find a thin, nerve-ridden woman standing in the doorway. She came forward, her arm stiffly extended long before I could get to it and shake her hand. "I'm Fiona North, head of Classics. Did you find us easily?"

I assured her I had, then she perched on a seat opposite me and talked about the teaching of Classics at the school. She seemed capable and intelligent in a neurotic way, and tactfully I asked why her post was becoming vacant.

"I've had ME, you know that virus which leaves you washed out for months. Also, my mother's getting frail, so I've decided to live near her and teach part-time."

I made commiserating noises and thought how I had been spared the cramping obligations that throughout the history of mankind existed between adult children and their parents.

She was holding up a hand, as if to ward off my sympathy. "I want to go!" Her tone was almost peevish. "I've never been right since a bout of 'flu! By the way, if Mrs. Carrick offers you the post and you take it, will you need accommodation?"

"Ah, not in school, thank you!"

"I didn't mean school! I've got a flat on the outskirts of Oxford. When I leave, it'll be on offer to absolutely anyone. But if you or whoever comes here would be interested..." Her voice trailed off, as if too exhausted to continue.

My reply was soothing. "It's certainly worth bearing in mind."

She looked at her watch. "Oh, goodness! We'll have to dash through the sights or you'll be late for Mrs. Carrick. Come on, I'll give you a whistle-stop tour."

She was not the best guide, and when I was given a seat outside the head's door there were many questions which I still wanted to ask. I waited and waited to be summoned, just catching the rise and fall of voices beyond the wall; evidently the head believed in making applicants sweat.

When at last she called me I did not like the woman. The stoutness of her frame was accentuated by a dress which made her look like a homemade lamp-shade. She had grey hair scraped back in a french pleat and a gap between her front teeth. She wore glasses and a surprisingly bright lipstick. I labelled her a cold fish.

Attend one interview for a teaching post and you have attended the lot. They were all the same, and most interviewers had no idea of interviewing procedure. They would ask such risible questions as: "Why do you want to come and teach here?" and "What can you bring to our school?" These deserved the facile answers: "You sounded promising!" and "Myself – what else do you expect, you mutt?"

It was difficult to say how I had fared, and as I waited (again) this time in the bursary for my travelling expenses, I decided many school principals would do better selling corsetry and used cars.

At last I was on the open road heading back to Dons. Within a week I should know whether Whitemeads offered me the post. If they did, because of Alex I would accept.

# CHAPTER XXVI

*tam Venus otia amat (R.A. 143)*
*"Love so likes leisure"*

Did the façade of Dons reproach me as I parked in its drive later that day? Did I not feel a pang of regret as I entered its imposing hall which breathed antiquity and tradition, qualities which Whitemeads lacked? Was to leave what I wanted? Not really. I wanted Alex and Dons, but since I could not have both, I was ready to risk all – and hold on to neither.

On my way to the staffroom Nisbet and I crossed paths. He paused to look at me with his usual inscrutable expression which I, in my present frame of mind, interpreted as, "Silly woman." I stooped and ran my fingers across his back, murmuring, "I know!"

Seneca was in the staffroom pontificating about the sacking of incompetent teachers to three others, who attempted to read mail or mark or do both in the proficient way of academics. He was saying, "How do you define 'incompetence' anyway?" while both hands twiddled deep in his pockets. No one answered, so he turned as I came in and sluiced his oil in my direction. "Ah, Mrs. Farthing! What's the Latin derivation of 'incompetence'? Do elucidate."

My reply was terse. "Probably from *competere*, 'to suit, correspond, agree, coincide.'"

"You see?" He rocked triumphantly before the others. "Why doesn't everyone learn Latin? What a lucky lady you are, Mrs. Farthing."

He was patronising me and I was in no mood for it. "Why?"

A hand worked harder at the money in his pocket. "Because you – and dare I say I in my own small way – have the benefit of a Classical education while so many don't." Perhaps he saw the glint in my eye, for he quickly reverted to incompetent teachers and his lukewarm audience.

At that point, one of the general studies staff ambled in. Whatever the temperature, he was always in shirtsleeves, and the tail would hang out like a blue or cream or striped tongue at the back. "I seek God," he murmured to nobody in particular.

A colleague said, "Not here. But the Chaplain's around."

"Oh!" Incompetent teachers forgotten, Seneca rounded on the godforsaken one. "That sounds familiar!"

The lost soul wandered deeper into the room. "Yes, I often say it."

"No, no, someone centuries before you was saying it!"

"And many in years to come will, too." He had a lugubriousness which, with his shirt-tail sticking out behind, I found endearing. Now he saw me and gave his sad fool's smile. "Hello, Jessica. I haven't looked upon you for a long time, and I need to pick your brains. The General Sixth want to know whether all Athenian men looked like figures on the Parthenon, or was that an ideal?"

Interesting! I answered with a question, "Do all Western males look like the models for Boss Menswear?"

"No."

"There's your answer."

He pressed his hands together and bowed slightly from the waist. "I've found God, and He's a woman."

I laughed as I went out, and had not quite closed the door when Seneca said in an undertone, "She doesn't like me, you know."

To which someone replied, "She doesn't like anyone!"

If that was what they all believed, then my subterfuge so far as Alex was concerned was proving a total success.

Francis Marks found me, some ten minutes later, in my office where I was being entertained by a paper on Classics howlers: *'The Greeks were a highly sculptured people,'* (read one) *'and without them we wouldn't have history. The Greeks also had myths. A myth is a female moth...'*; another said, *'Socrates was a famous Greek teacher who went around giving people advice. They killed him. Socrates died from an overdose of wedlock...'*

"How was the interview?" asked the Deputy.

"Hello, Francis. Nice of you to ask. Like most interviews, I suppose."

He leaned against the wall, arms folded. "Meaning?"

I blew out my lips. "Some questions were fatuous, with a lot of hanging about."

"Did we ask you fatuous questions?"

Briefly I thought back. "No. Men are better prepared."

He gave a smile. "I don't believe you, Jessica!"

*'Julius Caesar extinguished himself on the battlefields of Gaul. The Ides of March murdered him because they thought he was going to be made king. Dying, he gasped out: "Tee hee, Brutus."'*

"Did you like the school?"

I glanced up at him again. "It had a good atmosphere."

"You don't have to leave here, you know. I think you've been a bit hasty. No one can decide whether a job's right till they've been doing it for a year. Do you know what I think? I think Mrs. Farthing is ruled by her heart, not her head!"

*'In the Olympic games, Greeks ran races, jumped, hurled the biscuits, and threw the java...'* For one moment I thought he was hinting that he knew of my involvement with Alex. "It's been a long day, Francis, and I don't much like post mortems on interviews." I held my papers to my breast, and made for the door. "Will you turn the light out when you leave? See you in the morning." With a nod, I made off down the corridor.

It was the not the punchiest of exits, yet it got him off my back. Doubtless he was right; I was sometimes ruled by my heart, but it was none of his business.

In my experience, a school which was keen to appoint an interviewee did so immediately. The days went by, and no letter came from Whitemeads; and my application to the Suffolk school had been met with silence, which was quite normal for heads well-versed in paper-pushing and very little else. Then, just before exeat weekend Whitemeads School offered me the Classics post. The delay showed I had not been first choice. No matter; the job was mine. I replied at once, accepting.

In my letter of resignation to Dr. Graff, again I asked him to keep it confidential till the very last possible moment. "I don't want to unsettle the boys too soon," was my explanation. But it was Alex I really had in mind.

During the small hours that night I imagined the scenario where I told him of my decision to leave Dons, that I had accepted a post near Oxford, and planned to rent accommodation on its periphery. I saw his expression of delight, heard the plans he made for us, formulated while still at school. Then my imagination moved on in time to his first term at Balliol when he was telling me details of college life, lectures, new freedoms and friends. His interests were widening, and though I was still important small things were starting to convey a different message: fulsome excuses for arriving to see me late, or not at all; too much work; unexpected seminars; demands of friends. The Alex of Dons was becoming (as he should) a rather different animal; he was outgrowing Mrs.Farthing of school; put baldly, he was leaving her behind. That was how I imagined it, and it would be a worse situation than had I remained at Dons without him.

So much for things from my point of view. Now, what about his? Alex was not the ordinary run of youth. He was wiser than most; his upbringing and personal experiences had ensured that. His mind, too, was remarkably focused. If I was near him at Oxford he would start a new chapter feeling an obligation to me. That was no way to begin a university career; he must be free. The answer in that case was to tell him nothing; to allow him to go on believing as long as possible that my job continued at Dons. Of course, I would have to break it to him eventually. But not yet; I had lived long enough to appreciate the bliss in ignorance.

Martha was put out that I was not staying part of my weekend with her. "Given up your dancing?" she had asked with a tinge of sourness when we spoke on the telephone.

"Not at all. There's a lot to do here. It's that time of term."

She snorted genteelly. "I don't believe you. You're a dark horse."

"Occasionally. Isn't everyone?"

"No! I'm as transparent as glass. When I conspire everyone knows about it."

We both laughed, and a firm date was fixed for the weekend after.

Spring was well advanced in London. Grey city squares frothed a sudden blossom pink; window-boxes blared their trumpeting daffodils, and crocuses stitched purple seams across private lawns.

It was seven on Friday evening when I rang the bell to the Forsyth flat. Alex was at the door in a trice, and for a moment we gazed at each other in silence.

"At last!" he cried, taking my bag and closing the door behind me.

I said, "I feel desperately inhibited!"

He placed a hand lightly on my shoulder. "It's all that rotten keeping up of appearances at school. It's bad for you! Give me your coat."

As he helped me out of it, I murmured, "I think we do rather well, myself."

"Yes, and isn't this ridiculous. I long to kiss you at Dons, but I can't; now I can, you can't!"

"Alex! Give me time to unwind!"

He drew me into the sitting-room. "A glass of wine should help. Why do I rush you? Sorry! After all, we've got two whole days and two long nights together!"

I caught his mischievous look and laughed. But I was annoyed with myself. Had I been a girl of his age, by now we'd probably be ripping the clothes off each other and getting down on the floor, all devouring mouth and triumphant thigh. That wasn't my style; I liked slow sensuousness. But although he had never said as much, perhaps he preferred a certain frenzy? If so, should I work at it?

The cork popped as he pulled it from the wine bottle between his knees. "Would you prefer instant access, Alex?" I asked.

He grinned. "I never like a tussle with a bottle."

"You know exactly what I mean!"

"I suppose I do. What would it be in Latin – *visne adventum instantem?*" He was standing obliquely to me, a glass in one hand, the bottle in the other, and about to pour. I moved up to him. He opened his arms and looked down at me gravely.

Sometimes, a lack of response is guaranteed to arouse. His eyes and his manhood against me betrayed his arousal, pent up for weeks since our time together at Christmas. I brought his head down and whispered against his mouth, "Why do I suddenly feel guilty? Are you forbidden fruit?"

He murmured back, "At school, yes."

"But Alex, we're both classified as adult."

"Yes, so let's go by what Catullus said."

"He said lots of things."

"One of which was:

> *'rumoresque senum severiorum*
> *omnes unius aestimemus assis'!"*

My translation was somewhat free, "'Let's not care tuppence for the gossip of more starchy old farts'!"

"Could I put it that way in the exam?"

"No."

"Pity. You're the only Classicist I've known who's not like an undertaker."

"What do you mean?"

"Mr. Rowland wore a black suit and tie and carried a black case. Dons' present Classicists, bar you, seem to be in mourning for a dead language. I half expect them to come to school with a coffin in a hearse, into which we will throw all our Classics texts, declensions and conjugations included, and see them off for burial."

I was laughing against him. "Over my dead body!"

He jerked back. "I don't like the sound of that."

"Metaphorically speaking, Alex! For so long as I live and live to teach Classics, no one is going to bury the most civilizing subject on the curriculum."

"Good!" His lips brushed mine. "Exegesis over. Now, we were discussing something equally important." His mouth pressed a little harder. "Something about tussling with bottles or bodies and instant access."

I passed my palms across his back, feeling under the sweater the knots of his muscles. The flavour and scent of him was making me heady, long before I drank the wine.

"So, Mrs. Farthing, I'll take my prompt from you. If you want instant access, dinner can wait. On the other hand –" his lips pressed and pressed mine, "– we've waited long enough already, perhaps another hour or so won't harm?"

That first glass of wine took some time to be poured; and dinner was later – much later – than expected.

☙ ❧

By breakfast the next morning there was not a spring of tension in me. A good dose of Alex, Alex, then more Alex had guaranteed it. As I took a seat at the kitchen table I asked, "Are you stripping at *Henny-Penny's* tonight?"

He paused over the toaster. "I was going to discuss that."

"Don't. Go if you want to. How's the car-fund?"

He was bringing my toast carefully to the table, then arranged in a semi-circle round my plate the butter-dish, savoury spread, marmalade, teapot, milk jug, boiled eggs and salt-cellar. "What's this?" I wondered.

"Just me playing games. I'm happy. I love you. You're fantastic in and out of bed. I want you now, tomorrow and forever. You're clever. You've got a sense of humour. You're beautiful. Your love is perfect freedom. Cripes! Is that blasphemous?"

"Some would say yes."

"Shall I rephrase it?"

"I like it, but I'm not sure it's true."

He sat opposite and began vigorously to spread butter on his toast. "It is! You've never once made a demand of me."

I thought of the night before and some nights in Cumbria. "Ah!" I said.

"That demand's different! I was thinking of non-erotic requests. I mean, most women would whinge if there was the merest whiff of their man going off to strut his stuff in a hen-club or such like."

I shrugged. "You want a car, so you save for a car. It's something you planned long before I came on the scene. You'd probably have stripped last night if I hadn't been here."

His eye glinted. "I did strip last night!"

I glinted back. "Shall I pay you? How much? Fifty pounds?"

"This is sordid! Eat you egg, Mrs. Farthing."

Like a lamb Mrs Farthing ate her egg, but she reverted to his car at her third piece of toast. "Well, how is the car-fund?"

"Healthy. Another three hundred pounds to go, and I can buy something rather better than a banger."

"Then it's stripping tonight!"

He leaned forward. "I can't invite you here, then do a bunk in the evening."

"Yes, you can. I shan't run away." I watched his white even teeth bite into his toast, then added perhaps below the belt, "You want that car for Oxford and – taking out girls."

The chewing stopped. "Girls? I want a car to drive and see A Particular Woman."

We were approaching problematic ground here, so I chose my words before continuing, "Oxford will be an entirely new world for you. You should not hold yourself aloof from all the opportunities it will offer."

He pushed away his plate and leaned his elbows on the table. "Are you telling me that what we have is only temporary? Perhaps you don't want to see me after I leave Dons?"

I gave a sigh. "I'm only pointing out that we shouldn't make promises or have dreams that may possibly be broken." My hand found his. "You are the best thing that has ever happened to me. But I will not hold you back when you move on."

He was looking depressed. It was clear that he regarded my scruples about standing in his way as a wish not to continue our relationship after he left school. "You don't seem to understand, Jessica! I don't want to drink till I throw up, or attempt drowning in the river, or sleep with girls who wear their genitalia on their sleeves. I tell you, Virginia is right – I'm a fuddy-duddy."

I couldn't help laughing. "Virginia can see only as far as Jasper. Just promise me you will leave the door ajar for the possibility that the impossible may happen."

He pulled his plate back and resumed eating. "You don't have confidence in how I feel about you, do you?"

I told him I did (under his present circumstances). "But," I added, "as a senior member of the Sixth Form at Dons, you're living a circumscribed life. Oxford will be a totally different kettle of fish."

He stuck out his jaw at me. "I'll show you, Mrs. Farthing. I'll prove to you that despite what you think, I will feel the same way at Oxford as I do now. And I'll buy that car and come and see you!"

His was a heartfelt speech, and I wanted to believe him. But I was cynical about love.

That day, at any rate, was ours. We went to Hampstead Heath and tramped for miles, avoiding West Heath where ancient Greek sexual practice without its aestheticism was indulged up to the hilt. It was bright weather with moments of sharp sunshine and, when a cloud rolled up, an equally sharp breeze. I loved the ash-brown of the trees against a moody sky, the sudden lime ghost of leafing willow and storm-cocks singing on the wind.

We lunched then at a small restaurant off omelettes and salad and a bottle of rosé wine. Alex could not eat a meal before his show at *Henny-Penny's*, so I bought some food locally for my dinner and our Sunday lunch, and after a latish tea he left the flat for Soho.

I saw him off at the door. "Are the women particularly rabid on a Saturday night?"

"Nothing the bouncers can't deal with. What price a car, eh?" He paused, looking down at me. "Will you be in all evening?"

"Yes."

"Will you answer the 'phone if it rings?"

"If that's what you want. What would you like me to tell them?"

"Simply that I'm out, and if they want elaboration, I'm at the gymn."

I thought perhaps he had in mind Virginia. We clasped hands, then he was gone.

☙ ❧

I had brought some school work with me. Francis had asked me to write a job description ready for applicants interested in my post, since it would shortly be advertised; and I was engrossed in it when the telephone rang. Wondering if Virginia would recognise my voice and how I could explain my presence this time in her parents' flat, I rose to answer.

"Hello?"

There was the slightest of pauses, then a well-spoken male voice began, "That's definitely not Alex, and I know it's not Virginia. This is their father here. May I ask who has answered?"

Could guilt be detected in a voice? Calming myself I replied, "Good evening, Mr. Forsyth. This is Jessica Farthing speaking, Alex's Classics tutor."

"Mrs. Farthing!" Recognition warmed his tone. "I've heard quite a lot about you! How's that son of mine getting on?"

My composure returned. "Very well. I expect a top grade in both his Latin and Greek."

"Splendid! I was rather fond of the subjects myself when I was at school. I gather you've brought some colour to Dons. You were new last term, weren't you? How do you find the place?"

I liked his impeccable English, and his voice sat with gentle authority on the ear. "It's a good place to work," I said, which was essentially true.

"And that son of mine's revising hard?"

"Sometimes too hard!"

He laughed. "Well, he'll be able to relax soon enough. Is he about?"

"I'm afraid not. He's gone to the gymn."

"'*Mens sana in corpore sano*,'" Mr. Forsyth quoted, before adding, "You know, it's not easy supervising one's children from a distance. But I dare say he's too old for that now. Is he looking after you all right?"

I assured him that he was, and we carried on a conversation – he in Bogata and I in London – as if it were quite usual for Sixth Form young men to entertain female tutors in their parents' flat. No reference was made to the reason why I was there nor to the nature of the relationship his son and I shared. I admired Mr. Forsyth's diplomacy, but I could not help wondering how much he knew.

Now he was saying, "Will you be so good as to tell him his father 'phoned? His mother's got a slight cold, but we're both fit considering the weather here. Oh, and please tell him I got his letter today, and that I'll be replying soon."

"Of course. He'll be sorry to have missed you."

To that came the simple reply, "He's a good lad." He paused, then concluded, "It's been nice talking to you, Mrs. Farthing. I hope we can meet one day."

I expressed the same, and our conversation ended affably.

For some time I drifted round the flat, unable to settle. In the master bedroom, I picked up the group photograph where the youngest child, Gavin, who had died so tragically, looked fresh-faced out at me. Last time I had examined it, I had wondered who he was. Now, with knowledge, I could see a slight resemblance between him and his mother. I knew Alex, had met Virginia and just spoken with Mr. Forsyth. Mrs. Forsyth, however, remained an enigma.

Alex returned at about midnight. I was on his bed, reading. He came to the door in that silently compelling way of his and said, "You look clean and goodly!"

I smiled. "How did it go? Did they paw you?"

He unbuckled his belt and dropped his trousers. Three red weals rose angrily on his outer left thigh.

"The sluts!" I cried, snapping shut my book.

He kicked off shoes, socks and trousers, and pulled his jumper over his head. The only hair he had on his upper body was in his armpits. I could not desire a pelt-chested male. His physique never failed to quicken me, and my pulse was galloping now. I dragged away my eyes as he moved about tidying his things. Then he said,

"Since I've known you, this stripping-thing gets harder."

I looked at him in silence watching, as he stooped and straightened, the muscles of his solar plexis bunch and relax with each movement. "I've got an idea," I said at last. "Tell me how much more you need for a car, and I'll give it to you to save your being groped and kneaded by a lot of nymphomaniacs."

He came to the bottom of the bed and leaned towards me. "I want to kiss you but I'm polluted. You're very generous, Mrs. Farthing – I wouldn't dream of it! Now, I must shower."

I didn't believe he would accept. "Can I get you something to eat?"

"I don't think so, thanks."

Only when he came to me later, and we were re-acquainting ourselves with the idiosyncrasies of our respective nude bodies did I tell him about his father's telephone call.

"Good old Pa. I think I fixed that rather well."

I lifted my head and stared at him. "Fixed what?"

He grinned. "I said that you were staying with me in the flat over exeat, and if he wanted to find out what you sounded like, he should 'phone on Saturday evening."

"You devil! How much does your father know?"

"Not much more than before. That we baled each other out at Christmas and that you invited me to stay on in Pomeroy when I was pushed for somewhere congenial to go ..."

"And?"

"And that you stand *in loco parentis*."

I sat up. "But I don't!"

He agreed.

I lay down again, becoming increasingly inattentive to his caressing. At last I said, "We'd better stop this."

His hand passed down the small of my back where it was most sensitive. I drew in a slow breath.

He smiled, and repeated the action. "Why?"

"Because we're crossing unwritten boundaries."

"Good. I shall get better grades because of it. I associate so much of my reading with you that I'm positively inspired."

"But you need to express facts, Forsyth, not inspiration!"

"I will." He saw me leaving him. "Where are you going?"

I draped his dressing gown round my nudity and made for his bookshelf. "If you don't get your grades and lose your place at Oxford, it will be my fault. I know it's late, but we're going to revise now."

It was his turn to sit up. "I don't want to share my bed with the Greeks and Romans! Come back!"

I was searching his books. "With Aristophanes and Catullus."

"Not more Catullus!"

"With Aristophanes, then."

"Tomorrow. I promise, after breakfast I'll put my head down and revise."

I glanced at him over my shoulder. He did look tired. Perhaps I was going too far. "Very well. Now we sleep and tomorrow you study." I eased back in beside him, but kept myself to myself.

He began murmuring, "*In loco amantis* not *parentis*," and I felt such a heel and he felt so good that sleep was deferred after all.

# CHAPTER XXVII

*utque viro furtiva Venus, sic grata puellae (A.A.I.275)*
*"secret love delights a man and woman"*

We had a staff-meeting that Monday after school and held it in a civilized manner sitting over sandwiches and tea. I wanted to be outside; sunshine glanced in through the leaded panes and a blackbird was singing ecstatically from an oak.

First on the agenda was mock exams. "Someone has suggested to me that we hold next year's mocks not in the Lent term but at Michaelmas," began Dr. Graff. "Are there any comments?"

Unfortunately, Seneca was sitting beside me. He swallowed noisily from his cup then sucked his teeth. His dullness and ignorance were becoming increasingly tedious and, like a cat which knows you do not like it, he invariably placed himself next to me. Invited to comment, he now spoke. "Head Master, at my last school – wonderful place, always at the top of the league tables – we had mock examinations at Christmas. The benefit is that you have the whole of the spring term to pull the boys up by their boot-laces. The down-side is that many staff haven't finished their syllabuses by Christmas."

"We couldn't finish by Christmas," put in Archimedes. "We have practicals and theory, and they both take longer than subjects which require mere reading."

Head of English swung about in his chair and glared at head of Sciences. "I take objection to your use of 'mere'. We don't dish out novellas and tell our classes to put their feet up and have a good read, you know!"

Archimedes removed his bi-focals and breathed on them. "Point taken. I retract the use of 'mere'. But you know what I mean. You don't require your candidates to assemble the mechanics of book-writing and prepare a novel in two years."

Head of English looked round at his departmental colleagues. "Support from the ranks!"

Support came. "It's strange how difficult pupils find essay-writing," put in one teacher, blandly. "You could say an essay is a mini book. You need a beginning, middle and end, and all kinds of ingredients – let's call it a formula if you like – to make it good."

Archimedes returned his glasses to his nose. "But you don't have explosions and have to start again."

Everyone laughed.

"Gentlemen!" cried Dr. Graff.

Squeaked Miss Johns, "Head Master! There are some ladies present too!"

He bowed his head. "Apologies. Ladies and gentlemen! We are drifting from the point. Putting aside formulae, explosions and best sellers, who of you feels we should have mock exams at Michaelmas?"

It would not affect me, but I raised my hand with about fifteen others.

"And who feels we should continue as we are?"

They won the vote, and we passed on to a new topic which was Harrison Senior. I thought of the fourth-former with his chewed thumbs, acrid smell and gender-bending of pictures in the Latin texts. "He isn't back from exeat," Dr. Graff was saying. "His mother thinks he's got glandular fever, and will confirm it tomorrow. Naturally his work will suffer if that's his trouble. So, will all those who teach him collect the books he needs and write a list of what he must work on at home." He turned to Francis. "Will you chase this up and put a package together?"

The Deputy nodded.

Beside me, Seneca burped, quite genteelly for him, and I caught a waft of salmon sandwich.

"The governors have been twitching about our smoking policy," resumed Dr. Graff after consulting his agenda.

There was a groan from head of Games and a heavy sigh from the careers tutor. Both smoked, and were necessarily covert about it. On a walk round the games fields one day, I had come across them in the groundsmen's cubby-hole, puffing away like two third formers. "Want a drag, Jessica?" one had asked. I declined and the other said, "Can you see smoke signals from the window?" I said, "No," they had grinned and I left them to it.

"Does our present policy really need reviewing?" wondered Francis.

"The governors think so. We last discussed it some three years ago."

"We can't stop the boys smoking," said head of Games. "Some come from a home environment where both parents smoke and it is regarded as acceptable behaviour. To demand they stop a habit the moment they're in school is unreasonable. I know!"

We smiled, aware of his addiction.

"Quite," answered Dr. Graff. "But we must be seen to be upholding the policy."

I suddenly raised my hand. "Head Master, may I voice my views here?"

He turned indulgently to me and, next to him, Francis sat up straighter. I flushed slightly and began,

"I've never smoked after one or two disenchanted attempts in my teens. But considering the implications the act of smoking has for youngsters – adulthood, independence, peer esteem and all that – we should move with the times. Young people today are well-informed about social evils. Surely part of their education is decision-making." I paused, wondering if it were wise to draw attention to myself, given my illicit penchant (and someone in that room, apart from the Chaplain, knew of it) for a Sixth Former. But I had begun, so I would continue. "May I suggest smoking be allowed from the Lower Sixth up, that a special room be set aside where smoking is permitted, and that being caught smoking anywhere other than in that room carry punishment."

At first this was met with silence. Then everyone spoke. I had opened a can of worms. I heard "Ridiculous notion!", "Highly irresponsible!", "Brilliant!", and a longer grouch from, I thought, Mr. Sproat – "We've got girls coming soon and there'll be plans for a sex parlour next."

Dr. Graff tapped his knuckles on the table. "Please!" Quiet returned. He looked directly at me. "Mrs. Farthing, I like your idea. How do you see this smoking-room?"

"Unattractive. Poky. In the bowels of the building. With windows that can't be opened."

Someone snorted rudely. "A veritable black hole of Calcutta!"

I continued, "In effect, Dr. Graff, it would be a bit of a dive. And when smokers came out they would reek, and their non-smoking peers would in true male fashion make no bones about saying so. We should be seen to associate smoking with an unhealthy atmosphere and a bad impression. Our message would be: we condone it but do not advocate it."

It was an avant-garde notion. Dr. Graff and his Deputy were exchanging looks, while the rest of the staff jabbered like macaques. I felt strangely ostracised.

The Head Master drummed again. "I doubt our governors would agree, Mrs.Farthing. Your suggestion belongs to the twenty-first century and we aren't quite there yet." He sent me a smile. "But I do like your idea. I shall put it forward at the next governors meeting ... For the moment, however, can we discuss under the existing policy the penalties for smoking at all."

Said Seneca, "I was beaten at school for having a box of matches in my pocket."

Dr. Graff raised an eyebrow. "We don't go that far! But we need to think in terms of one warning, then loss of privileges and finally a fine. No one likes parting with his money."

Half an hour was spent in thrashing out a system of punishment which was stronger than the one in existence. Like a tide, agreement ebbed and flowed, and I gradually lost interest.

After the staff-meeting, it so happened that I passed Harrison Senior's classroom. It seemed a good opportunity to collect his Latin textbooks and devise, that evening, a scheme of work for him while he was ill at home. The room was empty of pupils and, like all in Dons, was furnished with tables for two. No sloping chunky desks as I had when at school; your desk was a personal burrow inside which you kept a tidy house or, as often in my case, a pig's breakfast. It was your sanctuary to which you fled, like a god-fearing Roman, to escape the wrath of your tin-god teachers. You cowered or sat triumphant at it. Sharing your trials and successes, it supported while it harboured you. Its lid was a unique surface for exercising your need to write graffiti; where you drew hearts with arrows through them and wrote JS at the butt and JL (or some such) at the point, with large gouts of blood – preferably etched in red – dripping down the wood; or *I hate maths* or *Miss R is a b.* Sometimes, the grain of wood suggested all manner of fantastic shapes: animals, curlicues, funny faces, and in a bored moment (Maths) of which in my schooldays there were several, you would etch deeper and more fantastically, hoping that next term you would recognise your desk and claim it once again. The lid was good to hide behind, too, either to weep a tear of humiliation (Maths, naturally) or to whisper to your neighbour something about the teacher's person. Keeping it up with your head left your hands free to rummage frantically for books for the next lesson, and if the teacher swept into the room before you had found the appropriate texts, you held the lid almost closed with a thumb while the fingers of your other hand surreptitiously groped.

At Dons, boys kept all their books in a row of lockers at the back of the room, and carried school bags on one shoulder, laying the foundations for a generation of spinal curvatures. I ran my eyes along the row, looking for Harrison Senior's. He had stuck a peremptory notice on his locker-door: *Keep out! Private! Sniff off!* which was in character. I could not like the boy; his physical failings apart, he had a bad aura.

Ignoring his courteous message not to look inside, I opened the locker-door. Messy little tyke! He had stuck numerous excrescences of chewing-gum to the inside which looked as if they were about to suppurate. Folders, dog-eared papers, a men's magazine, used tissues, Mars Bar wrappers and text-books blotched with ink and ear-wax had been thrust higgledy-piggledy into the locker's maw. And it smelled.

Reluctant to touch this unpleasantness, I found a ruler and began poking about for his Latin books. As I prodded, the front page of a tabloid newspaper fell doubled to the floor. Squares in the headlines had been cut out. I picked up the sheet to thrust it back in when numerous individual letters cut from the print showered round my toes. Finally, a blank piece of notepaper fainted to the ground.

My heart quickened. Knowing now what I was about to find, I twitched over the sheet and saw staring up at me the beginnings of an anonymous message:

DO YOU TALK DIR

Heat went to my face. Not the Deputy, but Harrison Senior ... not Sproat or the Three Graces, but Harrison of the fourth year was the sender of my anonymous notes. A pupil! I had not properly considered it. And what was his reason? Surely not a hatred of Latin or me?

I tossed away the ruler and began searching his locker with my hands. I found his Latin books, and something else. Tucked right at the back in a brown paper cover, on which was scrawled *Holy Bible,* lay a small volume. I opened it, and saw a diary. The first entry was dated 20th September, six months ago.

Footsteps were approaching in the passage outside. I picked up Harrison's Latin books, all the accoutrements of his anonymous note-writing and his 'Holy Bible' as Archimedes walked into the room.

"Hello, Jessica! Great minds think alike! Is that Harrison's locker?"

I hugged the books to me as I turned. "It's more of a litter-bin."

He blew through his teeth as he advanced. "Filthy little devil! Oh, well, let's get down to it."

Bidding him a good night, I left the room. I had business to do among the boys' files, and I might just get to the school office before it was locked for the day.

Dr. Graff's secretary was tying on her head-scarf in fishwife fashion. She looked at me like a goose about to bite. "Oh. Mrs. Farthing. I'm just about to leave."

My voice was soothing. "I know. We've been in a meeting, and then had to find Harrison Senior's books. I need some clarification from his file. Would you leave me the office key, and I'll lock up and put it somewhere safe when I've finished?"

Her goose-glare hardened; sacred geese had guarded and saved Rome once, as she was guarding the citadel of Dons now. She thought a moment, her fingers twitching at the knot under her chin. "Well, I don't like to ..."

"Just suggest somewhere safe," I coaxed her gently.

She sniffed. "I have a spare. Put this key –" and she handed it to me, "– under the door when you're done."

She dithered as I laid down my burden without disturbing the papers on the desk. Then she gave me a tight little good-bye, and I was left in peace to find Harrison Senior's details. A grey filing cabinet marked A-I stood with several others against one wall. I wrenched open the drawer marked H and searched for Harrison. There were two, John – a nice little lad in the second year – and his brother, Ian, or Harrison Senior.

Staff were permitted to consult pupils' files. Various kinds of information were available there, whether parents were divorced, separated or dead, last school, IQ test results, special difficulties and similar. All these details helped staff assess, evaluate and understand the boys in their care. Housemasters were more likely to need this information than teachers like me. Now, I was not sure what I hoped to find in Harrison Senior's file, but I would know it when I did.

I read that his home-life was difficult. His father had run off with a nurse and his mother had a live-in lover, a man and a situation which, apparently, Harrison Senior detested. According to a letter his mother had written to the school, Harrison had been a day boy near home in Lancaster; when her boyfriend moved in, Harrison refused to sleep in the same building and retired at night to a summer-house at the bottom of the garden. In winter and wet weather it was unhealthy, and she had had no option but to place him in a boarding-school. I glanced at the date of this letter; both Harrison boys had entered Dons the same term as I.

Other papers showed his housemaster's comments. Harrison Senior was described as a loner with few strengths, save an 'ingenious, if somewhat obsessive, turn of mind.' And he was taking medication for bowel difficulties. All of this did much to explain the boy with whom I had classroom contact; and soon I discovered how he had managed to see Alex and me that Christmas at Haweswater. A further note on file stated that he had grandparents living near Penrith with whom he chose to spend most of his holidays. What I could not deduce from these details was his precise reason for sending me anonymous notes, but it was made clear later that night when I read his 'Holy Bible'.

Under normal circumstances it would never have occurred to me to pry into another's diary. But these were not normal circumstances. I had been subjected over the past few months to the attrition of some particularly unpleasant messages. At times, I thought I would break. Had it not been for the Chaplain, that might well have happened. Now I felt I was justified in reading Harrison's diary.

His first few entries when he was new to the school revealed an unhappiness. He disliked the masters, hated boarding, found his peers 'frightfully, frightfully' (he wrote) and loathed everything and everybody, especially the 'Swine' whose relationship with his mother was the cause of his present misery. And he detested sex. It was 'filthy', he could not understand 'how two people could do that to each other. Bought a men's mag to find out more' (continued one entry in late September) 'and it talked about positions and timing, things we aren't told in PSE. Hate the whole bloody idea of sex, sex, SEX.' (*sic.*) Then as the weeks passed, hatred of all things subsided and there entered references to 'he' and 'him': 'Met him in the passage. He's OK. Nicer than most in the Sixth. Saw him twice today. He supervises prep. Wednesdays. Must ask chaps his name.' Next, Harrison was referring to this Sixth Former by his initials: 'AF is cool. Found out he's a fitness freak. Saw him in gymn. Wish I was like him.' AF was, of course, Alex, and as I leafed through one page of that diary after another, things fell into place. 'AF is brilliant at Classics. Penny-farthing wiped the floor with me cos I handed in some tatty prep. Couldn't do the bloody stuff. Asked AF after. He put me right. AF's tres COOL.' Intrigued, I read on: 'Oct. 1st. Found out AF has tutorials with Pen-Fart in her rooms. It's sick. They should be properly in school. Asked him what he thought of her. He said she's OK. Rumour has it the Marxist fancies her. Sex again. Always bloody sex. What's she doing in a chaps school anyway? Looking for a man? Slag!' Well, I thought; this was one way of finding out how others saw you.

The references to AF continued, generally understated, but constantly at the centre of Harrison's entries. And by the end of the Michaelmas term, Alex was clearly an obsession. I began to feel sorry for Harrison; here was a lad whose domestic life had crashed about his head; who had none of the normal absorptions on which boys of his age concentrated. He disliked sport and was not particularly academic; sex disgusted yet held him fascinated; his loathings of people spat acid, and yet he felt Alex's attraction keenly.

It was his entries after Christmas which I found most revealing. I judged from the dates that he had not taken his diary to Penrith; and his first comments on returning for the Lent term made everything plain: 'AF and Pen-Fart are having AN AFFAIR. It's disgusting. I went with Gramps to Haweswater. Was minding my own business in the car, when who came down the fell but AF and her. The pathetic bitch slipped (on purpose?), she put her arms round him and AF had to carry her off. Feel sick. What's going on? The fucking cow must have got her claws into him up there in her rooms. That's why she's here. To fuck all the sixth she can while teaching Classics. And the masters. Everyone. Hate her guts. May her overies (*sic*) rot and her eyes drop out. Must think what to do.'

He thought, and came up with anonymous notes. I read on: 'That silly old fart the Chaplain talked to us about fancying other boys. What does he know about it? He only fancies god and he doesn't exist. He can't, cos what sane god would invent SEX. What's wrong with fancying a male? I fancy AF. He's made like me, he functions like me and he hasn't got claws like that fucking cow. Have thought of a way to shrivel her up. The Marxist caught me pinching newspaper from the library. Old sod. Watch this space!' Later that same day, Harrison had added: 'Found out why AF went AWL from the Carol Service. Someone said that three years ago to the day his brother was run over by a train. Don't believe it. AF's so cool. Put a Mars Bar in his rugger boot, well, I hope it was his.'

Poor Harrison. He struck me now as burdened, burdened by imperfect knowledge, misconception, solitariness and worse, by his own self. Here was a boy at that crucial stage of development, stunted and warped through lack of guidance. His father had failed him; his mother, unable to discuss her needs with him, had packed him off to boarding-school as the easy way out; and Dons, with all its educational facilities, was failing him, too. His love for Alex wasn't doing him any good, either, for it had stung him into vengeful acts on me.

Feeling that I had read enough, I skipped some pages to two entries later in that term: 'She's not giving anything away, that fucking cow. She's had four messages now, and she still ponces into class like a made-up tart with her Salvete, pueri and all that crap. She looks knackered sometimes, but I bet it's cos she's been having it off with someone. AF? No chance. The Marxist? OK, but hands off AF, you slag.'

The final entry I chose was one of the most recent Harrison had written: 'Saw AF in the gymn. Everything he does is cool. He saw me. Told me to piss off. Can't.'

I closed Harrison Senior's 'Holy Bible', wondering how he was getting on stuck at home with glandular fever. There would be no sleeping in the summer-house at the bottom of the garden under those circumstances. Would he be back in school at all, now it was so near to the end of term? Perhaps he intended convalescing with his grandparents in Penrith. Alex and I hoped to spend part of the Easter holidays up there, too.

My tutorials with Alex were now geared to exam technique. We had finished the Classics syllabus comfortably and needed only to brush up on final areas. It was a day or two after I had read Harrison's 'Holy Bible' and I was giving Alex his usual lesson. The tutorial had almost finished, and across the roof-tops came the frantic whistle of the games coach which shrieked end-of-play.

Said Alex, "So, Harrison Senior's got glandular fever."

I looked up from my books. "Yes. It's been confirmed."

"At least it's not meningitis. One of the fifths started a rumour that it was, but that's been knocked on the head. It's quite a relief."

"That he hasn't got meningitis?"

"Actually, I was referring to Harrison's absence." He paused. "Do you remember my telling you some time ago about a fourth former's sneaky observation?"

I knew all about that now. "Yes."

"The creep was always around when I practised in the gymn. I didn't like to say then that it was Harrison."

Our eyes met. Calmly, I said, "He hero-worships you."

He shrugged. "He's nuts. He sent me a note once saying that if ever I wanted my shoes cleaned, my tuck bought or letters posted, he'd do it. I wouldn't trust him as far as I could spit!"

I kept silent. Harrison's interest in Alex would probably sort itself out in time, but jealousy of our relationship was no excuse for sending me anonymous notes.

Alex was studying me. "Do you think I'm being tough on him?"

I gave a smile. "Not at all." With a lowered voice I added, "If I was a lad at this school, Harrison wouldn't be the only one wanting to clean your shoes."

He grinned. "I'd let you clean my shoes any day!"

The bell for lesson-end rang. Oddly subdued, we put our books and papers away and stood almost at a loss for words. I said, "Only three more weeks till the holidays."

He pulled on his shirt cuffs. "Does that invitation – you know the one I mean – remain?"

"Pomeroy?"

"Yes."

"It does."

He chewed on a knuckle. "I'll have to spend a little time with my uncle and aunt in Wiltshire."

"Of course."

"Two weeks in Pomeroy and two weeks with them?"

"As you wish."

"Which two weeks?"

"Easter in Pomeroy!"

"Done!"

I moved towards him, he put out his hand and I checked myself. "Look, you've forgotten your pen," I cried, picking up a ball-point from among my papers.

"So I have!"

I slipped the pen and my fingers under his hand. We exchanged pressure, then broke apart.

# CHAPTER XXVIII

*ignotas cogor inire vias (R.A.578)*
*"I am forced to enter uncharted seas"*

When my post was advertised in the papers, I called a departmental meeting. The Three Graces entered the office, looking sheepish. We were squeezed as usual together, but I had taken the precaution to open the window so that any Catullun 'rank he-goat under someone's armpits' had the means of escape.

I surveyed all three men before speaking, and pity took hold of me; pity that the subject I loved should rest in their uninspired hands, pity for all the boys in that school who would labour over *amo, amas, amat* and the paradigms of Greek verbs with frowsty teachers like them.

"Gentlemen," I began at last, "You may have seen my post advertised in the press." They swung their heads like fourth formers and avoided my eyes.

Allan spluttered into voice. "Jessica, I'm sorry."

It remained a mystery why he felt sorrow: was it that I was going, or was he ashamed of their concerted resistance to me? I let his apology pass. "The Head Master and I have agreed that the best time to interview is on Wednesday 14th March. The upper school will be out on charity work and the juniors and middle-school have a long-distance run."

Bowtie looked surprised. "Why the secrecy?"

I expressed one reason. "My leaving so soon might unsettle some of those taking public exams next term. I would appreciate it if you all would keep this confidential."

They nodded, and I believed they would. Teachers, like the military, were good at closing ranks.

"One further point," I continued, straightening some papers that shifted in the draught from the window. "Does any of you feel he'd like to apply for my post as head of Department?"

As I suspected, none did; they wanted to be led, but led by someone of whom they approved. Well, they would have their chance to meet short-listed applicants; but the final decision rested with Dr. Graff, Francis Marks and me.

The remainder of term raced by. I wrote to Miss North at Whitemeads School, whose post I was inheriting, to suggest a day during the June exams when she could show me the flat she was vacating. And applications for my own post flooded in.

The closing-date came, and Dr. Graff, Francis and I met to draw up a short-list.

"Still determined to leave?" asked the Head Master in a jocular way.

I spread my hands like a continental.

He waved his folder at me. "This, Mrs. Farthing, contains twenty-two applications. We've got to choose five out of this lot by tomorrow. Have you tea-ed?"

"Not yet."

He went to the door and Francis and I heard him ask for three teas and a plate of 'sticky cakes'. On his return he gave a schoolboy grin. "The task ahead demands sustenance!"

We sat in easy-chairs, Francis looking remarkably glum and Dr. Graff resigned to the fact I was leaving. I did not like to examine my feelings.

"There's the usual rubbish here," observed the Head Master, leafing through cv's and typed letters. "Young teachers who can't spell and first-jobbers trying to persuade me that what they lack in experience they have in enthusiasm. Here, take a look." He gave a sheaf to me and to Francis. "One man has even sent me a photograph. What does he think that'll gain him? This is not a beauty contest. But that lot's more encouraging." He prodded a slimmer pile. "I've asterisked the possibles. See if you agree."

Among these were six men and one woman applicant. I looked up at Dr. Graff. "You don't like the sound of the woman?"

"Remind me of her name."

"Carlotta Schabedli."

He rubbed the ball of his thumb across his left side-burn. "And her academic vital statistics?"

We exchanged a grin, and I read, "Single, thirty-five, has twelve years' experience in the independent sector, is presently at a co-ed in Wales..."

He interrupted, "Asterisk her. I think her name put me off."

Wryly I asked, "Do we all have to be Susan Smiths and Harry Browns before we are considered for our jobs, Head Master?"

He grimaced. "It helps." He turned to Francis. "You're very quiet, Deputy. Feeling all right?"

Francis shifted uncomfortably. "Fine, Head Master."

It took us some time to whittle down the applications to five. Letters for references and invitations to interview were sent out the next day, and over the week replies came in. From nine o'clock on Wednesday 14th the school emptied. Senior boys were sent off to Deme to do shopping for the elderly, dig their gardens, sit and talk to them, or walk their dogs; while the younger boys pounded away on a cross-country run. The first candidate was interviewed at ten.

Out of the five, I liked one man and the only woman best. Both were well-qualified, intelligent, lively and professional. But it was male versus female. Dr. Graff and Francis would doubtless choose the former, and get round the equal opportunities rule by insisting the successful applicant should help with rugger and housemaster's duties.

We had a working lunch in the Head Master's study. I held out for the female candidate, while they felt the better choice was the man.

"How did your colleagues take to her?" asked Francis, who looked like a dog who desperately wanted a walk.

I thought back. They had been stiff, but polite; it had been the same when I came for interview. "Can I be frank, Head Master?" He inclined his head and I went on, "If girls are coming into the Sixth Form soon, then I think we should choose the woman. How many female staff have we got? About five. The ratio of men to women should be increased if we are serious about a mixed Sixth Form. Further, I cannot help thinking that if the male Classicist is chosen, my present colleagues may feel they have exercised a power of veto which is not really their privilege."

Francis was nodding in agreement while Dr. Graff appeared to waver. "But ultimately your colleagues have to work with the chosen applicant," he observed.

"Of course. However, if you remember, you once said to me that you would not be bullied by your staff. I have nothing against the male applicant. But if the decision were mine to make, I would choose the woman." I sat back. I had said my bit. The rest was up to them.

Dr. Graff looked at his Deputy. "Francis?"

Francis was torn, I could see; perhaps he wanted to indulge me for reasons I could divine, yet felt he should let the Head Master decide. In the end he chose to sit on the fence. "I like the sound of both."

"Have another cake," urged Dr. Graff, thrusting the plate towards us. "Very well. Let's offer the post to Carlotta Shewadiwadi –"

"Schabedli," I gently corrected him.

He smiled. "– and if she declines, to the man."

☙ ❧

I had unfinished business with Harrison Senior, but it was unlikely that he would return for the last few days of term. I did not relish the thought of a confrontation hanging over the Easter holidays till we all came back. So, great was my surprise when I entered the fourth year classroom to find him sitting at his usual place. Considering the circumstances, I was nice to him.

"*Salve,* Harrison," I said. He looked thinner, ringy and not very happy.

His eyes slipped from mine as he mumbled, "*Salve,* Mrs. Farthing."

"*Valesne?*"

His look was blank. *Oh, come along, do!* The other boys were prompting him in stage whispers, "Psst, Harry! 'Are you well?'"

"Huh? Yes, thanks."

I corrected him, "*Ita, gratias.*"

He swung his head helplessly and the whole class chanted, "*Ita, gratias!*"

He mumbled something which sounded like 'up your arsias', but I gave him the small benefit of a large doubt. I now pursued the matter of his Latin-work, in English; he wasn't worth the waste of the others' time. "Did you complete the exercises I set you while you were ill, Harrison?"

He nodded, but could not or would not meet my eye. I wondered if he had been to his locker, and found various items missing. Now he was holding out his exercise book with two hands, as Oliver Twist held his bowl.

My tone was curt. "I'm sure your legs are sufficiently rested for you to bring me your book," and I put out my arm.

Drawing himself together like a moribund spider, he rose and approached the staff-desk. As he returned to his seat I added, "Come to my office at four, please, and I'll go over your marked work." I had every intention of going over something else, too.

Alex had not yet spoken to me of the tragic circumstances of his brother's death, and I would not speak of Harrison's anonymous letters; everyone had a right to some secrets, and however terrible Alex's loss, it was irrelevant to the way we conducted our affair, just as were Harrison's disgusting notes.

The fourth former was five minutes late, yet I let that pass. He had also 'forgotten' his text book, but I had mine and did not make an issue of that, either. I offered him a seat opposite and beyond my desk; anything closer, and I would have felt contaminated. First, we went through his work which, as usual, was incorrect as well as lacking care. If he genuinely did not understand the grammar, I would have been lenient; but it occurred to me that he got things wrong wilfully; it was his way of punching me in the eye.

"What haven't you done, Harrison?" I pointed with my pen at the top of his work.

"I've got it wrong."

"It's to do with presentation."

He fastened his ragged thumbs round the book and with a fruity sniff peered at the page. "Huh? No page number."

"Yes. What else?"

"No exercise number."

"And?"

"Too many crossings out?"

My patience was wearing thin, but that is what he wanted. "Look at the translation, Harrison!"

"It's wrong!"

"Not all of it. The spacing!"

He thumped his brow in a dramatic gesture. "I've not written on alternate lines."

"Exactly. Why do you think we ask you to do that?"

"So you have space to write corrections."

"That's it. Remember next time, please." I shot him a look. There was an underlying disrespect in his whole demeanour, from the bored expression on his wooden face to his body language; for he sat, one ankle balanced on the other knee, his chewed fingers playing with a shoe-lace. "Have you any questions?"

"Nope."

"I must be going deaf. What did you say?"

"Nein."

"I don't teach German. If you can't manage it in Latin or Greek, try plain English."

"No, Mrs. Farthing."

I closed his exercise-book and pushed it at him. He rose. *Oh, no you don't*! "Just a moment, please."

He waited, standing. That would not do. He was a tall boy, and to have him looking down at me while I dealt with the next piece of business would psychologically put him in a position of dominance. I had had enough of that over the weeks.

"Sit down, please."

Now our eyes were level. I calmly unlocked the top drawer of my desk and drew out a clean folder. Passing it closed to him, I said, "Yours, I believe."

Uncomprehending, he slid the folder over and opened it. I have never seen a youth turn such an apoplectic red. I continued to stare at him and his eyes just brushed mine. The heat spilled to his neck, and the shirt-collar stood out brilliant white. I extended my hand. He could not get rid of the evidence fast enough.

Opening the folder, I took out the piece of newsprint with its square holes and screwed it into a ball. Pointedly I held up the sheet of paper glaring its foul unfinished note, then tore that into shreds. And all this was done in silence while he sweated it out, shoulders rounded, head down like a gnome with stomach-ache.

There was one piece of evidence which, for the rest of my time at Dons, I would keep as insurance. "I have your 'Holy Bible', Harrison," was the only reference I made to it, for one does not enter into formal treaties with under-age schoolboys. Then his eyes did meet mine. They were turgid with hate and fear. "Right, you can go."

He jumped to his feet and shot out of the door. I called, "Harrison! You've forgotten your Latin!"

His soles squeaked like brakes on the floor outside. He dived back in, snatched up his book and vanished.

I was sure my confronting him with what he had been doing gave him a shock, and the anonymous notes would cease. Of a photograph I had found no evidence – he and the photographer at Haweswater must have been unrelated. Harrison was cunning enough to realise that, with his notes and a revealing diary in my possession, I needed only go to the Head Master and he would have been expelled. Dons might not be the right environment for him, but anything was better than an unhappy home-life. And Alex was still in the school.

☙ ❧

Carlotta Schabedli accepted Dr. Graff's offer of my post, and no one except a very few was any the wiser.

Now, at the close of the Lent term, there were house matches. Dons was divided into four houses: Raleigh (Sir Walter), Nelson, Jonson (Ben) and Watts. Each personage represented exploring, naval, literary and inventing endeavours in the male human spirit. It was quaint but traditional, and the boys supported their houses with a fierce loyalty. I happened to comment to the Chaplain in the staffroom that I wasn't a feminist in the strict sense of the word, but with girls entering the Sixth Form, something should be done to introduce a woman into the house-system.

As usual, my quietly-spoken asides always seemed to catch Seneca's ear. He oozed up to us, tinkling the money in pocket, and said, "Who do you suggest, Mrs. Farthing?"

Unfortunately, several knots of staff sitting over their coffee heard his unctuous voice and turned. I paused a moment before replying, "Mary Wollstonecraft?"

Seneca threw back his head and laughed, and I saw the gaps in his upper jaw. "Why don't you call the girls' house Frankenstein and be done with it!"

Some of the others, like the sheep they were, took his cue and laughed too, so that I felt my sotto voce conversation with Mr. O'Hare had become open to public ridicule. I let them guffaw their fill, then continued, "She had talents which, with respect to the men providing the house-names here, they appear not to have possessed."

The Chaplain supported me. "Actually, Cotton, it was Mary Wollstonecraft's daughter who wrote Frankenstein."

Seneca looked stupid for a moment, then recovered himself. "Well, I don't really think the young ladies would like to have an association with Frankenstein however remote. The boys would tease them to death."

"And –" I continued, "Wollstonecraft was an educationalist, a radical, a translator and a publisher's reader."

Those colleagues who had shown initial interest returned to their own business, while Seneca thought he would join Mr. O'Hare and me. He sat, leaning forward, elbows on bony knees, pressing together his palms in a praying gesture. "I think Elizabeth the First would be a good choice, myself. Now that was a remarkable lady!"

We were in for a History lesson for which I was in no mood, and Seneca's superiority was so insufferable that after a brief spell of it, I excused myself only to be caught as I left the room by head of Games.

"Jessica!" His voice pounced on me. "The Staff versus Sixth Form rounders match. Will you play?" His track-suit reeked of cigarette smoke; he had probably spent break in the groundsmen's cubby-hole.

I replied on the defensive. "I haven't played rounders since my school-days."

"It doesn't matter. We've got up a rugger team between men and boys, but want the women staff to have their little fling at a gentler sport. Will you?"

I wavered, secretly liking the idea of playing rounders again. "So long as I don't have to wear a ridiculous get-up – you know, hair in bunches..."

"Jessica, you could never look ridiculous!"

On the strength of that piece of chivalry, I consented.

It appeared I could go nowhere that day without bumping into everyone save the only person I really wanted to see. For the Deputy accosted me not much later, and the moment I saw him I felt a pang of remorse. How could I have suspected him of anonymous notes! Since receiving my resignation he had barely spoken to me, perhaps because it was now a *fait accompli* and he was getting used to rejection. I resolved to be specially nice to him.

"I hear you've suggested a new house-name for the girls," he began, with a soulful expression.

"My word, news travels in this place! Heaven knows what would be the speed of malicious gossip! Just an aside, Francis. Nothing to get excited about."

He looked more than ever like a walk-weary retriever. "Why not? You're an exciting person."

I dismissed that with a laugh. "I'm sure a better idea will crop up nearer the time."

"I don't think there could be a better one. It sounds exclusive, different."

"It was only a passing suggestion, Francis. I was just making a comment to the Chaplain, and suddenly it has grown like the biblical mustard-seed!"

He tentatively placed a warm paw on my arm. "You see how good you would be for the school if you stayed. Dr. Graff says he will put that suggestion forward at the next governors' meeting, too."

"Heavens! What else can I suggest before I leave?"

He left me with an eloquent look.

The Staff versus Sixth Form rounders match promised to be 'a giggle', to use Miss Johns' term. Our team was made up of most women teachers, kitchen staff, Chaplain, the Head Master and drama teacher who, for health reasons, could not be too energetic. A motley crew, we stalked through the building at twelve o'clock on the penultimate day of term. Miss Johns had tamed the snakes of her hair into a Medusa plait, she wore a short pleated skirt, socks and trainers, and her knees were red to the wind. The others had attired themselves in various degrees of 'scruff order', while I was dressed in a pullover, trousers and walking boots. We sauntered out into a typical March day; big clouds like misshapen mushrooms puffed across the sky making a Bo-Peep of the sun; a wind, scented with broken grasses and routed earth, blew now shrill then dulcet. I felt Mad Hatterish, confident that we women would dawdle round our posts, a source of kindly fun to the junior boys, while the rest of the school was intent on the macho ruggerites. Not so.

Over five hundred boys and non-playing staff crowded at the edges of the rounders pitch where the opposition were already gathered. And the opposition included Alex. In fact he was bowling, but I did not know till I saw him tossing the ball back and forth to his peers. On we paced to the whistles, cat-calls and cheers of hundreds of lusty young men. I said, "Oh, cripes!" and Miss Johns, wobbling beside me, burst into a panic of titters.

It was the first time Alex and I were seen by the school in close proximity. So, I felt vulnerable because of our illicit love, and was convinced all that we had done and shared must have been transparent. Surely it was written over my body, in my face and expression, in my eyes and voice. And when some third years yelled: "Go for it, Penny-Farthing!", I wished Pluto in his chariot would rise from the ground and whisk me to perdition.

Alex and I exchanged not one look, which is not to say we did not look at each other. I tried to conceal myself behind the hefty proportions of the kitchen staff and carry on a sane conversation with the Chaplain, but everyone kept shifting and interrupting, and in the end I thought 'What the hell!'

The Sixth fielded first. I manoeuvred myself into the middle of our team, dreading my turn the nearer it came. Alex was kind, bowling gently to the women. I dared not look too closely at the way his fine physique moved to each throw. And when Miss Johns ran, red knees bobbing round the posts, another member of the Sixth ran on the spot, giving her time to reach her goal. It was different when I took up my position.

My colour increased with the cat-calls. The fielders braced themselves, and Alex (the devil) dramatically flexed his muscles. *Oh cripes! How much do the Sixth know, and what are they going to do to me!* Then I prayed that their anticipation would not end in the anti-climax of my missing the ball.

I stood poised, adrenalin coursing like a hare round my blood. Alex stepped forward; I drew back my bat; released from his hand the ball came on. With a satisfying thwack, I sent it whizzing through the air.

"Oh, good shot!" said he, while I ran.

It whizzed forever. It created a Red Sea cleavage through a tide of boys. I ran on, round one post after another.

"Penny-Farthing, Penny-Farthing!" cried the juniors, leaping up and down.

Then, at the penultimate post, as the ball seemed to have got lost, I played to the gallery and sauntered up to the finish. Behind me I heard a shout of delight. The ball was returned to Alex, and play resumed.

My success was short-lived. At my next turn, the ball bounced off the bat right into the hands of the backstop. I was out. Needless to say the opposition won, though the Head Master had a good innings and we others fielded very well.

Then it was on to watch the Staff versus Sixth Form rugby. The boys triumphed there, too; but it was good fun and lunch sustained us all before an afternoon of house matches. And when at day's end I sat weary yet strangely exhilarated in my rooms, I decided that a staff versus school match was more nerve-wracking than a dance class in London.

# CHAPTER XXIX

*Spes tenet in tempus longum (A.A.I.445)*
*"Hope endures a long time"*

Alex and I met in London the day we all broke for the Easter holidays. We spent the night at his parents' flat, then drove up to Pomeroy. As usual, we took it in turns at the wheel, with regular breaks at motorway cafés.

Our last stop was in Lancaster where we shared crumpets oozing with butter and what seemed like an urn of tea.

"Did you get my message on the rounders field?" he suddenly asked, aiming with accuracy the ball of his napkin into a rubbish-bin.

"You flexed your muscles at me!"

"Of course."

I tried to look indignant. "But you shouldn't have. I was weak at the knees already without you rippling."

"Nervous?"

"Terrified! Then you did your little act and I thought everyone would cotton on. Don't do it again in public, Forsyth."

He grinned. "It was only a bit of fun, Mrs. Farthing. All part of the match."

"Hmph. Do your friends in the Sixth know anything about us?"

"Absolutely not. No one knows."

I kept silent; *Harrison Senior and the Chaplain knew.* I said, "Anyway, I'm always on the qui vivre where you're concerned – and you know it!"

In answer, he took my hand in both his and chewed gently at the wrist. I watched his lips nuzzle my skin and had an urgent desire to make love to him. But my next words betrayed none of this. "Mrs. Medic," I said.

His mouth moved to my palm, much to the interest of an obese truck-driver who clearly found these oral explorations more to his taste than the ballooning girls on Page Three of his paper.

"What about Mrs. Medic?" Alex was progressing up my sleeve.

I tugged gently. "This is getting personal! Can't you wait till tonight?"

At the word 'tonight', the trucker closed his paper and stared.

Primmer than a maiden aunt, Alex sat back. "You mentioned Mrs. Medic, I believe?"

"Yes. Will she be around when you stay in Wiltshire?"

"Probably. But I've solved any problems there. I've asked to sleep in the main house. Virginia can have the flat over the stables, if she comes."

What could I say to that? I turned reflective over my mug of tea, remembering a conversation I had once had with Antony about the 'regrettable reality of the other person.' It must have been a Sunday evening for he was cleaning his shoes; he had always cleaned shoes late in the weekend.

He spat precisely on the toe of one shoe then said, "What are you talking about, Jess?"

The way I had often to qualify a perfectly simple (to me) observation was sometimes a source of irritation; Antony and I did not speak the same language. Hiding a sigh, I replied, "When the romance fades, you are left with a person who after all, eats and breathes like you."

He began vigorously polishing. "What of it? Really, Jess. For a practical woman, you can be remarkably chimerical." He looked pleased with his use of a word grander than his usual choice of vocabulary, then added, "Life can't be one long romance."

I had agreed. "But the other person's table-manners may not be yours, their use of grammar may be annoyingly unsyntactical, they may snore as they sleep and break wind, and there's little you can do about it."

Looking shocked, he had dropped one shoe and taken up another. "For heaven's sake! Am I to start apologising for holding my cup a different way to you –" (I winced, saying to myself: different *from*, Antony!) "– for snoring and farting in bed?"

I had laughed to take the tension from the moment. "I'm the one who usually calls a spade a spade! All the same, the Victorians had something with their separate bedrooms."

At this, he thumped his shoes noisily about the floor. "So, now you want us to sleep apart?"

My answer had been cryptic. "Perhaps I was a Victorian in a previous life."

"'The regrettable reality of the other person' indeed!" Placing his shoes in the cupboard with pedantic care, he muttered on, and the subject had never been raised again.

In all, I had spent only six nights in the same bed as Alex. Either he, or I, had returned to our separate rooms and no objection had been made. The seventh night we spent together was the first of the Easter holidays in Pomeroy. I doubted there was a 'regrettable' reality to Alex.

All that week the days were sky-bright with a saw-toothed wind from the Pennines. We toured those Lakes we had lacked the time to see at Christmas, and disagreed as to the nicest. He liked Derwentwater; I preferred Rydal. Then, as we skirted Patterdale on our way home and saw Ullswater, now sullen now bright in the evening sun, I suggested we stop and walk up the fell.

Sienna-brown oaks were turning ruddy which meant the sap was rising; grey-green lichen clung to their branches and at their base glowed the foxy red of ferns. I loved the way Lakeland valleys shone with iridescent pastures; then, as we climbed, the colour drained from the steeps and became numb-grey scree.

Above a farm we watched a shepherd and his dog drive their flock, like so many buttons, down to the barns. Every so often, the farmer gave coaxing whistles then a piercing imperative; and the dog, in response, sank on its belly to watch, or nosed the 'buttons' onwards till eventually sheep, dog and farmer disappeared behind the buildings. All we heard then was the cadence of bleating protest.

Suddenly Alex flung an arm round my shoulders. "You said once, Mrs. Farthing, you'd like a dog. So would I. And that's the kind of dog I'd have."

We laughed into the wind and stamped on up the fell.

During that holiday Alex began to talk of Oxford. He'd live in hall for the first two years, he said, then find his own place for the remainder. "By the way," he continued, "Which was your University?"

We were having tea in the sitting-room where the light at that time of day was brightest. I had picked some yellow crocuses, and they were spreading their petals to the sun. Their faint honey scent mingled with that of toast and Earl Grey.

"I went to University College, London."

"Is there any more tea in the pot? Were you happy there?"

As I poured the last dribble into his cup I though of my bitter-sweet experience with one of the Classics lecturers. The recollection now was neither bitter nor sweet, just vaguely nostalgic. "Generally speaking, I was."

"And were you a good student?"

"Define to me 'good'!"

"Did you party and booze, or work and attend lectures?"

"I was a good student!"

"Hah! So, don't encourage me to waste my time at Oxford! I shall lead what Virginia calls a fuddy-duddy life."

I looked doubtful. "You'll probably end up teaching your year how to do Henny-Penny routines. Just enjoy yourself, that's all!"

"Right. I shall get legless at weekends, sleep with a different girl four times a month and stay up till dawn sorting out life, just because you told me to!"

I caught his eye and we both smiled. But I thought it a possibility.

"And you, Jessica, will you miss me at Dons next year?"

I rose to put another log on the fire. Here was the perfect moment to tell him that not only was I leaving Dons in the summer, but also taking up a teaching post not far from Oxford. But again I shrank; it could seem that I was chasing after him or, worse, manipulating circumstances to suit myself. Once more, I procrastinated.

With my face in the wood-basket, I replied, "I shan't be able to teach anyone else in my rooms after you."

It was neither a direct answer to his question, nor the reply had had probably expected. I turned back to him, our eyes met and his just as quickly dropped from mine.

When he spoke, his voice had flattened. "Who's coming up in the Lower Sixth and good at Classics? Marlowe?"

I sat down again. "And Peterson. They're both able. But my rooms won't hold two, so you see I couldn't possibly take them there."

An under-boiled raspberry from the jampot sat on Alex's plate. With his knife he began to press it flat, but it was hard and grainy. "How will we be able to meet? I can't really turn up at the school other than on Old Boys' Days."

He clearly mistook my hesitation as reluctance to see him. A dull colour went to his face and he knitted his brows. And my answer, slow in coming, did nothing to reassure him. "I really don't know, Alex."

The hurt shot into his eyes. He tightened his lips, not long ago so soft and pliant, and said no more. He began helping me to clear away, and his demeanour, cheerful all day, became depressed. I felt he was shutting something out; not me, but the hurt I had perhaps inflicted. His silence continued till he took a schoolbook and sat distant, uncommunicative, by the fire to read.

While I moved about, I looked covertly at him. His eyes were open but not following the print on his page. Once I passed behind; the angle of his head was so poignant that I stretched out my hand to touch him. But I checked the impulse; present cruelty would be a future kindness to us both.

From that moment, self-doubt entered his part in our intimacies. He was always tender and considerate, but his actions lacked something I could not define. He would lie back, an arm across his eyes with only his mouth maddeningly visible. I gave no hint that anything was different, and encouraged him in the subtle ways we liked best. He responded, but with a desperation.

I cannot say what gave me the idea that I knew his mind better than he; perhaps it was my older years, a cynicism about love, or plain arrogance – or was it all three?

Just after Easter, when we were into the second week of the holidays, Martha telephoned to say she was bored with London and could she visit me in Pomeroy. It was almost a relief for me and probably for Alex, too, since a barely perceptible restraint had entered our once so easy relationship.

Of course I said she could for I owed her some hospitality. But how would Alex react? "She is a relative by marriage," I quickly explained. "Will you mind very much if she stays?"

His answer, so diffident, wounded me. "Not in the slightest."

I wanted him to mind, to say that he much preferred to spend his last few days with me, alone, before travelling down to Wiltshire.

"Shall I sleep on the couch in the sitting-room?" he asked after a pause. "I mean, does she know about me?"

My tone was indignant. "Certainly you won't, and no, she doesn't know of you!"

He raised a hand. "Then where shall I sleep? She will need the spare room."

I looked miserably down at the floor. "I would like you to sleep with me."

Our eyes suddenly met and held. His showed no emotion.

"Then, shall I make myself scarce when she comes? There'll be only three days before I leave."

I went up to him and placed my hands on his shoulders. "Alex! I'm not ashamed of our relationship. There's no need to keep things secret here. I love you, and I don't care if Martha knows it."

I should have wooed him more, but now I felt constrained. He laid his hands lightly on mine, then turned away. "I'm going for a walk," he said. I let him go alone.

Alex stayed back when I went to pick up Martha from Pomeroy station. She came the same way as he had done, on the Settle-Carlisle line. When we met on the platform she thrust a bunch of daffodils into my hand. "Jess, I do hope this isn't inconvenient. I've got the spring blues."

I assured her it was not, adding, "It's lovely to see you again. A bit of Pennine air will put you right." I opened the passenger door of my car and saw her in. "You must be ready for some tea!"

She smiled and nodded through the window, and as I went round the other side, I hoped Alex had not disappeared. He was revising steadily, but it was not sensible to milk his set authors dry.

"Why on earth didn't Antony like it up here?" Martha wondered, when we had driven through the town and were stopping outside my house. "He really was a bit of an old stick, you know."

I took her in, saying, "It was the town mouse and country mouse syndrome. Give me your coat. Oh, these daffodils are lovely! I'll just find a vase."

She went into the sitting-room where the fire blazed, and I noted with satisfaction that Alex had set a tray with three of everything.

"Tea for three!" she exclaimed. "Who's the third?"

I felt, rather than heard, a presence behind me.

"I am," said Alex.

Martha spun round. She stared at him and murmured, "Well, hello!"

I became brisk. "Martha, this is Alex Forsyth. Alex, meet Martha Verall."

They shook hands affably. Now, Martha liked to survey a new person rather as one surveys a sculpture in the British Museum. It did not win her friends, but it was done with such naivety that the broad-minded soon forgave her. She could not walk round Alex because he stood in the doorway; but her eyes travelled slowly over his person, then came to rest on his face.

"Well!" she said once more, and folded her arms under her breast. "Are you local, Alex?" She turned briefly to me. "Jess, I feel brighter already!"

He smiled, showing his white teeth. "No." He sent me a glance. "Where do I come from, Mrs. Farthing – Sussex, London, Wiltshire, Bogata?"

This ruffled me slightly, but I replied, "Sussex," and thrust my arm through his.

Martha absorbed our proximity, but Alex's 'Mrs. Farthing' had conveyed a mixed message, and she looked confused. She sat, pulling off her gloves, for once at a loss for words. I went to make tea.

When I returned, they were talking unreservedly about London and the country, Martha's journey and rail travel in general. I was glad to hear that she was not pumping him for personal details. She would pump me later instead.

"Thank you for making the sandwiches, Alex," I murmured, passing him his plate. It was spoken with a certain intimacy, and catching Martha's eye I saw the curiosity of a cat.

"A pleasure," he quietly returned.

Martha had a nose for the scent of romance. We all chatted gaily over tea, but I observed that she could hardly wait to put the critical questions: who was Alex, where did we meet, how did it begin and how far had it gone. Then I saw things from Alex's point of view: two older women, obviously quite close, who might put their heads together when he was out of earshot and gossip about his potency and experience.

Was it his inborn diplomacy? After tea, he said he was going to telephone his sister from the town. Martha waited a while when the front door had closed behind him, then had her moment.

"You are a dark horse, Jess!"

I was going to the kitchen with the tray. "I can't see it myself."

"You wouldn't. Now, if he's from Sussex, then he must be at your school. I know!" And her face lit. "He's a junior master! What does he teach?"

From the doorway, I said, "He doesn't teach anything."

"I'll start again. With a body like his, then he's a...a life-guard?"

I hung back in my exit. "No."

Her expression changed to one of alarm. "He's not a pupil!"

"He's in the Upper Sixth and is Dons' Classics Scholar." I went out.

"God, Jessica!" She followed, her demeanour twittering though her voice was firm.

"I don't see what God has to do with it."

She ignored that. "Why do I think I've seen him before? Do they know? Is that why you're leaving? Have they sacked you?"

I put the tray on the table. "I doubt you've seen him before." I had in mind *Let not thy right hand know what thy left hand doeth.* I would tell Martha only so much. "And no, I haven't been sacked."

"Then where are you going when you leave?"

"To hell."

"Don't be so melodramatic!"

I faced her. "Something'll work out."

She looked in my eyes. "Jess, you're living on your emotions – you once so cerebral, so firmly in control of your feelings! I remember you saying some time ago that you often thought like a man, that you used your – how did you put it? – left-hand brain more than the right, like most men do. Jessica Farthing, come back into the women's room!"

I had to laugh, and my tension eased. Then I told her, briefly, how things had happened between Alex and me, that for the present we were both serious though all that would end in the summer. And as I spoke, she sat or rose and roamed about, twiddling this and that. She seemed unnerved, and I think it was the thought of him.

At last, she settled. "Well, there was I thinking you had shut yourself in a boarding-school away from real opportunities. How wrong I was. He's absolutely stunning. So manly. So mature. Lucky you!"

"There's one thing you must promise me." I looked at her gravely.

"What's that?"

"Never breathe to him that I'm leaving Dons when he leaves."

"Why shouldn't he know?"

"He might think less of me." It wasn't the truth, but it would do.

She gave a snort. "If he does that then you're wasting your time. Right, Jess, I shan't say a word."

When we retired for the night, she grew a little stiff on discovering that Alex and I would sleep together. But that was all we did. I don't believe Martha's proximity inhibited us; it was simply that our intimacy was so great that it could transcend sex.

Attempting to be to each of them what they wanted, tired me and when Alex's final day came I felt I had failed both. I could not show him love because it would have excluded, and been discourteous to, Martha; and I was unable to talk to her in the way women do, or he would have felt left out. Christmas had proved the better holiday, and now this one, almost over, was probably my last with Alex.

He had made no further reference to our slight contretemps before she arrived; nor did I. On our last night I was desperate, desperate for some demonstration of love that might not come again. We lay together in the dark, barely touching. Then he rolled over and faced the wall. My exclusion was complete.

Mercifully, the voices which once plagued me, had for some time gone beyond my hearing. But now they returned. *Make love to him!* urged Aphrodite. *Don't be so selfish,* said Athene; *he's asleep and has quite a journey tomorrow. Ha!* sneered Aphrodite; *since when have you felt mumsie? Listen to his sigh. He does not sleep!* I lifted my head; Alex was lying very still, the sort of stillness which is pregnant with thought. Should I make some move?

My hand was warm, and I slipped it gently under the collar at the back of his neck. He made a small sound. Encouraged, I move nearer, slowly pulling his pyjama shirt from the confines of its trousers. My palms found bare skin. Still no rebuff – in fact a turning to me. And I did what Aphrodite advised.

Silently I made slow love to him, smothering his low groans with kisses. It was a thank you, a plea for forgiveness and a farewell all in one.

☙ ❧

He returned south via Penrith. I drove him to the rail station, and Martha came too. Next to her twittering, he seemed in amused control.

"If ever you're at a loose end in London," she cried, thrusting a piece of paper between his fingers, "here's my telephone number."

"Thank you, Martha." He took it and left the car. Then, heaving his bag on to his shoulder, he bent towards her at the window. "It's been nice meeting you. 'Bye!"

I went with him on to the platform. Above us, rooks whirled in ragged circles, their raucous cries caught and tossed by the wind. "I don't like to ask you to write to me, even once," I began, "But will you?"

He put down his bag and twined his arms round my waist. "I'll write and 'phone!" His eyes went to my mouth. "It's turned out all right, hasn't it?"

Did he mean the snag in our relationship, or Martha's visit? "Yes." I released a hand from its glove and ran a finger lightly across his lips. "Will you 'phone me tonight to say you've arrived safely?"

A sharp north wind was blowing. He stroked away a strand of hair which crossed my face. "Let anyone try and stop me!" We rocked each other a moment, then he added, "Just think, in four months' time I'll have left school and we won't have to worry any more about keeping up a pretence. In Oxford, when you come and see me – you will come? – we can walk hand-in-hand and lie close on the grass. Professors, readers, lecturers, provosts and deans bugger awf!"

A distant roar warned us of the train's approach and the ground beneath us juddered. The rooks widened their circle and rose on the wind. Alex and I hugged fiercely. Then the train thundered in.

He boarded. A fat woman with several bags stood by the window, obliterating him from view. He passed down the train, I following along the platform, to the next carriage. There he opened the window and leaned out.

"At Dons next, in two weeks time!" he called as the train began to move.

My voice would not function. I nodded and smiled and my eyes blurred. That would never do. "Safe journey!" I cried and the train pulled away.

"Thanks for everything!" He waved till the last moment and I was left standing horribly alone. Even the rooks had gone.

I returned to Martha and sat for a few moments composing myself.

Gently she said, "You really care, don't you?"

"Too much."

# CHAPTER XXX

*sume animos (R.A.518)*
*"play hard to get"*

The third years were on a high, presumably because it was Trinity term, they were glad to be back (though they would not admit it) and because they were intelligent. We had just finished Cocles defending the bridge, a simplified version of Livy's story.

I picked on a lad called Goodhusband, a russet child with fascinating green-gold eyes and a nose as I imagined Puck's might be. "Tell us this story in your own words, Goodhubby." (He had asked me to address him as his peers did.)

A flush clashed with his natural colouring, and glowing like a copper pot he began, "Horatius Cocles is facing the Sabines."

"Etruscans."

"Etruscans, then. They are advancing at one end of the bridge while he and the Romans block their way at the other. They are outnumbered by the enemy, but telling his friends to shield him, he begins to back along the bridge. Then, just as it is on the point of collapsing, he prays to Father Tiber, jumps into the water and swims safely to his friends' side."

I nodded approvingly. "I couldn't have told it better. Now, in the few seconds we have left, suggest to me what is heroic in this tale."

They had forgotten my rule about not calling out. I heard: "He's brave!" "He's Roman, of course!" "He's prepared to die for his friends!" "Patriotic!" "He's quick-thinking." "Cool!"

I covered my ears. "Gentlemen, please!" And they sank in their seats in mock contrition. "You're far too noisy. I'll teach you some listening skills, and that's a threat!"

They perked up. "Listening skills, Mrs. Farthing?"

"Next lesson. Now here's your prep."

It had struck me some time before how people were fast losing the art of listening. There was no silence any more. At home were shouting, music, television, computer games; in cars the radio or cassettes played at full blast; in shops you bought as you tap-danced; in streets cars roared, 'planes whined, breaks screeched, people bellowed; in gardens children shrieked, dogs barked, lawn-mowers and strimmers chuntered. Even at night clocks ticked and cats hummed their hymn of hate.

In a spare moment I had devised a listening skills exercise which contained the following: 1. How do you listen? 2. What do you like to hear? 3. What don't you like to hear? 4. Demand silence, tell them: 'Write what you can hear NOW.' 5. What things are important to hear? 6. What happens if you don't hear important sounds? 7. Give them permission to talk. Teach them. 8. Class feedback. Ask: 'Did you hear what I just taught?' 9. Gag them. Repeat thing just taught. 10. Class feedback. 'What did you hear of my teaching?' 11. Finally, 'What has this exercise taught you?'

The next time I took the third years, I entered with an oddly-shaped plastic bag.

"What's in that bag, Mrs. Farthing?" they asked.

"A ferret."

They grinned and one lad said, "Ferrets go up your trouser-legs."

"Not if you tie the bottoms," observed another.

"Shall we tie our bottoms, Mrs. Farthing?"

I quelled them with a look and without more diversions of this nature put my exercise into action. I told them step-by-step what to do, then began, "Now, everyone, how do you listen?"

"With our ears."

"With our eyes, too."

"Some people with their mouths!"

That brought a laugh and I smiled. "Tell me, what do you like to hear?"

"End of school bell."

"My parents' voices."

"Hens."

"My dog."

"Waves."

"Pop music."

"Evans crunching sweets, because that means I'll get one too."

By the time I had reached point three – what did they not like to hear – the class was well into the exercise.

"The rising-bell."

"Teachers cross."

"Loud bangs."

"Whingeing sisters."

One boy referred to breaking wind and burping which caused a moment of ribald mirth, but I took that in my stride.

Next I asked for silence and told them to write down all the things they could hear at that time. I made a list, too: scratching pens, footsteps, the groundsmen on their tractors; a slammed door; throats clearing; a raised voice from the class next door; birdsong; a bee banging itself against the window; empty stomachs; and a 'plane.

This was shared with some glee, after which we passed on to noises it was important to hear and the consequences of ignoring them. But into the next part they entered with aplomb. I told them I was going to teach them the passive perfect, but they could talk to one another as I did so. Thereupon, I asked them to open their books at the relevant page. Some, out of habit, obeyed. Others ignored me. I proceeded to explain the principles of the passive perfect, speaking through their voices but never once raising my own. Most of them were in profile chatting animatedly to their neighbours. So, this was what it felt like to be out of control of a class.

After some moments, I called a halt. They paid attention, grinning. "Well, did any of you hear what I said?"

"No, Mrs. Farthing."

"Good." I lifted the plastic bag on to my desk.

"The ferret!" came a voice, but to their astonishment I began taking out long strips of material.

"Cripes! What are those for?"

"Bondage! Mrs. Farthing's been reading dirty magazines!"

"They're gags," I said, walking between the tables and dropping a remnant in front of each lad. "Will you now please gag yourselves, making sure your mouth is well covered."

Giggling, they proceeded to do so.

Some needed help, but I did not assist; had I, it might have got out that I was abusing boys. "No, Forrester, you must be able to breathe. Just your mouth!" Soon I faced a class of twenty boys, swathed and speechless. Their eyes, in relief, were curiously alive. "I'm going to repeat what I taught you five minutes ago about the passive perfect. Page forty-nine, everyone."

Almost verbatim I gave out the same information. They looked at their texts and listened, and watched me till I had finished. "Gags off!" I cried.

"Ugh! Mine's got spit on."

"Slobber-chops."

"Now, what have you heard about the passive perfect?"

They gave all the right answers, I praised them and we finished the class with an examination of what that little exercise had taught them.

In some curious way, the staffroom came to hear that very afternoon of what I had been doing. For Seneca oiled his way towards me as I examined a notice-board.

"You have a fertile imagination, Mrs. Farthing."

I glanced over my shoulder. "Really?"

"The Head Master's wife told me she saw you teaching a classful of gagged boys."

I hardly knew Mrs. Graff, but she had struck me as a bonny sparrow of a woman. "That's right," I said evenly, picking up the paper and making for a seat.

"May one enquire the object of the exercise?" pursued he, thrusting his hands in his pockets and standing square.

"Listening skills."

His glasses flashed in a strong burst of April sunshine. "Do you think the Spanish would listen to me if I adopted your idea?"

I liked the American way of expressing incomprehension or disbelief. "Excuse me?"

He gave a laugh. "I thought everyone knew. I'm going to Spain in the summer to research the plight of wolves."

Seneca and wolves seemed incongruous, but here was a side to the man which for once appeared genuine. From then on I softened a little towards him; he was often dull and at times ignorant. But like the rest of us he had his story.

For the fifth years upwards, exam fever was mounting. They would sit their first public examinations in May, and the hall was already being prepared with rows of single tables and chairs.

I could count Alex's remaining lessons now on the fingers of one hand. We continued as before, to all intents and purposes tutor and taught, and I found this easier to deal with than the wariness which had entered our relationship at Easter. Sometimes, he looked preoccupied, and I thought it was the onset of exams.

Towards the close of our penultimate lesson (it was the end of April, now) I asked, "What do the fifths and sixths do when their exams are over?"

He looked up. "Some go on work experience, but most of us go home till we return here for Prize Day."

I consulted my diary, a hollowness widening inside me; no more lessons with him would be a punishment. He was gradually loosening the bonds of first youth and moving, as he should, away. "Prize Day's on Wednesday the twelfth of July. Tell me the format, Alex."

He hooked an arm over the back of his chair. "In the morning we have prizes and an address. Then there's lunch for those whose parents can't come with picnics. In the afternoon, we hold sports events, and in the evening is the Sixth Form Ball. Will you dance with me?"

I gave a little laugh. "Would it be wise?"

His posture stiffened. "As wise as it would be to dance with Grundig or ... or the Marxist."

"Should we give anything away, ever?"

"Why are you always so controlled!"

I willed his eyes to meet mine as I said softly, "Not always!"

His tension eased. "Well, all right, not when we're alone. So, you won't dance with me?"

I looked away, my silence implying a negative. "What about your parents?" I continued. "Will they be over for Prize Day?"

"No. Their long leave begins later in the summer."

I said I was sorry. "Aunt and uncle, perhaps?"

He shook his head. "Too busy with the farm."

Of course he did not yet know, but I had awarded him the Senior Classics Prize; how much nicer for him if some member of his immediate family could have been there to see him collect it.

"One of the chaps in my form has set me up with his sister as dance partner. Do you mind? If you do, I'll get out of it."

I fixed a smile to my face. "Enjoy yourself! You see, how could we possible dance together when you're meant to escort her?"

He shrugged. "Like most girls she'll be going off every five minutes to powder her nose. We could slip in a dance then."

"She's never met you? There'll be no powder-room for her! She won't let you out of her sight."

He muttered one word, "Suffocation!" and said no more.

I changed the subject. "Where will you be between exam-end and Prize Day? London?"

"After a few nights at the flat I'll go to Wiltshire. July's a busy time on the farm. My uncle's asked if I'll help as usual. I said yes, and he's paying me, too."

I gave a smaller "Ah!" than usual and began putting together my papers. Since our minor conflict at Easter, I had not had the courage to ask whether Mrs. Medic had been around when he spent the rest of his holidays at the farm; and he had not mentioned her in his letters. I had no right over him; men and women everywhere were being thrust together, enjoying each other's bodies and then drifting apart. Opportunity meant much more than commitment. For Alex and me the chance, the place and the time had synchronised. They were now raggedly breaking at the seams.

Suddenly he had moved to the edge of his seat. "We need to talk and arrange things!" His voice was low and urgent. "Damn this purdah!"

But what was there to arrange? I had tutored, and fallen in love with, him. The tutoring was over, and there was work to be done now at falling out of love. I would rather have lost my tongue than say, "Alex, I'm leaving Dons when you do. I've got a post near Oxford, and a flat as well. Yes, let's arrange things!" This would delight him now, but later? How soon would his pleasure become pretence? We would end by changing one form of duplicity into another. To see him grow offhand would be more than I could bear.

Our eyes met. He had been watching and waiting all this time. Hurt sprang into his face again, and the urgency died.

"We have both so much to do over these next weeks," I began lamely. "You must concentrate on your exams."

He leapt to his feet. "Blast the exams! Don't you want to see me any more?"

"Yes! Please keep your voice down!"

He thrust both hands in his pockets and swung round at me. "Exeat weekend?"

"I have prospective parents to see."

"Half-term, then?"

"You need to revise for Greek Paper 2."

"Don't keep telling me what I need to do!"

I rose hushing him. I went to the door, opened and looked out. Only Nisbet sat at the bottom of my stairway, gazing up, his funny little puzzle-face wearing a look of astonishment. The kitchen was the most sound-proof place to finish what Alex and I had to say. I beckoned him in and closed the intervening door.

He stood apart, his fingers pulling at a thread. "I need to have you behind me to do well in my exams," he was saying. "Don't you realise? You've been behind me all this year. It's been wonderful. I've felt so supported. You don't know what it's like having both parents across the world, seeing them only occasionally, keeping in touch only by letter or 'phone. You've done so much for me!" He stared fiercely at the ground, flushed and agitated.

No, I had no idea. This revelation shamed me. Caught up in what he had done for me, I never paused to consider what I meant to him. I moved close and took him in my arms. He buried his face at my neck. His pulse was racing.

He could do without all this now. It was a tense time; so much depended on his exam grades. Quietly, I said, "Half-term it is." We stood embracing. "Alex –" I continued, as his heart-beat slowed, "– this probably isn't the right time, but I want you to know that I heard why you vanished at the Carol Service and – I'm so sorry."

His embrace tightened. "No, I'm sorry. I left you in the lurch. I wouldn't have done it now." He paused. "Who told you?"

"The Chaplain."

"Better coming from him than anyone else, I suppose."

I looked up at him. "But fancy their choosing the very carol your brother sang and you still in the school! Couldn't they have waited till next Christmas?"

He moved away with a shrug. "I told you, people's memories are short."

"When did you 'chicken out', and where did you go?"

From the window he said, "I was sitting at the back of the Chapel and near the aisle, since I was a reader. The moment those familiar chords began, I thought Christ, it's happening all over again. I lost my nerve and left, and cooled off in the grounds."

I wanted to go to him, yet I sensed a bubble of private space which it was not wise to invade. My next question was invasive anyway, and he could refuse to answer it. "You rarely speak of your mother, Alex. Don't you get on?"

He turned to me, his expression inscrutable. "There have been... communication problems."

I pursued my point. "Since your brother's tragedy?"

His eyes fell. "Since then."

"She doesn't hold you responsible!"

He seemed to struggle with loyalty to his mother and to the truth. "I think she feels I should have been travelling with Gavin. She doesn't realise that chaps don't sit with their younger brothers. But had I been with him, he might not have fallen out of the train. He was the youngest and her favourite, you see."

I didn't see. Parents shouldn't have favourites. Now I had little sympathy for Mrs. Forsyth; it appeared to me she had turned her back on her remaining son and daughter, and left it to her husband to be both mother and father. For Alex's sake, I said, "In that case she would take it badly."

Somewhere, it seemed a long way off, the school bell rang. I put out my hand to him, and he clasped it warmly.

☙ ❧

I had always prided myself on my strength and organisation skills. The latter, part of the professional's brief, did not fail me now, although everything in my life was slowly falling apart; but I was having problems with inner strength, and this had more to do with my role as a human being.

In the days that followed, I found myself going quite often to the school Chapel. Haste and regimentation stopped at its heavy oak door; the atmosphere within was serene. There I would reflect and sometimes pray; once I cried.

After lunch one day when the school was deep in public exams, I went there again. Sunshine poured through the stained glass window and cast port, sherry and green wine splashes on to the grey paving. I thought myself alone, but the Chaplain was going about his business.

Hearing my quiet step, he turned from tidying the hymn-books. "Mrs. Farthing! How nice to see you here!"

I advanced. "I'm not a complete pagan, Mr. O'Hare."

"I never thought you were." He tapped the side of his nose. "We men of God can sense a religious turn of mind, and despite all those *numina* you consort with, you're no heathen."

I passed slowly down the aisle, murmuring, "It's nice in here." When I returned to him, I asked if he remembered the problem with which I had come to him some time before.

"Yes, I do. I've often wondered how it ended but didn't like to ask."

"Let's say circumstances revealed the sender."

"And was it whom you suspected?"

"No."

"But the nastiness has stopped?"

"Yes, thank God."

He smiled. "Trust can take one a long way, Mrs. Farthing."

"I regret I was wanting there."

"Surely not! You believe in Some One, don't you? You don't just blunder through life from one day to the next?"

"Not often."

"There you are, then." He came a little closer and lowered his voice. "That other thing you mentioned – the question of affections. Has that resolved itself, too?"

He obviously referred to my involvement with Alex. Forcing a cheerfulness I said, "I think it will soon, and for his own good."

He nodded. "Sometimes one has no option but to follow a certain course. Well, I'll leave you with your thoughts." Straightening a hymn-book which was determined to act drunkenly, he left the Chapel.

The atmosphere was peaceful but my thoughts grew no happier. A great weariness came over me, and the idea of a change of scene far from the oughts and ought nots of everyday existence seemed very tempting. But I had shot myself in the foot; home was where Alex had been, where we had warmed, grown hot, and loved.

The Chapel failed me this time, and I came out more disturbed than when I went in.

I had invigilation to do, and I turned my steps to the Great Hall. With so many candidates sitting exams, three members of staff were needed at any one given time. We were allowed to do nothing save keep an eye on pupils, checking that they did not communicate with each other or cheat over their answers. Our task was periodically to walk up and down between the rows of desks, and hand out paper as necessary.

I took over from Bowtie on the dais. There were boys taking GCSE's and A levels. Among the latter sat Alex at work on French. I forced myself not to look his way too often; but just once I happened to glance up to find his eyes on me. We showed no special recognition, yet I thought that neither of us felt bruised by the other's apparent lack of response.

Above me in the arched window outside, a collared dove wheezed its reedy note. Nearer, someone dropped a pencil. Beyond the Hall, a swell of voices approached only to be hushed by another. In front of me, a boy sneezed three times; I had read in the paper that the pollen count was climbing.

The hush, the down-bent heads, the shiftings and sniffs and despairing sighs soothed my ruffled spirit. A weekend with Martha and my usual dance class in London was a bright prospect.

# CHAPTER XXXI

*nec causas aperi quare divortia malis (R.A.693)*
*"do not reveal why you choose to separate"*

Holding a post mortem on an examination is not a good idea, but Alex came to my school office ten days before half-term ostensibly to discuss the Latin paper he had just sat but, so I liked to believe, to see me.

I gave him a seat and left the door ajar; our conversation would not be private. "Well, Alex!" I began briskly. "Four done, two to go. Did you like the Latin prose?"

He had his question paper and placed it on the desk at an angle so that we could both look at it. "It wasn't too daunting. Is that a bad sign?"

I smiled. "Not necessarily. Do you want to tell me what you did?"

The piece for translation into Latin had a good story line: it was about a school-master who during the Roman siege took his aristocratic young pupils ever further from home, intending to hand them over to Camillus, the Roman commander. His action, however, rebounded on him for, disliking his treacherous methods, Camillus gave the boys some rods and bade them whip their master all the way back. The art of Latin prose is to link as many actions together using accurate idiom and a variety of syntax, and to make people, rather than abstract ideas, carry the action.

Alex told me what links he had made and the grammar he had used. "But I could not for the life of me remember at first what a rod was," he added. "I kept thinking of the Greek βακτηρία. Then in a flash it came. It's *virga* isn't it?"

"Excellent! Now, remind me when your last exam is."

He drew from his inner pocket a small diary, the one I had been tempted to open in the Michaelmas Term when he had left his jacket in my rooms. It seemed longer ago than just six months. "Thursday, the twentieth of June."

"And that's when you leave for Wiltshire?"

"Well, London first for a few nights –", he looked at me significantly and I knew he was thinking of *Henny-Penny's*, "– then I'll be back here for Prize Day and the Ball on the fourteenth of July."

My eyes fell from his and I nodded. "I see from the staff notice-board that in the meanwhile we are invited to the Sixth Form house for tea?"

He put away his diary. "Yes. Next Thursday at four-thirty. Then on Friday it's half-term." With another meaningful look he leaned forward. His back was to the door and he whispered, "London, in the flat at seven?"

A figure had filled the doorway. It was Francis Marks. He seemed harassed. In my professional voice, I answered, "Exactly, Alex. Then it's half-term."

The Deputy came in. "Excuse me, Jessica. Hullo, Forsyth. How's things?"

Alex stood. "Hello, sir. All right, thanks."

"Good." He turned back to me. "Jessica, you haven't signed up for the Ball. We desperately need women partners. You are coming, aren't you?"

Alex and Francis gazed down at me reprovingly, Alex probably because he wanted to dance with me and couldn't, Francis because I had not signed by the deadline which had passed. Tickled by their expressions, I laughed. "I'll come and sign now!"

Alex slipped out and his firm footfall down the passage spoke his annoyance. Escorting me in the opposite direction, Francis complained,

"I feel like a collie-dog with a lot of erring sheep!"

The Chaplain rounded the corner. "That's my line, Deputy."

"No, no, Ryan, you're the pastor. You just whistle and wave your crook. I do the running."

❧ ❧

I was driving to London after the Sixth Form tea. They had done it well, assiduously handing round plates of salmon-and-cucumber sandwiches, madeira cake and chocolate squares. It was a formal 'good-bye' to the Upper Sixth, many of whom had started at Dons aged eleven and now, as young men, were leaving to shake the world. It must have been a wrench for those members of staff who had cajoled, bullied, wooed and thrust them through numerous school and public exams.

Now, as I was driving on the approach road to London and Alex, streams of cars were making their exodus from the city. It was Whitsun weekend and the evening was fine. Dons had four days of half-term, after which it was a downward gallop to the summer holidays.

It had gone seven when I entered Park Mansions, and I had barely released the Forsyth bell when Alex opened the door of the flat.

"Virginia and creep Jasper are here!" he said in a low voice. "And she told me she wouldn't be!"

I thought quickly. "How long will it take you to pack the essentials?"

His face lightened. "Three minutes flat!"

"Does she know I'm coming?"

"Alexander?" His sister's rather sleepy voice came from the room beyond. "Who is it?"

Calling, "A neighbour," he stepped into the corridor, drawing the door to behind him. "No, she doesn't."

"Tell her you've come up with other arrangements. I'll wait for you in the foyer downstairs." As I returned to the lift, I could have rapped the knuckles of all the pestilential Virginias of this world who said one thing then did another.

Alex joined me downstairs with a small bag. "I told her two's company but three's a crowd. She went on chewing her gum and said she got there first. Girls! They're all the same. Where are we going?"

We left the building while I told him of a small hotel in Bloomsbury, not far from Russell Square, where I sometimes used to stay during my graduate studies. "And I'll pay for us," was my conclusion.

There now began a good-humoured argument about why I, not Alex, should foot the bill, and we were still debating the point when we approached the hotel in question. The management had given it a new cream wash, painted glossy black its railings and filled the window-boxes with cinerarias.

"Nice!" commented Alex as I parked the car.

There was only one twin-room available on the top floor, and it was clean and comfortable. Turning to me, Alex caught my hands.

"I'm sorry about the change of plan, Jessica, but I really couldn't see all four of us in the flat. That bear, Jasper!"

"We'll do very well here." I returned his clasp reassuringly. "I'm getting peckish despite the Sixth Form tea. Who made the sandwiches?"

"The school kitchen."

"And the madeira cake?"

"The school kitchen."

"The chocolate squares?"

We chorused, "'The school kitchen'!"

I gave him a playful thumb-screw. "It's time cookery were placed on the school curriculum."

Over dinner we intended making plans for the next few days. In fact, we spoke very little, catching the romantic mood of the candles on the table and a blackbird singing wistfully outside. It was silent companionship which Alex and I shared that evening, communicated by look, hand-touch and his legs pressed against mine under a capacious tablecloth.

Even our drive back to the hotel was quiet. In the lift up to our floor he came close, placing his palms against the wall on each side of me. When the lift stopped, we lurched out in mid-embrace like virgin honeymooners who cannot wait for consummation. With one hand, he unlocked our door and we waltzed inside. Beneath the open window a taxi purred by. Alex nudged the door shut with his foot. We leaned against the wall.

"So many nights at school I lie awake thinking of you," he whispered. "It's like having hornets all over me."

My fingers began unbuttoning his shirt.

"Once, I couldn't stand it any more," he continued. "I got up – it was two in the morning – and walked the length of the school till I came to your door. I almost went in, but sat on the top step instead, sweating."

My lips found the warm skin of his breast. What he had confessed was immensely gratifying. So, I gave away my secret about trying on his jacket and exploring the pockets. He kissed me then, fit to draw the soul out.

At last he said, "Do you have any fantasies?"

I thought a moment. "I've told you one, and we acted on it! But no, perhaps not so many as other people... I do like a man in dark trousers with a buckle-belt, bare-chested and barefoot."

He began slowly to remove his shirt. "Is this man any particular build?"

"Tallish, muscular, no spare fat."

"Age?"

"Youngish."

"Bearded or clean-shaven?"

"Definitely clean-shaven."

"Light or dark hair?"

"Dark."

He slipped off his shoes and socks.

I protested, "The floor..!"

"Hang the floor!" He stepped back in the gloom. "Do I approximate your fantasy?"

On a sigh, I said, "Each time."

Still he held back. "Before you met me, did you have a different sort of man in mind?"

I wanted to fill my arms with him, but restrained myself. "A man with brains, a sense of humour – and clean fingernails."

He paused. "Is there a connection between brains and fingernails I've missed?"

Neither of us seemed eager to turn on the lights. I went up to him, and walked slowly round, drawing my index finger across his shoulder-blades and down his right arm. He drew in a protracted breath of pleasure.

I disregarded it. "Is there a connection between brains and fingernails," I repeated. "No... not that I can think of." I turned away, fully aware that I was teasing him mentally and sexually. I stooped between the beds to turn on a lamp, but he caught hold of me and the light remained unlit.

When later we lay together, he asleep and enjoying the repose of satisfied youth, I listened to the dull roar of a London night. And I asked myself what love was. The same question had been put to several drinking guests in Plato's *Symposium*, one of whom claimed it was a heightened sense of honour and self-sacrifice. By contrast, the comic poet, Aristophanes, also at the symposium, suggested human beings had been cleaved in half and that they spent their lives pursuing their lost half in order to make the whole; but in their division, their private parts remained on the outer side of their bodies which, for reproductive purposes, ensured more of a miss than a hit, and resulted in propagation via the ground 'in the manner of crickets'. I paused at this point, surprised and not a little dismayed that the Greeks, over two thousand years ago, knew more about the courting procedure of the cicada than did I.

I was at that stage when sleep is not far off and before which I had started on a coherent line of thought; but now that thought was trailing like the wispy wake of jet-stream. So, I fell asleep, my question unanswered, save that in a dream I was trying to get under Socrates' cloak as he lay, among the potsherds and wine-leas, telling me what love was; and in front of us his lover, Alcibiades, jumped up and down shouting petulantly: That's not love! That's not love!

❧ ❧

"If I give you a Greek and Latin unseen to do this afternoon, it will help you revise and salve my conscience."

We were at breakfast in the hotel restaurant which looked out on to a garden full of roses. Alex gave me an old-fashioned glance. "Why? Are you going shopping?"

I smiled. "No."

He helped himself to some more marmalade and I looked at our fellow guests. They were remarkably interested in us which irritated me: this modern obsession with categorising people! What label were they thrusting on Alex? And what was I? I thought of appearing in a *chador* next morning.

"Then is it Martha?" Alex wondered.

"She doesn't know I'm here."

"What, then?"

I leaned across the table. "For the last few months I've been going to modern dance classes on Saturday afternoons."

"Good for you! The unseens can wait. I'll come and watch."

"No!"

"Why not?"

"Because I will teach you Classics and share with you things of a delightfully intimate nature, but I will not have you watching my gyrations."

"You've been to *Henny-Penny's* and seen rather more than my gyrations."

"I left *Henny-Penny's* before I saw the 'more' – if you follow my drift. By the way, are you going there tonight?"

He finished his toast. "They'd like me to. But I'm not going to leave you if you want me."

"I always want you."

He widened his eyes. "In the bath?"

"I think of us that time in the shower."

"When you cook?"

"Of you weeping over onions."

"When you're talking with the Marxist?"

"'Comparisons and you are odious.'"

"Ha! After John Donne! I like him. But I much prefer you!"

"So, while you strip in Soho, I'll mark your unseens here."

He groaned. "This is Mrs. Farthing at her toughest. You're so brisk in the morning! Tomorrow we should order breakfast in bed, then I'll have The Other Woman longer."

"I thought you liked the strong, firm, controlled Mrs. Farthing."

"I do, I do! But not when she threatens me with Greek and Latin unseens when there are seen things I'd much prefer translating!"

I liked his innuendo and pressed his foot lightly with mine. "Do you know what I'm frightened of, Forsyth? I'm terrified that we'll get so immersed in each other that your exams are put on the back boiler. I will not be responsible for ruining your career prospects!"

He pushed back his chair and crossed his legs. "Then I'll become a full-time stripper at *Henny-Penny's*."

The word 'stripper' hit an unfortunate lull in general conversation. Faces turned our way. I glared back. Then a mobile phone bleeped, and the faces moved reprovingly in its direction.

"We'll compromise," I said at last. "If you do my unseens first, I'm happy for you to go to *Henny-Penny's* later."

"Done." He stretched out his hand and we shook on the deal like third formers.

I lent him my reader's pass which gave access to Senate House Library where he could work undisturbed. And just before we parted for the afternoon, he said casually, "It's very useful having a lover of one's Classics tutor. I'd recommend it to all sixth formers."

"Would you now! Why?"

He hitched his bag more firmly on to his shoulder. "I was looking over the Latin unseen you gave me while you were powdering your nose –"

"An unseen, Alex, is meant to remain an unseen till the moment it is seen and translated!"

He rubbed my arm. "I know, I know, Madam Control. Anyway, I saw the word *nugae*, and thought ah, yes, the plural of *nux*, meaning 'nut'. Then I thought, hold on, what the heck has 'nuts' got to do in the context of love, putting modern slang aside? And I remembered one intimate evening in Pomeroy when you talked about 'sweet nothings', which of course is *nugae*. So, I'll chuck out the 'nuts' and put in the other. See?"

We were momentarily separated by a twittering throng of Japanese girls with their goldfish-bowl faces. Over their heads I called, "I see!"

Each time Alex and I met and loved now, I believed it the last. That half-term, passing too quickly, was memorable for rather more than his air of cheerfulness. And I? I tried to be spirited, too; and since he never noticed the effort, it must have been a brave attempt.

We kept off talk of the future, both knowing from previous experience that there conflict lay. His was the optimism of youth; reality subdued me. And reality was staring me all too boldly in the face on our return to Dons. I would teach Alex no more. His only reason now for staying in school was to take his exams.

With the fifths upwards intent on GCSE's and A levels, and all other boys sitting school exams, I had more spare time. One day I went to Oxford to settle the question of accommodation and to revisit my new school. At Dons I catalogued all the Classics texts in the stock-cupboard, a task, apparently, which had not been tackled for years. Then there were trips to the Roman Villas at Bignor and Fishbourne for the lower school, with which Mr. O'Hare and his wife kindly agreed to help, since my departmental colleagues acted true to form even now and pleaded too much marking.

Spring gave way to summer. The cricket-ball hitting willow sounded regularly from the games field; swallows dived over chestnuts tiered with candle-flowers, and evening merged with night as a sylph glides into a depthless pool. Concerning my future I was philosophical. I had a good job to go to, a flat near Oxford and the knowledge that Alex would be somewhere among those dreaming spires. On the other hand, life was not all work. I was only thirty. He had given me almost one year during which I had been truly alive. When he left me – not consciously, you understand, but seductively drawn by the ploys of freedom – I would return to what I had always believed was the one route: the life of the mind. I would look into becoming an external student and work for a higher degree.

Meanwhile, Francis Marks was astonished at the way I was throwing myself into extra-curricular events. When I offered to help with team teas on Wednesday afternoons and to accompany the juniors on local rambles, he said,

"This is very generous of you, Jessica. Are you perhaps regretting your decision to leave us?"

"Not that I'm aware of." But I rather think I was.

It seemed that only senior staff and my immediate colleagues knew I was leaving. I had never entered into staff-room gossip, for gossip has the peculiarities of a frog: hop into the thick of it, and in due course it will rebound on you. Certainly the boys did not know I was leaving, and the diplomatic time to tell Alex had, I felt, come and gone. Now, intent on his exams, he could do without that kind of distraction.

I hardly saw him. But he would telephone me from outside the school, either during jogging sessions or when he went into Deme. Several boys in the upper school were looking strained; yet he sounded calm and centred, and during one conversation told me he wanted me to meet his parents when they came on leave in August.

With some anxiety I chewed on my thumb-nail. "How will you introduce me?"

His reply was prompt. "As my Classics tutor which, in the context of school, you are."

"Ah! And where will this introduction take place?"

"If it suits you, in London at the flat. My father will take to you no end. If I told him you and I were lovers, he wouldn't have a fit."

"Not so soon, Alex!"

He made an exasperated sound. "Why not? We are. And once I'm out of Dons I don't care who knows it." On my quotation that discretion was the better part of valour, he replied, "Youth is the time for indiscretions, and chaps of my age are expected to sow wild oats."

I was silent; unintentionally he had bruised me. And after his 'phone-call, I began to wonder if that was what I was becoming to him: 'an indiscretion' and a handful of 'wild oats'.

The school gradually emptied as we proceeded to the end of June. Having finished their exams, the fifths struck out on work experience, and the Upper Sixth also left save those whose parents lived abroad and Dons was to them both school and home. Alex sent me another bunch of flowers, ostensibly from 'Sandy', as a thank you for everything, then went to help out on his uncle's farm.

Martha visited Sussex for a few days, and stayed at the local inn in Deme. I teased her mercilessly, "Now own up, you haven't really come to see me, but to catch a glimpse of Alex!"

She laughed and blushed, and I knew I was right. "Nonsense! Though, if he is about, it might be rather nice to see him."

"He's in Wiltshire, so you'll have to make do with me."

"What's he doing there?"

I told her, then she eyed me severely. "You look palely loitering, Jess. I think you need a holiday. How are things with you-know-who?"

"Couldn't be better!"

We were sitting in the pub garden; it was six-thirty and not far away a group of colleagues had settled at a table to order a meal. Martha inclined her head towards them and me, and I nodded. "I thought so," she whispered, "They look like teachers!"

I didn't want to talk about Alex, and started a debate on what made teachers look as they did. But Martha had my well-being in mind, and soon lost interest in the physical shortcomings of educators. "Go to Italy, Jess. Stay in my flat in Rome. Eat pasta by the kilo, drink wine by the litre and flirt with a couple of men. Stay till you get bored, then come home when you're ready."

For a while I considered it. When I eventually replied, my comment sounded irrelevant. "Ovid – you've heard of him?"

"Isn't he the Latin poet who's supposed to have seen Augustus's daughter in the bath and was banished to the Black Sea?"

I smiled. "That's one of the hypotheses. Well, Ovid advises the young man who wants to fall out of love to immerse himself in the country."

"You aren't a young man, and the country you'd immerse yourself in is alive with Alex. Oh, really Jess!" She put her hand on my shoulder and gave me a little shake. "Go to the Italy of your beloved Romans. What's holding you back?"

What indeed?

She continued. "When's the earliest you can leave Dons?"

"The night of the Sixth Form Ball."

"Well, when it's in full swing, slip away. Come here for a few hours' sleep and take an early flight the next morning. Is there a local travel agent? Why don't we make enquiries tomorrow?"

Within twenty-four hours of that conversation I had booked on a 'plane for Rome.

# CHAPTER XXXII

*i procul (R.A.214)*
*"go away"*

Each class I taught that final week of term demanded Latin 'hangman'. It was a word-game, initially presented on the board by a series of dashes corresponding to the number of letters in the word the player had chosen. Every letter suggested by the class was either inserted into the dashes or, if inappropriate, formed the construction of the gallows and, eventually, the shape of a hanging man. It was played *ad nauseam* until I was so bored with dashes and swinging bodies, that I suggested mimes of events in the history of Rome which non-participating members had to identify. This went down well with the third years in particular, and they made of their tables an ambush known as the Caudine Forks. Then, in their excitement, they forgot the essence of mime and give out such blood-curdling battle-cries that Dr. Graff's head was seen looking in at the glass-paned door. Moments later, an *extempore* fire-drill called everyone to order, and the battle of the Caudine Forks remained unresolved.

As the boys grew in high spirits, so we staff slumped into exhaustion and might be seen sitting speechless, teacups in *rigor mortis* hands, as we gazed into the middle distance. "I hear you're leaving us, Jessica," began Archimedes. It was lunchtime two days before term-end.

I surfaced from a brown study and looked at him. He lay in an arm-chair, spectacles perched above his brows, his shabby feet stretched out in front of him.

"Yes, I am."

"She doesn't like us any more," put in childish Miss Johns.

I turned my attention to her. She was fastidiously picking with blood-red talons at a sugary cake. She had grown fat over the year and sat, her tree-trunk legs crossed, so that there was an expansive view of lardy thigh. "I like you all well enough!" I protested with some energy.

Archimedes held up a hand. "No need to justify your reasons. We'll miss you. I've always thought of you as a piece of Dresden china in a box full of seconds."

I laughed, and Miss Johns gave a slightly sour smile.

"Where are you going?" she asked.

"A girls' school near Oxford."

Archimedes sat up. "Not Whitemeads?"

"Yes."

"My niece goes there! She's in the lower fifth. So, Miss North's leaving? No bad thing. She gets scattier by the term."

Seneca had now drifted on his oil-slick into the room. "Who's getting scattier?"

I hid a groan. The man was verbal viscosity. I drank my coffee and rose.

"Don't pick up fag-ends, Cotton," cried Archimedes.

Seneca stood squarely in the room, hands in pockets and bent a little at the knees. "I always pick up fag-ends. No one ever tells me anything, so this is how I find out things. Mrs. Farthing, before you slip away, who was it who wrote *dulce et decorum est pro patria mori*? I keep thinking it was Cicero."

"No, Horace."

He jingled his money and dipped further at the knees. "You sure?"

"It would be a sad state of affairs if I wasn't."

"But what does it mean?" wailed Miss Johns, with a last suck at her sticky fingers. "I never did Latin at school."

In tandem, Archimedes and Seneca said, "'Sweet and fitting is it to die for one's country.'"

The door opened again. This time two of the Three Graces sauntered in. "Who's dying for their country?" asked Bowtie.

I could see it was going to be a picking-up-of-fag-ends conversation each time the door let in someone else, and I made my escape. I felt tense and, simultaneously, distracted. Prize Day was now only forty-eight hours off; Alex would receive his accolade with all the other winners, then Dr. Graff would make known the names of those staff who were leaving. I dreaded how Alex would react at the Ball. I really should have told him, face-to-face.

Reports had been written and checked. We collected text books and piled them high in the stock-cupboards. Book prizes were inscribed with the recipient's name and the subject in which he was being honoured. As well as the silver cup, Alex would receive Apuleius' *The Golden Ass*, a rollicking story about a man who has all kinds of adventures (some painful) in the guise of an ass, and how he communes at last with the Egyptian goddess, Isis.

Excitement burst in the school when maintenance staff were seen erecting an open-sided marquee on the lawn for tea after Prize-giving. Then the next day, local electricians set up strobe lights and amplifiers for the Ball, and the band dropped in for practice. I had a ballgown, a midnight-blue lamé sheath dress which fitted over one shoulder and arm, leaving the other bare. I had worn it only once at a function in London with Antony, and he had been unnecessarily irritated by the way everyone stared.

"I'm not altogether sure I would like a celebrity for a wife," he had grumbled as we slid over the floor in a (sort of) waltz. It was not the best compliment a man could give his wife and my rejoinder had been a trifle acerbic, "Never mind. A wife with a face like the back of a bus would have gained you no stares at all." Now, at Dons' Sixth Form Ball I would be neither the property nor the questionable enhancement of any man.

The staffroom had clubbed together to buy me, and two other leavers, presents. At break the day before we finally ended for the holidays, I was given a handsome crystal vase. A brief speech was obligatory.

"Thank you, everyone, you have been most generous." Here I paused to steady my voice, for it was an emotional moment after an emotional year. "When I arrived at Dons last September," I continued, bolder, "it was with the intention of staying rather longer than I have. But you know what they say: the best made plans of mice and – I must be politically correct here – and persons." That raised a laugh. "Some of you may like to believe that I am leaving to get married again. It's nothing so simple as that!" I smiled round at them all. "However, rather than bore you with my reasons, may I just say how supportive you have been. It's not easy for a woman to enter, and hold her own, in a mostly male environment. So I go with some fond memories and, I think, with a broader character than when I arrived."

This went down surprisingly well, and everybody's reaction looked sincere. It was ironic to discover that now I was leaving I had more colleagues in the true sense of the word than had been clear during the previous nine months.

One or two tricky moments followed in the final classes I conducted that day when some little boys with endearingly tousled backs of hair asked me what I was teaching them next term. Then a group of fourth years stood round me, a hand in one pocket as they were permitted to do, expressing hopes that I would take them in their fifth year. It struck me how my relationship with Alex was exposing me to myself: here was a woman full of imaginings and capable of moral cowardice. The decent thing with him would have been to say a long time ago, "Alex, I'm leaving Dons. I've taken a teaching post near Oxford. I'll be there for you at any time, but I will never intrude on your new life unless you invite me." And the decent thing would have been to tell these guileless lads, "I'm sorry, but I won't be here next term to teach you." Now that I was on the point of doing so, I did not want to leave Dons at all. The experience of loving Alex, as I had never loved another before, had enriched me just as the experience of anonymous letters – though terrible at the time – had given me a new kind of strength. My first year teaching in a boys' school had, despite the difficulties, proved a success. But Francis Marks was right: my heart did rule my head; and as Martha, too, once said, I should return to the women's room.

Too late I realised that if Alex grew out of me, as I felt he would once he entered dizzy university life, then my new post with its broken dreams would be worse than had I stayed at Dons nursing those that were sound.

That afternoon, the eve of Prize Day, the school was full to capacity; the fifth years were back from work experience and the Sixth had returned to carry out, among other things, obligatory duties. During his absence in Wiltshire, Alex had telephoned and written without fail. I wondered if he would search me out on his return, and I hung about in my school office tidying what could be no tidier. Some twenty minutes before the supper bell there came a knock at the door. Without looking up I called, "Come in!"

He stood in front of me. And he looked stunning. A few weeks labouring in the sun had turned his skin dark gold and it glowed against the dazzling white of his school shirt. His eyes, that arresting combination of hazel brown and blue, looked into mine in such a way that Sappho's reaction became my own: *'a subtle fire runs beneath my skin, my eyes go sightless and my ears are roaring...'*

"Have you seen a ghost or the spirit of Christmas Past?" he asked with some uncertainty.

A heavy flush spilled into my cheeks; I, ten years his senior, a professional woman, once married now widow, felt embarrassed before him. In a low voice, I said, "You strike me dumb."

He closed the door. "I'm the same Alex Forsyth, Mrs. Farthing – yesterday, today and tomorrow!" Our eyes met again. At that moment I would have done absolutely anything he asked me. I swallowed a dry swallowing. "Have a seat, Alex. How are you? You look fit!"

He sat in the chair obliquely to me and crossed his legs. We were visible through the glass-windowed door, but it hardly mattered now. "I feel fit. And you, are you well?"

I gave a little smile. "Yes, I am. My word, the sun must have been hot in Wiltshire!"

He opened and shut the flaps of his school blazer like a streamlined penguin. "It was shorts and nothing-else-weather. We were up at six and had done two hours work before breakfast. My uncle was reluctant to let me leave but I've assured him I'll be back in two days' time."

My eyes stroked him, then peeled off one layer of clothing after another to the bronzed warm skin beneath. "I suppose you're that colour all over?"

He grinned. "In the tractor I wore indecent shorts – apart from my masculinity and the soles of my feet, yes, I suppose I am."

I fidgeted with some papers, feeling hot, cold, frustrated and despairing by turns. "Mrs. Medic around?"

His teeth, white and even, showed. I think he liked it when I showed mild jealousy. "Oh, she left the area two months ago. She and her husband have gone to a quieter practice in Dorset. Things should work out for her now."

"I bet she went kicking!"

"Not at all. I've been a bit *noli me tangere* since Christmas – I wonder why?" His eyes caught mine, and I understood. "You know what I mean –, avoiding her like the plague, sleeping in the main house, clinging to the horses' bellies like Odysseus when she came to the stables sniffing me out."

I gave a low laugh of delight, comparing hairy Odysseus, stinking of brine and whey as he clung to the underparts of the Cyclops' sheep, with smooth Alex skulking beneath his aunt's horses.

Now he asked, "Mr. Marks behaving himself?"

Despite my denials, Alex still believed that the Deputy and I had had a penchant for each other. "The perfect gentleman!" I replied extravagantly.

"That's the problem. You go for the gentlemanly sort!"

"Not always. Once on holiday in Bavaria I fancied a Mancunian waiter who said bath with a short 'a' instead of our barth, and ruber instead of rubber."

Alex cocked his head. "How on earth did baths and rubbers enter your food orders?"

"You'd be surprised!"

"Hm. I want to hear more of this one day. Now, for the third time of asking, will you dance with me tonight? Please!"

I sat helpless. "It wouldn't be wise. Body language gives away so much. If I'm close to you pulsating suntan and throbbing tractors I might forget myself completely."

He chewed on his lower lip. "Then can we meet tonight? I'm starved of you! The heat is on my flesh like nettle-sting!"

"That's sunburn."

"God, you're cynical!" He sat back with a gesture of despair.

I changed the subject. "Have you met your dancing partner for tonight? Is she pretty?"

He gave a shrug and pulled at his tie so that it lay askew. "Grundig – it's his sister – showed me a photo of her. She's passable but looks thick, and I hate thick girls!"

Softly, I said, "She'll fall for you hook, line and sinker."

"Really? Well, I'm not up for grabs, as they say." He leaned forward again. "Look, it'll be difficult to talk together after this, so can we confirm our time together in the holidays?"

He told me he would be working with his uncle till the end of July. Then, for three weeks in August his parents were due in London on leave. After that, he had been invited back to Wiltshire till he went up to Oxford in October; could he and I have a fortnight together before I returned to Dons?

Here was another opportunity to tell him the truth. I let it pass. I 'chickened out', and for reasons just as valid (in my view) as those which had made him avoid the Carol Service. It would probably offend him deeply to hear the news like an ordinary member of the school next day. But while I was too weak to tell him there and then, I had the strength to risk the consequences.

☙ ❧

That evening I packed. Nisbet must have smelled a rat because he scratched at my door till I let him in. Casting the odd look at me over his chewed-into shoulder, he stalked about my rooms, sniffing my case and thrusting his nose fastidiously at the wastepaper basket till he finally leaped on to the windowsill. There he sat, haunches surrounded by his tail, dabbing half-heartedly at a gnat absailing down the pane.

My guilt extended even to him. "I'm sorry!" I said repeatedly. He merely glanced at me then returned to his chastisement.

At dusk I went out for a walk. The oaks, green giants, loomed above me as I paced quietly down the drive. Bats squeaked high and thinly as they spooled their threads of flight. D.H.Lawrence had described batwings as *'bits of umbrella'*. Where in the school did they hang *'disgustingly upside down'*?

Behind me the clock-tower chimed ten. The lights of a car arched in through the gates ahead and I slunk round a tree trunk out of sight. It passed, loud with thumping music; one of the Sixth Form perhaps.

Outside the gates I crossed the road and found the footpath where all those months ago Alex had jogged past me. It had been autumn then, and we were nothing to each other. In the field to my left cows shifted heavily through the grass. One coughed a human cough; another urinated profusely. I moved on towards the river beside which not many days before the third years and I had rambled. We came across an opening in the bank which led to a miniature beach, and because it was hot the boys had tossed off their shoes and socks, pulled up their trouser legs and waded in.

"Mrs. Farthing! It's deep enough to swim!" they cried. "Can we skinny-dip?"

I said, "Of course not!" But they had been only teasing, and threw me louche backward looks.

Now, at dusk, the air was like a stuffy cupboard. As my calves ached from too much standing, I followed the boys' example and bared my legs and feet. Feeling the occasional stone with my toes and recoiling as sludge oozed between, I waded in. How different were these rivers from those in Cumbria; up north they had *loquaces lymphae* – 'chattering waters', to quote Horace; here they flowed deep, silent, somnolent.

"Jessica!"

I jumped as my name was stage-whispered behind, and turned to see a figure approach through the gloom. "Alex! How...?"

He stood on the bank. "Grundig was driving back from Deme. He said he thought it was you."

I went up the little beach, anxious that at the eleventh hour they might all suspect. "Do they know you've followed me?"

With a spring he was at my side. "No. Anyway, there's such a coming-and-going in the Sixth Form house that no one can keep tabs on anyone else." He grasped me by the shoulders. "You shouldn't be down here alone!" The urgency sank from his voice, "But since you are ..."

We had not kissed for weeks. Eventually, I let him go, and he asked if the water were cold.

"Gloriously!"

"Well, I'm hot. Feel me!" Pulling up his T-shirt, for like every pupil he wore home clothes after six, he placed my palms against his torso. He radiated heat.

With both hands, I began to explore his breast. "Solar panels!"

He laughed against my throat. "We've never swum naked. Let's do it now!"

Dons could hardly sack me at this late stage, and I doubted there would be a search party so early in the night. We began to undress each other, not the rabid clothes-tearing that many give in to, but a slow methodical disrobing which because of its deliberate nature is all the more sensual.

After much nudging and many pleasurable sighs, we stood together naked. Then, in one firm movement, he lifted me and eased into the water. When he stood waist deep, he lowered me bit by bit: feet, ankles, calves, knees, thighs, groin... As the coolth travelled like shock waves beyond my navel, I gripped him in spasms.

He laughed low and long. "Mrs. Farthing, you're so sexy!"

I drew my knees up round his thighs. "Words fail me what you are, Forsyth!"

He dried me with his T-shirt as an elder brother would dry a sibling.

"Is the nettle-sting better now?" I asked, running my fingers up his spine as he bent over his task.

He straightened, tossing the wet hair from his eyes. "Much! ... Are there any secluded bathing areas round the River Eden in Pomeroy?"

"At night, plenty!"

"Good." And he returned to his drying.

When we were both dressed, I touched the hair at the nape of his neck. "How will you explain this?"

"Easy. I've just come from the shower!"

We strolled through the muggy dark the way we had separately come. At the road, he insisted I went up the drive first, and we parted with no more than a hand-clasp.

☙ ❧

Sports events began at eleven o'clock the following morning. It was a typical English summer's day with clouds like mushrooms and deep skies in between. The sultriness of the previous night had gone, for a breeze – at times quite stiff – blew from the north-west. Somewhere on the games field Alex was competing, but as he had said he preferred me not to watch, I hung around the junior events and talked to parents.

By one, the sports were over. Mothers opened hampers and families sat between car doors, fighting gusts of wind and the nosy wasp. For staff and boys without guests there was a special lunch, and then we flapped into our gowns.

Prize-giving began at two. The Great Hall was packed; more than five hundred boys sat on one side; parents, friends and governors on the other. Staff, resplendent in gown and hood, would have the stage. The Hall had been so built that two wide doors opened at its left and right; and as the school clock chimed two, we members of staff entered by both doors, snaked our way up the side aisles, mounted the stage steps and came together in a semi-circle. In front of us were seats for Dr.Graff and the visiting speaker, and a huge table bearing prizes.

The entire Hall stood in silence, save for the obligatory cough and throat-clearing, as the Head Master, his Deputy and Sir Bertram Wolford, our guest speaker, took their places near the trophies. At a sign from Francis Marks we all sat, save Dr. Graff who paced to the lectern.

"Ladies, gentlemen and members of the school," he began. "Here we are at the end of yet another academic year." He spoke of new building developments, of special achievements among particular departments and the proposal, now fully ratified, of opening the Sixth Form to girls, and he mentioned old boys whose talents had brought them to public notice. Then he wound up his address with a reference to prize-giving itself. "It is time once again to recognise those boys whose abilities have been outstanding and who have set high standards for others to follow. But before they are commended, a word of comfort to those who do not receive awards this year: often the striving is more character-forming that the accolade." Some pompous hear-hear's sounded among the guests, after which Dr. Graff added, "And to those who are receiving prizes, may I remind you of the Roman practice to keep the triumphant general on an earthly plane: a slave stood with him in his chariot, saying, 'Remember, you are only a man!'" Everyone laughed, and when the humour had subsided he turned to Sir Bertram Wolford, and gave him a formal welcome.

Sir Bertram had been a boy at Dons many years before and, so he told us, had won no prizes at all. He left to study at the University of London where he surprised everyone by gaining a first in politics and economics. "After that," he explained, "I went on to build an empire based quite simply on packaging." Now he proceeded to entertain us with the forms of packaging with which we were all familiar: the box of sardines which would not open, the packet of cheese which neither tooth nor nail could puncture, the bottle of oil whose top, after numerous serrations with scissors, knife and opener tore the skin so viciously that eventually if poured both blood and rapeseed. His peroration was short and pithy, "So, boys, whatever you do in life, it is sometimes best to keep it simple – I did!"

A round of applause followed as he took his place near the table, where Dr. Graff and the Deputy prepared respectively to announce and hand him each prize. Dons had a reputation for academic excellence, particularly in languages. English awards were given first, followed by Classics, then modern languages. The junior

Classics prize went to a little lad in the second year about whom the Three Graces and I had agreed unanimously. As head of Department, I made the final decision on whom to confer the senior Classics prize, and while Alex strode up the steps and across the stage to receive his award, the boys' response showed how popular he was. But that was not the only accolade he gained; he came up again to take the senior Athletics Cup.

Archimedes, who sat on my left, leaned towards me during the applause. "An all-rounder, that one!" he exclaimed over the noise. "He wasn't bad at science either!"

Gradually the table was cleared of trophies, and when it stood white and bare it looked like some puritanical altar. The rite of prize-giving was over. Now my malaise began. The Head Boy give Sir Bertram a vote of thanks, then Dr. Graff took his place at the lectern for the final announcement.

"Ladies, gentlemen and members of the school. Before I invite you all to take tea, I must end on a sad note for us as a school and, I hope, a little sad for those members of staff who are leaving. Mr. John Ridgway, head of Geography for six years, has decided to go part-time at a school nearer home. Dr. Bill Creddle, head of History for a decade, is taking early retirement. And Mrs. Jessica Farthing, head of Classics for one outstanding year, is taking up a post near Oxford."

Did I hear a concerted gasp from the boys? I looked down, feeling nauseous, and Dr. Graff concluded,

"Could we all show our deep appreciation for what these dedicated teachers have done for us while at Dons." He turned towards our semi-circle and led a tremendous round of applause.

Taped pieces of light music were played as we staff made our exit via the stage doors. Boys and parents trailed through the side exits into the sunshine. There were so many of us that tea was divided between dining-room and marquee. I felt too apprehensive about Alex to want any, but Francis attached himself to me and we strolled towards the tent.

"So, Jessica, the die is cast!"

Entering the marquee, I said. "No going back now!" Cautiously, I looked about me. Members of the Sixth had been allocated in school and out to hand round plates of food. Some were in the marquee already, going from one knot of guests to another. Francis edged his way to the table where local lasses in black were pouring cups of tea. He took two, and passed me one saying, "We'll have to circulate in a moment, but before we do, can I meet you in the front hall at eight and escort you to the Ball?"

I managed a smile. "Thank you, I'd like that."

Meanwhile, he ate while I sipped and when after ten minutes Alex had still not made an appearance I assumed his duties were inside. My tension eased slightly, the nausea subsided but a headache took its place.

Now boys and parents were coming up to me, the more uninhibited crying, "Mrs. Farthing, I didn't know you were leaving!" I was obliged to offer some sort of explanation, and since I was getting rather good at dodging the truth and infinitely better over deceiving myself, I said an aged parent needed me closer to home. After about an hour of all this, I felt enough was enough and began edging my way out of the marquee to find peace in my own quarters. And always, always I was looking out for Alex.

In my rooms I finished packing and took a bath, then from the east window watched boys leave for the summer holidays. Car after car rolled up to the front door. Caught up in the bosom of their families, the juniors laughed, older ones swaggered. Prefects and housemasters called, advised and directed. Approaching the youngest with good wishes, matron and her assistants in white bent and straightened like four doves. Doors banged, engines revved, and having swallowed lads and luggage, cars large, small, high, low-slung, retreated down the drive. And my apprehension over Alex grew.

I might never see him again. He might be so offended that he avoided me as he had avoided Mrs. Medic though she, poor woman, had done nothing to deserve it. And he would leave me like a piece of script on a computer page which, because the ink has run out, tails off unfinished...

Immersed in these dejected thoughts I hear running footsteps approach my stairway. Someone's in a hurry, takes them two at a time. There's a pause – for breath? Next comes an urgent knocking. I remain still. Alex – for I know it is he – knocks again. A hiatus, filled with an anguished groan. Now a board creaks as he shifts weight. Silence. Then sounds of tearing, and a slip of paper tongues its way under my door. Taking the stairs, this time one by one, the steps slowly recede.

I pounce on the note. He has torn out a cheque and used the back to write: *Why didn't you tell me? Where are you going in Oxford? I don't understand. AF.*

What was the point of protracting it all? I thought of going at once. But my colleagues wanted to toast us leavers, and Francis was set on meeting me in the front hall at eight. To sneak off would have been the easy way out – yet what a back-door way to go.

There was a certain brilliance in my look that night; increased blood pressure has its moments. At seven-thirty, I heard the band start up, and just before eight I made my way to the front hall. Francis, in formal dress, was waiting as I came down the stairs.

He gazed up at me in open admiration. "Jessica, you are superb!" Holding out his hand unnecessarily, he eased my final descent.

I smelled alcohol on his breath. "Thank you, Francis. And you look debonair!"

"Hungry?" he asked, opening the door to the passage. "You had nothing at tea, bad girl!"

"What will there be? A buffet?"

"*Par excellence*, excuse my rotten French. The caterers do us proud. My word, I'm a happy man tonight!" He had put an arm behind me and was ushering me into the Great Hall, miraculously changed to an expansive dance-floor. On the stage sat and played the band. At the far end was the white-clothed table again, this time solid with refreshments, and beside it tables and chairs. Beyond the open doors, hung Chinese lanterns among the trees, and still more tables and seats offered an invitation.

Couples were already on the dance-floor. All the men, including the Sixth Form, were in dinner jackets. The women wore evening gowns or short dresses. A quickstep engaged them, some not successfully, and the mood was lively. I dared not look for Alex.

"Would you like a drink, Jessica?" Francis was asking as he put his hand under my elbow to guide me through the crowd. "Shall we see what there is?"

As my head still ached, I had an innocuous shandy; and soon all the staff had gravitated to our side of the room and the toasting began. It was done according to length of service, so the other two leavers were wished well first. Then it was my turn: "To Jessica!" they all cried. Up went their drink hands and down went the toast.

Pulling at her skirt which kept wrinkling round her fat thighs, Miss Johns yapped at us to go to the table. "While the Sixth are still busy!" she added over the music which had increased in tempo. I looked round at the dance-floor; scores of young men and women were wriggling, twitching, scuffing to the beat. I wished I could see Alex and his girl.

Kindly, Francis took Miss Johns under one arm and me under the other and we approached the buffet. Greed got the better of Miss Johns' manners, for she soon outstripped us in the indiscriminate ladlings she heaped on to her plate.

Smiling indulgently, Francis meanwhile continued, "A little rice, Jessica? And what about some tomato salad and salmon?"

Slowly we made our way down the table, I holding my plate while he dabbed on portions of this and that. There was something for every taste, from gross carnivores to pernickety vegetarians. More people joined us and soon the entire table was surrounded like a trough by squealing girls, shaking their hair over the food, and merry youths with spoons.

Francis, increasingly pedantic, fiddled with lettuce leaves and slippery olives. And as I watched, a hand I knew very well, bronzed and finely-shaped, was stretching across from the opposite side of the table and deftly skewered a sausage. My eyes flew up. I was face-to-face with Alex.

He wore a set expression.

"Jessica," Francis was saying, "Would you like a vol-au-vent?"

I grew agitated. "Yes, no, perhaps yes!"

Then Alex spoke, his voice tight. "Abigail, would you like a vol-au-vent?"

She would be an Abigail! What right-minded parents would call their daughter *'Serving-maid'* if they knew it was used in the context of *'any that pisseth against the wall'*. This Abigail was clearly besotted with Alex already; she hung possessively on his arm which held her plate. And, like so many eighteen-year-old girls out to party, she was skimpily clad, her bare round arms dark with a bloom of hair and wrists ajingle with bangles. Upstart breasts, uncorsetted beneath their bodice, quivered at every disjointed movement she made. About her shoulders the brown hair shone like a shield with silicon dressing. She had the blubbery look of young unrefined womanhood and the lips, half open and slightly damp, that might shriek with laughter or wail at a whim.

Yet she read between Alex and me something which no one else noticed. Was it in the way our eyes met and held for that searching moment? Or could it have been in his forceful impaling of the sausage? Or in the way he asked her, immediately after Francis had put it to me, whether she wanted a vol-au-vent?

For, as the Deputy gently ushered me down the table, she cried in a peevish tone, "Who is that?"

To which Alex answered tersely, "Mrs. Farthing, departing head of Classics." He leaned on the word 'departing'.

Miserably, I declined any more food which Francis, in blissful ignorance, pressed upon me.

The band was now too loud for conversation, so we moved to a table beneath the trees. Sixth Formers and their girls, staff and their partners came and went, cradling drinks or brandishing platters. Everyone looked at me, men indulgent, women with a toss of the head. Of Alex and Abigail I saw nothing.

Francis and I talked about school, our holidays and plans for the intake of girls. He became a little stuttery although he was making his drink last, and when we finished the first course, he said,

"I want you to know I s..still think you and I would make an excellent team here, that if your new post doesn't turn out you only have to tell me. There may not be vacant the same job you've held this year, but one of the three existing members of your department is bound to move on s..soon." He looked at me like a retriever begging for a titbit. "Will you always remember that?"

"Thank you, Francis, I shall – though I rather hope this new post will work out."

"So do I, of course I do! But you never know." The titbit denied, he metaphorically shook himself. "Now, can I fetch you a pudding? There's raspberries and cream, meringues and a lemon gateau. Why not s..stay here while I get it?"

I chose the raspberries, and as he went inside I mused on how cunningly he had arranged to be my evening escort. But we were all cunning in our separate ways and for different reasons – he to claim me for the Ball, I to avoid telling Alex of my plans.

Near me, a fumbling moth zoomed up and down the lantern-side, desperate for the light; I turned to look at it. It shivered and vibrated with energy, the frippery patter of its silken wings whirring frantically.

"Have you seen my note?"

On an explosion of alarm, I straightened. Alex leaned on the back of Francis' chair, his knuckles white.

"Alex! Yes, I did. Are you enjoying..."

"Why did you never tell me?" His voice was low and tense. "There was ample time, even last night. Am I, after all, just another member of the –"

"Forsyth!"

He turned irritably in mid-sentence.

Francis was stepping out of the Great Hall, a bowl of raspberries in both hands. "There's a young lady in here looking high and low for you."

Alex made an exasperated sound as Deputy and Abigail came towards him.

She dodged round Francis and laid proprietorial hands on Alex's arm. "I thought you'd ditched me!" she cried, stroking with stubby little fingers the sleeve of his dinner-jacket. "Let's dance!"

Francis had reached the table and was saying, "One raspberries and cream for you, Jessica dear, and because they looked s..so nice, one for me as well." Intent on setting them down, he probably missed Abigail's words as she shunted Alex off,

"What is it between you two?"

I heard no reply.

Inside the Hall the tempo quickened to a disco beat. Francis and I ate our pudding in silence. I wondered whether Alex would clear the floor with his dancing. For a while I fidgeted, the energy fizzling inside me. Desperate to see, I could bear it no longer. I rose. "Would you excuse me a moment, Francis?"

He raised himself from his chair. "Of course."

It was now half-past-nine. The lighting inside had been dimmed and strobe lights flashed their neon shades over the dance-floor. I made for the drinks-table and asked the waiter for a mineral water. Then I raked the dancers for Alex. Half way down the room he and Abigail were moving, but his gyrations were what might be termed 'low gear'. He was no exhibitionist (unless paid to be so), and his hip movements were, at that moment, restrained. But each thrust he made was spot on the beat, and occasionally he could not help executing a jazz turn which delighted all those around him. Fumbling, I took my drink. I longed to get in on that circle, to dance just once with him, to show him that the tension had quite gone from my movements, that I could thrust my hips and isolate my pelvis like any rhythmic dancer.

Francis rose stiffly from his chair as I returned to him. "I th...thought Tarzan had got to you!"

I sat down. "Tarzan?"

"Forsyth, then."

"Ah!" and I gave a mirthless laugh.

He jerked his head at the beat which thumped out through the doors. "Not my kind of music at all. I leave that to the young!"

But it was mine. Even as I listened to it, my blood began to race, my pulses throb. I knew with a strange atavistic knowing how to move to it. The thought of sitting the night out in Francis' heavy company depressed me so much that I looked at my watch pointedly. "Good heavens, it's that time already!"

He gave me a benevolent look. "And what time might that be?"

I was inaccurate. "Ten o'clock! I'll have to be leaving."

A dogged expression slipped over his face. "Why?"

"I'm due in London by midnight."

"This goes on till dawn. I'll get you s..some breakfast later. Meanwhile, I like sitting with you."

*Sitting?* Who wants to sit, when the Forsyth Tarzan is swinging on musical lianas, the life and soul of dance!

Francis must have seen the vibrance in me, for he began to droop at the corners of his eyes and mouth, just like a dog which has anticipated a walk but finds that his owner is leaving him behind.

"There's Dr. Graff and his wife!" I cried, raising my arm as if to long-lost friends.

A little surprised at this encouragement, the Head Master and Mrs. Graff came towards us. Allies! They pulled up some chairs and sat.

"Remember last year, Francis?" began Dr. Graff, swotting at a mosquito.

"It rained."

"Poured, I should say. But this is grand weather and you, Mrs. Farthing, look grander still!"

Before I could reply, Francis said, "Try and s..stop her from leaving. Says she's got to be in London by midnight."

All eyes turned to me as if London were the den of iniquity and I iniquitous to want to go there.

"Tut-tut!" said Dr. Graff with a twinkle.

The men were hopeless, so I appealed to Mrs. Graff for support. "My late husband's cousin's waiting up for me. We're off to Italy at seven!"

Now she looked wise. "Well," and her tone was matter-of-fact, "if Mrs. Farthing says she must leave, then we shouldn't stop her. Francis, you'll have to let her go!"

That was my cue. I rose, banging my head on the lantern so that the moth, still at it, bounced. The men rose, hands were shaken, good wishes exchanged, and I was free.

I could have gone to my quarters without entering the Hall. But I didn't. Instead, I made my way into the pulsating gloom where the music was now so loud my breast-bone quivered. I edged along the wall, avoiding couples gyrating and bobbing madly, till a hand behind me was laid lightly on my wrist. No, not Alex, but one of the Upper Sixth, a nice lad and a passable Classicist.

"Will you dance with me, Mrs. Farthing?" he shouted over the beat.

"Thank you, Willis, I'd like to!"

Astounding myself, I joined him under the shooting lights whose spasmodic fires made dancers momentarily recognisable. I did some hip isolations, and a bit of clever footwork learnt at classes in London. Willis's teeth grinned in appreciation, and nearby arced a wolf-whistle.

I'm not sure what happened next. But a dancing male figure had moved close to Willis and put his face to his ear. Then there was a deft shifting of places, and Willis was dancing with Abigail and Alex faced me.

If his movements had been controlled before, he now let out all the stops. He wasn't stripping, but he performed many of the sensual moves he did for *Henny-Penny's* shrieking clientèle. Bursting with love and desire, I loosened up completely and danced to the beat of my heart and the surge in my veins.

Suddenly Abigail left the floor. Alex hesitated, and went after her. Willis rejoined me, but my fire sank low. I danced a little longer then cried, "Thank you, Willis. That was good!"

He nodded, raised a hand and made a threesome nearby.

Sweating, I picked my way out of the Hall and through the deserted school. In my rooms the music came only as a dull thud. I undressed and put on easier clothes, and packed the last of my gear. Two of my cases were already in the car. Quickly, for I wanted to be off now, I went into each room, bidding it good-bye. Then, on the threshold I paused, contemplating the chairs that Alex and I had occupied over the year as we shared and explored Classics. With a sigh I switched off the light, drew the door to, and left.

# CHAPTER XXXIII

## *domina in Urbe (R.A.291)*
## *"in Rome, the world's mistress"*

There was one little task left that related to Dons. I posted it from the airport next morning. No covering note, just it in a brown envelope. Someone's 'Holy Bible'. The Harrison experience was over.

At the same time, a rather more personal communication went into the post: a letter to Alex in Wiltshire. I hoped I explained things adequately. Only one point I now kept from him: where I was going for the next two weeks. He might have construed it as flippant behaviour.

I slept throughout the flight and telephoned Martha, as promised, on my arrival in Rome. I thought she sounded – odd.

"The caretaker's been in?" she asked, which was fair enough. And, "How are my geraniums on the balcony?" which was normal. Then, "Was the flight smooth?" It wasn't what she said but how she said it; she sounded like one who is talking in a public place: warily.

Her flat was small but up high. I could see some famous landmarks and a piece of the Tiber. There were unfamiliar smells – garlic, oil and onions, and sounds – farty motorbikes, car-horns, canaries; and the feel of hot sun.

I had arrived during Rome's high season. At about this time, two thousand years before, Augustus' poet laureate, Horace, avoided the dog days by sheltering on his Sabine farm; and rich families would have packed their bags to head for seaside villas at Herculaneum. But I welcomed the heat, and after a light lunch in a bar just up the road I slept through the hottest part of the day.

I had last visited Rome ten years before. I was then a second year degree student, and with a group of fellow Classicists spent part of April cramming in as much as I could so that my cerebral studies back home came alive. But things increase their dimensions as you as a person develop; my first thirty-six hours in Rome this time were richer and fuller than that fortnight ten years earlier.

But while my senses were focused, mind and spirit tangled; Alex, always Alex. Was he back in Wiltshire? Had he received my letter? How would he react? Had he realised at the end that I was only another sowing of wild oats, lush and fruitful initially yet, lacking rich soil, soon to wither?

I spent some time sitting at the top of the Spanish Steps, soothed by the scent of cool water on hot stone and the patter of sightseers' voices. They passed me speaking in a variety of tongues: drawling Americans garlanded with camera equipment, bandy-legged Japanese exclaiming in their staccato way, lobster-red Dutch with greasy noses, black-robed prelates cool and collected, gesticulating nationals, moaning British, big-haired Greeks. They glanced at me, looked away and glanced again.

On my third day, I changed my activities. Rather than close the shutters and lie down with a book through the heat of noon, I walked to the café nearest Martha's apartment. It was in a quiet street, visited more by pedestrians than wheeled traffic. I sat at a table under the dappling shade of a grape-vine and ordered a beer. Then I looked about me.

Not far off lounged a solitary Italian in a pair of raffish sunglasses which blocked out the thinking part of his face. Although I could not determine the direction of his gaze, his posture showed interest in me as a solitary woman.

For some twenty minutes we sat at separate tables, hunted and hunter. I wished I had something to read; a woman alone is rarely allowed to be busy with her thoughts, and if she is personable she must be selling.

I shifted position and looked the other way, which left me wide open to approach. A shadow crossed my table and the Italian was asking in a thick accent,

"Excuse me, Signora, but would you like a drink?"

Tensing, I gestured to my glass. "No, thank you. One's enough."

I hoped this rebuffed him. He swaggered off, making for a flower-seller sheltering with her blooms under a brown umbrella, and bought a white rose. Then he came back, laid the flower on the table and said, "For an English lady who looks so sad." Next, he eased into the chair opposite, raised his hand for the waiter and removed his sunglasses.

As Italians go he was personable, if you like the blue-jowled look and turgid eye. He smiled, showing perfect teeth save for a gold filling in a canine. "You are tired seeing our beautiful city, yes?"

I felt sharp, so gave a sharp reply. "No. I came here to think."

He found this amusing; apparently women weren't thinkers but doers. "To think makes beautiful women frown when they should only smile!" he said.

I managed to smile and frown simultaneously which appeared to disarm him. If his coffee had not come, I think he would have left. He fiddled in his pockets to pay the waiter then resumed,

"You wait for your husband?"

"He's at a business meeting."

I sensed this had scotched one plan, but he quickly went to work on another. He poured the sugar into his cup and stirred and stirred with the spoon. "Your husband knows the city? Perhaps you and he would like a guide to show our beautiful Rome?"

"We've seen it."

"But you want to go with a guide just for you, because then you can ask all the things without hurry. For example –"

On he spoke, persuasive hands moving with persuasive tongue. I ceased to listen. Pedestrians passed, others followed our example; chairs scraped back, voices gabbled, a moped screeched its brakes. My nerves were on edge, and I turned my attention from people to nature. Three dusty sparrows settled round a piece of bread and pecked hungrily. One had lost its tail, another had a bare head. Then two lead-grey pigeons joined the feast until a pair of feet sent them packing. Aware that my companion had mercifully stopped his gabble, I was left watching the feet and crumbs.

The feet stood still. What now – a street-photographer to fend off? My eyes moved from the shoes up a long pair of legs to a big-buckled belt; up the torso to a brown throat athrob with its pulse; from neck to mouth to the eyes. Pale and exhausted under his tan, Alex was looking at me.

In silence he came forward, hitching a bag higher on his shoulder. His voice was quiet even stern. "If you want nothing more to do with me, just tell me to my face and I'll never bother you again."

The blood swayed into my cheeks and fell back. I rose, holding on to the table, for I felt dizzy. "*Scusi,*" I said to the Italian, and putting my arm through Alex's I walked him away.

He must have been in agony, poor chap, wondering why I said nothing. But I could not. My mouth twitched uncontrollably and my eyes filled. We went round the corner, then I pushed him into a doorway and embraced him. And giving way to my tears I cried, "Darling, oh, my darling!"

We pressed together in that doorway, under balconies festooned with shirts, geraniums and caged birds. And I assured Alex I wanted absolutely everything to do with him. His body against mine felt so good, but then it always had, and I hugged and kneaded him in disbelief.

"Did you get my letter? And how did you know where to find me?" I asked at last, moving to the top step so that our eyes were level.

He stroked my hair. "What letter? I haven't been to Wiltshire at all. Just because I danced with you, that dratted Abigail had hysterics in the school grounds and threw up for good measure. By the time I could sort that lot out and get to your rooms, you had gone. I spent the rest of the night in Dons, then 'phoned you first thing at Pomeroy. I thought you might have driven there overnight."

I leaned back, looking into his tired eyes. "And then?"

"I had to go to London anyway, to dump some things at the flat, and I 'phoned you again. You still weren't home! Then it occurred to me Martha might know. If you remember, she gave me her telephone number last holidays." He paused for breath. "God, was she cagey! She knew where you were, but said she wasn't sure she should tell. I lost my cool, I'm afraid, and told her if she didn't say, she'd be responsible for two very unhappy people!" He scrubbed at an eye. "So, I contacted my uncle and said there was a change of plan. Then I booked the first available flight to Rome. The wretched 'planes were packed! In the end I had to take a first class seat or I'd never have got here. I arrived three hours ago."

I felt mortified. First class travel was dear, and he was saving for a car. I stroked his cheek in contrition. "It's eaten into your funds?"

"Bloody hell, it's swallowed, eaten and digested some bite!" He gave my hair a tug. "Mrs. Farthing, why didn't you come clean with me? It would have saved a lot of hurt and energy, not to mention time. I've been sitting outside your door here for what seems hours!"

I came down from the step, took him by the hand and said, "I will come clean. But first, let's go in."

We passed the café where I had been sitting. The sparrows and pigeons had returned to the crumbs but of the Italian there was no sign. Only his white rose lay wilting on the table.

Alex looked at it suspiciously. "Who was that man?"

I pressed his hand. "A Roman opportunist."

He freshened up first and I made him something to eat. Then he sat back, less drawn by this time, and said, "You're running away from me, aren't you?"

"No."

"Yes, you are!"

"No, I am not. I'm running away from my feelings for you."

"That's crap!"

"I wouldn't have put it quite like that."

"Don't you be too clever with me!"

"I am older."

"Well, I don't like it!"

"Then stick to your Annabel."

"Abigail – and I could do worse!"

"She'll bore the pants off you – if she's got it in her to get them off you."

"That's crude!"

"I can be crude."

"We're arguing!"

"Yes."

"We've never argued!"

"No."

We stared pugnaciously at each other, but our mouths were soft.

"Now," I began gently, because his eyes showed love. "Will you give me the chance to come clean, or not?"

"It's got to be squeaky clean!"

"Ah!" And so I explained why I had not told him I was leaving Dons for Oxford, that I wanted to but kept procrastinating, that it did not seem fair to lumber him with a bit of the past (me) when he was starting out on a brilliant future (Balliol); he would feel constrained and that was the last thing I wanted to do to him.

He listened to all this in silence, then rose from the table and stood gazing at the geraniums. "So, you thought I was too wet behind the ears to know my own mind?"

"No. I thought I knew your mind better that you did."

He looked at me under his brows. "That's a bit of a nerve!"

I lowered my eyes. "Yes. I have been told about it before."

"Well, listen next time people tell you!"

I picked up a crumb and worried it. "Just look at it from my point of view. At school, trammelled by bells and rules, an attachment can grow out of proportion –"

"You sound like Goddy!"

I smiled. "Perhaps I've missed my vocation."

"I've fancied you no end as my tutor, but if you turned up in dog-collar and cassock, I'd get down in the pews with you at a twitch!"

"Who's got fantasies now!"

He grinned. "Perhaps we can discuss those later. Anyway, out of proportion you were saying."

"Yes. Well, university does funny things to people: they commit suicide, become stressed, fornicate, drop out, take to drugs and alcohol, fall for their lecturers, all because these green pastures of freedom have no cosy enclosures like school."

He looked amused as he absorbed all this. Then, "I know more about life than you credit me with," he said, gravely. "I have a father I think highly of but hardly ever see, a mother who can't communicate with me because my only brother fell out of a train when I should have taken care that he didn't, I've had two affairs with married women (well, one married, the other widowed) and I've stripped to the buff countless times for female hyenas. I may be nineteen, but how many nineteen-year-olds have all that behind them? I've grown up pretty damn quickly!"

I flicked away the crumb. "I'm sorry, Alex. I've been too engrossed in what I feel for you."

"But when you planned to slip off without telling me your intentions, didn't you *think*?"

My voice lowered. "That was the problem – I didn't think, I felt."

He came back to the table and stood looking down at me. "Right, this is how I see it. All this past year we've known each other, you've been in control of our relationship. I understand and appreciate how circumstances dictated those terms. But from now on, Jessica, you and I are free. You don't need to be in control any more. Let me be as responsible for our relationship as you. Don't be a control freak!"

I withdrew a little; he had never criticised me before and it smarted. But he was right. I was a 'control freak', and I would have to curb it. I glanced up at him, and noticing my expression, he approached to crouch by my chair.

"Jessica!" His tone was urgent. "I know you've had my well-being at heart. I know you're older. But let things unfold as they should. Trust me!"

I nodded and we clasped hands, and were silent a while. When he rose it was to say, "I'm dog tired. Can't we lie down?"

Martha's room was pleated with light and shadow from the closed shutters. Alex and I lay together on the coverlet, and he said, "Don't underestimate me. Please!" Then he fell asleep.

I pause here in my narrative, for although I remember precisely what happened after that meeting, my recollection of the sequence of events may be faulty. I'll have to ask; he'll know. A whistling tells me he is about.

I exclaim, "I need you!"

A man, now in his late twenties, enters the room. He's a notary by profession, specialising in European law. "What can I do for you, Mrs. Farthing-Forsyth?" He calls me that at jocular moments, though I am still Mrs. Farthing. He comes up behind, pushes aside my hair and starts nuzzling me.

"Alex," I say, smiling, "When you ticked me off for controlling our relationship..."

He blows down my collar softly and I squeeze my shoulders up round my ears. "I didn't tick you off!" He blows again.

"Well, you made one or two things clear which I was too dense to see. After that day you arrived in Rome looking for me, did we stay in Martha's flat or go immediately down to Sorrento?" He nuzzles on. I put my right hand up to caress his jaw. His teeth close on my index finger. "If you damage that," I warn him, "I won't be able to type your book."

He releases my finger. "My book?"

"Yes, it's all about you."

"I thought you were working on your MPhil."

"Mostly, but not always."

Over my shoulder he scans the page and reads out loud the recent lines I have written, *"Alex and I lay together on the coverlet, and he said, 'Don't underestimate me. Please!' Then he fell asleep."* He makes a noise in his throat. "Fancy sleeping at that crucial moment. What a goop I was! But, to answer your question: we had a few days in Rome, then went to Sorrento, then we returned, then it was home to England and you gave me your car, then I went to Nuncle in Wiltshire, then I stayed with you, then you met my parents and Pa smelled a rat and was delighted by it, then I got in to Balliol, then –"

"Stop!"

He bends right over my shoulder, his lips moving across my cheek in the direction of my mouth. "You see," he murmurs in his travels, "I may have done Classics well, and taken off my clothes for the delectation of many, and for you, Mrs. Farthing, in particular, but I'm not a creative writer. Too many 'thens'." We kiss lingeringly and he leaves me.

I watch him saunter out through the french windows into our garden. He has barely changed. He has still that muscular physique which he hones with hard work, clean living and exercise. Periodically, he asks me if I will marry him. I have always refused. There is that little bit of me which still feels I know his mind better than he does, that I should leave him free for someone younger. But for whom? The Abigails, the *Serving-wenches* of this world?

As I gaze at his backview, he turns and catches my eyes upon him. Slowly he takes off his jacket and loosens his tie and begins a sensual rotation of the hips. I laugh. I get up. I go to him.

If he asks me to marry him now, there can be only one answer.